Twisted Legacy

Heartless Heirs of Canyon Falls

Dakota Lee

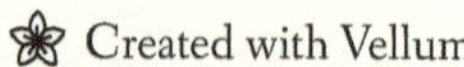 Created with Vellum

CONTENT WARNING

The following subject matter may be discussed in passing and/ or be described in detail on page:

* Drug Use ((Prescription and Recreational)
    * Alcohol Use
    * Why Choose
    * Graphic Sexual Descriptions
    * Child Abandonment
    * Talk of Loss of Child
    * Student/ Teacher Relationship
    * Bullying (By Harem Members and Others)
    * Knife Play
    * Blood Play
    * Manipulation
    * Non-Con
    * Dub-Con
    * Somnophilia
    * Breath Play
    * Primal
    * Violence

* Graphic Assault (Physical and Sexual)
* Depression
* Trauma/ Trauma Responses
** Rape/ Attempted Rape

Your safety and well being is important to me. Please carefully consider these warnings before reading this book.

No sense of time
The darkness fractures your mind
Your hope dissolves with each shaky breath
In this coffin you lay, it's judgement day
Your shattered soul now put to rest

Prologue
Paxton Cox

I roll over onto my back and stare at the embellished ceiling above the bed. It's all I can manage right now, as I let the guilt and disgust consume me. I never talk to the guys about these little side projects my mother has me doing.

I have full discretion about how far I go. It was fun in the beginning, now I hate it. I'm a sum of body parts. Fingers. Mouth. Tongue. I've become the means for them to be selfish. They happily please themselves without worrying if I had a good time, too. The transactional nature of sex has even leaked into my interactions with girls my age. These women use me, so I use their daughters, sisters, nieces. I feel hollow after every hookup, and that's not likely to change, because once I'm married, the only reason for sex will be to produce an heir.

Mrs. Baker snores beside me. Blissfully satisfied and oblivious. I'm fighting the urge to heave her and the bed out the window. But I can't. Instead, I crawl out of bed and do what I came here for. There's an item I'm supposed to get. One Mr. Baker has refused to let out of his possession. He's away on business, and this little tryst with his wife has given me the opportunity to steal it. I have a replica to replace it with. If he ever finds out about the switch, he'll never know it was me. His wife wouldn't dare admit she may have let a thief in her house. Or admit to our affair. She values her prenup too much for that.

I dress quickly, tiptoeing through the house toward the fish tank. I have the woman snoring upstairs to thank for making my search easier. She complained all night about her husband staring at the saltwater tank. Without that clue, I'd be wasting time looking in the wrong place. I slip on my gloves and grab the net from the hook next to the tank, disrupting the sand until I find what I'm looking for. I scoop out the stone, replacing it with the fake, and let the eel on the bottom disperse the sand to cover it again.

Once outside, I walk a few streets over before calling a car to take me to the secure drop zone where I'll leave the stone. I don't know who contacts my mother to set up these jobs -but once or twice a month; I show up for Sunday dinner, -and she hands me an envelope with a picture, a name, and an item to retrieve.

I've dropped off the stone and I'm in the car on my way back to campus when I get an automated alert from Prospectus. It's the fraternity rankings. Rho Beta Psi is in the lead for challenge points, but we're in the lower 30th percentile when it comes to community involvement and outreach. Finn's our social guy. He needs to do something about that.

With my side project done, I switch my attention back to the rest of the night. Time to cause some mayhem.

Chapter 1
Pax

Holden, Finn and I pick our way across the last few feet of dirt and gravel towards our destination. We were ramping up for our biggest prank of the night when we got the text summoning us to The Tomb, the official headquarters of The League of the Daggered Ravens. The structure is built into a cliff wall, completely underground, and hidden from sight. We parked our cars a quarter mile from here. The only way to access The Tomb is on foot. We step through the doors and I take a quick look around the meeting hall. I've never seen this many people in this room before.

The hollow clank of the inner sanctum doors locking puts me on edge. The sound of chains unfurling drags my attention to the ceiling, and I watch as they lower a cage to the floor. I lock eyes with Finn and Holden and jerk my head to the side, indicating we should move to the back corner of the room.

When they bring out the cage, that means somebody has a grievance to address. A position they want to fight for. Odds are highly likely that someone wants to challenge The Trium for control of the school.

I'm still scanning the crowd when my gaze settles on a familiar face. "What the hell is Wade Bishop doing here?"

The doors directly across from us open, and the council members enter, wearing their ceremonial robes and masks. Wade's presence is now the least of my worries.

"Shit." Finn whispers beside me. "What the fuck is even happening right now?"

That's a great question, because the upper council doesn't get dressed up in ceremonial garb for challenge nights, and the lower council members are the ones who supervise it. I look up to the third level, to where my grandfather stands. He's masked, but I get the impression he's looking right at me.

The orator opens the ceremony and asks everyone in the room to reaffirm our oath to The League. When we do, my grandfather steps forward and takes control of the meeting.

"I know you're all excited about this evening's challenge. We have some serious grievances to address and we don't want to deny our members the opportunity to do so. But first we must tend to some pressing matters."

He looks to his left and right. "As you all know, we are a brotherhood of tradition, of the highest esteem and order. When we make our oaths, they're forged in fire. Bonds that cannot be broken until death."

Members nod, smiling at each other.

"However, there are consequences for those who betray The League. We prefer not to administer the harshest of those punishments, but sometimes it cannot be helped. Some time ago, we shunned one of our most trusted members. The shame his family brought upon us was too much to overcome, and he withdrew from our rolls. This individual had no appropriate heirs in whom we could trust, so ultimately, his familial line was frozen."

My friends and I look at each other. This is the first we're hearing about any kind of shunning. We went through a month long class which covered the rules of behavior and etiquette for The League. That's why Holden knows the bylaws by heart. There were weekly tests and essays to write. If The League is upset with you, they take your money and maybe demote you in rank. They definitely put you on bullshit types of duties during different social functions. But you're here and you're a member. Not once did anyone ever mention removing your name from the membership list and freezing your bloodline.

My grandfather continues, "It would seem, however, we may have acted hastily in his dismissal from our walls. Some new information has come to light."

With the mask on, I can't tell if he and the other high council members are happy or pissed about this information they've found. Whatever it is, it's important if he's addressing it here and now.

"We have recently discovered that the circumstances regarding his infraction may have been an elaborate scheme of which he had no knowledge of. As is his right, he has asked for a review of his status, which we are in the process of doing. In the meantime, we believe the information we've uncovered so far is credible. More than that, we're happy to announce that there is a legacy heir to continue his bloodline."

I scan the floor, trying to spot someone who looks unfamiliar, or like they've been put on the spot. Everyone looks calm and curious. Someone hands my grandfather a scroll, which he unfurls and reads, "By the order of the high council of The League of the Daggered Ravens, we do hereby decree that a formal inquiry shall commence to validate the bloodline of the female child, Theona LaReaux, of the Laurent family line."

What in the actual fuck?

"As confirmed and agreed by the majority vote of the high council, we do hereby decree that the female child, Theona LaReaux, be afforded all rights and courtesy's as due a legacy heir, in the interim while the official validation of her bloodline and a determination of her lineage's standing is in progress."

This can't be happening. This is the worst thing they can do. It positions her perfectly to do what my dad is afraid of.

"As discussed and decreed by the unanimous vote of the high council, we will appoint a liaison to the female child, Theona LaReaux, to assist with her transition from unaligned status."

His head lifts, and now I know he's looking at me. "We have assigned this official action to first year prospects, Finley Jefferson

Rhodes the Third, Holden Sullivan, and Paxton Cox. Do you gentlemen accept this assignment?"

I took an oath to protect The League. If I say no, they'll assign someone else to this job. Someone who doesn't know just how malignant her presence here would be. I need to make sure that doesn't happen.

My voice rings out as I answer, "I accept the assignment."

Finn speaks next. "I accept the assignment."

It's on Holden. He can say no, and Finn and I will still do it, but then our unit would be under scrutiny. We've agreed to never be publicly at odds.

A few seconds after Finn answers, Holden's voice rasps out, "I accept the assignment."

My grandfather continues, "Our prospects have agreed to take on this task, without coercion, without hesitation. Let the record show their acceptance and notify the resource center to provide them with whatever they require to complete the task."

The high council melts back into the shadows, and the orator transitions control of the sanctum to the lower council to begin challenge night.

Chapter 2
Finn

Of all the colossal fuck ups. I rake my fingers through my hair, working through the urge to hit somebody. Getting into a fight outside of The Tomb tonight would've raised some questions, and likely triggered an application to air my grievances. I'd love to beat the shit out of someone, but I can't exactly explain why I'm mad without revealing what we did.

There were so many things we have done and could have done wrong over the years, but ultimately, nobody questioned us. They've even commended our actions. But *this* is where our reputation goes to shit? Over a favor for Malcom Cox?

We've been working so hard to orchestrate Thea's downfall. Now we have an official assignment to do the opposite of that. Talk about being set up to fail.

Malcolm Cox Jr is a mid-level council member. I've never heard of the name Laurent, but he would have. There's no way he didn't know Thea is connected to a league family.

The Trium's always been untouchable. Insulated. Protected. But if word gets out what we've been doing... *shit*. Malcolm's never gonna admit to asking us to get rid of her. Not after his father, a high council member, just sat there and gushed about finding a lost heir. *Fuck.* The more I go over things, the worse it gets. Holden found that birth certificate through illegal channels. That means somebody went through a lot of trouble to hide it and we dragged it out, and threw it in Thea's face, dust and all.

"Guys, what if Thea didn't know?"

Pax is shaking his head before I can even finish my thought.

"Seriously, Pax. What if Thea didn't know who her parents were?"

He cracks his knuckles. "She knew. Just because the council didn't know about her, doesn't mean she didn't know about us, or her connection to The League. It makes even more sense that she'd be here working against us. The truth coming out just helps her cause. Long-lost family member. *Abandoned.* And not one high council member in The League knew about her? It's the perfect setup to make the other families doubt the leadership, which is why I said yes to being her liaison. We're gonna get rid of her once and for all."

I can't believe he's defending his dad and sticking to this narrative that Thea was trying to sabotage The League. Half the time he doesn't even like him. "What do you think, Holden?"

Holden passes his phone to me. The screen is on a text message from his dad.

DAD

> I don't know what the hell is going on, but please tell me that when I start digging, your digital signature won't be anywhere near this.

If Holden's father is digging, that means The League's security council has a few questions. That's just as bad as the NSA and CIA having questions. What could they be looking for? If the high council says Thea's one of us, shouldn't that be enough?

I need to stay objective. Blindly accepting what someone said is what got us into this mess to begin with. My head's hurting from trying to work this out. Okay, let's go with what I know. The high council made an official announcement in chambers with the entire senior leadership present. They don't randomly put shit out there that can be disproven. That would definitely call their leadership into question.

Okay, so operating in good faith, their intel is valid. So what do I need to do to complete this assignment? Earn Thea's trust and bring her in alignment with the other legacy students. That's easy. We can do this. I glance over at my friends. Uh, *I* can do this. Pax will fuck shit up worse than it already is, and Holden... I'm not sure how he'll play this. He and Pax have always been two peas in the pod. Like twins separated at birth, sharing the same fucked up brain cell, so I can't assume he'll see this my way.

He looks just as conflicted as I feel. I could tell Holden was interested in Thea, but I never got the chance to talk to him about it. Finding that birth certificate derailed all my plans. How badly did I fuck things up? It should be salvageable, right?

Maybe that's the angle I should play. Thea and I connected. It was real. I just have to remind her of it and apologize for being an ass. Girls like that. Maybe I'll throw in a gift, too. Eloise is always complaining I don't buy her enough stuff. I'm usually looking at her like she's fucking crazy when she does, because I've never brought her anything. Any gifts she's ever gotten were picked out by one of my dad's assistants.

But this is different. We have to get on Thea's good side to make The League happy, and there's nothing I won't do to make The League happy. Gifts and orgasms. My Pet loves coming. I can totally fix this.

"Finn!"

"What?"

"You wanna pretend you're listening?"

I really don't. I usually find letting Pax stress about every little thing leaves me free to worry about nothing. "Can we do this tomorrow?"

"We need to have a plan, in case we get called in front of the disciplinary council for not warning them about Thea before they made this big announcement."

I pull my hat off and shove it in my pocket. "I get that, but whatever you're thinking about right now, I don't want to hear it. We still have five hours left in Mayhem Night, and half a dozen challenges to complete. I'm trying to focus on that."

"But-"

"No, fucking *buts,* Paxton. You were bitching earlier about our outreach numbers being down. If we don't get back to campus and join the frat, you'll be mad about our challenge numbers too."

He nods. "You're right, man. One thing at a time. Let's go finish up Mayhem Night."

Chapter 3
Pax

My head's spinning from the high council's announcement about Thea. I pushed it aside last night for Mayhem Night, but now we need to deal with this assignment before her presence here becomes a bigger problem. I know what The League thinks, but until I've talked to my father, we need to operate as if she's still a threat, and I need my boys on board with that. We need to stick to our plan.

I chug my drink, then stalk back over to the pull-up bar to finish my workout. The gym door squeaks open. I catch sight of Holden and Finn through the mirror, but continue my reps, counting down from thirty in my head. When I'm done, I hang for a second, stretching out my shoulders and lats, then drop, landing softly on my feet.

"I'm ready to listen to your suggestion now." Finn grumbles, walking over to the treadmill.

I meet Holden's gaze in the mirror. He must've had something to do with Finn's calm demeanor. He's usually more hostile this early in the morning after no sleep. I turn to face them. I'm not a coward, and I stand by everything we did. That we're even having to discuss this shows just how problematic Thea is.

Holden's brows furrow, and his jaw ticks when I say, "We should've gotten more information about Thea before confronting her." Looking over at Finn, I say, "There was probably some merit to your suggestion that we get closer to her, and we should have implemented that sooner. I didn't trust her. I still don't, but maybe we would have gotten some more insight into who she is and why she's here."

He pushes his hair back off his forehead. "She hasn't really done anything to make us distrust her."

I see the strain on his face. He's still strung up pretty tight, and clearly refusing to see what's so in front of his face. "Hasn't she? Why is she using a false identity? We never found out why she was on the Southside of town the night of the painting challenge, when she almost ran you over. Remember, *that's* what started it all."

Holden interjects. "Malcolm knows something. That's the night he ordered you to spy on her, right? If anything's suspicious, it's how she got on his radar before she ever came to school."

"My father is looking out for The League, like we've all sworn to do. He's always following up on rumors he hears about threats. This one was credible."

"Possibly. But isn't it *also* possible he used your relationship to manipulate the situation? To cause confusion? What are we doing, Pax? Are we in the right, and we continue with our current course of action to protect The League? Or was Malcolm wrong? This is why the bylaws forbid us from accepting personal assignments from family members. He presented it as a favor, and we went with that because who wouldn't want a council member to owe them one?"

Holden holds up his hands before I can jump to my father's defense. "I concede it's highly likely he was looking for dirt on Thea or her family to present to the high council. But other than the birth certificate, I haven't come across anything suspicious about the Hughes to warrant a deeper look, so you need to be willing to accept that it's possible he failed to share some pertinent information with us, about why he thought *this* girl was a threat, and we won't know the answer to that until we talk to him."

Holden gets it. That's exactly what I've been thinking. Finn scratches the back of his neck. He looks like he wants to argue about this some more. I'm right. I know I am. I steer the conversation onto safer ground.

"There's no sense in arguing about what we've already done. Now we have a new task from the high council. An official task, but before we do anything, we're gonna go back over the rule book and make sure everything from here on out is in strict accordance with the by-laws." I look each of them in the eye. "And we won't mention the favor we did for my dad. Agreed?"

I haven't heard from my father. My mother says he's still on his business trip. I doubt he'll tell anyone what he had us doing. He won't want the scrutiny until he has absolute proof that he's right and everyone else is wrong.

"Agreed," Holden says, going to take up his spot in the corner. Finn turns on the treadmill and starts running.

"Finn?"

We're the Trium. We have to be in agreement on everything. We never leave room for anyone to form a wedge between us. It's what makes us unbeatable. Unstoppable. If Finn wants to go a few rounds in the ring, because he's pissed we're in this situation, we can, but ultimately he's gotta get on board. "Are you in or not?"

"I don't want the council on my ass any more than you do. Of course. I'm in."

We finish our workouts in silence, a stifling heaviness in the air between us. The longer Finn runs, the looser he gets. Exertion is his happy place, and he's never been one to hold a grudge. That means the vibes I'm getting are coming off of Holden, who internalizes so much shit. I walk over to where he is. He transitions from downward dog into cobra. His movements seem forced. He's definitely not feeling the zen.

"I wasn't implying you didn't do a good job on the intel, Holden, but we took Malcolm's word for it and never thought there was anything else to look into. That could bite us in the ass. We need to make sure it doesn't."

"I'll take care of it." He exhales, releasing some of the tension from his body. I'm done working out, so I go back to my room to get ready for our first appearance of the day at The Rock. We may have had a fucked up weekend, and we're currently at odds with each other, but no one will know anything's wrong when we step off the elevator.

Chapter 4
Holden

Pax and I walk into The Rock, and I debate walking back out to save my ears. Everyone's still talking about the pranks we pulled over the last week, and wondering how big the party will be when we celebrate the initiates crossing over. I think my friends would agree, we're not in a party mood.

Someone fucked up last night. Starting with the dorm check that didn't happen and ending with the gate guard not manning his post. Protocols are in place to prevent people, like Thea, from stumbling across sacred rituals, like Epsilon Tao doing their secret circle jerk.

I was in the graveyard spying on Epsilon Tao, donned in one of their ceremonial masks and robes. Thea's lucky I'm the one who caught her. It would have been a nightmare trying to explain to The League how she wound up in the middle of Epsilon Tao's slam fest on Mayhem Night.

I've been out of sorts all morning. I could barely concentrate on my yoga and it's more than the tension between me and the guys. This sense of unease started this morning before I went to the gym and it's only gotten worse post-workout and shower. I can't pinpoint what it is or why, but something feels off. That's why I'm providing my own ingredients for an omelette today. Spinach, mushrooms, onions, peppers, and a carton of egg whites.

I've learned to trust my gut and embrace my need to question everything. The one time I didn't, I almost became a kid on the milk carton. I was seven, and I knew all about not walking off with strangers. Nobody could show up at school and lie about the nanny sending them to pick me up. I wasn't going to help any strangers find their lost puppies. I was prepared for all those dangers. But nobody told me that there was a simpler way to get me to go with them. A way that no one would suspect. By poisoning my food at a kid's birthday party.

I didn't want the piece of cake the member of the wait staff insisted I eat. But it would have been rude not to have a slice. In our world, manners are everything. The sedative took effect during a game of hide and seek. I was always a good hider, and very observant, so I hid in the one room of the house that was always off limits to everyone. It was the perfect spot. I don't know how long I was unconscious before Pax found me. Or how long it took for an adult to reach my parents before getting permission to take me to the hospital. I just know when I woke up, Pax was there. He stood guard over me, refusing to let anyone come near me. Not even the doctors.

It was never in the papers. The police were never called, but I know the kidnappers were caught and punished. That's the first time my parents sat me down and explained the life we live is different. That my father's job and associations put me and my sister in danger. My near kidnapping led to our first conversation about The League of the Daggered Ravens. My father was a field agent in the FBI, working on one of the biggest cases of his career. Little did he know his investigation would implicate a legacy family with ties to the cartel. They planned everything. Where to approach me, how to gain access to the party, and when to drug me. My curiosity about the wall to ceiling bookshelves in Mr. Winston's office saved me. I'd stolen the spare key earlier in the afternoon and planned to hide in the office to escape the party. If I would have gone anywhere else, the people hired by the cartel would have found me, shoved me in the back of their van and driven off with me, never to be seen again.

I was trusting back then. Insulated. Never again. Which is why I genuinely question everything. I do a quick scan of the tables. Cataloging who's sitting where. Everything seems normal. Everything in its place. I reach the counter, order my food, and pass over the basket with my ingredients. Making note of who's working today. It's one of the cooks I usually trust, but today I'm feeling off, so I grab a hairnet and go into the kitchen to watch him cook my food. I collect my plate, put it on a tray and carry it to our table myself.

Eloise's shrill laugh draws my attention to the table. She looks all recovered from her run-in with Thea. I wish I could have been there when Thea tore through the sorority house right before she quit. Everyone thinks it's because Zeta Nu was about to drop her, but that doesn't make sense, since Thea was high up on the leaderboard.

The Zeta Nus are trying to keep things quiet, but I know all about Layla-Jean's chastity vow ceremony. Somehow she wound up in an actual drug den, no pledge master in sight to monitor or control the test, seconds away from being forced to turn tricks. Thea never came out and said anything, but I know that's why she attacked the sorority house. I think it's admirable that she felt so protective of her friend. I don't know what Eloise and the pledge masters were thinking. The purpose of the initiation tests is to push the pledges to the edge of comfort, to see how they act, and assess their critical thinking and problem-solving skills and their ability to improvise and work as a team. None of them are supposed to be in any real danger. As Interim President, Eloise should have been called to appear in front of a campus tribunal. If you ask me, she got off easy. She knows the pledge games she's playing. She's been through them before and knows what it takes to score high on the board. Her biggest challenge is having to watch Finn flirt and hookup with other people while she's celibate. I grimace as I slide into my seat. She's sitting here without a care in the world, hanging onto Finn like they're some kind of celebrity power couple.

She smiles up at Pax when he motions for the girl holding two trays to set one down in front of her. I dissect that little exchange as I cut into my omelet. Finn and Eloise are getting married. They go through these phases where they spend all their time together and then avoid each other. But this behavior is out of the norm for Pax. It's been happening for weeks, but I've pretended not to notice. He's making sure her food is delivered, and has people carrying her books when Finn's not around. He even blocks off the seats so no other girls can sit near Finn. First, I chalked it up to pledge season and us having to spend more time with the members of Zeta Nu, but this is something different.

I've been watching Eloise too, and she seems to have a lot more power around the school than she did at the beginning of the year. Power that only comes when you have a Trium backing you. I guess she and Pax have finally called a truce.

I don't have much of an appetite, but I force myself to eat, ignoring the conversations going on around me, trying to get lost in my book. It must work because the next time I look up, the table is emptier than when I sat down.

I finish my meal and jerk my head towards the door, letting Pax know I'm heading to the library. Everyone else will be going back to the dorms to sleep in. This morning's breakfast meet up was just to soak up the alcohol or drugs in their system.

Chapter 5
Finn

I ditched the guys this morning, feeling the need to walk to the dining hall alone, then skipped breakfast altogether. I know we have to present a united front in public and we will, but for now, I need some space. I'm crossing the circle when an ambulance comes screeching by heading down the road that leads to the infirmary. There's a crowd gathered on the side of the building near the ambulance bay, so I go to check things out. I slip through the bodies, coming to a stop next to Eloise, who's at the front of the crowd. "Hey Ellie, any idea what's happening?"

She turns and flings herself into my arms. "Oh, god, Finney. I just heard. It's Zeus."

"Zeus, what?"

"I don't know the details, but that's him in the ambulance."

"Well, Zeus takes big risks and tends to go overboard on Mayhem Night. It was only a matter of time before something happened."

She links her arm through mine and rests her head on my shoulder. "I was just heading to breakfast. Walk over to The Rock with me?"

There's no use in me standing around here, listening to everyone talking about poor Zeus. He's one of Mikey's frat brothers. I can't stand those dudes, so yeah, I've got zero sympathy for him sustaining a boo-

boo last night. As I'm turning away, something else catches my attention. It's Thea's friend LJ, pushing her way through the crowd, like she's looking for someone. She spots us and walks over, her eyes red-rimmed.

"I know it was you."

It's hard to determine which way the accusations are being hurled. Could be Ellie, could be anyone else standing around. I'm guessing the students have begun uncovering the destruction we left behind last night. That could go on for a few more weeks. We're thorough and insidious. I can't wait for The Dean to find what I left for him.

"I know you did this and I swear to god I'm going to find a way to make you pay." She lunges at Eloise, grabbing the collar of her shirt. Someone drags her away, but not before she leaves a tiny scratch on Ellie's perfectly made-up face.

I ignore the cut and ask, "Eloise, what the fuck was that all about?"

"How do I know? She and her bestie are psychos. They keep attacking me." She wails, falling into me again.

I hear The Dean's voice at the other end of the crowd. "Make room. I said, make room!"

Instead of everyone dispersing, it seems like more people are showing up. The crowd now extends into the street. A break in the bodies reveals a cop car and a second ambulance. "Eloise, was anyone else other than Zeus hurt in whatever shit they were doing?"

She doesn't answer. I grab her chin, making her look at me. "I asked you a question. Was anyone else hurt?"

"From what I hear, it was nobody important."

Something about her tone puts me on edge. "What are your spies saying happened?" She gives me a bright smile. "What does it matter, Finn? God, it's not like you're a doctor and can help or anything."

"It matters, because The Trium don't know anything about what the hell is going on right now, and that's unacceptable. You're withholding information from me. Now talk before you need a medic."

"Don't threaten me, Finn. It's done, okay? The problem's been taken care of, and I expect my reward."

"What's done?"

She nods, looking over her shoulder. "Right. We probably

shouldn't talk about it here." She looks around the crowd again. "Where is Pax, anyway? He should be here acknowledging that I fulfilled my end of the deal, so it's time for you to make good on your end."

I grip her arm and drag her away from the crowd. "What fucking deal?"

"Let go, you're hurting me."

"No, I'm not. But if you don't start talking, I am more than happy to make that a reality for you. I've been dying to see your blood on the outside of your skin."

She pales, then starts babbling. "The Trium wanted that bitch to be taught a lesson. *I* made it happen." She points to the gurney being wheeled past us. "Now I want my compensation for that."

Thea's strapped to the bed. Pale and unmoving. Her face a swollen, bloody, unrecognizable mess. An officer walks by holding a bag with what looks like torn and bloody clothes. Her friend Layla-Jean clings to her hand, sobbing.

No. No. No. This can't be happening.

I've never wanted to knock the shit out of Pax as badly as I do now. I called an emergency meeting for him and Holden to stop whatever they're doing and meet me back at the dorms. He's leaning back in his chair like he's the goddamn king of the castle without a care in the world.

I stalk to the kitchen to grab a drink to calm down. Fuck that. Day drinking won't help. I walk back over to him and slam my fist into his jaw.

He rubs it, and I do it again. Before I can swing a third time, he's on his feet. "What's up your ass?"

"As if you don't know."

"If it's about the girl from last night, my bad. I didn't feel like a group fest."

"You think I'm pissed because of that? What do I care whose ass you ream?"

"Aren't you? Since you and Eloise haven't ended her chastity vow yet, I figured—"

"Fuck, no. You're welcome to all the legacy bitches on campus. I'm done with them. *Especially* Eloise."

"Then what's your problem?"

Is this really how he wants to play this? "My problem is you sitting here acting like you don't know what's going on. Damn, Pax. I know you're a ruthless mother fucker but this doesn't bother you? Not even a little?"

"Probably not, but how about you explain which situation you're talking about?"

"Thea! I'm talking about Thea."

Hit sits back down with a shrug. "Fuck that bitch. You're right, I'm not losing any sleep over her."

I lunge for him again. This time he gets to his feet and body checks me. I crash into the wall with a thud. We wrestle back and forth, getting an equal amount of blows in. I'm faintly aware of the door slamming and then Holden's in the mix, pulling us apart.

"Is this about the girl from last night?" Holden asks, a frown marring his face.

Pax walks over to the fridge and grabs a drink. "That's the same thing I asked."

"Well?" Holden stares me down, waiting for my reply.

My chest heaves, my hands itch. I can hardly see through the haze of red, let alone answer the question.

"He says it's about Thea."

Holden dips his head to look me in the eye. Ready to dig into my psyche. "What about her?"

"Ask Pax, what about her."

Pax comes back into the living room. "Finn, I don't know what the fuck you're talking about, but I'll be straight with you. Whatever it is, I. Don't. Care. She's our enemy. We'll do what The League wants, pretend to guide her to joining." He chuckles, "Because karma's a bitch, and I want a front-row seat when The League finds out what she's really up to."

I cock my head to the side. "Right, and maybe you helped karma along by introducing her to a wall, or someone's fists?"

They both look at me like I'm crazy. Pax asks, "What the fuck are you talking about?"

"I'm talking about the ambulance that pulled out of here ten minutes ago."

The smile on his face slips. "Somebody got hurt last night on campus?"

Holden nods. "I heard about it as I was coming back from the library. Zeus got hurt trying to pull off a prank in the training room. Students are saying a weight fell on his junk."

Fuck Zeus and his swollen penis. I want Pax to tell me what he did to my pet. "Thea was in a second ambulance."

Holden looks from me to Pax, then me again, as he digs out his phone. "You sure?"

"I was there when they loaded her gurney onto the second ambulance."

Pax leans forward in his chair as if he's expecting me to come at him again. I might. "Why are you looking at me like I know something about that?"

"Because Eloise was there, and she says I owe her for handling our problem." I'm getting angry all over again. My hand instinctively curls around my blade.

Pax eyes my hand and frowns. "Calm down Finn, and just tell us what happened."

"I told you. Eloise said our problem's been taken care of, and seconds later, they paraded Thea's body in front of me on the way to a second ambulance."

"And you think Eloise had something to do with it?"

"I'm sure she did."

He's still watching my hand. Smart, because if he takes his eyes off of it, he won't have time to defend himself against my attack. "And what does any of that have to do with me?"

"Who told her Thea was a problem, and to get rid of her by any means necessary? Because it sure as shit wasn't me."

He doesn't even blink. "I told her to send a message that she's no one. So she'd stop walking around with her nose in the air. I told her to show Thea who runs this school. It's the same speech we've given to the legacies countless times before. We've always let the Zeta Nus handle the women."

"Right, but Thea fought back, didn't she? I'm sure that would've prompted a second conversation. Kinda like the one we had where you said, 'Let's get creative'".

He juts his chin out. "You're right. I did. So what?"

"So, you basically gave Eloise a blank check, and she cashed that fucker in."

He gets to his feet, holding his hands out in front of him. "Are you seriously standing here bitching to me about your fuck buddy getting a few bumps and bruises? She went after Eloise in Zeta house, so it sounds to me like Eloise got even. She's well within her rights to do so. And an ambulance? Really? I hear another con coming on."

"Are you even listening to me, Pax, or are you already working out excuses in your head to come out of this untouched? They carted Thea off in an ambulance, and Eloise was there with a very convenient story about the whole thing."

Holden's frowning at his screen. "Zeus was taken to medical this morning with a severe laceration to his penis. He's in the infirmary, but Thea's been taken to the hospital."

That gets Pax's attention. Most injuries are treated at our fully functioning medical center. Only the worst injuries are transported off campus.

"Guys." Holden looks up, a worried look in his eyes. "Her records are sealed and the only thing I can see in the school transport log is that she was found unresponsive at the scene."

"She was more than that. Her face was bashed in. There was blood everywhere. It didn't even look like she was breathing." I pace back and forth. "We haven't been at the dorms this week. She might've been here hurt. Has anyone seen her since we took possession of her accounts again?"

Pax says, "It's not on us to keep tabs on her."

Holden's more quiet than usual. He's got this look in his eye. The one he gets when he's keeping information from us because he's not sure how reliable it is. "Holden, do you have something to add to this?"

"Why would you ask me that?"

His left eye twitches, ever so subtly. Whatever he's thinking about isn't making sense in his complicated brain. "Come on, man, what is it? Maybe we can help you work through the problem."

"The dining hall isn't the last place I saw Thea. She was out last night."

"Say, what?" I ask at the same time Pax says, "Are you sure?"

"She was the person getting chased at Tao Epsilon's crypt. "

Oh shit. I croak out, "Did you?"

He shakes his head, knowing where my thoughts are leading. "I scared her. That's it. I gave her the opportunity to run, and I let her get away. She was fine and heading towards campus."

I hurl my knife at the wall. The thud of it embedding in the plaster calms me a little. "Okay, so we know whatever happened was between last night and this morning and it was more than Eloise getting even for some bitch fight at the sorority. We empowered her. Encouraged her. We let Eloise run things, but she took this too far. You..." My voice breaks. As much as I want to lay all this at Pax's feet, I didn't speak up when we decided to make an example out of Thea. So this is on me too. "We're The Trium. We removed our protection from Thea, and we didn't stop to think just how many people she's pissed off on campus or how many people would be looking for a way to win favor with us. We didn't think about what that would mean so close to Mayhem Night." I look at Pax. "I asked how we'd know if things went too far. This is it."

I can't be around here. Around them. Pax calls out to me as I open the door. "Finn, we may have called open season on Thea, but you know this isn't what we meant."

My head drops as the weight of what we did lands on my shoulders. "Maybe not, but it happened."

Holden

Pax stares at the door, long after Finn walks through it. He may not show it, but I know he's taking Finn's words to heart, and is worried about what he'll do. I try to reassure him. "He'll be fine."

"I know, I just." He turns my way. "How did this happen? How did this happen and we not have any idea?"

It doesn't matter how it happened. It *shouldn't* have happened without us knowing. Finn says Eloise admitted to having a hand in it, but that might not be the truth. She's always looking for ways to make Finn pay more attention to her. If she thinks saying she handled a problem for us will get that attention, that's what she'll do. I share my thoughts with Pax. "The only thing we know for certain is that Thea was injured. We don't know when, where, or how. Finn didn't make it seem like Eloise had any bruises on her, did he?"

"Nah. Sounds like she was fine."

"Okay, then. The first thing we need to do is find out exactly what happened. Then we can find out who was involved." I'm speaking with a calmness I've perfected even when I feel anything but calm inside - just like now, I'm furious- because Thea's been hurt by someone who isn't me.

Pax gets to his feet. "We need names. Somebody saw something. Somebody heard something, and they kept this from us. It's too late to get ahead of it since the dean already knows, but I don't want any council members asking questions we don't have the answers to."

He doesn't need to explain why that would be a bad thing. Last night we took an assignment after being told Thea's from a legacy bloodline. We should have immediately gone to her and started the process of explaining what that means. We didn't, because we were too focused on fraternity rankings and winning the most points for Mayhem Night.

I head out, leaving Pax alone with his thoughts. The first step in unraveling the truth, is finding out exactly when and where she was hurt. Somewhere between the time I let her get away and now, someone got their hands on her. I settle into my chair in front of my computers and pull up the camera feed for this floor. Thea never came back to the dorm last night. It wouldn't be the first time she's stayed out all night. Sometimes she crashes in Layla-Jean's room. Eloise destroyed Thea's stuff, and she's been slow to replace it. Us stealing her money didn't help. I guess that should have been our clue that Eloise was getting out of hand. She came up to our floor and destroyed a Legacy Four room. It doesn't matter that a fourth doesn't actually live there. Eloise crossed a line, and we didn't say anything about it.

I don't know how the guys will react, but from now on, I'm putting Eloise in her place. I don't care if she's engaged to Finn. Until they're actually married, she's just like any other daughter walking around here. No power outside of what we give her. It's time someone reminded her of that.

I get lost in the process of searching camera footage on campus and through people's phones, trying to come up with an idea of what happened. It's slow going. We have our phones with us all the time and the students love taking and uploading videos, but there's an electronics ban in effect on Mayhem Night. It looks like most of the students adhered to it. I keep looking, because I know there has to be at least one person who wanted some footage to relive the experience.

While I'm searching on this screen, my other screen is tracking Rescue 822. I wanna know where it's taking her, then I'll get into the hospital system to find out exactly what's going on with her treatment.

I let Thea out of my sight once. I won't do it again.

Chapter 6
Finn

My father, Finley Jefferson Rhodes Junior, is about as straight an arrow as you can get. I'm what everyone calls the polar opposite of him. I can't stand numbers, and boring ass business meetings, but he gets off on that shit. I guess that's what makes him so good at his investment banking job. We spent thirteen years overseas. Four in Italy, four in Japan, three in Paris, and two in England, before moving back to the states. Talk about a culture shock. I was used to being the new kid in town, but because of the military bases nearby, I wasn't the only new kid in school. I also thought it was pretty weird that nobody spoke more than one language. Latin doesn't count. I learned that shit in church.

I was a scrawny kid, but being multi lingual and world traveled made me a catch. I said a few words, smiled, and the girls let me finger them. Sometimes do more than that. I knew how to sweet talk the ladies. I was mischievous, with a knack for sneaking in and out of places. I learned that trick from a guy at the parkour course I hung out at. Dad paid the membership dues, because he thought it was a good outlet to help me burn off some of my excess energy. But given the fact that I use these skills for campus challenges, I no longer believe it was just a coincidence that I was always surrounded by navy seals and thieves.

My dad is type-A, but there's no better man than him on this planet. I walk into the skyscraper where his office is held and ride the elevator to his floor. I didn't make an appointment or call and say I was coming. I never do. My dad stops what he's doing to see me. Each and every time.

Today's no different when his assistant announces I'm here. He tells me to go straight back. Dad's finishing up a call when I walk into his office. I head to his beverage cart, ignoring the look he gives me, since I'm not old enough to drink the scotch and soda I just fixed. He buzzes his assistant. "Hold all my calls for the next two hours."

I don't need two hours of his time. He's busy and I shouldn't be here now, taking him away from his work, but I'm so glad that he said that. He gets up and closes the door before sitting back down behind his desk. "What can I do to help?"

That's it. It's always what he says, without knowing the situation or if I'm the one who messed up. "I need to know if... Thea. How sure is The League that she's this missing legacy kid?"

He chuckles. "The high council loves their dramatics, don't they?"

"So it's a test?"

"Oh, no. Her family was once very active in the league, but there's a lot of confusion about her parentage. The birth certificate on file at school says Hailee LaReaux is her mother. No known father, and Scott Hughes is listed as her uncle on her admission application." He gives me a look. "But we're all fairly certain that's a lie, because the Hailee we're familiar with isn't a Hughes, and she's related to the wife, Moira." He sighs. "That's what triggered The Leagues' interest. Years ago, Hailee was pregnant, or The League was led to believe she was pregnant and lost her male child. She never came home after giving birth. She ran off to heal and disappeared into her grief."

He leans back in his chair before continuing. "So when Thea showed up at school and ended up on your floor, nobody cared about what we assumed was a computer error. Then the complaints started coming in from some of the other legacy families. We fully expected the housing office to transfer Thea out of the dorm next semester. Getting her moved wasn't a priority until Malcolm Senior visited Pax on campus. The residents of Vale Tower were quite vocal about the housing issue."

"I'm sure they were."

"Once the council agreed on upping the priority, it didn't take long to find out that her birth certificate has some discrepant data on it."

This sounds a lot like Malcolm's theory. I nod. "She forged it and came here with an agenda."

My dad surprises me when he says, "I don't believe so. I've seen some of the files the researches have collected. Her history, it's all documented. She never once went by a different name. We've spoken to people who have known her at different stages of her life, and a woman going by the name of Hailee LaReaux raised her until she went into the system. I found one file photo. It's the Hailee I grew up with."

"Then what the hell's going on?"

"That's a good damn question, son. Scott and Moira brought her here, but I don't think they expected anyone to pay attention. They certainly didn't consider The League would dig into who this girl is, since everything we were told and all the paperwork we've seen documented that the baby Hailee gave birth to was a boy who was stillborn."

How many levels of lies are surrounding her birth? Is the birth certificate Holden found legit or not? "Is she Moira's niece?"

He smiles at me like he knows I already have the answer to that question. I won't admit it and get Holden into trouble.

"We were willing to let that narrative play out."

"But?"

"But as of an hour ago, that's no longer an option. Moira and Scott needed to establish a medical proxy for the girl. They couldn't do that if she's nineteen and not legally responsible for her."

I have a sinking feeling in the pit of my stomach. "What did they do?"

"They submitted to DNA testing, and provided a copy of a birth certificate listing them as her parents. And since she's only *eighteen*."

He's confirming what I already know. My Pet's entire life is one big lie, right down to her age. I need another drink.

The last text I got from Thea said she was going to grab some stuff from her aunt and uncle's place. The next time I saw her, she was drunk and begging me to fuck her. I know what hiding from your feelings looks like, but I was too mad to ask why. If she learned the truth while digging through her belongings, I understand why she was drunk.

"Now, son, I'll ask again. How can I help?"

I want to say, *you can help by finding Malcolm Cox, Jr. and making him confess to dragging us into this shit.* But I can't throw Malcolm under the bus without implicating ourselves, and casting The Trium as disloyal. To Malcolm, for admitting he had us do a side job without permission, or to The League, for not holding our brother's secrets.

"You already have. I had questions about Thea, and you've cleared them up as much as you can. Where does the family fall in the council hierarchy?"

"There was a bit of an upheaval following Hailee's departure. The family hasn't been active in seventeen years. In fact, the head of the family line doesn't even live in town anymore. That explains why Moira and Scott were able to bring Thea here without raising any red flags sooner."

"And all this, with the council's announcement, was because of complaints?"

"That's right. I don't know what's going on at school, but I haven't wanted to interfere. The Trium is the ruling authority there. But, I'll be honest, Finn, all the grumblings... pretty soon the high council is gonna notice. If a Trium has to be micromanaged, that doesn't say much for any of your futures here."

"We have it handled, dad."

"Do you? A student's in the hospital in serious condition."

I look away. I was hoping I'd get out of here without having to talk about how much we don't know about what happened.

"Finn?"

I amend my statement. "I'm gonna handle it."

"The Dean is saying it's a sorority prank that got out of hand. It's lucky that a faculty member was out in the graveyard. A little longer and the girl might've run out of air."

My blood freezes in my veins. Now I have no problem meeting his inquisitive gaze. "Did you say they found her in the graveyard?"

"That's right. In a coffin, in a freshly dug grave. She must've drank too much and passed out, so she didn't dig out like the other pledges did."

I stand. My mind's still a jumble of information and questions regarding Thea's parentage, but one thing is clear. This was no sorority prank that she volunteered to be a part of, because Thea wasn't pledging a sorority.

Dad doesn't need to know that. He also doesn't need to know that I'm going to get to the bottom of what happened and when I find those responsible, they won't be climbing out of their graves unassisted, either.

Chapter 7
Deacon

I'm staring out the window that overlooks the loading dock of the hospital, but my mind is on the woman hooked up to machines, in the bed behind me. Thea's been in and out of consciousness for three days. Nobody knows what happened or how many people were involved. Zeus has taken sole responsibility and says it's a prank that went wrong. I know a beating when I see it, and minus his dick being damn near bit off, he didn't have nearly enough bruises on him for it to have been a fair fight. The injuries Thea sustained, tells me she was jumped, and as soon as I find out who was involved, I'm gonna make them pay.

Her aunt and uncle are pacing the halls, trying to get answers from the school administration. I'm sure a cover up is already under way. Layla-Jean hasn't left her side since she showed up at the infirmary. She's sitting in the chair next to Thea's bed with bloodshot eyes. She's been downing coffee and energy drinks, like she's afraid to fall asleep.

"Breland, you need to head back to campus. I'm sure you have classes tomorrow. You should get some sleep."

She whips her head up and glares at me. "Thea isn't going to classes, so neither am I."

"Thea's in a hospital bed recovering."

"Exactly, and I'm gonna stay here until she can walk out of this place. She's my best friend, and I wasn't there to protect her. I'm here now." She narrows her eyes at me. "You're the one with assholes to train on how to beat up women. You're the one who should leave."

Her shoulders slump after that show of strength. I remember Breland from when I've subbed for a class or two at the high school. I don't remember that she ever had a backbone. This has to be Thea's influence.

"It's obvious you care a lot about her. But you've been here the whole time, sitting in that chair. How do you think she'll feel if she wakes up and sees you sleep deprived and starved?"

"When she wakes up."

"Huh?"

"You said *if*. *If* is not an option. Thea *will* wake up." She stares at her friend like she's willing her to do that.

"Yes, she will. LaReaux's too damn stubborn not to."

Thea's aunt comes into the room. She startles when she notices me. "Coach, Wolfe. I didn't know you came back."

"I never actually left."

Her husband walks into the room. He looks just as confused as his wife to see me here. Obviously Thea hasn't told her guardians anything about me. Training her, that is. I can't imagine any scenario where she mentions me fucking her in an alley an hour after we met.

"Coach Wolfe, did the school send you to follow up with the investigation? Because, as you can see, our daughter is still unable to tell you what happened, and we won't be signing any waivers of liability until we get her side of things."

"I'm not here on school business. I'm here for LaReaux."

His chest puffs up. "Excuse me?"

"I said... I'm here for Thea. I won't be leaving the hospital until she wakes up and tells me it's okay to leave."

"Look, we appreciate you finding her and bringing her in, but I believe your job as a teacher is done. So if you're here to harass us-"

"I'm Thea's coach at school. She takes my Physical Enhancement class, and I'm her trainer. She's been working out at my gym for about a month now." I point to the unmoving body on the bed. "I don't know how involved you are or aren't in her life, but since you look shocked to know that I'm training her, I'd say not much."

"You're not very good at your job, since it looks like she was attacked."

Smart mouths must be a family trait. I ignore the jab Mrs. Hughes just hurled my way. "I'm excellent at my job and Thea's one of the top fighters in my gym and a top student in my class. Which is why I'm staying. Because this..." I point to the bed again. "Whatever happened to her wasn't a fight. It was a brutal beat down, and more than one person was involved. In fact, I'll go as far to say that at least two people held her down, while everyone else used her as a punching bag. Now, before you ask me how I came by that number, I'll say this. It's because I train her to fight men twice her size with the same amount of experience and she bests them, almost seventy percent of the time. If I have her fight two at a time, they're still working hard to put her on her ass. So in case you're not following, it takes more than the pimply kid with the ice pack on his flaccid dick to do this to her. We won't even go into me finding her in a coffin in an unmarked grave. Sorority prank, fraternity fuck-over, Mayhem Night Mischief. I don't care what label the school gives it. As far as I'm concerned, your niece was targeted. It could be because of you and whatever you do for a living, or because she has a smart ass mouth and pisses people off. Who's to say they won't come here to make sure she never tells us what happened? LaReaux isn't safe if she can't defend herself. Now, if you don't want me here, fine. Get a security detail. Make sure it's someone you know and trust. Don't accept anyone the school sends. If you need help vetting a team, I can recommend some people."

"That won't be necessary."

The uncle's an idiot. After everything I laid out, he's willing to risk her safety? "You don't want a security detail? That's your choice. But like I said, I'll leave when she wakes up and tells me to."

"Deacon Wolfe, right? You own Wolfe Pack. That's the gym you mentioned. You train fighters, but your students also have the highest scores at MISTIC, and your grandfather owns Dire Wolfe Security."

"Did you just google me?"

"My daughter was missing. We hadn't heard from her in three days, and the school said they didn't know anything. Then we get a call yesterday, saying you're the person who found her. What kind of man would I be, not to suspect that you had a hand in her injuries?"

The school let them worry for three days, trying to get their story straight. I found Thea early Saturday morning and took her straight to the infirmary. I'm glad he's not blindly accepting their version of events, but he's not in the clear himself. Why was it three days before they noticed she was missing? It's not lost on me that he's calling Thea his daughter, when all her paperwork says he's the uncle.

I've caught bits and pieces from the phone conversations and discussions I've heard when I've gone to get coffee. It all boils down to one thing. They've been lying to Thea about who they are. I hope they're prepared for the shit she's gonna put them through when she wakes up. She's really gonna love the part where she finds out she's eighteen again, for a few more weeks. Fuck, I dodged a bullet on that one.

"I assume your research revealed I'm not a threat to LaReaux, and that's why you haven't had me escorted off the premises yet."

"That and since you brought it up, we'd like to hire you."

His wife side eyes him. "We would?"

"To teach you self defense?" I was just spit balling that they're the reason Thea was targeted, but maybe I'm not way off.

"We want you to protect Thea while the school investigates what happened, and we determine it's safe for her to go back."

"I don't do that type of work."

"We're hoping that you'll make an exception."

"I can give you names, better candidates than me."

"The doctors are saying she'll need therapy for the hand and shoulder. Thea doesn't strike me as the type of person who will do well with therapy. You're already training her, so you know her strengths and her limitations. It says here you have a degree in kinesiology. I can't think of a better candidate than you, and Thea isn't big on people. She's not gonna let anyone near her, even if it's for her own good."

Breland cuts in. "Please, Coach Wolfe. Thea won't care if she's in danger. You know she won't let anyone help her that she doesn't already like, know, and trust."

"What makes you think she likes and trusts me?"

She stares down at her friend. "She does. I can tell by the way she talks about your training sessions. She's tired and pissy and calls you a sadistic prick. She says you don't give out compliments easily."

"None of this is winning me over to the side of wanting to say yes, Breland. If anything, it strengthens my reasons for saying no."

"She says those things, but she keeps going back to your gym, and she hasn't cut you yet."

"She's threatened to."

"Yeah, but she hasn't done it yet." She grabs Thea's hand and squeezes. "Help her Coach. She trusts you."

I look over at the aunt, uncle, parent mashup. "Got anything to add?"

Mrs. Hughes tips her head back, her eyes so similar to Thea's roaming over my face before locking with mine. "I think LJ has summed it all up rather nicely. Are you in or are you out?"

That's definitely a Thea-ism. I want to hear her sass me again. I want her knocking men on their asses and staring up at me when she executes a move we've been working on, daring me to critique it, and I want to see the look on her face when I call her a good girl for doing it correctly. None of that'll happen if she winds up with an idiot and sabotages her own recovery.

"When Thea wakes up, as long as she doesn't have an issue with me, I'll do it."

I'm lying. Of course I'm lying. She can have all the issues she wants, but now that I've said yes, there's no way I'm letting anyone else watch over her.

"Okay. Thank you." She shares a look with her husband. There's something she's about to say, and they've already discussed it. I get the feeling I'm not gonna like it.

"We're moving Thea."

"To a new room?" LJ questions from her post by the bed.

"To a new location. If what Mr. Wolfe says is correct, then we don't want her where anyone can reach her."

"Let me know when the medical team is ready to go."

"There will be no team. Just you, Thea, and a nurse."

LJ gets to her feet. "Mrs. Hughes, you can't move, Thea. Didn't the doctors say she's not out of the woods until she wakes up? They're in here every half hour checking on her. We can't just leave it up to a nurse and Coach Wolfe. What if she has complications or needs surgery again?"

"Thea's strong. She'll survive the transport, and we have a medical team waiting at her final destination. We don't want a bunch of people coming in and out, and knowing where she is."

Breland looks at the bed. "But I'm not people. She's *my* best friend. If she's going somewhere, so am I."

Mrs. Hughes walks over and grabs her hands. "I know, LJ, and I don't want to assume to know Thea's feelings about you. She's a complicated person, and I know she likes you. But we can't risk you knowing either."

The machine's beeping increases, drawing all of our attention. The medical team rushes in, pushing us out of the way. Mrs. Hughes looks at the doctor and asks, "What's going on? Is she waking up?"

"Her heart rate is elevated."

Thea thrashes around in bed as more people crowd into the room, touching her. "There's no sign she's waking up, but we'll need to run more tests to find out why she's convulsing like this. Please clear the room."

"Thea! Thea!" Breland calls her name, trying to be heard over the beeping monitors.

"Please leave. We need to sedate her and keep her calm so she doesn't hurt herself."

I drift closer to the bed, taking in the pained look on Thea's face. I bark out an order. "Back up." The doctors and nurses ignore me. "I said, back up! She may not be awake, but she senses there are too many people in here. Back up, give her space."

"Sir, that's not likely."

"I will put you on your ass if you don't move." I motion LJ over. "Go sit, hold her hand like you were doing."

She immediately does that, and says, "It's okay, Thea. I'm still here."

The monitors slowly quiet, and I point at the screens. "We don't know what she's been through, but I do know that on any given day, Thea doesn't like people messing with her friend, or touching her."

I look over at the aunt and uncle. "There's your answer about who's in this little circle of trust. Breland goes."

Thea mutters, *Big Bad Wolfe*, in her sleep. I resist the urge to smile. That's right sweetness, and I'm gonna chew up anyone that tries to hurt you, again.

Chapter 8
Deacon

It took a few days to make the arrangements, but we're finally in an ambulance heading towards our new location. Thea had several more episodes. The doctors haven't been able to find a physical cause for the spike in her blood pressure and heart rate. So they settled on a psychological one. She's having nightmares and panic attacks. I don't have a medical degree, but I already knew that. The more people in the room, the more stressed out and agitated she becomes. Her mind is fighting, even if her body can't. The only thing that seems to help keep her calm is LJ talking non-stop. I finally convinced her to go home and pack a bag, since she's coming with us. The caveat is that once Thea wakes, LJ has to go back to classes.

We both know she'll be pissed if her friend messes up her education because of this. I'm on the spare gurney in the back of the ambulance with my eyes closed, going over my checklist in my head. The kitchen of wherever we're going is supposed to be fully stocked to limit our interaction with anyone from the outside.

We didn't tell anyone we're moving Thea. Not even the school. Until she can tell me who's not involved in her attack, everyone is a potential threat. We've also left Thea's and LJ's phones behind. Scott and Moira are staying in Canyon Falls, but I have a burner phone they can reach me on.

"Are you sure I can't have my phone, Coach?"

"I'm sure if anyone comes looking for Thea, you'll be the first person they use to get to her."

"Why, me? Why not her aunt and uncle, or you?"

"If anyone's gonna keep track of her, it'll be you. You're clingy, like that."

"I'm not clingy, I'm concerned."

"They'll notice you missing first and rightly guess that you're probably wherever LaReaux is. Since her aunt and uncle have already contacted the school once about her being gone, it'll be easier for them to pretend she woke up and signed herself out of the hospital without telling them. As for me, nobody cares where I am. I'm the asshole Physical Enhancements instructor. I'd never waste my time babysitting a student."

"Your family's in security, right?"

"Yeah. But I'm not, and I've been very vocal about not joining the family business. That's why I'm whipping entitled brats into shape at C Falls University. Besides, I take breaks all the time. I've been overdue for one, and since it's almost the end of the semester, nobody will question where I went. Even if they do, they won't suspect it's to a safe house to baby-sit chatty princesses."

She snorts. "Oh god, please let me be there when you call Thea a chatty princess to her face." Her next question isn't so cheerful. "Why would somebody do this to her?"

"You'd have a better idea about that than me."

"You see her in class. You train her. Thea minds her business, and despite what lies the Zeta Nu's might be spreading, she doesn't go out of her way to bother people."

"She's not in the habit of making friends either, but you're right, Breland. Whoever did this was working through more than just an angry little spat."

She sighs as if she was hoping I wouldn't confirm Thea was attacked. "They canceled classes for the next few days, but the school's saying it was a sorority prank that went too far. Nobody's gonna ask anymore questions once the official ruling comes out. She won't get justice."

"Don't worry, Breland. If I know anything at all about LaReaux, it's that she doesn't need an official investigation from the school to get justice. She's her own little avenging angel."

The safe house is a townhouse in Palisades Shores. It's been a while since I've driven through this town. It's more upscale than I remember. Then again, it could be the side of town we're on. I'm not here on vacation so unless there's a reason for me to go across town, I won't get to see firsthand if the gentrification extends beyond this area.

The medical transport company and nurse gets Thea settled into the master bedroom. LJ takes the one right next to her, and I'm at the end of the hall. It's still early evening, so I inspect the grounds while LJ unpacks her stuff. Our neighbor across the street has a dog that barks every time a car drives by. That's a useful early warning system, and annoying if he does it all night. There's not much to see on my short walk. This is a newer neighborhood. The entire block of houses behind our street is empty.

When I get back inside, LJ's glaring at the fridge. "Something in their making you mad?" I ask.

"I can cook basic stuff. Spaghetti, Mac and cheese, microwave a pizza." She waves at the freezer. "None of that's in here. Why are you looking at me funny?"

"I'm a little surprised to hear that you cook."

"Thea started teaching me when The Trium messed with her dining hall account. We started with the important stuff. Carbs." She waves her finger at me. "There's some suspects I know the school wouldn't even consider."

I push her to the side, pulling steaks out of the freezer, and things out of the fridge for a salad, and find potatoes in the pantry. "I'll take care of the steak and potatoes. You do the salad." She pales when I say, "And tell me why you think The Trium could be to blame."

"It was a joke."

"Maybe, but there's a reason behind it, and you're gonna tell me what it is."

I'm just stepping out of the shower when Thea screams. It's a blood curdling sound filled with anger and pain. LJ pops her head out of her room and rushes towards Thea's. I pull her behind me, entering first. "Someone screams you don't go running in first, Breland!"

"It's Thea and nobody's here but us."

"We assume nobody's here but us, but you still treat things like there might be an intruder. Got it?"

"Got it."

I walk inside first, LJ close on my heels. Thea's thrashing around in the bed, in the middle of another one of her dreams.

"Do you think the doctors are wrong? That maybe we should try to wake her."

"No. Something tells me that would be a bad idea, but she needs something to make her feel safe."

"I can hold her hand like I did in the hospital."

"We need something that'll work when you're sleeping, too."

"A knife."

I arch a brow at her. "You wanna cut me for saying you can't hold her hand all night? She really is rubbing off on you."

"No. I mean, what if we give her a knife? Thea always has one with her, but when I asked, Moira and Scott said Clint wasn't in any of her things. Maybe she'll feel safer if she has a knife."

"Okay. Go grab one."

She runs downstairs to the kitchen and comes back with one of the biggest ones in the butcher's block. I have to stop her again from approaching Thea. "I'll take it over, just in case she reacts in her sleep."

"Okay, put it under her pillow."

I walk towards the bed, holding the knife handle out, slowly slipping it under her pillow, then place her hand firmly on top of it. "Is this what you need, sweetness?" I feel her hand close around the handle.

Slowly her breathing calms, the monitors quieting. I move back to the door. "Good call, Breland." I put my hand on her shoulder and steer her into the hall. "Now go get some sleep."

"But Thea might need me."

I shove her forward. "I'll sit with her. If she needs you, I'll come get you."

I collapse onto the chair in the corner of the room, tilting my head back, trying to work through everything I still need to do. Thea's restless, and cries out in her sleep again. This time it's not as loud as before. I think her grip on the knife helps. But I won't be any good to her if I'm dead on my feet. I walk over to the bed and kneel down beside it, pushing her damp hair off her forehead. "I don't know what's happening in that head of yours, LaReaux. I'm guessing a lot of bad shit. But I don't want you worrying about any of that right now."

I slip under the covers, leaving some space between us, and toy with a loc of her hair. "I need you resting and healing. Now settle down."

She whimpers, the sound cracking through the wall of my heart, making me relive the night I found her. Shuffling closer, I repeat the words I told her when I pulled her from the burning coffin. "You're safe now, sweetness. I've got you."

Chapter 9
Thea

There's a beeping noise, and it's driving me nuts. There's also a thumping noise and a whirring sound. All of them are happening at once, and I have no idea why they're in my bedroom. I'm fighting to open my eyes, so I can turn them off. It's harder than it should be. The moment I crack them open, the lights send a sharp pain shooting through my eyeballs and into my head.

A hand rubs up and down my back, and somebody's saying something to me. I focus on the voice instead of the other noises. "It's okay, sweetness. Take your time. I've got you."

My hand closes around a smooth surface. The familiar chill of metal rests against my palm. I've got a knife. I can protect myself. The repetitive motion of the hand and the soothing voice lulls me back to sleep.

I'm hot. That's the first thing I notice before I'm pulled completely out of my dream. The second thing I notice is that I'm not alone. My left hand curls around the hilt of a knife. My eyes pop open as I yank the knife from under the pillow. The movement jostles my shoulder, sending pain through every nerve ending in my body. Even my teeth hurt.

"Don't stab me LaReaux, you might pull out your stitches."

My right arm is in a sling, and there are wires coming out of my left one. It takes a considerable amount of effort to turn around, but I ignore the pain enough to do it. When I do, I find Deacon Wolfe lying on his back, his arm thrown over his eyes.

"Why are you in my bed?"

"Because on your journey back to the land of the living, you've been making pit stops in hell -screaming loud enough to wake the whole goddamn neighborhood- and cutting through the linen. It wasn't until I got into bed with you that you settled down enough for LJ to sleep."

At the mention of her name, I look past his shoulder. The paint on the walls isn't the paint in my dorm room. "Where are we?"

"Palisade Shores."

"Why?"

"I'm hoping you can tell me, but how about I change your bandages and get some coffee before we launch into that?"

I raise the knife. "How about you talk now, and if I don't cut your throat open, you can drink you coffee when we're done."

He's not even looking at me, but he grabs my hand, pushes me onto my back, and rolls on top of me. I panic and thrash around, trying to free myself. "Let me go, let me go!" I can't breathe. Why can't I breathe?

"Thea, look at me! Look at me!"

My eyes pop open. "That's it, sweetness. Just look at me." My vision clears and my lungs inflate. "Good girl. It's just me, LaReaux. Look at me. Hear my voice. I would never hurt you."

"Wolfe." My voice sounds small. Timid. I hate how scared I sound. I can see him, but I can't move. I can't tell him I know he won't hurt me, because right now, he feels like a threat hovering over me.

"I'm gonna move. Okay?"

He rolls off of me and slowly climbs off the bed. My muscles loosen and the beeping in the room slows.

"Since you're up, I think we can disconnect you from that thing."

"You said LJ was here before. Is she coming back?"

"Breland's right next door, with noise canceling headphones on. I'll go get her."

I keep my eye on him until he steps through the door, then inch myself backwards so I can sit up. I'm halfway up when LJ comes running through the door. "You're awake!"

I am, but the longer I am, the more I wish I wasn't. I'm stiff and sore, my body feels like a dump truck hit the forward and reverse over me and then did it again. I let her help me into a sitting position, then slowly ease my legs over the side of the bed. "I wanna see."

"See what?"

"What I look like." I swallow, trying to wet my throat. "I wanna see the damage."

"No. You don't." She walks over, putting a hand on my shoulder. "Lie back down, Thea. You're still healing."

"That's exactly why I need to get up and see what I'm healing from."

"Thea, please."

My face hurts, the familiar throb of taking a blow to the jaw. My mouth isn't wired shut, but that doesn't mean I don't have structural damage to it. Like my nose. I can feel the brace on it, which means it's broken. My ribs too, but I want to look at myself and see the damage while it's still at it's worse.

"How long have I been asleep, and what kind of drugs did the doctor give me to get me here without waking up?"

"It's been seven days since Coach Wolfe found you. You were unconscious and rushed right into surgery. You never woke up."

"Seven days?" Now I know I need to get up. "Did they say I have a brain injury?" I try to work through things, see if there are any obvious holes in my memory.

Coach Wolfe comes into the room and leans against the door. "You obviously remember Breland, and who you are. I think we've established you remember me. Your recall of people's names seems to be intact. Do you remember specific details about the last time you saw each of us?"

The last time I saw LJ, we had breakfast in my room, and I had just told her I was going to Nags Creek for winter break. The last time I saw Coach Wolfe, he had Tank pinned to the mat working out a new move. "Yeah, I do."

LJ smiles. "Good. What about the first time you met each of us?"

"We met outside the auditorium and you told me about the Coxsuckers."

"Good, and Coach Wolfe?"

My eyes slide over my trainer as I recall our first meeting. He's standing there, arms folded across his chest, and he's shirtless. I've seen him without a shirt plenty of times at the gym, but right now it seems indecent, and there's no way I can tell LJ about the first time we really met. "I remember his crappy welcome speech in class."

"And you remember your life before you came here?"

I remember the lie I lived before I came here, which leads to Finn trying to humiliate me and wandering through town then... my body shakes, and I break out into a cold sweat. The machines are beeping again. I want to be okay. I tell myself that I'm okay, but my body locks up, unable to do anything about the hands touching me.

"Easy, sweetness. Just breathe. You're safe. Come on. Breathe for me. Just breathe. In and out. Ten breaths."

I try to do it. My mind says to do it, but my body won't listen. "Come on, sing for me LaReaux. Count those breaths."

"One, sir. Two, sir. Three, sir." By the time I get to eight, I'm not as rigid in his arms. The habit of counting the way I do when we're training is natural. My body easily falls into it. I get to ten and sag against LJ.

"Good girl."

I swipe at the tears with my good hand. "Help me to the bathroom. I need to see. Whatever happened has messed with my mind. I need to see my body, too."

LJ shakes her head. "I don't know if you're ready yet. Just talking has triggered you."

"LJ, help me or I'll hurl myself on the floor and crawl in there myself."

Coach steps forward. "I'll let you see, but you're not walking. You're weak, and the last thing we need is you falling down and hurting yourself further before the nurse gets here. If you want to see, I have to carry you."

He gives me a minute to work it out. Considering I just freaked out and did the same thing earlier when he touched me, he's probably thinking I'll change my mind about getting out of bed. I want to say forget the whole thing. The idea of touch makes me sick to my stomach. But I won't be this pathetic thing. Not right now. I can cry about it later when they leave the room. So I suck it up as much as I can.

"Okay."

He drapes the blanket over me, wrapping me up in it from head to toe, before lifting me. No part of his skin touches mine. Through the thick quilting of the comforter, I can't even feel his hands. LJ rolls the monitor and IV bag into the bathroom with us. He puts me on my feet with my back to the mirror, then backs away.

"Hang onto the counter. Call me when you're ready to get back in bed." He turns and walks away without waiting for me to agree.

LJ asks, "Do you want me to leave too?"

"You don't mind?"

"No. This is your moment. I don't need to be here. I'll close the door behind me, just please do what Coach Wolfe said, and hang onto the counter."

"I will."

I wait until the door is closed before turning around. Nothing I could have imagined would have been enough to prepare me for my first look at the bruised and swollen flesh on my face. Seven days and my cheeks are still puffy, my lip twice the size it should be. This is ten times worse than any damage I've ever gotten in the ring.

I prop my hip against the counter and ease my shirt up, working my arm through the sleeve and slipping it over my head, letting it hang across the sling on my useless arm. LJ said I was in surgery. The scar extending from the side of my neck across my shoulder is the least alarming thing on me; but weaved in through all the superficial bruising it adds to the grotesque image in front of me. I'm not a vain person, but seeing the damage to my body cuts me deep. Not because I've been hurt, but because I don't know how I got hurt, and however it happened, I wasn't strong enough to fight back.

Holding onto the counter, I cry. I cry silent sobs, for the girl I was before my attack, and for the girl I was before I found out the foundation of my life was built on lies.

I cry for the Thea LaReaux I was when I came to Canyon Falls, because I have no idea who I am now.

Chapter 10
Pax

My father's back from his business trip. His car is parked in front of the dorm when I get back after class. I climb into the backseat, steeling myself for whatever he's about to say. He waits until the driver is back behind the wheel and the partition raised before speaking.

"I hear your grandfather has a theory about the girl."

He's been gone for two weeks, but that didn't stop him from staying in touch with what's happened in his absence. It's just his family he couldn't be bothered with. "You think he's wrong?"

"It doesn't appear that he is. Though I've only just begun looking into things myself. As a member of the legacy validation committee, I think we need to be certain of this girl's origins before we go around making certain claims. Even if she is the daughter of this ostracized family line, that doesn't mean she isn't here to sew discord in our ranks. This bit of news just puts her in a better position to do it, don't you agree?"

It's the same thing I said to the guys. Hearing it repeated back to me just strengthens my resolve. I don't want to be my father, but I respect the way his brain works. "I do. I agree."

"Good. So nothing's changed. She's still to be watched, and at the slightest sign of anything suspicious, you let me know."

"Don't you mean the high council?"

He pins me with the stare that makes men cower in their loafers. "Are you suddenly high enough in rank to get a direct line of contact with them? Did a promotion happen while I was away?"

"No, sir."

"I'm on the validation committee, and a prospect chair member. Coming to me with your concerns is the correct thing to do. Now, I'm told the school will wrap up their investigation shortly, but there are still some parents who have questions about how the girl was injured. Others worry about what this means for the safety of their heirs. This little problem will not be the thing that brings the news vultures to our doorsteps or tarnish our reputation. It's on you and the other Trium members to get things back under control. I expect it to happen quickly. The League will be watching how you handle things, and with your grandfather's interest focused on this girl, it's more important than ever that you show you can lead outside of the campus games and challenges. The Trium is the ruling faction, and family members of the twelve are members of your court. Make sure you're spending time with them, strengthening their support. If our suspicions prove true, we're going to need it."

"Understood, sir."

"Go on, then. I have a flight to catch. Your mother expects you home at five for dinner on Sunday."

I'm assuming he just got back to town because this is the first I've seen or heard from him, and now he's leaving again? He said my mother expects me, which leaves it unclear whether he'll be there as well. I wish I could skip dinner, but if I do, I'll never hear the end of it. Maybe I can convince the guys to go with me. Misery loves company, after all.

I walk through the doors and pass the crowded lounge, catching snippets of conversations as I head towards the elevator. It's just as my father said. They're gossiping about Thea's accident. Finn is sitting in the middle of it all. He has his headphones, his head bobbing to a beat only he can hear. It looks like he's not all that invested in the conversation flowing around him, but I know he's still trying to piece together what happened. When Finn gets an idea in his head, it's hard for him to just let it go. Someone will need to show him evidence to prove he's wrong. I don't know if he'll get that in this situation. The school isn't obligated to share their findings with students. Whatever soundbite they give to the news outlets is it.

An initiation prank gone wrong, maybe hazing on campus. Whichever organization is blamed for it will get a fine, and some type of school administered sanction. Depending on how many infractions they've already received, they may have to move their operations off campus. That last part isn't all that bad. Very few of the Greek houses are on campus to begin with.

Finn tips his chin, acknowledging he's seen me, before looking back down at his phone. He's probably recording everything. I'm sure he'll fill us in on what he's heard when we meet up for dinner. Right now I'm going up to my room to change, then I'm heading to the gym. For the next hour, I don't wanna see, hear, or talk to anyone.

I don't get to the elevator fast enough to ride it alone. The girls who get on blush when they see me. I'm not in the mood to deal with them, but it's all about keeping up appearances. I give them both a once over - slowly stretching my lips into a cocky smirk- that suggests I know exactly what they're thinking. That makes their cheeks even redder. They get off on the third floor, giggling, giving me one last appreciative look before the door closes. Thankfully, they didn't actually try to talk to me. I put the car in private mode so I don't have to deal with anyone else.

I change quickly and head to the gym on the ninth floor just so I can get to my workout quicker. As I go through my warm up, I let my mind wander over everything we've learned these last few months. I was anxious to talk to my father after my grandfather's announcement, because I thought doing so would provide some clarification. After our conversation, it feels like we're back in the same situation as before. There's still no definitive answer about who Theona LaReaux really is and she could still be a threat to all our futures.

I drop onto the floor and set my alarm for two minutes, knocking out as many pushups as I can. There *is* one thing different. We have The League watching us, and her. The minute she makes a move against them, they'll intervene. I climb to my feet and walk over to the heavy bag, and start working on punches and slips. Maybe we're putting the focus on the wrong thing. Instead of waiting to see if she's a threat. Maybe we should push her to reveal that she *is* a threat.

Going over what I know about her that might be easier to accomplish. She's secretive, which makes it easier to hide what she's doing. But she's also reactive when she feels threatened. Getting her to lash out won't be too hard. Now I just have to figure out what to do to make her feel like The League is the threat she needs to fight back against.

Chapter 11
Finn

The school is full of gossiping idiots. Everyone has a theory, an idea, a story, a speculation about what happened to Thea, but nobody knows for sure.

I take that back. *Somebody* knows, but they're not talking. And despite what I suspect about Eloise, I can't take action without proof that she was involved because of this damned marriage contract. It doesn't matter how I feel about her. She's going to be my wife and, according to the rules, I already have an obligation to protect her from threats. In this case, it means not torturing the truth out of her.

I tune out whatever she and her friends are talking about, replaying some of my favorite action sequences in my head. Pax told me about the complaints some of the council members had, regarding my treatment of the annoying little princess, so now I have to play the role of perfect little prince in public. We can't give anyone in The League a reason to think I won't do what's expected of me when we graduate.

That's the reason I'm letting her hang onto my arm like Sannakji wrapped around chopsticks. She's happy as shit about it, too. I'm resigned to having to put on this public show of being her boyfriend while my nut sac dries up. Since her damn chastity vow is still in place, even the most basic of sexual adventures with her isn't even an option.

Her presence is like pussy repellant. The girls at the table are too afraid to fuck me behind her back, and I haven't been able to ditch her long enough to find someone who isn't.

Thea wouldn't care. She'd be happy to cut out and fuck like animals just because it would piss Eloise off. I need my pet to come back so we can clear the air about everything. "Holden."

He looks up from his tablet and waits for me to explain why I'm interrupting whatever he's doing. "Any new information?"

He's been glued to that thing since the moment he realized Thea's medical records aren't in Canyon Falls General's database, and is trying to figure out where she disappeared to. He repeats what he's been saying all week.

"This is a professional level blackout. Whoever is helping her has to be the same people who kept her off The League's radar for eighteen years."

I inwardly groan, as he brings up her age. Thea and I went from being the same age; to her being the baby of the group.

"I logged onto dad's server at work but didn't find anything. Maybe she's working with the CIA or the NSA."

"Yeah. That would explain it. Thea's a spy." I chuckle at my own joke.

Holden pins me with his stare. "Her movements are cloaked in shadows and secrets which lend to spy like tendencies."

My jaw hinges open because he's serious. Which means he's seriously considering hacking those agencies. We don't need those issues right now. "Holden, she's not a spy."

"I agree, Thea's probably not a spy, but someone with expert level computer skills is definitely shrouding her movements. She's a fucking ghost right now. There are no camera clips, credit card transactions, or anything else to clue us in on how she got out of the hospital and where she went afterwards."

Pax picks this moment to join our conversation. "Do you know who'd be able to hide her tracks? People who are trying to tear The League apart. They'd have plans and contingencies to protect their assets. And those people could be a government agency, or a corporation with deep pockets. We can't rule anything out."

Of course he thinks her disappearance is ammunition to support his theory that she's our enemy, but I think this is just one more thing that makes her so fucking hot. A real life action hero whose pussy feels like heaven? Sign me up for more of that.

Someone walking by says into their phone, "Can you believe we haven't crossed over yet?"

The complaint is one I've heard several times this week.

"I don't know what the holdup is. I think somebody should go ask The Trium why they're sitting on their asses instead of doing something." He looks over his shoulder and catches me staring.

I'm not in the mood for this shit, but since he's talking loud enough for everyone to hear, I'll have to address it. I pull out my knife. "Go on Everdeen. I know the words are on the tip of your tongue to volunteer as tribute. And once they fall, I'll happily take your tongue so you never wag it in my vicinity again."

He scurries off, clearly not man enough to get the deed done. The thing is, we *have* asked what the holdup is, and the answer is simple. Nothing can happen while Thea's "accident" is still under investigation. The Intercollegiate Fraternity Council was on campus a few days ago. They're trying to decide if any of the Greek clubs broke the basic rules they agreed to uphold when they joined the ICC. We're all getting scrutinized. Thea was dropped from Zeta Nu's pledge roster, but that doesn't mean another fraternity or sorority didn't use her as a willing or unwilling pawn in an initiation prank that went too far. Willing. My Pet? Not likely. But that's the narrative we're supporting. As long as nobody actually confesses to anyone, *other than me*, about what happened; the ruling that it was an accident should stand, and we can get back to finishing out the pledge season.

"He's right, you know." Eloise pouts. "Our entire season is on hold because of that stupid bitch. She probably did this just to mess with us, you know? Since she wasn't Zeta Nu material, she's made it so all the worthy pledges can't claim their place."

Pax chuckles. Is he agreeing with her? Holden lowers his tablet. I think he's about to say something, but he gets to his feet and walks to the exit.

Every day Thea's gone is one more day we risk the high council taking a closer look into what's been happening at school. We have a job to do -and it's important that we succeed- but for now, as long as the investigation is underway, Thea's absence is working in the school's favor.

My molars grind together as I raise my left arm over my head. I'm trying to regain some fluidity in my stiff body. I've been through fights before, and I've lost plenty, so I know what it feels like to be pulverized. But none of those losses have ever felt like this. I'm not just talking about the aches and bruises. I feel like there's a weight on my chest that has nothing to do with the broken ribs. I'm still piecing together what happened between walking into Moira and Scott's house and finding those photo albums, and waking up here.

My mind stalls on my stupid decision to go see Finn. He's always been a bit of a jerk when he closes ranks with Pax and Holden, but he was never cruel until that night. There was no hint of the teasing we usually did. It was nothing but anger and him trying to humiliate me. I owe him for that, and I won't feel better until I've gotten payback.

Deacon gives me a pointed look. He doesn't think I should be doing anything more strenuous than eating and sleeping. "I'm fine, Coach."

"We're not at school, or the gym, Thea. You don't have to call me coach."

"Right. I just figured with everyone else flipping the script on me, you have, too."

He leans against the wall, wearing a white tee and his hair's damp like he recently showered, his arms folded across his pecs. He sleeps in my bed, but he's been clear about where we stand in this power dynamic. Same place we did before. He's the coach, I'm the student. I'm tired of looking at him, and I'm tired of being here. I need to figure out my next moves and I can't do that with him hovering.

"Why am I here?"

"Because you need to heal."

"Last I checked, doctor wasn't on your resume."

"Then you didn't look close enough, because I have EMT experience."

"Seriously. Why did you bring me here instead of leaving me at the hospital or the school infirmary?"

"Your injuries were too severe for the school. You needed surgery. As for why you're not in a hospital; your aunt and uncle thought it'd be best not to leave you in Canyon Falls General, and risk all the questions that would come with that."

That tracks. "So the liars shipped me off again."

"I don't know what that means."

"Moira and Scott. The liars. They're not my aunt and uncle."

"Blood relations don't matter. They care for you, and that's the title you've given them."

"No, I mean, they're really *not* my aunt and uncle. Turns out they're my parents. *Surprise,* it's a girl." I study his face, waiting for a reaction. He doesn't have one. "You don't look surprised."

"Unexpected paternity reveals are why I'm so meticulous about sanitation at the gym. I don't want the gym shutting down for people taking involuntary DNA samples."

"This isn't funny, Deacon."

He shrugs and asks, "When did you find out?"

"Before... before that night."

"Were you that upset that you went looking for a fight? Were you trying to prove something?"

I can see where this line of questioning is going. "God, no. I didn't break your stupid fighting rule. After I found out, I wanted to be alone. I went for a walk, stopped to get something to drink, and…"

"And what?"

"And after I made it a third of the way through a bottle of vodka, I went to see Finn. He was back on his bullshit. I don't know how he found out the truth about me, but he did and acted like I betrayed him."

"What happened?"

It's my turn to shrug. Fuck that dude. "He let me know he was such a cliche. I was his chance to walk on the wild side to up his bad boy street cred. Then he kicked me out and slammed the door in my face."

"He kicked you out?"

"That's right. Now that I supposedly come from money, my time and pussy were no longer of interest to him."

His jaw clenches, and the vein in his temple throbs. He's probably about to call me out on drinking. I definitely consumed more alcohol than I should have, but your life imploding warrants drinks, and lots of them.

"LJ mentioned you've been having problems with The Trium. Do you think Finn and his buddies could have been behind what happened to you?"

"On Mayhem Night? I don't know. It's all fuzzy in my head."

I've been going over that night, and it doesn't matter how many times he, LJ or the doctor asks, I don't have any new information to give him. Did I mention I hate shrinks? Because I do. I'm being forced to see one now, just like I was all those years ago. This time it's worse. He expects me to just spill my guts after knowing him for five minutes. It took my old shrink years to get me to talk, and we kept it simple. I told her how close I came to stabbing someone that week, and she told me why she thought I felt stabby. But this guy doesn't seem to want to get on board with the way therapy with me works. He keeps telling me I'll feel better if I open up about everything that has ever happened to me in my life. I tell him I like feeling crappy and bottling things up until I explode like the firecracker I am.

My sarcasm is wasted on him. After our first session, I told him not to come back. He didn't listen. The second session, I left him sitting in the living room for fifty minutes. He's coming back today even though I have nothing to say to him. Which brings me to this little hallway meeting with Wolfe. He caught me trying to sneak out of the house.

"Now, if you'll excuse me, I need to finish holding this wall up with my good hand."

He pulls me away from the wall and lifts my shirt to check my bruises. Then he slides the collar of my shirt down to look at my scar. I avert my gaze. I've been avoiding looking at myself. I've gotten okay enough to let him check it for me, and as long as it's not infected, it's good enough for me.

My breath catches in my chest. There's nothing sexy about him looking at my ugly ass scar, but I'm acutely aware of how close he's standing and the way his lashes sweep against his cheeks when he blinks. The thing I'm most aware of is the weight of his hand on my shoulder, and the way his fingers press against my skin. I don't want to talk about my feelings with the shrink, but getting my pussy devoured would probably do wonders for my mood.

"Why are you looking at me like that, LaReaux?"

"Like what?"

"Like you're imagining me naked."

"Because I am. Wanna show me if the fantasy matches reality?"

"It doesn't."

"Selling yourself short, Wolfe?"

"Mmm." He pulls away, finished with inspecting my scar. "It's healing nicely."

"You're avoiding the subject." The intensity of his gaze lights me up inside. I press for an answer. "Well?"

"Trying to bait me into fucking you won't work."

"Who's baiting? Tell me you haven't thought about that night. You can be honest. It's just us here. No school, no rules. Just you and me giving in."

LJ appears at the top of the stairs. Her gaze shifts between the two of us. "Uh, is everything okay?"

"LaReaux's scar is fine. Is her doctor here yet? If he is, show him to the backyard. Maybe the fresh air will make her more talkative."

"I don't need a shrink. If he is, shove him into the fountain on the back patio. Maybe the water will convince him not to come back again."

LJ shakes her head and scurries back down the steps, calling out, "I'll go ask if he wants something to drink."

She's been around for enough of our arguments that she's learned to stay away until they're over. They usually end with Wolfe walking away. But instead of him yelling at me in his trainer's voice, he says, "Thea, I want you to work just as hard on your mind as you do everything else."

"I'm good."

"You were attacked and got some disturbing news within days of each other. You're strong, but you're not invincible."

"I said, I'm *fine*."

"If that's true, then why are you suddenly throwing yourself at me?"

He's got me there. But I play it off, like what I said to him was a joke. "Don't get a big head. It's not you, specifically. I'm in the mood to fuck. If you let me out of the house, I'll go throw myself at someone else."

I smile up at him and purr, "Wouldn't that give the shrink something else to jot down notes about?"

"You're not taking that eighteen-year-old pussy out of this house to give to anyone. You're gonna march your ass downstairs and talk to the man your people are paying to get you well."

"I said-"

"I don't give a fuck what you said. I'm telling you this is happening. Someone hurt you, and you don't remember the details. You're blocking them when you're awake and reliving them in your dreams. LJ and I would like to survive this without you crawling out of bed and murdering us in your sleep."

Rolling my eyes, I scoff, "You're being overdramatic."

"I'm being reasonable and considering all sides of this. I'm training you, just like I agreed to. Just because it's not physical work doesn't mean it's not important. The first thing I told you in the gym was you had to be strong of mind. Remember?"

He reaches around and tugs my ponytail, forcing my head back to look at him. "I wanna find out who did this to you, sweetness. Don't you wanna know? Don't you want to tell me which punk I should make miserable for the rest of their lives?"

"I don't need you fighting my battles."

"I know you don't. I'm actually thinking of letting you fight each and everyone one of them. In the ring, of course. Don't you want me to give you permission to fight?"

My eyes flutter closed thinking about that. "Yes."

"I need you to do the work, and that starts with the guy downstairs. Prove to me you don't need his help, and he'll never come back here again."

My nipples pebble. It's so unfair when he talks to me like this. I don't need to be handled. I have my own mind. I know what I want, but when Wolfe does this shit, all I want to do is make him happy. Please don't say it, please don't say it. I need to stay strong on this.

"C'mon, sweetness. Tell him one real thing about how you're feeling today."

"I feel like I want to go out and get hammered and fuck some stranger in a bar. Oh wait, I've already done that. Maybe we should talk about that."

He steps back, his gaze shuttered. He's back in full coach mode, and I have no way of knowing how he feels about what I just said.

"If that's what you choose to discuss, that's your business. Eventually your body will heal, but until you can talk about what happened - and deal with it- our training is on hold."

"What? You can't do that."

"I can do what I want, and I'm not putting you up against any of my other clients, or students with that bomb ticking in your head. You're one flashback away from hurting someone. Maybe even yourself. You don't wanna talk to a professional? Fine, then talk to LJ, or anyone else you feel safe enough to confide in."

He retreats into his bedroom, leaving me standing alone in the hall. I can either go into my room or downstairs, where I hear LJ making small talk with the doctor. I make a choice. The right choice *for me*, and go to my room.

Chapter 13
Deacon

Thea ignored everything I said and skipped out on her therapy session again. The screaming at night is how I know she needs to talk it out. I want her to confront whatever she's blocking, but I can't force her to do it. I climb out of bed and walk over to her room. When LJ sticks her head out the door, I shoo her back to bed. I know she's worried and wants to be there for her friend, but I'm still the better person to go in there and disarm her when she gets violent in her sleep. Some nights it's just screams and others, she's clenching the knife we left for her.

I stare down to see if it's a knife day. It's not. Not yet. I climb into bed, draping my arm around her waist. She stiffens when I touch her. I hate that it's still happening. "It's me, LaReaux."

She's shaking but slowly relaxes into my hold, allowing me to pull her into the curve of my body. "You're safe. Get some rest." I draw figure eights across her skin, and listen to her breathing even out as she falls back to sleep.

Thea, mumbling my name, wakes me a few hours later. "Hmm?"

"Don't leave me."

"Never, sweetness. You're stuck with me."

I'm not quick to make promises about my time and intentions, but with Thea, I'm clear on this. I want what's best for her. I want her to heal, and I want her to face down the punks who did this to her, and let them see she's stronger and better than before.

She shifts in my arms, her ass rubbing against me. That brings up another truth that I'm trying to ignore. "Be still, LaReaux."

Thea's gorgeous. Sexy as hell and I love that she's honest about her sexuality. The memory of her picking me up in a bar and fucking me in an alley lives rent free in my head. I'm no saint. It wouldn't take much for me to push her onto her back and feast between her legs.

I let out a pained groan when her ass brushes against my dick. It's not getting the memo that we're not going there with her again. When she rolls over, things get worse for me. She hooks her leg over mine and grinds against me in her sleep. It takes every bit of resistance I can muster not to grab her and help her get off.

I fist the sheet behind her back while she dry humps me. Letting whatever she's dreaming about play out. Grateful that at least for now, there are no memories terrorizing her in her dreams. My cock brushes against her when I finally decide to move away.

"Fuck." I pant on a soft breath. I need to get out of this bed, out of this house, away from her. I've already come to terms with the fact that I can't have this girl. Staying here is messing with my resolve.

I put more space between us, and turn, swinging my legs over the side of the bed. Her soft whimper almost makes me change my mind. *Almost.* I grab a blanket from my room and stretch out on the floor at the foot of her bed. This way, I'm keeping my promise and protecting her from all the shit I'm fantasizing about doing to her.

I've slept on floors plenty of times. It doesn't bother me, but I'm having a tough time winding down and getting comfortable. My dick is standing at attention, begging for relief. I grip the base, trying to relieve the ache. "I know, buddy. I know. But she's asleep, and she's hurt." I say, trying to overcome the desire to make her dreams my reality. That doesn't help, so I focus on the fact that she's only eighteen. Way too young for me.

That thought makes the throbbing in my dick ease. Slightly. The other part of my brain rationalizes that eighteen is still legal and I've already fucked her. I close my eyes at the onslaught of memories. Fuck! If I don't get control, I'm either going to fuck my hand or crawl back into bed and let her rub her ass on me again.

I think about her horrendously timed flirting earlier and remind myself of the words she used when I didn't cave. She'd be happy to fuck anyone if I let her out of the house. She was wasting time, avoiding having to talk to her shrink about all the damage her attack has caused. That thought deflates my dick. I yank my hands out of my sweatpants. Thea doesn't need me lusting after her. I'm here to get her started on the road to recovery. This isn't us playing house or moving our relationship forward. I shouldn't be thinking about how fucking adorable she looks, walking around barefoot in a tank top and sweatpants.

When we leave here, things will go back to normal, and I'll be just as professional as I was before.

LJ squeezes my hand as we drive the last stretch of road leading to campus. I give her a small smile and lean my head back against the seat, staring out the window at the trees. Has it only been three weeks since the last time I walked through campus? It feels like a lifetime. LJ and I wanted to come back last week, but the stupid head doctor refused to release me back into society. He said he couldn't diagnose my current mental health state since I refused to talk to him.

I'd still be stuck in Palisade Shores, bored out of my mind, if it weren't for LJ. I took Wolfe's suggestion and talked to her, letting her record our conversation, then gave permission for her to play it for the shrink. He was concerned about my desire to stab people until LJ and Wolfe explained that's my normal base line. They may have also promised to make sure I continue therapy. I've agreed to no such terms, but it seemed to appease him and here I am. If he's happy to take Moira and Scott's money while I sit there and stare at the walls or clean my nails for an hour, then so be it.

My stomach flips, thinking about Deacon Wolfe. Despite my attitude and our many arguments about therapy, he's been a steady source of strength during my recovery. We played board games, sat in silence, and ate his amazing cooking. It was like the three of us were in our own little world. The only thing that would have made it better, is if Sasha could have been there too. I lost my phone, but hers is one number I remember by heart. Deacon let me use his burner phone so I could let her know why I probably won't be coming home for Christmas like I planned. I reluctantly agreed with everyone who said it's probably not a good idea for me to travel with one arm. Nothing's changed in Nags Creek, and I'd be signing my death warrant by walking those streets with my dominant hand out of commission.

The warmth in my belly slides lower, as I think about Deacon crawling into bed with me every night. He's the only one who knows just how bad my nightmares are. Every night, he held me down, and risked getting sliced open, until his voice penetrated the terror in my brain, then wrapped me in his arms, holding me close. It felt so good to be pressed against him. But no matter how many signals I gave or how much I rubbed against him, he wouldn't let his hands wander across my body.

I don't want a domesticated life and I've never seen myself in traditional gender roles. I think everyone should do what they're good at or most comfortable with. There's no sexier sight than Wolfe in the kitchen, his jeans hanging low on his hips, hair wet as he handed me a cup of orange juice, and a bottle of water, before letting me have coffee.

I huff as the cab comes to a stop in front of my dorm. We're back at school now and no matter how cozy things were in our house, he's still my teacher and clearly not interested. First step in stopping the fantasy of us being together, is to stop thinking of that building in Palisade Shores as *our* house.

It's the middle of the evening and there's always a few people hanging out around the first floor lobby area. I've had my mask off at the house. I didn't need to hide my thoughts from LJ, but here, here I do. I slip my bitch don't care in place, pull my hoodie down over my head and put my sunglasses on before sliding out of the cab. I sling my bag over my good shoulder and strut to the doors. They hiss open, announcing our arrival into the empty lobby. LJ holds up her phone, answering my unspoken question. "There's a party. That's where everyone is."

Isn't there always a party? I breathe a sigh of relief as we make our way over to the elevator. At least I won't have to face anybody until I go back to class in a few days. I let us into my room and lock the door behind us, double checking the lock's engaged before going to my bedroom to offload my bag. When I come back out, LJ tells me to relax while she takes care of dinner. My lips twitch, because taking care of it leaves a lot of room for interpretation. She knows how to cook a few things, thanks to Deacon, but she's still not the best at it.

"Oh, don't give me that look. I promise your dinner the first night back is edible." She pulls containers out of a bag. "Deacon made us enough food for the first few days." She looks over at me, a sardonic grin on her face. "Guess I should go back to calling him Coach Wolfe since we're back at school."

"Good luck, with that." I flop down on the couch, pulling my feet up and tucking them underneath me. "I'm not changing anything up."

"That's because you were already addressing him informally. You dropped the Coach from his title and just call him Wolfe."

"He insists on calling me by my last name, so I'm returning the favor." In my dreams I've called him other things, but for the sake of our friendship, I won't mention that.

"You okay, Thea?"

"Huh? Yeah. I'm fine." I put an indifferent look on my face.

"It's okay to miss him, you know."

"What's to miss? Him bossing me around, demanding I talk to the therapist? I don't think so. I'm glad to be out from under his thumb. Why are you staring at me like that?"

"You're such a liar."

I bang my forehead against my hand. "I know. But it's stupid, right? How can I miss his overbearing ass, when all he ever does is tell me I have to 'do the work'? Plus, it's only been a few days since he came back to campus. That's not enough time to forget all the ways he irks me."

"It makes sense to me. You've seen him every day, for almost three weeks."

"I saw him in class and at the gym too and it didn't feel like this."

"That was a strict routine with clearly defined boundaries. You weren't sharing meals with him, watching him cook." She arches a brow, "Sleeping in his bed..."

"Look here, messy missy, it was *my* bed, and you know it wasn't like that. He was there to make sure I didn't hurt myself in my sleep."

"Thea, you drool a little bit whenever you see him."

I thought I was better at hiding it. "Have *you* seen him? He's kinda hot. I've got eyes, and I noticed. My appreciation of his physique doesn't mean anything."

Her back is to me as she leans over to put our dinner in the oven to warm up. "Does him calling you sweetness, not mean anything too?"

"I don't-" The lie dies on my tongue. I don't want to be dishonest with her. "It doesn't mean anything, now."

"Did it mean something before your accident?"

I bite at a hangnail on my thumb. "Way before. Like before my first day of classes here."

She walks over and plops down on the couch next to me. "Girl, have you been holding out on me? Did you know Deacon before you came to Canyon Falls? Is that why he was at the hospital?"

"No. I met him when I got to town. My first weekend on campus I went to a bar and picked him up."

"You mean he picked you up?"

"No. I said it the right way. I picked him up, bought him a drink, we played a little pool, and I fucked him in an alley without ever knowing his name."

"Well, damn."

"I walked into my Physical Enhancement Class and that's when I found out his name and what he does for a living."

"Well, damn."

"You already said that."

"Uh, huh, but I think it bears repeating."

"Don't go romanticizing it, LJ. He was a jerk in class, from day one. I had to literally fight for a slot at his gym, and the only reason he gave it to me, is because he didn't want me making my way through the illegal fighting circuit without a coach, or hurting someone on campus with my awesome skills."

"That might explain him training you, but why did he just move into a three-bedroom townhouse with you for three weeks, and tell your aunt and uncle that he didn't trust anybody on campus to handle this investigation correctly?"

"That's easy. I'm his prized fighter. He wanted to oversee my recovery and make sure I didn't try to get revenge on who did this."

"Do you know who did it? I mean did you remember something?"

I see flashes sometimes, but those come with headaches like my brain refuses to let me remember. "It's still spotty. Just flashes that I can't be certain of. I've had run-ins with several people on campus. I think I'm just projecting faces onto blank canvases to make it all make sense."

"You know what the doctor said. If you take time to sit with it, it may come to you."

"Fuck that doctor. I've never been one to sit around and mope about the bad shit that's happened in my life. I'm not about to start now."

She laughs at me. "It's not moping. It's therapy."

I shrug and pull a pillow into my lap, hugging it to my chest. "I don't need him for therapy. I've got the ring and I've got you and Sasha." She shifts closer and pulls my head onto her shoulder. "I don't need to cry on your shoulder because some cowards attacked me and left me in a pine box, or because my parents gave me away, and I've been lied to all my life or because the Coxsuckers never fail to live up to their name, and Finn dogged me out the one time I actually let myself think about needing someone else, or because Deacon Wolfe's sexy ass pretends, I didn't rock his world when we fucked."

"Wow. That's a lot to not care about. But anyway, I'm hugging you and being mindful of your bad arm." After a few moments of silence she says. "And there's nothing wrong with crying on somebody's shoulder. If you ever did need to let loose about any of those things, both of mine are always at your disposal."

This is why I love this girl. She knows I just unpacked a lot of shit that I'm clearly not okay with, but she doesn't push me to say anything else about it. "Thanks, LJ."

"For what?"

"Deacon's not the only person who moved into a townhouse for three weeks. You gave up your Thanksgiving break, too." I lift my head to look at her. "I haven't met a lot of people who selflessly do shit for me. In fact, it's just you and Sasha. I know I'm not all chipper and bubbly, or pouring out my feelings over tubs of ice cream, but if you need to cry on my shoulder some time, I'll sit still and let you do it. If you still needed to, after I stabbed whoever hurt you, of course."

"And I've never had someone offer to maim and kill on my behalf. So we're both in unchartered territory, but if you remember who hurt you, I'll be right alongside you with the fighting drills you've already taught me."

That gives me an idea. "Speaking of. I need to get you back into training. Clearly I can't do it and demonstrate, but I know who can."

"Uh.. wait. No, there's no hurry."

Nodding, I say, "Yes. Yes, there is. If you don't train, you'll get rusty. We need you flexible and ready to go, since these pussies on campus like to attack women." I pick up my new phone from the table, banging out a text with my good hand.

"Who are you texting?"

"The Big Bad Wolfe to let him know you'll be taking my spot at his gym."

Chapter 15
Deacon

I glare at my phone. Who the hell is texting me during the hours everyone knows I work out? My mood shifts when I see it's from Thea. I gave her my personal number in case of an emergency.

She should be just getting back to campus. I'm on edge as I unlock my phone, preparing myself to read a message about someone fucking with her already.

Do I really think she'd text and complain about that? Hell no. She'd try to handle it with her one good arm, but that doesn't stop the part of me that feels responsible for her from wanting to know. Responsible might not be the right word. I feel territorial. Possessive. In a, *I don't want anyone else to look at her*, kind of way.

This is uncharted territory for me. I thought my interest was residual lust, then I attributed it to me training her and wanting to see her reach her goals, the way I do any other fighter I work with. But after sharing a house with her, I can admit it goes deeper than that. This woman challenges and tests me. She has a way of making me laugh and cuss at the same time. I own my reputation as one of the meanest teachers on campus, and she's not put off by it. If anything, she goes out of her way to push my buttons.

I've been back at work for a few days, and I'm distancing myself from my coworkers more than usual. Three weeks away did nothing to curb my rage. Probably because I spent the entire time watching Thea recover from her injuries, and there's been no progress made on the investigation into what happened. The school gives the legacy students a lot of leeway because they have no way of keeping track of everyone's affiliation with The League.

That's why nobody batted an eye when I told them I found Thea buried in a coffin. I was on safety patrol because of my EMT experience, but I didn't think I'd need to do anything more than tell someone to slap an ice pack or band aid on a bruise.

I wandered into that plot and found the grave with the new coffin in it. Closed up and on fire. Whoever dosed her didn't want her to wake up in time. If I hadn't been there, she would have burned alive. I'm lucky the bastards left a shovel behind. I used it and my shirt to put out the flames. The amount of panic I felt, seeing her limp body in that box... I force air into my lungs. Thea needs to work on her feelings about what happened, but so do I. I may be running around pretending I'm okay, but nothing is okay about what happened.

That's why I didn't mind taking her off the grid for almost a month. Thea's aunt and uncle, or whoever the hell they are this week, dug into my background, but I looked into them too. They haven't come right out and said it, but I wonder if this was a message to them from The League.

It's also why The Trium are my top suspects. They're the top prospects, the highest ranked Wrens in their group. Their parents are mid level league members and around campus, The Trium is the ruling faction on campus, and the faculty generally bows to their whims.

Everyone is being tight-lipped about where The Trium was and what they were doing on Mayhem Night. And for now, Thea doesn't want to remember, so I don't have a lot to go on. We might've shared a home and a bed, but she's on edge around me. It's gonna take some time to get her to let down her guard enough to trust me again, and when she does, she's going to tell me every single secret she's been keeping.

I stare at her text. She wants me to give her training hours to Breland, to keep her slot open at my gym.

. . .

ME

That's not how it works. If Breland wants to train, she can submit an application to join my gym like everyone else.

THEA

Why? You have an opening since I can't work out right now.

ME

There's a waiting list. She can't just jump to the front of the line for personal training.

THEA

I did

ME

That was a special situation

As far as the other fighters are concerned, Thea was waiting for a slot to open up. I can't have them thinking I was biased or giving out preferential treatment, although clearly I am. Because I'm telling her no, when I'm already thinking about a training plan for Breland.

THEA

> I need LJ to be able to protect herself and I don't want her going to somebody else's gym

That's about as close to a request for help as I'm gonna get out of her.

ME

> You can't just demand people do what you want, LaReaux, and how are you even typing? Your sling better be on and ice better be on that wrist.

Her number flashes across my phone.

I answer it before it finishes its first ring. "Yes?"

"I'm one-handing it."

I'm unable to hold back the groan that barrels its way up my chest. "Are you calling me to come lend you a hand?"

"The text message, Wolfe. I'm typing with one hand. Not whatever you're imagining, you pervert."

I smack my phone against my forehead, recalibrating my brain. I bring it back to my ear and try switching gears. It's hard to do since all I've been thinking about since I left Palisade Shores is her, finally giving into my urges since there's no chance of her hearing me waxing my dick to fantasies involving her on her knees. When I'm in my shower, I think about how I've been inside her body and yet I've never seen her naked.

"Momentary glitch in the matrix. I'll go back to pretending you're not a woman now. What can I do for you, LaReaux?"

"You can tell me you're letting LJ have my spot."

"No."

"Dammit, Wolfe. Why do you always say no when I ask you stuff?"

"Why don't you ever ask me something I want to say yes to?"

"Something like what?"

Nope. Not going there. "Moving on. Why can't Breland just apply like everyone else?"

"It's not that she can't. It's more like she won't. You know how she is. Oblivious to the dangers of the world. She's walked around all these years and never had to worry about fighting."

"That's because Canyon Falls is a relatively safe place to live."

"Tell that to my shoulder, ribs and psyche."

I let her have that one.

"Just because it has been, doesn't mean it still is, and what about when she leaves here? What if I was just the warmup, and whoever jumped me plans to do it again? I need her to have a fighting chance."

"LaReaux, you've had years of experience fighting and you were still hurt. Even with your experience, my recommendation would have been to run from the danger, not confront it head on. That goes triple for Breland."

"I know that, dammit. Don't you think I *know* that? I'm not saying she's gonna be assassin level in these short weeks, but if she knows the steps and it's second nature to fight back, maybe she can do that and surprise them or incapacitate them long enough that she has a chance to run away."

"There are self-defense courses offered at other gyms, and the campus has a seminar twice a year."

"I don't want some raggedy ass old man telling her to use pepper spray and stab someone with a key, or some creep pretending to show her how to fight. I want her learning correctly and improving and you're the only one that can do it."

"LaReaux..."

"You're the only one I trust to do it, okay? Just you. It has to be you."

That gives me pause. Does she even realize what she just said? I know trust for her has to be hard, especially now. "Fine. If I do this, you'll have to do something for me."

"Something like what?"

Like drive two towns over, meet me in an alley, and let me fuck your brains out, because pretending it didn't happen isn't working.

Pretending I don't want it to happen again isn't working. Of course, I can't say that. "Answer a question. How did you sleep the last few days?"

"Fine. I'll let LJ know when to meet you at the gym."

"LaReaux, answer the question, honestly."

"I did."

"I can hear the strain in your voice. You sound tired. Did you sleep at all?"

"No."

"You know you need sleep to help you heal."

"Tell that to my nightmares. I woke up screaming and scared the shit out of LJ. I didn't want to keep her up too, so I decided not to sleep at all. I can't have nightmares if I'm awake."

She'd been tossing and turning, but it had been almost a week since the last time she woke up screaming. That's why I came back to campus before them. "I thought they were getting better."

"So did I, but I guess not."

"Do you think something triggered them the last few nights?"

"I'm not a shrink, and before you say something, no, I don't want to tell him and hear what he has to say about it, because the only thing that I did differently was finally having my bed to myself."

The implication of that hangs heavy between us. "I'm sorry I wasn't there to keep your night terrors at bay."

"What are you apologizing for? I'm a grown ass woman. They're just dreams, and eventually they'll go away. It's not like you can sleep in my bed and wake me from my nightmares forever. I mean, how would that even work here at school? Where would-"

I cut into her rant. "Thea."

"What?"

"If your dreams get too bad, just call me."

"Yeah, whatever."

"I mean, it. It doesn't matter what time it is. You call me. Understood?"

"Wolfe-"

"That's an order, LaReaux."

"Fine. I won't need to, because I've got it handled, but if I do, I'll call you."

"Good, girl."

I don't miss the whimper from her end of the line. I give her a second to pull herself together before telling her, "I'll work out a training plan for Breland. She can start next week."

"Thank you."

"Don't thank me yet. She'll probably quit after the first session."

"That's a very real possibility. Every time I leave the gym, I'm a boneless, exhausted mess."

"Good, because if you've still got energy left over, then I'm not doing it right."

"No problems there. You definitely know your way around my body."

"I don't know about that, LaReaux. I think there may be a few things left to discover."

Roger Dale, from the math department, walks into the gym, prompting me to wrap this call up. "I need to go. I'll touch base with you later."

I disconnect the call and shove my phone into my pocket. It's a good thing I had to cut our conversation short. I had been trying to convince myself that I could do this. That I could continue to pretend like I see her the same way I see all my students. As a sack of flesh to mold.

That lie burned away the minute I heard her voice, and now I'm wondering how she would have responded to my comment about her body if the conversation would have continued.

Chapter 16
Finn

Thea's here. I'd gotten used to walking in class and seeing her seat empty, but today she's here. A sling on her arm, her beautiful face marred with bruises so bad the makeup does little to cover them.

Thea was missing for three weeks. None of us could get any information on where she was. Not for lack of trying, but the administration office insisted they had no idea where she was or if she was coming back to school.

One minute we knew she was in Canyon Falls General, the next she'd vanished. It wasn't until I overheard a conversation between Austin and his buddy Corey that I learned she was away and submitting assignments remotely.

I couldn't very well demand to know how he knew that, because I'm not supposed to give a shit. Or at least that's what I keep telling myself, because she's been lying all along. But then I remember High Councilor Cox saying she's part of a deactivated legacy family, and my father's explanation of why that happened. Holden can't dig into the rest of the story, so we're trying to get our information the old-fashioned way. By attending dinners with our families and steering the conversation to Thea's family. Although a quicker way to get answers is to demand she give them to me.

The look of disgust Thea gives me quickly squashes that plan. Okay, so we had a disagreement. Words were said. Assumptions were made. Isn't twenty days' enough time to be ready to talk about it? She's the one who was lying to me. She owes me an explanation. I gave her my trust and let her play with my knife.

In his own little way, Holden started trusting her, too. Or at least that's what I assume his little experiment with kissing her was all about. He never would've done that if he thought she was a threat.

Pax is the only one who never quite warmed up to her and doesn't seem willing to change his position. Which makes what we're supposed to be doing even more complicated. We're trying to keep it a secret that we got into bed with Malcolm without the high council's permission. We alienated her, and now we have to regain what little semblance of trust she had in us, and convince her we're not that bad. The League's attention is on her and us, this little house of secrets can come crashing down on us at any moment.

I steal a look at her. She doesn't look sorry for lying. She doesn't look like she cares what we think about her. Were the weeks we played our games, and that night at the Breland anniversary party the act, or is it this indifference?

She's next to Austin, leaning in to hear what he's saying. Her body language with him still seems the same. Making me even more confused. If she was attacked, shouldn't she be tense? Or is Eloise right and Thea was a willing participant in whatever happened?

Holden is on the other end of the class, in his usual seat. He's not letting her presence distract him. Lucky bastard. Few things let me hyper focus. Parkour, lock picking, playing with my knives, extreme sports, and learning a new language. Fun shit. Everything else is static and annoying. I breeze through my statistics assignment, then turn to stare out the window, fantasizing about doing a forward tuck through it and landing on my feet before walking away to do something else. My phone chimes with a text from Pax in our group chat.

PAX

I heard the troublemaker is back. We need to discuss next steps.

Next steps? The step we're currently on is confusing enough. But he's right. We need to decide what we're doing and how to undo the devastation we caused after finding out Thea's secret. If she was attacked, it's because we gave the green light for people to torment her. I'm thinking, "oops, our bad," won't quite work in this scenario.

Class ends and Thea bolts from her seat. Austin is right behind her like a guard dog. I follow them, curious to see where they're going. Coach Wolfe is at the other end of the hallway talking to Mr. Corbin. His eyes flick towards me, then Thea, before turning his attention back to the teacher.

Coach Wolfe is the one who found Thea. If he were any other teacher, I'd just go up to him and ask what he knows about that night. But I know he's one of the few faculty members on campus who don't give a shit about us or our position, so it's doubtful he'd give me a straight answer.

I'm on edge, wavering back and forth between blind solidarity with my brothers and continuing to punish Thea for her alleged deception, and consoling her about her injuries. Just thinking about her being hurt makes me want to hurt others.

At the end of the day, it doesn't matter who Thea is or why she's here. She didn't deserve to be hurt like this. Zeus' dick injury is minor compared to how she looks.

I've been in and have witnessed enough fights to know that he couldn't have been the only one there that night. Whoever was involved, won't get the chance to hurt her again.

That means I'm back on recon, and when I catch the culprits, I won't show them any mercy.

Chapter 17
Thea

My favorite class is the now the most uncomfortable place on earth. I knew I'd see Finn this morning, but I didn't know it would feel like tiny shards of glass running over my skin, and this churning in my stomach, to hit back at him for that shit he pulled.

That's not it though. Mixed in with all that is this nauseating feeling, the thought of fighting back induces. Because what if I can't beat him? Verbal sparring and pranks wars were our thing, but what if he upped the ante? What if he was there that night? I fucked the guy, but I don't really know anything about him. That's not usually a problem when I don't see them again.

I think back over our time together at the movies and our interactions on campus. I try to think of something he's said that might be real or genuine. Something deep. There's nothing. It's all been superficial games.

"Hey stranger. Welcome back."

Austin smiles down at me, and a bit of the panic I'd just wrangled back slips out. I have to remind myself that I know it wasn't Austin. He was off campus when I was attacked. Wolfe and LJ have both confirmed this and shown me proof. Out of a school of roughly eighteen thousand students and twenty-two hundred faculty, I can rule out exactly three people.

I give him a tight smile and try to appear unbothered by the stares I'm getting from the students entering the classroom. I *know* I still look a mess. I don't know how I'm gonna make it through an hour-long lecture in their presence.

Austin is the only good thing about the class. His comforting presence and the normalcy of our interactions keeps a bit of my unease at bay. He doesn't comment on my stiffness or the way I wince every time I move my arm. Or the evidence of the beating I took all over my face. I put on some makeup, but you can still tell my lip is split and that I'm using concealer to cover how bad the bruises are.

I know about the statement the school disseminated on campus, and to his credit, he doesn't ask what really happened. It's nobody's business how I got injured. My focus is on acting like it's nothing.

My phone rings when I leave class. I answer it because I'm getting tired of it ringing.

"Thea?"

"Aunt Moira. Hi."

"Is everything okay?"

"Yeah. Why wouldn't it be?"

"You didn't check in today. Scott and I were getting worried."

"I just got out of class. Plus, I told you I'm not gonna call you every five minutes to tell you I'm okay, so let this be a blanket check in. I'm fine. I'm taking my vitamins and I'm staying away from unsanctioned fighting rings for now."

"That's not funny."

"It wasn't meant to be, Moira." I switch the phone to my other ear. "Look, I get that you're just being concerned, but I can't deal with appeasing your guilt right now. I need to make sure I'm not too far behind in the classes I couldn't do online, rest my body so I heal, and deal with the aftermath of what happened to me. When I'm ready to talk about how you threw me away like an old sweater and have been lying to me all this time, I will."

"Whatever you need, Thea. Just let us know if you need anything. We love you."

"Funny way of showing it."

She ignores that jab and ends the call with a soft goodbye. Too bad. I'm dying to cuss her out right now. Maybe that would settle me a bit. Just thinking about going to another class pisses me off.

I didn't ask to come here before, and I don't want to be here now. So why am I even bothering with this bullshit? I already know I won't be paying attention. That's how unmotivated I feel.

Yeah, fuck the rest of this day, and this campus. I catch the bus into town and then take a cab to the beach. I'll just spend the day in the sand soaking up some sun and listening to the waves.

Thea

I walk my usual route on autopilot. It's not until I'm standing outside of the hotel that I realize what I've done. This was a mistake. I shouldn't have come to this part of the beach. I'm trying to escape my moody thoughts, but I've walked straight into a reminder that I'm surrounded by liars. How did I not see I was being played?

Looking up at the hotel, my heart breaks a little more. Van told me this was a safe place, somewhere I could always come, and that's a lie too. She's Scott's mother. She had to have known all this time. I walk towards the side of the building and see her sitting on the patio, staring off into the water, just like I've often done. It's so tragically funny now to think about how similar we are in that regard.

She turns to face me, and my last shred of hope that she didn't know evaporates. "You should have told me."

"It wasn't my place."

"You let me come here and work for you, and talk to you and trust you, and none of it was true."

"What part wasn't true?"

"How much you... How much you cared about me, and my dreams and my goals. It wasn't true."

"Thea, it was *all* true. I do care about those things, and about you."

I shake my head, my hand clenched at my side.

"Would you have opened up to me, if you knew? Would you have felt free to talk to me if that truth was hanging between us? Or would you have hated me the way you think you do right now?"

"How could you let them throw me away?! How could they just throw me away?"

She shoves to her feet and moves toward me. I see the look in her eyes. A mixture of resignation and hope. "Let's get something straight, young lady. *Nobody* threw you away. They were trying to protect you. We were all trying to protect you. I'll give you a little truth, since I already know Scott and Moira haven't. Until they found you, your parents thought you were dead."

"If that's the case, then why did they keep looking for me, or was that part a lie, too?"

"They weren't lying. They kept looking, because sometimes logic and the deepest hopes of your heart don't always add up. Logic said you couldn't have survived the car accident when you were four. Their hearts said no bodies were recovered at the scene, so keep looking. I saw the photos of the accident site. Logic said you and Hailee burned to a crisp, because after that, there were no digital records of either of you anywhere. There was nothing but ash, nothing they could use to identify who was in the car that was registered to Hailee. None of us had any hope. But emotionally Scott and Moira weren't going to stop until they had proof."

"And it only took them roughly twenty years to get it. Oh wait, that's a lie too, since I'm repeating my eighteenth year on earth."

That shit burns, too. How the fuck am I only eighteen? I know it's a trend to lie about your age, and hang onto your youth for as long as possible, but I don't want to be younger than I am.

"So tell me, Van, what took you all so long to find a detective with any fucking sense?"

She snorts and rolls her eyes. "Scott and Moira didn't want to raise suspicion about what they were doing, and you're right. A lot of the investigators they hired weren't worth the toilet paper I use to wipe my ass. The only reason the last one got a decent lead was because of you."

"Me?"

"Yes, you. Louisiana is the last place we knew you lived, so that's where they were looking. The state systems don't talk to each other about immunization or school records. Even if we would have known you were in Nevada sooner, they wouldn't have found you. Somehow Hailee doctored your birth certificate, making you a year older, and you lived in damn near every city and town in Nevada. But one day, you finally stopped running."

"I wasn't running, I-"

A memory comes to me. One I hadn't thought about for a long time. One I've always dismissed as a remnant of a dream.

Thea. We have to go.

But why, mama? I like it here.

Because we've been here too long already. We have to keep moving. Always keep moving.

No mama. I wanna stay.

If we stay, they'll find you, and I can't ever let them find you.

She loads me into the car and asks me to sing our favorite song. I do, at the top of my lungs, loving when she joins in. We travel a long time, then mama finally tells me we're here. I don't know where, but I smile as I look at the cabin in front of us.

. . .

Is this our new house?

No baby, this is our playhouse. We're gonna play a game. You remember I taught you how to be invisible?

You sprinkle magic, then I sit in silence and don't make a sound until you make me real again

That's right, baby girl. So I'm gonna make you invisible and I wanna see how long you sit in silence and don't make a sound this time.

I can be invisible a long time

Really? She says, like she doesn't believe me.

Yes mama, really. I'm a big girl now.

Okay, but the last time you only stayed invisible for ten minutes, and this time I need you to do it for a looong time.

How long?

Very long. Like twelve minutes.

. . .

That does sound long. The last time I was invisible, my friends were outside playing, and I wanted to play too. This time I don't have friends so I can do it

I can do it mama. I promise.

Okay, baby girl. And I'll help you. She takes my hand and pulls me into the house and down the hall, pointing to a door. "You see this door?"

"Yes."

"This is a magic door. It helps with invisibility. I'm gonna put you inside and sprinkle you with magic dust and it's gonna keep you invisible for a long time."

"Twelve minutes?"

"Yes, maybe even longer if I do the spell right."

Okay mama, do it right. I wanna do the longest time ever.

Are you sure, baby girl? This is very important. If you can't do it, then we can play another game.

Mama told me when she says the magic word important, I have to listen extra hard because I'm her special helper.

I want to help mama. "I can do it. I can be a good helper."

"Good girl. Okay, let's go potty and then into the magic door."

. . .

I don't remember how long I was behind the magic door. I remember sitting quietly, then getting thirsty, and hungry, and crying softly to myself. I didn't want to be invisible anymore, even if it was important, but I couldn't turn the knob to get back on the other side of the magic door.

Eventually I fell asleep and when I woke up again, mama was there carrying me to go potty and then she tucked me into bed. She smelled like barbecue, but I was too tired to ask if she had eaten it without me.

The next morning, we went on a new adventure. Hiking and camping in the woods and mama taught me how to spell my name and I memorized my birthday.

That memory morphs into another one.

It's founder's day in Nags Creek and mama came home from work early to surprise me. We're going to the parade. We drive to the busiest part of town, and I'm in awe of all the colorful decorations. The car stops with a lurch; the seatbelt pulls tight around my waist, digging into my stomach. It was already hurting because I haven't eaten today. But mama said I'd eat later.

Her door opens and I watch as she gets from behind the wheel and grabs the brown bag with the bottle in it. She usually keeps the bottle covered, but this time she pulls it out, and flashes it around for everyone to see. It makes me feel funny. Mama's not acting like herself. Mama never lets people see her drink in public.

I get out of the car too. I have to help mama and hide the bottle. I ignore the people staring at us. When I get to the front of the car, I see that it's smashed in. Mama ran

into the fire hydrant, that's in front of a fire station. There's glass on the ground. It's red. I'll always remember the way shards reflected the lights from the cop cars that pulled up. And the way mama held up a piece of glass, cutting her hand, ordering people to stay away or she'd cut them too.

I'm crying for her when the cops grab her and throw her into the back of the police car. They can't take my mama away. I have to go with her too, but they won't let me. No matter how much I tell them, she needs me.

"Mama!" I pull away and run to my mother. Someone grabs me, holding me back.

"You remember what I told you, baby? Don't let them catch you. Never stop moving, Thea."

My mother went off to jail, and I was sent to my first foster home. When they released her and reunited us, we moved again. This time to Vegas. Until then, our moving was always like a game. A road trip. An adventure. But afterwards, it was fraught with paranoia. Panic that could only be subdued by the comfort of booze in her system. Years later, we moved back to Nags Creek.

The next time mom ever told me to stay on the move was the week before she disappeared for good. I was fourteen, and back in foster care, but I'd go to her place three towns over for a visit, even though I was supposed to be on my way to school.

The year before, started on anti-depressants to level out her moods. That morning, she was different. More alert than I had seen her in a while, but also more on edge. Almost manic. She'd been sober for about six months, had a new boyfriend, and was holding down a job. Mom had a new outlook on life and we were making plans for me to come home. But when I walked through the door that day, I could tell things had gone to shit.

The house was trashed. Her hair was greasy, like she hadn't washed it in days, and there were clothes all over the place. When I asked what was going on, she started talking about spies and being found. Then she told me we'd be leaving again. But instead of waiting for the courts to clear me to come home, we were taking off. She needed to get things in order. It would take a month for her to arrange everything and this time we'd go to the east coast.

She told me it was a mistake to put down roots anywhere, and that she finally figured out the system. Six months. That's the longest we could ever stop moving, because they always found us after six months.

Did I care that she was drunk and talking about changing her last name again? Nope. She was telling me I was coming home, and we were leaving the depressing ass town I lived in behind.

I was happy to go. It seemed like all our problems started when we were forced to stay in Nags Creek. I promised not to tell anyone our plans, and I went off to school, so my foster mother wouldn't get suspicious. When I came back a week later to check in with my mom, the house was empty. I checked back the next week too, and there was no sign she'd ever returned. I asked the neighbors if they'd seen her and they all said no. Not that I expected them to tell me if they did. Mom always picked places where people minded their own business.

I hunted the bars for her, the parks, anywhere I could think of. I stayed at her place, hoping she'd sneak back in the middle of the night. She never did. I finally accepted that she left me behind, off on her new adventure with her new name. A woman without a kid.

My foster mother reported me as a runaway and said I stole money from her, and I got shipped off to juvie. I spent two weeks there and then met Mrs. Sprout. I told her I was set up. I didn't steal money, cars were more my thing, and explained that I didn't run away, I was in Porter looking for my mother. It's the same thing I told the judge before he sentenced me, but he didn't care.

Mrs. Sprout listened, she went to mom's place, and told me there was still no sign of her. Her purse, phone, everything that a person would take if they were leaving the house, was still there. She even went to the police, but all they did was knock on a few doors the same way I did and got no leads. So I had to accept mom bailed on me and didn't take anything, because she really wanted to leave her old life behind.

I spent ninety days in juvie, then moved to a group home. Mrs. Sprout helped me pack up mom's stuff. Surprisingly, the rent was paid up six months in advance. I don't know where she got the money to do it. I didn't care. I packed up anything I wanted, and let the landlord trash the rest. I picked up Clint from Sasha's place and stopped thinking about my mother. I didn't need one. Didn't want one. I knew I could only rely on myself.

I didn't think anything of the fights I got into. The conflict with the group homes and foster parents. The number of times I went back to juvie over the years. But now I do. I think of all of it and see a pattern. I moved. A lot. Outside of juvie, I never stayed in a home for more than six months, until I got my apartment.

"I wasn't running. The places I was living weren't a good fit, and you still haven't explained why this latest investigator won the lotto on finding me."

"It was a Hail Mary, really. He was messing around with some aging software, scanned your baby picture in, and got a hit on someone who might look like you."

"On social media?"

This is why I hate those apps. I've never been into plastering my face all over the internet, but it looks like someone caught me in the background of a selfie.

"No." Her lips twitch. "It was a mug shot."

That tracks.

"Is Canyon Falls a good fit? Or have you decided to go back to Nags Creek?"

There was a time when I'd have said Nags Creek is the last place I'd want to live, but I built a life there. I had ways to make money. A little money or a lot of money. I know how to blend in on those streets. Stay hidden. Something I've been unable to do here, and now I feel like I'm under a microscope with Moira and Scott calling me all the time. It's suffocating.

"I don't belong here. Out of every place mom ever discussed us going, California never made the list."

"Hailee had a list? I was under the impression she was winging it."

I was too, but I'm not so sure anymore. "You say everyone was trying to protect me. From what?"

"It's not my place to tell you."

"Well, I'm not talking to your son or his wife at the moment, so feel free to spill the beans." She stays quiet. "Fine. All of you can continue to keep your secrets. But until somebody can be honest about what the fuck was so scary that I spent my life bouncing around from one shit hole to the next -while you all lived up here- then I've got nothing else to say to any of you."

I walk away, a tiny part of me sad when she doesn't stop me.

Chapter 18
Finn

I haven't seen Thea outside of class since she came back. She's never in the dining hall at the same time we are and has changed the time she leaves the dorm in the morning. She's probably avoiding us, but there's no reason for her to do that. We're not her enemies. Anymore. Though, I was never really her enemy to begin with. I swore an oath, and I honored it, but it was never personal.

Our last interaction wasn't the friendliest, so I can understand if she's still pissed about it. I operated on some information that may have been incomplete and I can admit I was too hasty to jump to judgement.

After talking to my father, I realize I owe her an apology. I can't keep putting it off, either. Saying sorry is the first step in implementing the plan the guys and I came up with a to gain her trust. I say gain, because I'm not so sure I ever really had it to begin with.

I enter the lobby of Vale Tower, slowing my steps when Thea walks out of the store carrying a bunch of bags. The handles are draped over the wrist of her left hand, and she's leaning a little to the side. A sling and an ace bandage are on her right arm. She didn't have those in class the other day. My eyes snap to her face. My stomach churns. She's not wearing concealer either, giving me a better look at her bruises.

"Who did this to you?"

Her eyes widen, then narrow when she sees me. She steps away when I reach for the bags. "Don't touch me."

"I'm trying to help."

"I don't need your help. I don't need anything from you."

"Pet, you're obviously hurt worse than you're letting on. You can't carry those bags by yourself."

"I *can,* and I will. And even if I couldn't, I'd rather struggle than to let you anywhere near me."

I follow as she shuffles to the elevator. As first interactions go, we're off to a horrible start. Nothing about her body language suggests she wants to talk to me. Once I put the car in private mode, she'll have no choice but to listen. I glare at the people trying to get on the elevator with us. They get the hint, and back away to wait for it to come back down. Thea's back is against the wall. The bags hang in front of her like an extra layer of protection.

"Pet, I know-"

"Don't fucking call me that."

We're back to her rejecting my name for her? This is like starting from scratch. "Fine, *Thea.* I want to clear the air about what happened the night you came to my room. People are always coming up to us because of who we are and what we represent, so it's hard to know who to trust. I thought we were friends. So you have to understand how I felt when I found your birth certificate and found out you'd been lying the whole time."

"I don't have to understand a goddamn thing. Whatever you felt when you dragged that document out of obscurity has nothing to do with me. It's your own fault for digging your nose into something that was none of your fucking business."

She's got a point. Isn't the caveat to be careful when you go searching for stuff because you might find it? "I get it. You feel violated, and I'm sorry for that, but there's an upside to this."

Her hair brushes her left shoulder as she tilts her head. "You're sorry? For which part? Shoving me out of your room with my pants down, for you and your friends hacking my bank account and draining it dry? Or is it the part where you had somebody change my grades which put me on academic probation?"

I can't refute any of that. We're responsible for all of it, and some other things she's not aware of yet. That reminds me to tell Holden to cancel those plans.

"So you can swallow your sorry, asshole, and choke on it."

The pain register on her face from her trying to wave her right arm. I ask her again, "What happened?"

The elevator dings and the doors slide open. Readjusting her bags, she steps into the hall. "That would be another thing that's none of your fucking business."

She drags herself down the hall to her door, then drops her bags on the ground as she fumbles around for her key fob. My anger rushes to the surface as I watch her drag the bags in one at a time.

She didn't answer my question. That part pisses me off more than her refusal to accept my apology.

Chapter 19
Holden

Thea's back. Her medical records aren't on the infirmary's server yet, but going by the bruising on her face, she was beaten to a pulp. I can feel my control slipping a tiny bit more every time I look at her. It's more than the bruising on her face. It's the vacant look in her eyes. The way she's staring through people. Staring through me.

After years of being ignored, I'd finally met a woman who looked at me, even when Finn and Pax weren't around. She teased me the same way she teased Finn and gave me an idiotic nickname. I never acknowledged it, but I liked her calling me Pretty Boy. I know I'm attractive, but nobody feels comfortable enough to say it around me. They're all too afraid of my reaction. So hearing her uncensored thoughts was scary, exciting, *liberating*.

I thought it would be safe to open up to her. At night I was open. As open as I could be, even if she wasn't aware of it. The hours in her bed, I felt a burden lift. I could talk and not be judged.

Finn and Pax don't judge me, but they're my brothers. My best friends. It was different to bare my soul to someone else. To share my thoughts with a woman wrapped in my arms at night. I felt comfortable.

Calm. I was even getting more than a few hours of sleep. To go back to the way it was before... that feels untenable.

Me and the guys are pretending things are normal. That's all we can do until we sit Thea down and explain how her life is about to change. So this morning, we're in our usual spot, watching the lingerie show. I wasn't interested in it before; and I don't pretend to be now. I'm here because that's what's expected of me. I'm trying and failing to concentrate enough to read my book. My attention keeps going to the elevator. I'm waiting for it to come down from our floor just so I can get a glimpse of her.

I don't have to wait long. My lungs inflate when the doors open and Thea steps into the lobby. Her hair is in a fishtail braid thrown over her shoulder, she's wearing black ripped jeans, and her favorite jacket and boots. This is the way she dressed when she first came to school. It's her armor. Her eyes scan the room with malice. A warning not to get too close. Her back stiffens when she sees us, but that's it. Her usual snark is missing. If anything, there's a moment of fear in her eyes. I feel the tension radiating off of her, as if we're all threats, and she's prepared for an attack.

She rushes out of the building and I force myself to remain in my seat, gripping the arm of my chair to keep from chasing her down and demanding answers. Starting with who helped her hide her identity all these years and ending with who hurt her.

I can't let the last question be the first thing I say to her because I'm barely holding on. The total identity blackout is a safer topic for me to focus on. But finding the perpetrators for the beating she took will bring me the most satisfaction. I push my bloodlust down. Business, first.

The League's reach is far and expansive, so for them not to know where she was... My gaze drifts to Pax. Is that a lie? *Did* the high council know about her? Is this a continuation of our test? *My test?* Did I fail The Trium by not finding that birth certificate sooner?

I add those questions to the hundred other thoughts that conspire to keep me up at night. No matter how much I go over everything that we knew before, and what we know now, there're just too many holes and missing pieces to weld a definitive story together.

I feel like chaos and confusion. An overstimulated ball of energy and doom. Dynamite just waiting for the smallest spark to explode. There is no off switch for my brain. I've learned to lessen the noise. Focus my thoughts, but now everything is too loud. *Too much.*

"Holden."

Finn and Pax are standing over me. Have they been calling my name long?

"We're heading to breakfast."

Another place where I'll be sitting around too much stimuli, listening to theories about Thea's absence and reappearance. That might be the thing that's bugging me the most. Where *did* she go for three weeks? Who was she with? How did she slip out of the hospital undetected? Did she have help from the person who's been hiding her all these years?

"I'm not hungry." I didn't even bring any ingredients down for the chef to use if I was. "I'm going to class."

I head towards my class, but change course when I catch sight of Thea hovering on the edge of the treeline she usually cuts through to get to her English class. She does that a lot. Cuts through the woods instead of taking the designated paths. I duck behind a tree to watch. I don't often come to the woods on this side of campus, because there's nothing over here. The stadium is behind us. There's an old storage shed about a hundred feet into the woods on the right, as well as the crumbling structure of the original groundskeeper's home. Neither of those places has been used in a hundred years, but the school keeps them around for historic sentimentality.

She's just standing there. Not moving any closer to her path. The shrill sound of a whistle through the stadium speakers causes her to jump. She turns and hurries back the other way, mumbling and typing something into her phone, veering off towards the library.

When she disappears through the doors, I head to class. Following her around for those few moments wasn't as big of a rush as when she ran from me on Mayhem Night, but it soothed a bit of the tension I've been feeling.

I've been telling the guys I'm fine. That I'm in control. But every day Thea was gone, I edged closer to the point where that wasn't true. I had free access to her. I let myself toy with her and teased the part of me that craves the chase and control. To have her go missing, and having to resist my urges, it was like uncorking a genie and trying to put it back in the bottle before it wreaks havoc.

Right now, the darkness threatens to drown me. I want to go to her and I want to find whoever had the nerve to put their hands on her.

My monster is awake, and I'm not sure there's any way to put him back to sleep.

Chapter 20
Pax

No one would ever call me flexible. It's common knowledge that I like plans and hate when I have to deviate from them. So, I grumbled when Finn insisted we change the time we usually eat. His rationale is that he's still on recon trying to find out what happened to his little toy on Mayhem Night, and he's not getting any leads from our usual crowds. Holden backed him, using our orders to get close to Thea as leverage. She's changed up her routine, so I had no choice but to agree with them.

This is the first time I've seen our neighbor from hell since her return. She's maneuvering around, avoiding crowds. Taking the long way around the cafeteria. She gets her food and sits at her *usual table*. They told me about the bruising, but this is my first time getting a look for myself. I put aside everything I've been told, everything I suspect, about the reason she's here and the threat she poses. I look at her like I would anyone else who came back to school with a ton of bruises after being attacked on Mayhem Night; taking in the way she's keeping her back protected. Her foot tapping. How she jumps at loud noises.

She's trying to pretend she's fine, but I can see she's not. She doesn't even look our way. I'm used to getting a reaction out of her, and dare I say, I looked forward to seeing the pissed off expression on her face whenever she saw me. It was refreshing knowing that at least one person at this school wasn't intimidated by us or our status. But I'm not getting any of that from her. She's here, but she's not.

One of my frat brothers asks me a question. I'm in the middle of answering when a scream pulls my attention back across the room. Someone's sprawled out on the floor, and Thea's hovering over them, her fork at his throat. Finn must've seen what was happening. He's already on the other side of the dining hall.

"Oh shit. She's gone psycho! Somebody call the cops before she kills us all!"

I ignore Eloise's hysterics and follow Holden across the room, mumbling, "I swear this girl attracts trouble everywhere she goes."

We make it to the center of the crowd. My heart rate slows as I assess the situation. Finn's trying to sweet talk Thea into letting go of her victim, but he's not getting through to her. If he gets too close, he's likely to get stabbed too. Ordinarily he'd like the chance to go blade to blade with someone, but even I can tell this isn't the time for that. I tip my chin towards the back door. Faculty is heading our way. Finn goes to intercept them.

"I wasn't there that night. I swear it. I was joking. It was just a *joke*." The guy on the floor looks up at me, pleading, "I swear, Pax. It was a joke. Someone dared me to say it. I wasn't really there."

Thea presses the tines to his neck, growling, "Then tell me who was."

"I don't know. Okay, I don't know."

I move in closer and give the signal to Holden. I grab Thea, pulling her away from Carter, while Holden drags him to his feet and shoves him towards the door.

She squirms, trying to break free. "Let me go!"

"I will just as soon as I'm sure you're not gonna stab somebody."

"You *can* be sure I'm gonna stab *you*."

"You can try. But I'll have you on your crazy ass before you get anywhere near my skin."

"You think so, tough guy? Let's test that theory."

I look down. The doctors here are supposed to be following up on her care, so Holden has access to her infirmary records. The tendons in her shoulder are shot to shit, and she has a fractured wrist, which is supposed to be in a splint. "Where the fuck is your sling and splint?"

"I don't need it."

She winces when I tap her shoulder. "You don't?"

"This is none of your business."

"Your newfound family status says it is."

"I don't have a family."

I see the sling sticking out the top of her backpack. I grab it, then slip it over her head and cradle her busted arm in it. "Whether you do or not, I'm not going to let you open the school up to a lawsuit because you're running around here re-injuring yourself while attacking another student." I tighten the straps and growl, "Leave that on, and wear your fucking splint, or you won't heal correctly."

"Why do you even care? If I need more surgery, that'll just keep me from kicking your ass for a little while longer."

I lean down, getting in her face. "I'm not afraid of fighting you, Nemesis. Heal up and I'll gladly meet you in the middle of the ring."

I lock eyes with her friend. "Get her the hell out of here."

Layla-Jean doesn't hesitate to do it, grabbing Thea's bag and gently grabbing her good elbow, guiding her to the exit. I turn back towards the room. Of course, people are standing around. Some even have their phones out. "If any of this winds up online, you'll have to deal with me."

The phones lower and a few go through the motions of deleting the footage. I'll have Holden run a search just to be sure nobody gets the bright idea to defy me.

I walk back to our table and dig into my food. I don't really have an appetite and it's cold, but I have to keep up appearances. Show that little tiff was inconsequential, and we're in control. I catch a few looks from around the room and hear quiet whispering. They're probably wondering why we intervened, and why I care if Thea's breakdown goes viral. It all goes back to The League. We have to explain what her being a legacy means, and the first step in doing that is making sure she gets the same level of respect as every other legacy student at this school.

That means nobody should be daring anyone to harass her, without our say so, and nothing embarrassing goes online. Finn comes back to the table, with two people following him. They place the trays they're carrying in front of us. It's the same meal I already have in front of me, but this one is piping hot. "Thanks, man."

As soon as he sits, Eloise slides down to the end of our table. Changing our dinner hours created a ripple effect. The other legacies did too, as if there's a rule that we always need to do this meal shit together. We don't, but once again, it goes back to perception. Eloise asks, "Wanna tell me what the hell that was all about?"

"No." Finn snaps, before digging into his food.

"What do you mean, *no*? Why would you jump in and help her after what she did to me?"

With a dismissive snort, he says, "We weren't looking at the same thing, because she didn't need any help."

Eloise drags me into their spat. "You forbade people from sharing the video of her going psycho. I'd call that helping. Violent people shouldn't be allowed to stay at this school with us. Those videos are the evidence we need to get her kicked out."

I feel a headache coming on. Who did I piss off in The League that I'm the one dealing with this shit? "Nobody's kicking her out, and my order stands. If any videos show up online, there *will* be consequences. Same thing if I find out anyone's threatening or harassing her."

Eloise won't let it rest. "She's a nobody. The Zeta Nu drop out. People can do what they want, remember?"

We have an audience now. More people listening in, trying to get some gossip. Finn looks at me. With a curt nod, I agree with his unspoken question. No time like the present to get this over with. He says, "Who she *is*, is Theona LaReaux, from a frozen legacy bloodline, and she's one of us."

Chapter 21
Thea

I'm avoiding my classes *and* the dining hall. I really can't do school right now. After failing to settle back into any sense of normalcy, I'm willing to concede that I came back too soon. I should still be in my house in Palisade Shores with LJ and Wolfe. Because this place is no good for me.

I don't know how to process everything that's happened. I'm mad my aunt and uncle have been lying to me for months. *Aunt and uncle.* Shit, I can't even imagine calling them my parents, even though they've already transitioned into publicly declaring it. In the week since I tried to skewer that kid in The Rock, I've gone from being the outcast at school to being sought out. I wouldn't say I'm popular, but people are saying hello. It doesn't make sense. I thought for sure they'd give me a wider berth.

Of course, LJ was happy to explain what sparked the change. Sadly, it wasn't my display of badassery when I got that twerp on his ass with one good arm.

There's a rumor circulating around campus- that I have ties to one of these pretentious ass legacy families- which automatically makes me funny, smart, and desirable. As if I wasn't *already* all of those things.

She broke down what being a legacy means and gushed about

parties and connections and status. All I heard were *expectations*. I had to calm her down and remind her that my life imploding doesn't make me want to go to anything planned, endorsed, or attended by the tiara wielding Barbies that live in this building.

At least Eloise isn't faking it. Her dislike for me shines brightly, like a beacon of reality, grounding me in my truth. Money doesn't mean shit. She's been my best teacher, showing me just how much I can get away with when I retaliate for what she did to my room.

It won't be a simple slap either, but I'm nowhere near ready to go after her. I'm still processing. Trying to find my footing. Whatever I come up with, I have to be physically ready to do it, and it'll be a solo mission.

A knock on my door interrupts my current hobby of staring at the wall. I snatch my steak knife off the table, gripping it tightly in my hand. I don't trust this place or the boys next door. I've been ambushed too many times already out in public spaces. They can do much worse by coming up to my door.

"Thea?"

Maybe I should put the wine down. I'm hearing things. Or maybe I'm so desperate for a connection to my old life that I'm conjuring Sasha's voice.

"Thea, if you're in there, open up. Don't make me pick this lock. I just got my nails done, and my knees are already aching from my date last night. If I've gotta stoop down and disconnect this electronic contraption, I'll be pissed."

I chuckle because I'm manifesting good. That's such a Sasha thing to say.

I hear some mumbling and then my illusion says, "Who the fuck are you? Oh, yeah... You're probably one of them, huh? Well I've got time today mother fucker. You can call security or whoever you want. They won't get here before I pump you with 50,000 volts."

Okay. I'm not *that* drunk. I run to the door and pull it open in time to see some kid I don't know on the floor floundering like a hooked fish. How did he even got up to this floor?

You know what... that shit doesn't even matter, because my best friend is standing over him feet shoulder width apart, her taser in front of her. Looking like one of Charlie's Angels. I look back down and spot the prongs connected to his dick.

Smiling over her shoulder, she gives me a cheeky, "Hey babe."

I stand blinking like an idiot as she unwraps the silk scarf from around her neck and leans over to pluck an envelope from the guy's clenched hand. "I'll take that, thank you."

He's coming down from his zap and wheezes out, "Crazy bitch."

"That's right. I'm crazier than Thea, and I'm in town. This is just one of the toys I brought with me. So tell your buddies from here on out, they can leave all deliveries at the front desk. Preferably in the trash."

She turns and, with a sassy swish of her hips, walks into my room. "That flight was the worst, babe. What are we drinking?"

I'm still at a loss for words, watching my best friend scope out my place before going to the kitchen and finding something to mix drinks with. She doesn't have to ask where anything is, because she knows how I arrange my kitchen.

"I'm assuming you're being more quiet than usual, because you're surprised to see me?" She glares at me. "If it's because I'm no longer the number one bitch in your life, I'm gonna use my taser on you to zap some sense back into your mother fucking brain."

I don't know what's wrong with me. Like, I really don't. I start sobbing. She finishes mixing the drinks, then walks back into the living room and sets them down on the table, before getting right up in my face.

"Who do I need to inflict a lifetime of pain on?"

That makes me cry even harder, because until she was outside my door, in the hallway screaming obscenities and threatening bodily injury to that guy, I didn't know just how much I needed her here doing that.

"I don't know. I-" I shake my head. "I don't know who did it."

"Okay, then. Let's sit down and drink and you tell me what you do know."

She drags me to the couch, shoves a drink in my hand and pushes it towards my mouth. "Go on, start drinking. I ordered pizza and wings while I was in the elevator. It'll be here soon."

The tears are still coming. I sniffle and ask, "How did you even get up on this floor?"

"Really, Thea? It's like you don't even know me anymore."

I just nod. She's right. It's a stupid question. There's not a mechanical or electrical contraption that Sasha can't infiltrate. I take a decent size gulp of my drink, concentrating on the burn instead of my feelings. Then another one, letting the alcohol and Sasha's presence calm me. "I can't believe you're here."

"Of course I'm here. These rich bitches fucked with you. That means they fucked with me."

She's always been my ride or die. "But don't you have to work? How long can you stay?"

"How long do you need me to stay?"

I can't take her away from her life, but after a few days with my oldest friend, I think I'll be able to step outside this room again. "The weekend. I just need you for the weekend."

"Okay, then let's get to it." She kicks off her shoes, tucking them under her on the couch and says, "Tell me everything. Start from the beginning."

Chapter 22
Finn

When I step off the elevator, I'm greeted with the sight of a woman standing over a body on the floor. I slow my steps, taking in the spectacle in front of Thea's door. She hasn't been to class all week. Holden did his thing and found out all of her professors have been instructed to let her continue submitting her assignments online while she recuperates.

With only a few weeks left in the semester, and they're waiving the attendance requirements, trying to mitigate any potential triggers she may encounter walking around campus.

Thea must be using her kitchen, because she hasn't been to the dining hall either. Not since the day Carter Turner set her off. I have no idea who the chick in the platform converses is -but Thea clearly does- doing nothing to stop her as she walks into her dorm room like she owns the place.

Thea's eyes meet mine as I draw closer to the door. I hate the look in them. Detachment. Like I'm a ghost, and she's looking right through me.

"Pet..."

That's the wrong thing to call her. The detachment turns to rage. I deserve her slamming the door in my face, but that doesn't mean I'm not pissed about it. I look down at the guy still holding his dick.

"What are you doing up here?"

"Delivering a message to Suite D."

There's a generic access code for the elevator, but it's for maintenance; and sometimes we give a one time code for food delivery, so we don't have to ride down to the lobby, and of course my laundry crew has a code to get up here for my clothes. This guy doesn't fit any of those categories.

"A message from who?"

"From The Prides, and The Lady Lions."

I advance on him. "Excuse me? How the fuck did you even get up here?"

He wheezes out a laugh as he climbs to his feet. "Somebody published an elevator code during last month's dorm challenge."

It wasn't me or the guys. That only leaves Thea, but she doesn't strike me as the type to indiscriminately share her code. LJ is the only person I've ever seen come up here, but they ride the elevator together. I look to Thea's door again. She was barefoot in sweats, and the girl had clearly just arrived around the same time as this idiot. She had to have had a code to get up here, too. There was a familiarity there and Thea let her into her apartment without hesitation. Did Thea hire security?

She doesn't need it. I'll protect her. She just needs to get over being mad at me and tell me who hurt her. But that's a later problem. The guy in front of me needs to give me more answers about why he's here. "What kind of message?"

He smiles again. "One that expresses our condolences for the brutality she endured during Mayhem Night, and our renouncement of Rho Beta Psi's endorsement of unsafe pledge practices."

"We had nothing to do with it."

"Everyone in school knows she dropped out mid-pledge season and caused a power struggle after airing her grievances in front of Zeta Nu's pledge committee. Which leads everyone to suspect that there may be some members of Rho Beta Psi who sought retribution for her actions.

There's also talk that your sister sorority is planning to invite her to pledge again."

We're the same height, but he still tries to stare down his nose at me. "If Thea is still inclined to join a sorority next term, Lady Lions invites her to apply to join their pack. The fierce sisterhood that embraces trust, loyalty, and respect."

There's no way Thea would be interested in reapplying to Zeta Nu. If they're petitioning for her to give them a second chance, it has nothing to do with thinking she'd be a good fit for their sorority, and everything to do with our announcement that she's from a defunct legacy family.

Active or not, legacy is legacy and we stick with our own. I highly doubt Eloise is supporting a vote for it to happen. We don't usually care what organizations people pledge, unless the council takes an interest in them. It's been pretty much a given that if you were a member of a fraternity before joining The League, then it was Rho Beta Psi, and the daughters were Zeta Nus.

The Lady Lions are one of Zeta's Nu's biggest rivals. They try this legacy recruitment shit every year. They want the loyalty and influence of a legacy student, forever tied to their organization. This wouldn't be a problem if Thea would have grown up here. The choice would be easy, and she'd automatically say no.

But, they're counting on a different outcome because Thea doesn't understand how our world works. Saying yes would cause a disruption around campus and set a dangerous precedent. Other legacies might decide to do the same, and if The Lady Lions advance to the number one spot on campus, The Prides won't be far behind.

It's not just the Lady Lions and Prides that will try to exploit this. Pledge season is supposed to be over, but with the delay, investigation, and possibly having to disqualify all pledges and start again... this may work to their advantage. After going through the shit the Zeta Nus require, how many pledges would choose a different organization if given a do-over?

"You've got thirty seconds to get off this floor before I help you off by way of the balcony."

I whip out my phone and text the guys. Our to-do list just keeps getting bigger. We have to get Thea to like us, teach her what it means to be a legacy student, and come up with a plan to make sure her joining the Lady Lions or any other sorority that isn't Zeta Nu doesn't happen.

Chapter 23

Thea

Last night, Sasha and I stayed in stuffing our faces with pizza and drinks. Today, we're heading out to the beach. After my run-in with Van, Sasha's the only person who could get me to go anywhere near that side of town. Her exact words were, "I don't give a shit if you're avoiding your family at the hotel. I want to see the water and have a huge slice of that pie you're always raving about."

LJ's meeting us there. On the drive, I keep telling myself that it doesn't matter if I see Van, because I don't care. She's a liar like everyone else. I have Sasha park the car at the end of the boardwalk so she can get the full experience of walking it.

I side-eye some of the shop owners we pass, wondering if they were in on the big secret too, but none of them look guilty. Although, that could just be because they're so good at lying.

LJ's holding a booth for us when we arrive. It's my favorite one with the view of the beach. She shifts over so I can sit next to her, facing the door. Sasha slides all the way over to the end of the booth on her side, shifting so her back presses against the wall.

"So LJ, I hear you're the girl I have to thank for nursing Thea back to health."

LJ ducks her head. "No, it was the doctors. I didn't really do much."

"That's not how I hear it. She says you're the one who was sitting by her bed and moved in with her."

"Coach Wolfe was there too."

Sasha wiggles her brows. "Yup, heard all about how *helpful* he was, too."

When LJ glances over at me, I say, "It's fine, LJ. She knows everything."

"Everything, everything?"

Sasha's face splits into a grin. "That's right, every sordid detail. I can't wait to see this guy in person."

Sasha has also convinced me to swing by the gym today so she can see where I was training. I told her I'd have LJ take her since she's going in to make up a workout she missed last week, but she insisted it be me. I get it. Trust doesn't come easy for either of us, and just because LJ's earned my trust doesn't mean it extends to Sasha.

Mel comes over with a couple of menus. I see her checking out my arm. Most of the bruising has faded, but I'm stuck wearing this sling for a little while longer.

"Hey hun, haven't seen you in a while. How you doing?"

That's a loaded question. "Depends on how gossipy this town is."

Tapping her pencil against her order pad, she says, "Now that depends on which part of town you're talking about. Up on the hill, they keep to themselves and hide their secrets. Down here in the cove we're a family. We look out for each other, but we also know how to mind our own business."

"So that means you heard about my initiation prank gone wrong?"

Mel snorts out a laugh. "That's the official line the spokesperson for the college gave to the news. Now if you wanna tell me something different. I'm all ears, and if not -then like I said- we're family on this strip, but we know when to mind our own business."

I get what she's saying. She's heard the official and unofficial version of what happened, but won't press me for answers or mention it.

"Now, what can I get you guys to drink?"

We place our orders, then settle back to talk. I let Sasha and LJ dominate the conversation, happy the topic is anything and everything but me. I'm glad to have a distraction from my problems. By the time we make it to the beach, I'm laughing and enjoying the time with my girls.

I let Sasha talk me into a game of how many new followers can we get. It's stupid since I don't use my social media account, but she's up for a laugh and I'm always up for a challenge. We even rope LJ into playing, which is actually good practice for her, since we're supposed to be working on bringing her out of her shell.

We're still in game mode when Sasha pulls into the parking lot outside of Wolfe Pack. She's in the lead because she honked at a guy at a traffic light two blocks over and held up traffic while they yelled at each other through the rolled down windows.

LJ laughs, "Girl, you are nuts. What happens when they hit up your direct messages and ask to see you again?"

Sashas's been telling everyone she's new to town and leaving out the part where she leaves tomorrow night.

"They don't need to know all that. And who knows… if whatever they're saying in the messages vibes with my vibe, then I might let them come to Vegas for a visit."

LJ looks confused. "I thought you lived in Nags Creek."

"Oh, I do. But rule number three of random hookups. You never take them back to your place."

LJ presses, "Okay, but why Vegas instead of a closer town?"

"I get a trip, a stay in a fancy hotel with room service, some black-jack, and *maybe* some stellar dick."

LJ looks over at me. I see the wheels in her head, turning. "Yes, LJ, that could work here too, and if I were doing a random hookup, that's the way I'd do it."

"You mean another one. Right? Outside of the one you've already had."

I drop my head. Shit, I didn't tell them about Finn. But only because I feel like that doesn't count. He turned into someone on my stab list.

"Thea?"

Only Sasha can say my name in such a way that makes me feel like I've done something wrong.

"Fine. Two. Okay? It was two, but I feel like we should just subtract the number from itself and say zero, because they don't count. One's an ass, the other's an off limits ass."

LJ, my ever inquisitive friend, asks, "Who was the second guy?"

Sasha laughs when I raise my head. "No. *No way.*"

I grimace, my eyes cutting to LJ. I watch as she puts it together. "One of The Trium?"

I nod.

"When? The night of my parent's anniversary party, you were very adamant that you weren't interested in any of them and they…"

She's worked it out and all I can do is nod again.

"You hooked up with one of them the night of the party. It was Finn, wasn't it? Shit. I was looking for you, and Pax and Holden were looking for him, but it never occurred to me that the two of you were together. Then you popped back up *drunk.*" She crinkles her nose. "Please tell me it wasn't in my bed."

"LJ, god, no! I would never disrespect your space like that. It was in the room you told me to decompress in, and the stairs leading to the wine cellar, and maybe the theater room."

"Maybe?"

"Like you said, I was drunk, and it was dark where I was hiding, but I'm pretty sure it had a huge screen."

"Hiding?" Sasha says between laughs. I turn to her and explain, "We were playing hide and seek."

She brushes at the tears running down her face. "Girl, this Finn guy sounds fun."

"He's not. He's a manipulative asshole, just like all guys, which is why we don't date them and keep them. The only thing men are good for is eating your pussy and sometimes a fuck."

LJ's mouth gapes open and I squeeze my mouth shut, because I know the look of horror on her face isn't from my crude language. She's staring over my shoulder. That means someone heard me. I square my shoulders and turn around, coming face to face with exhibit number one. I smirk at him, daring him to contradict my statement.

"Why are you loitering outside my building, LaReaux?"

"We're not loitering. We're having a private conversation before coming in."

He holds the door open. "Well, if you're done, are you coming in?"

LJ steps forward. "Hey, coach."

"Breland. Get changed and hop on the treadmill."

She groans as she walks inside, and I suppress a smile. It's nice to see I'm not the only one who has to start off running on that damned thing. Sasha checks him out head to toe. As she walks by, she says, "*Igi.*"

I bite down on the inside of my cheek to keep from laughing. Igi (I got it) is part of the shorthand we came up with years ago, for when we came into possession of certain things or information we didn't want to discuss with other people around.

He gestures towards the door so I can go inside. Our interactions have been stilted lately. Even when I text him, something's off about his responses. He used to argue with me, but now he's treating me with kid gloves. I hate it.

I storm into the gym and walk right up to the ring where Tank's sparring. He pauses and comes over to the rope to greet me. "Hey little girl."

"Hey big girl." I tease back, feeling the tension ease from my shoulders.

I don't even know why I was so nervous about coming here. Tank doesn't even blink at seeing my arm in a sling. He's a fighter. He gets it. Bumps and bruises happen, and nobody here is gonna make a big deal about it. They'll all probably just assume I got into a fight and took a beating. Which is true. We don't bitch about it. We heal, deal, and move on.

He smiles down at me and says, "Now don't be milking your time off because you're afraid to admit you're not ready to take me on."

"Puleeze. I'm ready any time you are."

"You think so? I got time now, little girl."

My face splits into a smile. "Let's go, big girl." I go to remove my sling, but somebody grabs the back of my shirt and pulls me away from the ring. "What the fuck?" I hiss, twisting away from the hold.

Wolfe tells Tank, "Stop bating her." And tells me to, "Leave that fucking sling on."

"My arm feels fine and Tank has a good idea. I should move around. Start working out again."

"You think you're ready for that, huh?"

"Yu-p." I pop the P because he hates when I do it.

"So if I call your par-" I glare at him, daring him to finish the word. "Guardians, they'll say you've been talking to your doctor."

"Yes. I've been talking to my doctor." I go to step around him, but he grabs my neck, yanking me back again.

"The one for your head?"

Dammit.

"Yeah, didn't think so. I already told you, if you want to train, you have to do the work." He taps my forehead. "Up here. It would be irresponsible of me to let you work out here and put my other fighters at risk while you're walking around with a short fuse."

"My fuse has always been short."

"That's true." Sasha says, chiming in. "I have a long fuse and can time my devastation out over years. Thea is the one you want for immediate and total destruction."

He looks over at her and asks, "Who the hell are you?"

"Me? Who the hell are you? Or maybe a better question would be how much longer do you think I'm gonna let you just grip up on the back of my girl's neck like that?"

"I'm Coach Wolfe. This is my gym, and Thea's a lot like an unruly pup. Sometimes the only way to get her to heel is to grab hold of the scruff on the back of her neck. Isn't that right, LaReaux?"

Sasha's baton comes out of its holster. "Did you just call my girl a bitch?"

I shake my head. Long fuse my ass. "It's fine Sasha. Wolfe would never call me that, because he knows I might not be ambidextrous, but I can still do damage to his favorite body parts without the use of my right hand." I bat my eyes. "Isn't that right, sir?"

His nose flares, and I smile sweetly up at him like as if I didn't just wave a red cape at a bull.

He smirks at me and leans forward. "Tell me one real thing about how you've felt this week, and I'll let you back into the gym."

You can't miss the tension in the room. The guys in the gym and LJ are used to Wolfe and I squaring off like this, but Sasha's not and I really don't want to turn this into a thing. "Forget it."

"Nah, ah. No running, sweetness. Show me you're woman enough to handle me. Tell me one thing, real."

"I didn't feel anything this week."

He searches my eyes, then nods, and lets me walk away. I go over to Sasha and tell her I'm ready to leave. Maybe it was a mistake coming here after all. It's just another reminder of what I lost. I used to have the gym and fighting as my outlet, but Wolfe's taking it away, because I don't feel the need to talk to a guy I don't know about all the things I don't feel.

We reach the door and Wolfe says, "LaReaux, I'll see you here on your next scheduled training day. Don't be late."

I turn to look at him and he mouths, "Good, girl."

Sasha turns to stare at me as soon as we get outside. I owe her an apology for what happened in there. "Look, I'm sorry I dragged you into my mess with Deacon. I didn't think of how that would-" I stop talking because she's laughing. "What? What's so funny?"

"Girl. Igi. I to the totally G. I.," she says as she pushes me towards the car.

"Get what?"

"The alpha vibes. The wanting to roll over and show him your soft underside."

"I don't have a-"

"Wanting to get on all fours and let him rut you. Yes, babe. I totally get it and I approve."

"Sasha it's not-"

"Yes, Thea. It's definitely like that. Now I know our motto, okay? Fuck em and leave em wanting more. But unlike you, I also know what healthy relationship dynamics look like. And that man in there growling at you and demanding you do the uncomfortable work, to get better, that's what someone does when they care about you. It's the reason I came here, and the reason LJ quit school to stand vigil at your bedside. It all manifests in different ways, but he's on your side, and it's okay to let him see you. All of you."

"No, Sasha, it's not. It's never okay. You know this. You know why."

She pushes me into the car and says, "I know. I know everything that you went through and Thea, I'm telling you, it won't matter how much you push back at him, how much you fight. He's solid. He's on your side."

"How can you be so sure after meeting him for five minutes?"

She gnaws on her lip.

"Sasha Abigail Prince!"

"Fine. Fine, okay. I know because he's the one who sent me an airline ticket to come here."

"What?"

"It came to the house with a note that said you needed me. No explanation or anything."

"You just hopped on a fucking flight after receiving an anonymous note? What if it was a trap?"

"Bitch, please. What am I, an amateur? Girl, you know I know how to handle my shit."

I turn to stare out the window as she starts the car.

"Look, the man's an asshole, for sure. And I wouldn't exactly go for all that high handedness, but you and I are not the same, Thea. You get off on the fighting and he recognizes that, so I think you're in good hands. But if he goes left, I'll be right back here showing him what the rod of justice and flames of pain can really do."

My lips twitch at the names she's given her baton and taser. With a sigh, I say, "I don't know if I can do it, Sasha. I feel like I'm drowning and I don't know if I can stay here."

"That's fine too, babe. If you really can't, then you send up the signal, and I'll send you a life raft."

Chapter 24
Thea

My steps falter as I enter the class. I almost walk back out to make sure I'm in the right room. Holden's sitting at the table to the right of where I sit, instead of in his usual seat. I lower myself into my chair and let the routine of pulling my stuff out settle me. It works until the students trickle in. I tense up as they walk by me on the right.

I focus on my desk, trying not to overreact. My head jerks up at the sound of a book hitting the floor. There's someone at Holden's feet. Out of the corner of my eye, I see everyone else is using a different aisle to get to the back of the class. Finn walks up and stares down at the guy on the floor, and mocks, "Are you going to spend the entire class down there or find another way to get your new seat?"

"My new seat? I always sit right there." The guy points to a chair behind me. Finn plops down in his usual spot, puts his bag in the chair the guy is trying to get to, and growls, "Now you don't."

The tightness in my chest eases and I loosen my grip on my book as I realize no one will be sitting directly behind me.

I don't know why Holden changed his seat, but his need to have space around him works out in my favor. For the first time since coming back to school, I'm not struggling to focus on the lesson.

When class ends, I wait in my seat for the rush of students to stampede towards the door. After a few minutes, I notice they're still avoiding this aisle because Holden's feet are back in the way. I pack my stuff and stand. If he thinks I'm taking the long way around, he's not as smart as I think he is. As soon as I'm out of my chair, he tucks his feet in, letting me by. Seconds later I hear books drop again and Holden says, "What part of this don't you get? While I'm in this seat, this aisle is off limits."

The deep treble of his voice sounds scratchy. A reminder that he rarely uses it. I steal a glance at him. The only times I've heard him talk are when I shared his workbook in class, the night he came to my room with Finn and freaked out on me, and the night in the hallway when he said I should leave school.

And I've never seen him talk to anyone other than Pax and Finn. Stormy eyes look back at me from under the brim of his baseball cap. A weird spark unfurls in my belly.

"Thea, you ready?" Austin asks, coming to stand beside me.

I nod and follow him out the door, trying to pay attention to what he's saying about his dad's football team and the latest trade rumors.

I've made it through back-to-back classes for the first time since I came back to campus. I only heard half of what the teacher said, but I sat through the entire lecture, so I call it a win. Now, I'm dealing with the lunch crowd at The Rock.

LJ worries her bottom lip, then asks, "Is it me or is The Trium acting weird?"

I look behind me to where Holden is holding up the lunch line, refusing to move or let anyone get in front of him. "They're doing their usual asshole routine. It would be weirder if they weren't." I'm just glad LJ and I got here before he did.

"I wonder why they changed their meal hours."

I hadn't given it much thought. LJ and I changed the times we eat to lessen my exposure to large crowds. But she's right, it looks like a little more than half of the legacy tables switched their meal hours too.

"Probably needed new people to boss around. The old ones might be on the verge of a revolt."

It makes me smile to think people might be pushing back against them. We grab our food and as we pass Holden, I raise my fist in the air and say, "viva la revolucion!"

LJ and I crack up as we slide into our seats, and Holden decides he's done being a premier Coxsucker, and goes to his table. He shoves his face in a book as soon as his ass hits the seat.

Chomping on a fry, I say, "See. That's that bullshit, right there. He didn't even get any food. He just stood there holding up the line to amuse himself."

The sound of something rolling across the floor snags my attention. One of the maintenance workers sets up a partition right behind me, blocking my back from the line. I relax my posture since there's something protecting my back. Too bad they'll probably move it before the next meal and I'll be on high alert again.

There's a free table against the back wall, but this one still has the best view and escape route. Plus, I'd hate to ask LJ to move just because I've lost my edge. My gaze drifts over to The Trium table. They're number one on my suspect list. They didn't mince any words when they told me they wanted me gone. Who's to say my attack wasn't the way they tried to make that happen?

I take a deep breath, trying to calm my too fast heart. The idea of a confrontation puts me on edge. This is why I need Wolfe to let me train. I can't keep walking around skittish like this. I have to be prepared in case they start their shit up again.

Going by the way they keep looking at me; that could be any day now.

Chapter 25
Holden

I study the security footage looking for blind spots on campus that need to be addressed. I'm not interested in the ones people use for getting high or fucking. Just the ones where Thea might feel cornered or triggered. She's trying to hide how bad her anxiety is. She's tensing up and trying not to freak out when people get too close or when her back is exposed.

I heard her talking shit about me in the dining hall. She thinks I'm just throwing my weight around. She's wrong, but I'm happy to let her think what she wants, because I doubt she'd be receptive to the idea of me running interference so she'll feel safe.

Finn told us all about her reaction when he tried to help her at the dorms. She's proud and stubborn, and I don't want to take that from her, especially since I know she's barely sleeping. She spends her nights sitting with her back braced against her bedroom door.

I know better than anyone how it feels to need to avoid your dreams. When my body takes over and forces me to sleep, I crash so hard it's difficult to wake me. In that state, I'm stuck in my dreams, and slow to react to outside stimuli. I don't want that for Thea.

When I feel my body finally shutting down, I let Pax and Finn know and one of them will come grab me if anything important comes up. I don't know if Thea has someone she trusts like that in her life, and I can't very well ask her. That would alert her to what I'm doing at night and I'm not ready for her to know *yet*.

I click my mouse, zooming in on another camera over by the tree-line near the stadium. It's a few feet from the spot where she was standing the other morning. She's done more than change her meal hours. She's switched up all her routines, and avoids the woods.

My father doesn't know much about what happened, but he shared someone found Thea in the cemetery and she doesn't remember the details of what happened to her. The cemetery is in the opposite direction from where she was heading when I chased her. That means she either doubled back or someone took her there after her attack.

Her aversion to the one place she loved so much tells me whatever happened went down in or around those woods. I just need to figure out where. And once I get a clearer picture of what happened, I'm gonna push her to confront her fears.

It won't be easy and will require her unwilling participation. I expect a bunch of cursing, yelling and tears. But when I'm done with Thea, she'll be stronger than before.

Thea

Another day of classes down, and three more weeks left in the semester. I'm still just taking it day by day and class by class. I psyched myself up into coming to the library. The building has way more open spaces and dark nooks than I feel comfortable being around, but the paper I'm writing requires sources other than the internet.

The Coxsuckers may have reversed whatever they did to my grades, but I missed a major test while I was recuperating. The teacher won't let me make it up, and now I have to ace this final paper to keep my A in ethics class.

I ignore the looks I get when I walk through the revolving glass door. This is another reason I avoid being out in public. All the fucking staring grates on my nerves. I just want to get back to my normal life. Or at least normal-ish.

I can't even process the train wreck my life has become in peace, because my family drama and attack is being gossipped about all over campus. But I can't avoid people forever. That would just give them one more thing to run their mouths about.

I am *not* a scared little bitch. I need to remind them of that, and the first way to do so is to stop hibernating in my room. I might not want the extra attention, but I've got it. Now I need to figure out how to cope.

I've just pulled out my notes for the paper I need to write, when a body slides into the chair catty-cornered to me. I wait all of a minute before asking, "Can I help you?"

"Thea..., right?"

He knows damn well what my name is. They all do. The guy looks vaguely familiar, but I'm not sure where I've seen him before. "Do I know you?"

He laughs. "No, I suppose not. I'm Archie Tucci."

Poor guy. Did his parents not want kids? "What do you want, Archie Tucci?"

"You know. I noticed that you don't get out much, and I was thinking it's a shame. A cute girl like you, you shouldn't be hiding out in your dorm, so I figured we could hang out. Maybe catch the new movie over in the Annex."

"Did you?"

"Yeah, now that pledge season is over and you haven't aligned with anyone, that means-"

He thought he'd shoot his shot. "Pass."

"Wha-what?"

"I said, I'll pass. As in, I don't wanna bang you. Cause that's where this conversation is going, right? You take me out to a movie, maybe grab something at a diner." I take in his clothes. "Or a three-star restaurant. Take me for a drive. And I'm supposed to put out." I turn my attention back to my notes. "You can save your money, gas, and time. I'm not interested."

"Wait. You think you can turn me down? You think you can get a better offer than me?"

"I just did, so yeah I can, and yes, I do."

"Look here, bitch, you're not important. I don't care what rumor you started around school. We all know you're still a nobody. The Zeta Nu Drop Out Pledge."

I'm successfully ignoring his rant until he sneers, "You think what happened with your chastity vow ceremony and Mayhem Night was bad? That was just the beginning. I was offering you a lifeline, you stuck-up bitch. A way to survive the people gunning for you after that shit you did to Zeus. You're not under The Trium's protection, so they will come for you. "

My body locks up at the mention of Mayhem Night, but I force my head up and words out of my mouth. "If anyone thinks they can take me, they're welcome to try." I size him up. "What d'ya say? You think you got what it takes to go toe to toe with me?"

I wait for him to answer. When he doesn't, I shoo him away. He climbs to his feet then grips my hand, hissing, "You need to be more appreciative of what I'm offering."

I look down at where his fingers are locked around my wrist, gritting through the pain as my newly mended bones grind together. My eyes snap to his face, and I let him see the threat in them. "Do you want to lose that hand?"

"Ooh, this looks fun."

Archies eyes widen, and his face loses color, as Finn slides into the seat he's just vacated. Casting a quick look behind him, he says, "Finn, hey."

"Heeey." Finn drawls. "Whatcha' doin'?"

"Just talking to the Zeta Nu Dropout. Reminding her of her place."

Finn leans back, putting his feet up on the table. I slide my book over so he doesn't knock dirt onto it. "And that place would be...?"

"On her back and knees." Archie quips.

Finn nods. "Righto. That's a good place for her to be." They share a laugh while I'm debating who to stab first. The guy who's still holding onto my wrist or my neighbor. Finn smiles up at Archie. "I believe there's an unanswered question on the table."

"What question?"

"She asked if you're attached to your hand."

Archie looks down to where he's holding me. Then darts his eyes over to my free hand. When he sees it's empty he smirks. "I don't have anything to worry about. I hear this is the hand she holds her knife with, *and* she doesn't have that knife anymore."

My heart lurches when he mentions Clint. Being without my knife feels a lot like losing a loved one. Or so I imagine, since Sasha and now LJ and Austin are the only people I'd be upset about losing.

Finn's smile slips, his wrist flicks, and he pulls Archie across the table, his arm stretched taut, a blade pressed against his medial nerve. "Let this be a reminder that you *always* have something to worry about. This is your throwing hand. Right, Tucci?"

That's right. He's a baseball player. Now this little visit makes sense. The guy Zeus must be his buddy. He should be happy his friend is injured. This guy was second string, now he's starting.

"I asked you a question, Tucci. Is this your throwing hand?"

"Yeah. Yes. It's my throwing hand."

"Are you attached to it?"

"Yes."

"Then I suggest you be more careful about what you're using it for. You know... stick to food, baseballs, and jerking off." Finn lets go, and Archie straightens with a grimace, rubbing his wrist.

"Finn, no disrespect, but this is none of your business. The Trium discarded her, shunned her, and turned her into the Zeta Nu Dropout Pledge, which means the rest of us can do what we want. That's how it's been. How it's always been. The team needs justice for Zeus, and since you aren't doing anything about it..."

Finn cocks this head to the side and asks, "Is that a challenge you're throwing down, Archie?"

I've heard that word thrown around before. In the quietest of tones. That simple phrase conjures more respect and fear about being over-heard than the whole secret society thing. I couldn't get one morsel of information about it, though. Not even from LJ. But Finn's throwing out that word, and I swear Archie looks like he's about to pee himself.

"No Finn, no. It's not a challenge."

"Then why are you still standing here?"

Archie shuffles off, giving me one last hateful glare. I blow him a kiss for his troubles. I don't care what Finn just said or inferred. Archie's not done with me. I'll add him to the list of people I have to watch out for. "I didn't need you to step in, Finley."

"Clearly, you had it all under control, Pet."

"I did. I can handle peons that think a little hand holding is intimidating." I stand, shoving my stuff in my bag.

"Pet, are you mad I helped?"

"Helped? You made shit worse. I've had enough spotlight to last three lifetimes because of you three and your shenanigans. And now, there's this rumor that someone started about me being one of you legacy twats. I know you probably can't understand this since you thrive on drama and attention, but I'm just trying to move on from what happened to me and be irrelevant again. I can't do that if you come over here, putting that big glaring focus back on me."

"Nobody's gonna bother you anymore, and it's not a rumor. You *are* one of us. We'll beat that knowledge into whoever needs it, and if you need to be punished, The Trium will be the ones to do it."

I stare at him for a second before blurting out, "Are you being obtuse or do you really not get it?"

Rubbing his temples, he says, "Fine. Explain why you think me defending you is a problem."

"Archie's a tool, but he's right. The *Trium* painted this target on my back. But even before that, I was dealing with all kinds of bullshit when you were pretending to be nice to me."

"What kind of bullshit?"

"The kind that's served with a good old heaping of slick ass comments from girls because they thought I was joy riding your dick, and a side order of obnoxious comments from guys because they thought, *I thought,* my pussy was too good for them."

"I've had your pussy and I can attest that it *is* too good for them."

"I know that, but if I want mediocre dick, it's my choice. Just like if I want to threaten to stab a motherfucker for touching me, or not stab them, that's my choice, too."

He holds his hands up in surrender. "I know, Pet. You're right. We put you in the crosshairs, when we found that birth certificate, because we thought... well, it doesn't matter what we thought. Now that we know what it means, we're trying to fix it. It's just taking some time because anyone who's not a legacy will drag their feet about accepting what they think is your overnight status change."

"You created this mess, but I didn't ask for your help to fix it, and I don't give a shit about this legacy crap. I want nothing to do with it, or you, so stop getting into my business." I lean across the table, getting right up in his face. "And yes, Fin-ley... that's a challenge I'm throwing down."

A shadow comes to a stop beside me. Holden's coffee bean scent tickles my nose. "That's not gonna happen."

I straighten and take a step back from the table. "What?"

"Staying out of your business. It's not gonna happen, and people will be more willing to embrace your position as a legacy just as soon as you do."

"Embrace?" I scoff. "Dude, I'm letting that shit trust fall right on the floor, and I'm gonna step all over it on my way out the door."

With that, I head across the aisle towards the stairs. They catch up to me on the second floor landing and Holden yanks me into an alcove. I freeze for a moment, then my fight-or-flight response kicks in as I swing, kick, and scream, "It was you, wasn't it? It was you?"

I'm dragged down the row and pushed into a study room. The door slams closed behind us. I launch myself at Holden. There's no way I'm letting them hurt me again. Pain ricochets through my shoulder and wrist, as I my fist connects with his jaw. I go to swing again, but Finn grabs me from behind.

Suddenly the room goes black, a heavy weight settles in my limbs. "Let me go. Let me go!"

Chapter 26
Holden

Something happened between the time Thea left the table and now to trigger her. The only thing I can come up with is when I grabbed her arm to keep her from leaving.

"Calm down, Pet." Finn soothes.

She struggles, trying to get out of his hold, and I tell him, "Let her go."

He does, taking a step back, but still blocking the exit. Thea darts around the tables, pinning her back to the wall. Her words come out in a choked whisper. "I guess you're ready to finish the job, huh? Bold choice in the library, but I guess this is the only place you could catch me."

Finn shakes his head, cutting her off. "We're not trying to hurt you."

She laughs. A caustic empty sound in the space. "I'd have to be a fucking fool to believe that. How many times have you threatened to put me in my place? What was it you said that night in your room? That I'd be choking on my own blood? And the threat in the dining hall about my impending doom? Well, that's exactly what happened, isn't it?"

It shocks the hell out of me when Finn doesn't try to bullshit his way through an answer. "You're right, Thea. I said those things, and I meant them. You have no reason to believe me right now, but I swear I was nowhere near you on Mayhem Night."

Her glare is now directed at me. "What about you? You gonna swear your innocence too and hope I'm stupid enough to believe it?"

"No."

Her mouth drops open. She recovers and twists her lips into a smirk. "Okay then, what's your method for pleading innocence? You planning to have your lawyer sue me for defamation or libel?"

"Neither. I'm not gonna lie to you. I *was* there."

She somehow pushes herself deeper into the wall, shrinking in on herself. "You what?"

"Mayhem Night. I saw you."

"You saw me?"

Her throat spasms. I should probably have used a different approach. Maybe had her friend holding her hand, but there's no time for that. If we're going to get Thea to trust us, we need to be honest about this. *I* need to be honest about this. "I saw you on Mayhem Night, and I chased you into the woods."

She blinks, then shakes her head. "Bravo. You almost got me. Trying to give me fake details so I say, *oh he's innocent*. Nice try but, I was in the cemetery."

"I know where they found you. What I don't know is how you got back to the cemetery. I chased you out of there and into the woods, and promised not to tell anyone I saw you if you made it back to the dorms."

"You chased me?" She queries like she's trying to work out the meaning or details. "Like we were racing?"

"No, Thea. I chased you like you were prey trying to avoid getting devoured by a predator."

Something about that phrasing emboldens her. She straightens her spine and says, "So you caught me and beat me! What kind of sick fuck-." She launches at me again. I let her get a few swings in before turning her away from me, pinning her arms to her side with her back to my chest. That makes her freak out even worse. But I don't let her go. I will, but right now she's gonna listen.

I inhale her scent. She still smells like warm apple pie. My lips graze her ear as I speak. "There are so many things I have done, will do and *want* to do to you, Thea. I fantasize about hearing you scream. I get hard at the thought of your tears. I want to break you into minute particles and watch you reform again. But I promise that when I do, you will remember and enjoy every single part of it." As I talk, I relax my grip on her, but keep her pulled close.

"You're delusional if you think I'd like any of that."

"What I think is that you're a person who would enjoy making me work for what I want."

"After everything you've already done, and after what you just said, why should I believe you aren't the reason I wound up in the hospital?"

"Believe *me?* You shouldn't. You should believe yourself. But first, you'll have to stop lying to yourself and pretending you're okay, when I can see plain as day that you're scared out of your goddamn mind."

"You don't know what the fuck you're talking about."

I bury my nose in her hair, filling my lungs with her scent. God, I've missed her smell. "I understand more than you think, Thea."

Reluctantly, I let her go, and back away, giving her space. "I know where we were when I started chasing you, and I know the direction you were heading when I let you get away. I don't have any more details other than that -yet-, but when you're ready to walk through that night, let me know, and I'll help you."

I tip my chin, signaling for Finn to move. He steps aside, giving her a wide berth so she can leave the room. When she's gone, he pulls his beanie off his head and scrubs a hand through his unruly curls. "Damn man. Do you think it was smart to tell her about chasing her when the plan was to lower her defenses?"

"Thea needs something to pull on. A reference point to start unraveling the details of that night. I've given her one and offered to help her look for more clues." I close my eyes, imagining I still feel Thea's presence in the room, even though she's long gone. "It's fine if she wants to fixate her anger on me for now."

"Let's see if you're still saying that when she tries to cut out your entrails."

"Thea fights because she's used to fighting about everything, and because mentally it makes sense that we're her attackers. But she *stopped* fighting while I was talking to her, and didn't move from my embrace until I was the one putting space between us. Logic says we're her enemies, but eventually, her brain will catch on to what her body already knows."

"Which is?"

"That I'm not the threat buried deep in her mind that she's too afraid to face."

Chapter 27
Finn

I've finally got someone to interview. Carter thought Pax dragging Thea away and us not asking questions meant the incident in the dining hall was forgotten. As if we'd just drop it. If someone dared him to say that shit to Thea, I want to know who it was. I slip inside the warehouse, letting the heavy door bang shut behind me. I've given him all day to hang around and think about what he's done. He should be ready to talk by now.

"Thank you for waiting." I smile up at him, letting him see that this is just a friendly little chat. His wrists are cuffed together and he's suspended by a chain attached to a hook on the ceiling. His ankles are zip tied together, so he can't do something stupid, like kick me. "I won't take up too much of your time. You just answer a few questions and you're free to go."

"Sure man. Whatever you want to know."

It's a good thing he wants to get right down to business. I'm having dinner at my parent's house, and don't want to be late. "What I want to know is who was there the night you attacked Thea."

He shakes his head. "I didn't attack her."

"You told her you did."

"Like I said, it was a joke. Just a joke."

"Right. Then I'll have the joke writer's name."

"Finn, man... I can't tell you that."

My brows shoot to my forehead. That's not the answer he's supposed to give me. "Why not?"

"Because it was a dare and, based on the rules, we're not required to disclose that information."

He's spouting game rules to me? Like I'm supposed to give a shit about how many points he racked up by traumatizing my girl? We've gotten soft. I can see it now. These punks aren't as afraid of The Trium as they used to be. I was hoping he'd just feel chatty, and I wouldn't have to get persuasive.

I look down at my feet and grimace. I'm wearing my new white sneakers. Now, they're gonna get ruined. "Are you sure you don't wanna tell me?"

"Game rules, man. Game rules."

"Uh, huh." I whip out my butterfly knife and jam it into his side. Not too deep and not enough to hit anything major, but it serves its purpose.

"I respect your loyalty to the rules. Now we're gonna play a new game. One where we pretend that I am a *Trium* and I make or break the fucking rules. Now, instead of just wanting to know who dared you, you're gonna tell me every other secret you've ever kept in your life, too."

I pull the knife out, and drag it down the length of his body, ripping his shirt in half. "I'm short on time. So let's get started." I step back, surveying his form. "I usually go from the top down, but maybe we'll switch it up."

I yank down his sweatpants and make tiny cuts on his left thigh. The design I have in mind is perfect. I'll take a picture when I'm done. I always take pictures of my art. Eventually, I'll have the pictures turned to sketches and I'll choose the one I like best for my next tattoo. I look up to see how Carter's responding to the cuts. The sting of pain can be a minor annoyance or feel like a million fire ants chomping on your skin. It all depends on your pain tolerance.

. . .

Carter broke fifteen minutes in. I wasn't even halfway through my design before he started blabbing. Other than telling me where his group hides their challenge items, he didn't have much to say. The person who dared him is a nobody. A peon at their frat, but I'll be paying him a visit too, and every other person who's outed until I get answers.

I'm sure someone will complain that I'm overreacting, but I'd be questioning people even if Thea wasn't walking around newly christened a legacy heir.

Nobody asked us if they could punish her, nobody notified us it happened, and nobody's come forward to take the blame so we can get pledge season back on track.

The Trium should have been the first call when this shit went down on Mayhem Night. We weren't, which suggests we've lost control. If the students aren't afraid of us, then someone else has convinced them they're a bigger threat. We need to find out who it is and prove that they're not.

That idiot Zeus is taking the blame for what happened, but unless he's suddenly hitting as hard as Pax or Holden, there's no way he did all that damage to Thea's face by himself.

Once I'm in my car, I shoot off a text to have someone pick up Carter, then drive to my parent's place. Carter's breathing. The cuts are pretty much superficial, but just in case he wants to make a big deal about me giving him a stern lecture, it's better if my dad hears about this from me.

My father's coming out of his office as I step out of the hallway that leads from the garage. Taking in my appearance, he says, "I suppose you'll be leaving the car here to be cleaned and detailed?"

"Yes, but I didn't make as big a mess as the Red Summer."

The Red Summer was two years ago. Right around the time we learned about The League. Somebody decided to publicly challenge my position as a Trium member, based on me living overseas for thirteen years, and things got a little messy. We had to reupholster the seats and replace the carpet because I smeared so much blood on them.

He looks down at the shoes I'm holding in my hand. I took them off outside so I wouldn't make a mess. "Why don't you toss those in the car too and I'll see if my guy can get them looking new again."

I backtrack to the garage and toss them on the driver's seat, then go to my room to get cleaned up before dinner. When I get back downstairs, I pass my parents in the hall. My dad has my mother pressed against the wall, devouring her neck. I roll my eyes, trying to block out her moans. "You guys have a room on the other side of the house for that."

"And you have a college campus on the other side of town you can eat at, if seeing me be affectionate with my wife is a problem for you."

Their marriage was a league contract, just like mine to Eloise. The only difference is, my parents *like* each other. A lot. I'm no stranger to their displays of affection, hence the reason I'm not an only child.

"Tonight is family dinner night or else I would be on campus, or out rounding up new leads."

My father drags his face away from my mother's neck, muttering. "He's always been such a cock blocker."

My mother laughs and steps out of his embrace, coming to slip her arm around my shoulder. "Tell me what you've been up to."

Some parents say that and don't really want to know, but my mother is just as active in my life as my father is. Of course, I spare her some of the more explicit details, though I'm sure my dad fills her in. I've never known them to keep secrets from each other.

Which is why I'm confused by their choice of wives for me. Eloise and I won't ever have a relationship like theirs. I thought we would when we were first matched. But the more I got into exploring what I like the less she wanted to do.

I'm giving my parents shit for dry humping each other in the hallway, but I'm not really upset about it. That's the way they've always been. The way I figured I'd be with my spouse.

"I had to interview someone today. He alluded to having information about what happened to Thea."

"And did he?"

"No. Someone dared him to say he did, and like an idiot, he took that dare."

"And how is the girl doing?"

I heft my shoulders. "She won't talk to me and just seems to get angrier every time I try to apologize. I don't know how to fix it."

My mother squeezes me to her side. "She's been through a tough ordeal. None of us know exactly what happened to her, and she has to be reeling from finding out that Moira and Scott are her parents. That's all a lot to contend with, don't you think? So maybe just give her some space to work through that, sit and accept her anger, hurt and frustration, before you go demanding she shares to appease your ego." She turns my face towards her. "And pro tip, women don't always need or want men to *fix* stuff. Sometimes it's more than enough that they just consistently show up and be there *if* we need help."

I ponder over my mother's words. Show up and help if needed. I excel at that.

Chapter 28

Thea

Holden says he saw me on Mayhem Night. I believe him, because he has no reason to lie about that. I'm just not so sure I believe he wasn't with the crowd that assaulted me. He and his buddies have been escalating their attacks all semester. It's a short jump from what they did to me at my chastity vow ceremony to beating me and locking me in a coffin.

I know I'm dreaming about what happened in those rare moments when I allow myself to fall asleep. I just don't remember the details when I'm awake. Of course, Wolfe says talking about what I do remember will help. *God,* if he doesn't lay off me about that, I'm gonna put that theory to the test and talk to a jury about why I offed my annoying ass teacher.

I've spent enough time in my room to know the guys' schedules by heart. Which gives me the opportunity to do what I'm about to do. I look over at the elevator door, then over to the corner where the ceiling and wall meet. It was Sasha who told me about the tiny cameras in the hallway. I had to call in a favor to scramble the feeds, and only have a short window of time to work. I use the exploit Sasha sent me and my lock picking kit to let myself into Holden's room. It takes longer than I would like because I'm out of practice and the dexterity in the fingers on my right hand isn't back up to 100 percent yet.

I stop short in the doorway, taking in Holden's living room. It looks nothing like I imagined. I expected pristine walls and disinfectant smells. Instead, I'm greeted with plants, soft lights, and a water feature that amplifies the woodsy vibe. I could totally see myself hanging out here. Why does he have to be such a Coxsucker?

With a sigh, I drag myself away from the living room. I'm not here to admire his decor. I've got a plan to get even with everyone who's been fucking with me, but I have to start out small, and Holden just happens to be the first target because of proximity.

I wander through his room, trying to figure out what might mean the most to him. He's got a thing for plants, but I do too, so I'd never mess with them. Nothing jumps out at me until I get to the spare bedroom with wall-to-wall computers and monitors. He must be a huge gamer. If I had time, I'd load all his games and delete the progress he's saved. But the clock is ticking, so I do the next best thing. I swap his monitors around, slightly alter the heights, and distance between them, and loosen the cords on his computers enough to break the connection, but not enough that he'll know before he has to troubleshoot why they won't turn on, and rearrange the batteries in his wireless mouse.

I glance down at my phone. Time's almost up. For shits and giggles, I snatch up his television remote on my way out the door. I stash it in my room and when the cameras come back online, I'm back in the same spot I was in when they went haywire, letting them capture me walking to the elevator.

I'm humming to myself during the ride to the lobby. What I did will be a minor annoyance to him, but it was satisfying. With my arm out of commission, I have no choice but to get creative on how I go about getting payback. Besides, it's been a while since I've had to use my B&E skills. These little missions I have planned out will be good practice for when I finally go after Eloise.

I make it out of Vale Tower and halfway across The Circle before the good vibes I was feeling make a crash landing at my feet. *Dammit.* I've conjured her up just by thinking about her.

Eloise walks right up to me, a sneer on her perfectly made-up face. "Oooh, look who decided to come out of hiding." She inspects my face. "I think you looked better with the bruising."

"So did you. Shall I give you more?"

She takes a step back, offering the fakest laugh ever. "This is why it's utterly ridiculous that anyone could ever think you'd fit into our group. You might be from a family that used to have some influence in this town, but now you're barely a step above the Taylors who are the bottom rung of the ladder."

"Good."

"Good?"

"That's what I said, *good*. I don't want to fit into your group so how about you keep saying it, maybe a little louder for the people in the back, and that way everyone stays out of my face and you get to keep your fake ass friends to yourself."

I shoulder past her and head towards the athletic building. I'm about ten feet away when the dread sets in. I don't feel like class today. I'm still on restrictive activities, anyway. I don't even know what happened. Last week, the doctor said everything was healing nicely and she would be ready to sign my release back to full activity.

When I went to what should have been my last check up two days ago, she gave me a slip of paper that says I can't do anything that puts pressure or strain on my shoulder or wrist.

Wolfe waved that note around like it was a winning lottery ticket, and now I'm still stuck sitting on the floor, walking on the treadmill, or his new form of torture. Arm rotations with a resistance band.

I would say it's punishment for not showing up at the gym. I tried to go. I *wanted* to go. I made it as far as the parking lot, but I couldn't walk inside. It's one thing to argue I'm ready to fight. But when I really thought about squaring off against someone, panic set in. Just the thought of letting anyone touch me makes me break out into a sweat.

Maybe I should have gone to Wolfe Pack and skipped this class, because at least at the gym, I don't have to deal with assholes snickering about me or giving me those pitying looks.

I walk in, barely sparing a look at my classmates or Wolfe, and go straight to the wall I'll be standing against.

Wolfe goes over the lesson, has two people demonstrate the moves, then breaks the class off into groups to practice, before walking over to me and dropping a set of exercise bands at my feet.

I'm supposed to start with the lightest one and work my way up. I do three sets of twenty-five each. By the time I'm done, my arm aches. He brings me an ice pack and I sit waiting for the last ten minutes of class to end.

Something has to give. I feel invisible. I know I just told Eloise I want to be left alone, but that's because the people coming up to me are as fake as the inflatable boobs on a blow-up doll. What I want is to feel seen, noticed, to have someone interested in me, just because I occupy the space.

I wait until class ends to walk up to Wolfe. When he sees me approaching, he says, "Decent effort today, LaReaux."

"Gee, thanks. That last rubber band almost had me."

"It would be easier by now if you'd show up for your training sessions."

I heft my shoulders.

"Why are you avoiding me?"

"I'm not."

"Fine, why are you avoiding my gym? I thought you wanted to resume your sessions. Didn't you argue me down about how ready you were?"

"I've been busy."

He tilts my chin up. "There's no shame in admitting you're scared."

I slap his hand away. "I'm not scared. I'm behind on a few assignments, and fixing my grades is more important right now."

Chapter 29
Deacon

Thea's so full of shit. She thinks I can't see through the tough girl act. I've trained enough fighters to recognize when they're afraid to get back in the ring after a serious injury. It's always a mental thing that they overcome just as soon as they stop being stubborn and confront what's making them afraid.

"Fine. Your shoulder's still healing, anyway. You need to continue working on range of motion outside of this class, and stretch."

"I stretch."

"Really? Because the cool down you did looked a lot like holding up the wall instead of the exercises I taught you." I tuck my clipboard under my arm. "I came up with a rehab plan for you and since you refuse to come to the gym, I'm allowing you to work the program during class. If you can't do that correctly, then your grades here will reflect."

"You can't flunk me for not stretching."

"It's my class and I can do whatever the fuck I want."

"You're being unreasonable." She balls her little fists at her side.

"I'm doing what I agreed to do. I'm training you. Just because it's not teaching you a combination in the ring doesn't make it any less effective."

"Then maybe I should find another trainer, because this arrangement doesn't work. That's why I haven't been to your stupid gym. Your training methods suck!"

I stalk forward. "Whatever lies you have to tell yourself to keep moving. But let's get one thing straight. There is no getting rid of me."

I grab her chin, forcing her to look at me. "They didn't break you, LaReaux. You're standing here in front of me as proof of that."

She tries to look away, but I won't let her. I keep her attention on me. "I know you probably feel like they took something from you, but they didn't. You're still you. You're still the same stubborn little shit that strolled into my class that first day and refused to leave when you realized who I was. The same fearless woman jumping into the ring with guys three times her size. The fighter I can't wait to put up against some of the hottest talent on the west coast. You're still you, LaReaux. They *didn't* break you."

Her voice is soft. Strained, when she whispers, "I feel like they did. They took something from me, and I don't feel the same."

"The only thing you lost was your knife."

"You don't get it Wolfe. I've got patches in my brain, these dark spots, and I don't know what happened or who was there, or how far they went, beyond them holding me down and beating me."

Her voice gets stronger when she says, "I wasn't good enough to fight them off, and it's your fault. If I didn't have to stick to your stupid no fighting rule, I wouldn't have been so weak and rusty. I could've been fighting at Club Dredd and I'd have been on top of my game."

I take the verbal abuse. That little bit of word vomit tells me a lot about what's going on in her head. Her rape kit came back inconclusive. There was no evidence of recent sexual activity, meaning no DNA in her vaginal canal, but there was bruising and tears at her entrance. That could mean someone's attempt was interrupted, or they used something other than their dicks. Zeus is the only person we can place at her attack, and he's not talking.

"Zeus has skin grafts on his dick, and eventually you'll remember who else was there." I can see that doesn't offer her any comfort. "How can you possibly think you weren't good enough when you did everything you could to survive?"

She pushes away, and I let her. "How can you know that?"

"Because I know you. Fuck, Thea. I know you, and I know the type of person you are."

She laughs bitterly. "You don't know shit about me."

"I know you had a tough life growing up, and it's only gotten shittier since coming to this town."

"You can keep your pity." She snarls, regaining her fight.

"Pity? Is that what you think I'm feeling? Why would I pity you? Fuck, sweetness, I have no room for pity in my heart, because I'm so goddamn proud of you."

She's back to mumbling again. "As my coach from school, right?"

"Yes, as your coach from school, and your trainer at Wolfe Pack." I pull her hands in front of her, knuckles on display, and I say, "Your knuckles were split wide open when I found you. You're always gonna wear these scars. That's the evidence that you took all your experiences from before, and the lessons we've had since you've been here, and applied them. You did everything you could to protect yourself."

I grip her shoulder, pulling her close again. "The Hughes want to wrap you up in bubble wrap and whenever I think of the state you were in when I found you, I want to agree. But as the man who admires your fighting spirit, even when I wanna strangle you because of it, and as the guy you met one crazy night, I shouldn't even be thinking about; I want to hunt down every last person that touched you and make them bleed. More than that, I want you to be able to look them all in the eye and show them just how much they *didn't* break you."

My hand slips to the nape of her neck, I rest my forehead against hers. "Come on LaReaux. Help me prove to these bastards that they didn't break you."

She doesn't agree. She doesn't have to. There's no way I'm letting her quit.

Deacon Wolfe is fucking with my head. That little speech yesterday was fraught with all kinds of sexual tension, even though I know he's not interested in me. If I thought he was, I would have shown him certain parts of me aren't broken by offering him a quick fuck right there in the middle of the gym.

Maybe an anonymous hookup is what I need right now. But I'll have to expand my net. The outskirts of Canyon Falls Annex isn't far enough away to escape running into people at this school. And I need an escape.

"It's her. It's her!"

"What the hell?"

LJ's unexpected outburst has me looking up from my phone. I instantly regret my choice to come to breakfast. Her cute little nose scrunches up as she asks, "Why is your face plastered all over the partition?"

I step around Holden, who is still doing his best wall impersonation, and gape at the sight in front of me. "A better question is why are there a bunch of people wearing cat ears sitting at our table?"

As we get closer, they all get to their feet and start some kind of chant. A jungle beat pipes through the speakers and lion roars mix with the bass, making the skin on my arms stand up. Somebody flips down the middle of the cafeteria and someone else jumps over him, landing in front of me on one knee, and presents me with an envelope. A second person does the same thing, landing in front of LJ.

I've gotten enough envelopes to know what this means. Taking a step back, I shake my head. Nope. No way. Nah, ah.

"Thea LaReaux, the esteemed members of the Lady Lions invite you to a hunt."

"A hunt?" LJ and I share a look and she asks, "What kind of hunt?"

"We will camp and prowl the lands, and at the end we will hold a celebration for all those who are successful in capturing their prey, and offer a formal invite to join our pack."

"Um, maybe you didn't get the memo, but I'm more of a lone wolf kinda gal. The last time I tried to join something didn't end so well for certain members of the pledge committee."

The girl standing in the front of the crowd who was leading the chant, smiles over at me. "I promise we're nothing like those entitled bitches in Zeta Nu, which is why we think you'd be perfect for us. And as a legacy student, don't you deserve to be a part of an organization that truly emulates pride and cohesiveness? A chance to choose what trails you prowl in life?"

Finn comes to stand next to me, glaring down at the guy who's still at my feet. "She's not interested. Now get the fuck out!"

I glance down and see the guy pushing a box towards me that I hadn't noticed before. It's like a cat dropping off a dead mouse. He looks up and my eyes widen. It's the guy Sasha tased.

He winks when he notices me staring at him, which sets Finn off. "Didn't I say get out? You can walk out or hobble out. The choice is yours."

The space around me gets smaller and I know without looking that Holden and Pax have joined the party. I scoot closer to LJ and look over at the girl in charge. "I'm not interested."

"How about you think about it and hold off on making a final decision until next semester?"

The guy at my feet is playing with the hem of my jeans. He rolls out of the way and springs to his feet seconds before Finn's foot connects with his ribs.

The girl lets out a whistle, and the group heads toward the door. The guy winks again and says, "See you soon, Thea."

Finn grits out, "Not if I cut your eyeballs out."

I straighten my shoulders and walk by Finn, settling into my seat to eat my food. Ignoring him and his friends is really the best response.

Chapter 31
Thea

I've had a fucked up morning thanks to that little display the Lady Lions put on. I get wanting to stick it to the glitter posse, but they ambushed me with all that legacy talk. Why can't people understand that I don't want anything to do with being a legacy? It sounds like a burden since nobody's actually given me a reason to be excited about slapping on that label.

Trying to go to classes added to my frustration. I'm in no mood to play nice, or deal with the fake ass civility I've been subjected to since coming back, so I'm taking a sick day for the rest of the day.

I'm not sure how long this medical pass is gonna last, but I'm using it when I need to. This afternoon, I need it, but I won't be sitting around. I need to move. Wolfe's little speech about getting back to training made some sense, but I just can't put myself up against anyone else yet. I need to assess my strengths and weakness on my own.

My mood worsens when I step into the gym and see Pax is here. I try to ignore him as I go straight to the speed bag. I'm not usually one to skip a warm up, but since I just walked across campus and took the stairs to get down here, I think I've warmed up enough.

My arm's stiff and my stitches pull every time I extend my arm. It takes me a few minutes to settle into a rhythm, but when I do, I have an easier time blocking out the discomfort. The familiar thud against the thick leather does wonders to help relieve the tension in my neck and shoulders. The sound and repetitive motion ground me in a way I haven't felt since I drove back into town.

A hand lands on my shoulder and my body locks up. This is why I can't let Wolfe train me anymore. His pride would go to disgust when he sees I can't fight anymore.

I play off my reaction and turn to glare at Pax. "Don't you know better than to sneak up on people?" I move over to the mirror, rubbing my shoulder before I go through some combos, trying to get back in the zone.

Jab, cross, half fan left. Jab, cross, upper cut, half fan left. I repeat the combos in my head. He's right behind me, making it hard to concentrate. I didn't like people standing at my back before my accident. I'm even less of a fan now. God, I wish I had Clint. I face him, and snarl, "Back off unless you want me to punch you."

"You're stiff and your reaction time is shit. You'd be lucky to land a blow."

"What will be lucky is if you don't choke to death when I knock your teeth down your throat."

He's staring at me as if unfazed by my threat. Why would he be? He's bigger than me, so he's probably confident he can take me. Right now, he'd be right.

"If you want a shot at me," He taps my shoulder, sending pain shooting through it. "This needs to fully heal. Pushing past your limits now is only going to make it worse."

He turns and walks toward the door, and says, "And stay the hell away from the Lady Lions."

"Excuse me?"

He exits the gym without answering, which keys me up all over again. Great, I'm still in a pissy mood and now my shoulder is throbbing. I might've gone too hard on my first workout, but it felt good to be doing something. I turn to face the mirror again, pulling up my shirt to look at my scar. It's red and swollen, but every day it gets a little better. So long as people don't tap me on it.

Why was the head Coxsucker even talking to me? He can't possibly think I give a shit about his advice on how far I can push my body or who I associate with.

I ignore the incoming call from Moira and send her a text response instead.

I'm fine

Geez, how much longer are they gonna require these check-ins, as if I'm a ten-year-old staying at home alone for the first time? The only reason I respond at all is because when I don't, they call LJ, and I really don't want them doing that. Especially not this weekend. She's got some family thing happening, and she doesn't need to be worried about my drama while her mom is playing pin the daughter on the bachelor again.

When I walk into the dining hall, it feels like the walls are closing in on me. The Lady Lions are back, but at least they're not sitting at my table. The Zeta Nu's keep glaring at me from their circle of hell and the Coxsuckers are in their usual spots. I should've switched up my meal hours since I'm eating alone.

Finn gets up from his table and comes over to me. "Hey, Pet."

He knows I don't respond to that name. I think he's only using it to get a response out of me, anyway he can. It's like a game now. He keeps trying to talk to me and I keep trying to ignore him. It's hard to do because he's so damn persistent. Still, I do my best to pretend like I don't even see him.

He hisses, "Back the fuck up. The only time I want someone this close is if I'm taking their ass, and since you're behind me, that's not what's about to happen."

My lips twist. And people say I have no filter. Out of curiosity, I turn to see who he's snapping at. I shouldn't have looked. I should've just guessed who'd be hanging onto him like a leech.

"Finn, how many times have I told you that's not an appropriate way to talk to me in public?"

"And how many times have I told you I don't give a shit where we are? I'm going to be me and do and say what I want, regardless. If you have a problem with me, then feel free to find a more suitable companion to annoy."

"I'm setting boundaries. That's healthy in a relationship." Eloise says, sounding like my shrink.

"So is pushing them. And by pushing, I mean through the tight ring in an ass, and massaging it from the inside with my dick until I blow."

I stiffen when Finn leans into me. "How do you feel about that, Pet?"

Before I remember I'm supposed to be ignoring him, I say, "Boundaries are for children, bosses, school zones, highways, and houses. Why bring them into bed?"

His warm breath fans my ear, sending a shiver down my spine. "My thoughts exactly."

Eloise walks off muttering about common sluts, and I tamp down the urge to go after her. Her day is coming. I just need to find the perfect way to hit back at her. I'm next in line and step to the counter to place my food order and fix my drink. When I turn back to wait for my tray, Finn's at his table with a tray already in front of him.

If he'd already ordered his food, why was he waiting in line? To annoy me? If so, that plan backfired because I was quite amused by the conversation he and Eloise were having. If anything, she's the one who flounced off, annoyed.

Walking to my table, I'm relieved to see maintenance still hasn't relocated the partition yet. I thought for sure they'd move it away, after the Lady Lions decorated it. I settle down at my table and plug my ears, letting my music distract me from the noise. As long as I can't hear, I can pretend everyone's ignoring me, and I can definitely ignore them. It works wonders and I get through my meal in peace.

Holden's standing outside of The Rock when I exit. His buddies are nowhere to be seen. Seeing him alone puts me on high alert. He admits to having chased me that night, but it's still unclear if the other Coxsuckers were with him.

I give him a wide berth. If I could walk backwards and keep an eye on him, I would. But I refuse to give him any hint that his presence unsettles me. He shifts, giving me more room to get by, but he's basically blocking the door.

I don't acknowledge him when he says, "Whenever you're ready to talk about it, come find me."

It's obvious what he's referring to. Were my thoughts written all over my face when I walked by? If so, it means I'm slipping and need to patch the cracks in my bitch mask. I just don't know how to do it without my usual weapons to protect me. My confidence in my ability to fight *and* my knife.

If I were the church type, I'd go to a service and pray for guidance. But I'm not. I believe there's something greater than me out there, but I don't think I have to sit in a building to touch base with it.

Maybe that's the problem. I am whole heartedly a commune with nature kind of girl, and I haven't done it. I haven't even thought about visiting my stream and have been avoiding the woods all together, even when it's a quicker way to get to class.

Maybe Holden chasing me through the woods that night would explain why. I don't remember what happened, but my subconscious does. Which is why I know I won't be going on any hunts. I can't go into the woods. I hate that he's ruined that for me.

I turn toward the parking lot. There's another body of water. A bigger one, that isn't tainted by the stink of that night. Going there means being near Van's hotel, but I can deal with that.

. . .

There's something calming about lying on top of this rock in the dark, staring down into nothingness. The fear coursing through my veins is the good kind. I've missed *this*. The quietness of the night juxtaposed against the crashing sound of the waves, drowns out the noise in my head. How much more quiet will it be if I jump, letting the water swallow me whole? I inch forward on my belly a little more, just to get that feeling of free falling. I brace my hips and let go, letting my arms hang free. If I move just a little more... it'll feel like flying. I do in small increments. My thighs are burning, holding my weight flush against the stone. I have to balance my weight just-so, or I'll slip. My stomach flips and my heart gallops in my chest. I taste the distinct tang of fear on my tongue. This is *it*. This is the feeling. I close my eyes, letting my upper body hang forward.

A hand closes over my ankle. I kick out, screaming, as I'm dragged back away from the edge. The rock scrapes along my back as I'm rolled over.

"What the fuck are you doing?" Pax slams his hand on the ground by my head. "You are the most selfish bitch I've ever met."

"Excuse me? I was minding my own business. If anyone's ego is taking up space here, it's you trying to be the center of everything. What are you even doing here?"

"I drove by and saw you climb the rock. I didn't know you were gonna be so stupid. You think your life is hard? From where I sit, it looks like you upgraded."

"Upgraded? It's been nothing but a shit-show since I came here."

"Oh, boo-fucking-hoo. You got caught lying, have mommy and daddy issues, and got hazed during Mayhem Night. Now you're crying about it instead of owning up to your part, and pushing away the people who are trying to help you acclimate to the changes. But if you ask me, you don't deserve their help. You don't deserve the legacy title."

"Their help? What help would that be? Do you mean when Finn kicked me out of his room after shoving a bottle in my cunt? Or the help Holden gave when he chased me through the woods and whatever else he did to me that night that he hasn't confessed to yet? Is that the help you're talking about?"

"Finn tried to apologize and you keep freezing him out, and Holden didn't hurt you."

"Were you there?"

"What?"

"That night. You say Holden didn't hurt me and sound so damn sure about it. Were you there? Are you the one who hurt me and the other two watched?"

"None of us were there for your hazing, and if you'd go to those therapy sessions -I heard you're skipping- maybe you'd be able to remember who was."

"Fucker, I wasn't hazed! I was beaten unconscious, my clothes shredded, and I was tossed in a grave; and if I don't want someone digging around in my head, making me relive that it's my choice!"

"It's not a choice, it's avoidance. You walk around here like you're so goddamn tough, but you're a coward."

I'm done with this conversation. "Why are you even here? You've been vocal about how much you despise me from the beginning. If I tumble off this rock, that just gets me out of your hair."

"I came up here because I'm not gonna let my friends fall into a guilt spiral because you killed yourself."

I snort out a laugh. "Kill myself? If I truly gave a shit about anything you just said, I'd be more likely to kill *someone* else. You know, like the people who wronged me."

"Then why are you hanging upside down off the rock, knowing it's nothing but jagged rocks and the ocean down there?"

"Because it's fun."

"Fun?" He shakes his head. "You're out of your fucking mind."

"I know, so leave me to my loopy thoughts."

He jumps in front of me when I crawl back towards the edge. "Move, Pax."

He doesn't. He just stands over me with his arms across his chest, ruining my chill. Every inch of stress I just released into the air is back. I climb to my feet and descend my pride rock, stomping my way back towards my car. Now I have to find somewhere else to go, because he's ruined this place just like Holden's ruined the woods. Why can't they just leave me alone?

Pax is less than a minute behind me. When he reaches the parking lot, I'm already in my car and gunning the engine. I shoot forward and he jumps out of the way to keep from getting hit. Big baby. I wasn't even aiming for him. I cut my wheel at the last moment, the back end fishtailing around his precious ride and squeal out of the parking lot, enjoying the smell of the rubber leeching onto the asphalt.

The head Coxsucker interrupted me, but I've gained some clarity. Now I know what I need to do to clear my head. I need the feel of the wind, the spaceless-ness, and the speed. I don't know why I didn't think about this sooner. The best way to defy death and gravity and eliminate the chance of anyone being able to stop me is on a bike. And I know just where to find one.

I park my car in the student lot and casually stroll over to the private parking garage some of the students use. I refuse to pay an additional parking fee to park my car here. Someone should tell these idiots that just because some rent-a-cop sits in a guard shack watching security cameras, does not mean their cars are better protected from theft or vandalism. Anyone with half a brain would just do what I'm doing, and enter and exit through the back door.

I stop in front of the beautiful machine I'll be borrowing this evening. Not using the front exit means it's gonna take me a little longer to walk the bike up three levels and then through the alley at the end of the building, but it'll be worth it.

There's a smart key system on this bike. That's convenient for me. Once I'm outside, I reach down and unplug the engine wire and let it sit for a few minutes, before plugging it back in, forcing it to cycle through a hard reset. I tap the app on my phone, letting it scroll through codes until it finds the correct one and pair it to my phone. Seconds later, I'm rewarded with a satisfying beep, beep. I press the button on the engine, and shivers run down my spine, as the bike rumbles to life. Voila! Time to peel out.

I kick my leg over the bike, adjust myself on the seat, and rev the engine. She's smooth and shoots out of the last twenty feet of the alley like a dream. Purring between my thighs like a contented kitty. My ponytail flies behind me, swinging left and right as I zip in and out of traffic.

I whoop and laugh as I reach the open highway, and embrace the truth that's settling through my spirit. I might be bruised, a little broken, and a whole lot confused about what's happening in my life; I might be directionless at the moment, but I'm *alive*.

Pax

It's hard to comprehend what I'm seeing. The spot where my bike should be is empty. I wouldn't have come down here tonight, but my mother called and said she wants to have dinner, *tomorrow*. Her request caught me off guard, and I couldn't come up with a reason fast enough, to decline. Our last dinner, and my honey pot assignment was just two weeks ago. I wasn't expecting another one so soon.

I needed to clear my head and thought a ride would help. Now I'm strung tighter than I was before. Heads are gonna roll, starting with the guard on duty.

Holden and Finn pull into the garage, their cars screeching to a halt behind me. I sent them both a text as soon as I saw my parking spot was empty. They thought I was joking, even though we all know I lack a sense of humor.

Their doors slam shut, and Finn's mouth falls open as he approaches. "Holy shit."

Holden whips out his phone. "Which one of the frats do you think did this?"

"I don't know!" I snap. "It's your job to find out."

Holden makes a noise in the back of his throat. I wince, because he's not the person I'm mad at. I need his help and things between us are already strained because of this Thea situation. I don't agree with him telling her he was chasing her through the woods. Especially since she brought it up the other night. It's something she can use against us. "Dude..."

Finn shakes his head, and points to the elevator. "Let's just talk to the guard while Holden goes through the security cameras."

I follow him up to the guard shack. The guard, *Walter*, jumps to attention when he sees us. "Good Evening, Mr. Cox, Mr. Rhodes. How's it going tonight?"

In a clipped tone, I answer, "You tell us."

"All quiet. Like usual."

"My bike is missing."

He smiles, then laughs. Why is everyone acting like I'm a fucking comedian all of a sudden? The smile slips when he takes in my face; the color draining from his. Turning to the camera, he says, "Sir, that's impossible. Nobody came by the booth on your bike."

"Maybe it happened when you were on a bathroom break."

Finn adds, "Or doing your rounds."

"Impossible. The gate would have been down, and they'd need a code to get it up, which is logged into the system." He stabs a button and shows no access in or out during the times he annotated he was away from the booth.

"Well, somebody was here, and my bike is missing." If they didn't ride by, did they load it onto a trailer so he wouldn't know what it was, or take it apart and sneak it out piece by piece the way we did Tyler's car?

That thought makes me even madder. Disassembling that beauty is the worst violation imaginable. If that's what happened, then there's only one frat that could be responsible. "Austin." I growl.

Finn points to the monitors, and says, "Show me the cameras."

The school installed cameras at the front of the building, because it's the only place for cars to enter or exit the garage. Vandalism isn't a problem here. Shit, I didn't think theft was either. At least not down on the lower level, because The Trium are the only ones who use that level. Sometimes we use the access tunnel to get down there, but even then, we still have to come this way to get out.

Walter speeds through the camera feeds. I don't see anything. I tell him, "Go back to yesterday." He does and still nothing. This doesn't make any sense. "Is it on a loop?," I ask.

"No, sir. These dates and stamps are in real-time. See the different cars going and coming?"

Holden joins us as Walter says the last part. The look on his face confirms the feed wasn't tampered with. Finn points to the screen. "I only recognize a few of these cars and jeeps, but none of them are Austin's."

"Maybe he borrowed someone else's," I suggest.

Walter's sweating when he swivels in his seat and asks, "Mr. Cox, do you want me to call the cops?"

I don't need that kind of attention. Especially since I'll be going after Austin myself. It's best to keep this between us. "That won't be necessary. I'll take care of it."

My friends and I head back to the lower level to look for clues. I jerk to a stop and bellow, "What the fuck is going on?"

My bike is back in its spot, and whoever had it definitely didn't come through the front of the garage while we were standing there.

"They must've put it in neutral and hid between two cars, or on a different level." Finn says, scanning the structure for movement."

Holden puts up his hand, when I take a step towards my bike. "Don't touch it."

Shit. Is this a prank or did somebody really do something to it, and hope I wouldn't know it was missing until it was too late?

While I'm thinking about that, Holden makes a call. He hangs up and says, "My dad's team will be here to sweep it clean within the hour."

An hour turns out to be ten minutes. Holden's dad rolls into the garage in an armored SUV with his bomb squad already suited up. They send in a remote controlled bomb sniffer to do an initial scan for wires, and heat signatures.

"Someone was definitely riding this bike, sir." The guy working the remote calls out. "The engines still warm."

But how? My smart lock is coded. I have the key with me at all times, and nobody knows the code for it but me. I didn't get any alerts that someone was trying to tamper with it.

"Proceed." Holden's dad says.

The last time I saw Parker Sullivan surrounded by this many armed agents, and looking this pissed, was the day Holden was almost kidnapped. It took him years to relax enough to let his son go out without an armed escort by his side. I think Holden's extreme distrust of people, and the tracker embedded in his watch, helped his dad feel comfortable enough to loosen the reins.

Parker being here, instead of just letting a team handle it, puts me on edge. I'm watching him watch the feed being transmitted by the bomb squad. He smiles, when he sees me looking. "It's okay, Pax. I doubt there's a bomb, but we want to be certain, and we're look for any other ways the perpetrator may have mechanically or electronically manipulated your bike."

"That sounds like FBI speak for bomb."

His smile widens. "That's overprotective dad speak for covering all the bases." He calls out, "Brex, make sure you sweep The Trium's cars when you're finished."

It takes an hour but the security team declares my bike and our cars are clean, with no sign of tampering. Holden scowls at the lead agent. "It *was* tampered with. By your own initial assessment, you identified the engine was warm which suggest someone was riding his bike without permission."

"What I meant was there is no evidence that his motorcycle is unsafe to ride. If he wants to file a police report that's below my pay grade."

Holden shakes his head as if he's disappointed in the agent. "Did you check for malware? How sure are you someone won't hack into his bike's computer system and drive him off a cliff the next time he goes for a ride?"

Parker passes his phone to Holden. He flicks his finger across the screen a few times, then hands it back to his dad, and asks, "You trust his report?"

"I do." All traces of humor are gone, when Parker says, "And if it turns out to be false report, and anything happens to any of you as a result of his deception, Agent Milligan's face will be on the missing person's wall at the station. I'll spearhead the investigation and all the leads will go cold. I'll sit around and lament how sad it is that I couldn't close the case, while he turns into worm food in a community garden."

Finn laughs as Agent Mulligan stammers, "It's an accurate report sir," before running off to join his team.

I find myself smiling too. I appreciate the fact that our bond with Holden means Parker has always included Finn and me in his overprotective dad routine.

Chapter 33
Deacon

It's hard to watch out for people who *want* you to have their backs. It's even harder when the person you're trying to protect won't take basic measures to protect themselves. Thea falls into the latter category.

It's not that she's doing anything overtly dangerous. Overtly *more dangerous* than what she was doing before her attack, like fighting. But I still think she should be restricted to class, and her dorm room, and only leave campus when she's accompanied by people who actually pay attention to her and give a shit.

But of course, it's not that simple with her. She finds the path with the most danger, the most resistance, and takes it. It's what I both admire and want to throttle her about.

Today, she's doing something super reckless. I heard rumors that Pax's bike was stolen from the garage last week, and wondered who would be stupid enough to cross The Trium. I should've known it would be her. The one person on campus that says *fuck you* in all caps.

I watch her inspect the new security lock on the back roll-up door of the parking garage. That must've been how she got the bike out of here without anyone seeing her. Sorry, not sorry, sweetness. Your joy riding days are over.

I keep to the shadows as I follow her, watching as she pushes the bike up to the fifth level ramp. If I wasn't watching, I'd never believe it. This girl is certifiable. She jumps on the bike, revs the engine, then goes careening down to the third level at breakneck speed and jumps the wall.

The bike lands on one wheel, and she holds the wheelie until she's halfway down the alley before shooting down the rest of it like a bullet out of the chamber of a gun. It's impressive and scary that she'd try something stupid like that when her arm's still compromised.

As a faculty member, I should be thinking about scolding her and reporting the theft. Instead, I adjust my now hard cock, run back to my car and gun the engine racing towards the back gate of campus, trying to catch up to her.

She's careful about taking back streets. Clearly, this isn't her first foray into grand theft auto. She's smart enough to know she needs to avoid street cameras. I'm expecting her to go somewhere specific, but she doesn't. She reaches the edge of town and just rides the open road, leaning into the turns until she reaches Red Bluff. Then she slows, turning onto a stretch of beach and stops, puts the kickstand down, leans back on the bike, her feet propped up on the handlebars.

She sits, watching the waves. No one comes to meet her, and she doesn't take any calls. She just sits, though I imagine I feel the thrum of tension in the air. It's in the way she's tapping her thigh.

Thea's bored. Restless. This little display must be her way of letting off steam. I have to get her back in the ring before she does something really stupid. Like... well shit, what would be stupider than stealing a Trium's bike and taking it for a joyride when your dominate arm isn't fully working? I don't know, but I'm sure Thea will figure it out and do it.

I have the thought that I know how to give her a thrill that'll curb the restless energy in us both. It starts with her mouth on my cock and ends with my cock buried in her pussy. I groan at the thought. Why am I abstaining?

I want this girl. I'm sure she still wants me, and clearly she's not worried about healing, the way she's hopping ledges and riding cliff walls. I beat back the caveman part of my brain that's screaming at me to go over there and fuck her right now. This part of the beach is deserted, but it's not safe. She's still here with stolen merchandise. Plus, there's the little matter of The League of the Daggered Ravens announcing that she's part of the legacy lines.

It's a double-edged sword. She'll gain respect, privilege, and notoriety, but her family isn't in good standing and if she gets caught with Pax's bike, The League wouldn't hesitate to punish her as a consequence for the Hughes' deception all these years.

Thea's not dumb. She knows she can't stay here all night. She straightens, starts the bike and takes a different route back to the garage. I'm wondering how she's thinks she's going to sneak it in, and then I see her go up to the roll-up door. The security lock is on the outside. She fiddles with her phone and then pushes the door halfway up. She ducks under the door, pushing the bike inside and then closes it back. I drive around to the front of the building and park on the first level, then walk over to the side of the structure to watch what she's doing. She calmly walks the bike back to its spot.

As long as she puts it back the way she found it, no one will know it was gone. She doesn't do that. I pull out my phone to warn her, but stop when I see her shoulders shaking. She's parked it wrong just to fuck with Pax. She's such a brat, and brats need discipline.

I hurry back to my car and drive to the faculty apartment complex, park it, then jog back across campus. I'm waiting by the back end of the library. The student made path through the grass is the best route to take if you're sneaking to the garage to mess with somebody's car or *bike*. I grab her before she even clears the last line of trees and push her back into the brush.

She freezes for way too long. I keep my grip on her, hating the delayed reaction. Finally, she pushes through her fear and starts struggling to get out of my hold.

"It's okay. You don't need to fight me." I whisper, dragging my lips across her ear.

"Wolfe?"

"You've been a naughty girl, sweetness."

She stiffens again, then tries to play it off. "I don't know what you're talking about. I haven't been fighting."

"Oh, I *know*. I was talking about your little field trip." I push my nose into the crook of her neck, tonguing her pulse. "You taste like the beach." Thea doesn't play coy or shy. She grinds her ass against me, prepared to tease me as much as I'm teasing her. "And you feel like sin." I loosen my hold on her. "How are you feeling?"

"Heated. Flushed. But this is good."

I chuckle, knowing where her mind is. "I meant your injuries."

"They're fine."

I give her hips a gentle squeeze. Pulling her against my growing erection. "Now, why does that sound like a lie from those decadent lips?"

"It's not a lie. I'm fine, but if you're asking so you can make me do some arm rotations or stretches to prove it to you, I'll pass."

"It's not about proving anything. It's about being mindful of your body. At this moment, I'm not your coach or trainer. I'm asking because I want to know just how hard I can fuck you without compromising your recovery."

Her gasp doesn't go unnoticed. I pepper kisses along her neck and pull the lobe of her ear between my teeth, slowly grinding against her. She may not care about how she's healing while she's out here playing real life grand theft auto, but I do. As hard as I am. As much as I want to slam into her wet heat over and over again and forget about everything for a little while, I don't want to hurt her.

"You remember how physical we got that night, don't you, sweetness?"

"Mmm."

"That's my default setting, so I need to know if I have to throttle back. Now give me the truth."

"My shoulder is a little sore, so no um. No direct pressure."

"And?"

"And my wrist is stiff."

"Probably stiffer since you were riding on one wheel for half the alley."

"You saw that?"

"Yes, sweetness. I saw that. You looked so fucking hot with that machine between your thighs. But we both know you'll look much hotter with my cock between them." I spin her in my arms. Suddenly desperate to taste her. "Kiss me like you missed me, LaReaux."

"Missed you?" She snorts. "I see you in class and all I can think about is bashing your face in."

"You mean in the class where I have to pretend like you irritate me?"

Shaking her head, she says, "I wasn't aware it was an act. *Everyone* irritates you."

"True, but you irritate me less than others." I tap my lips. "Come on, sweetness, kiss."

Thea's hard and soft. She likes her independence, and is used to taking care of herself, but in the weeks we were in Palisade Shores I saw how readily she melts with affection. I loved those nights in bed when she was soft in my arms. She'll never admit it, but I'm willing to bet she likes being kissed on these lips as much as those juicy ones between her thighs.

She presses her mouth to mine, in little nibbles. I let her feel out the kiss. Let her settle into it, and when the last vestiges of hesitancy evaporate, I deepen it. Gently nipping at her lips until she opens enough to allow me to slip my tongue inside.

Her reaction is immediate. Visceral. She grips my shirt, pulling me closer, moaning into my mouth. I suck on her tongue, my hands drop lower to grip her ass. She jumps up and wraps her legs around my waist, rocking back and forth. God, it feels good, but if I don't control myself, control *this*, I'll end up fucking her in these woods, and there are still too many people out.

I end the kiss and slowly lower her to the ground and set her away from me.

"Don't be a cunt tease, Wolfe."

I drop my voice, letting the words rumble through my chest. "I'm delaying, sweetness. As soon as you prove you're committed to your recovery, *nothing* will stop me from dragging that sweet pussy across my dick."

With one last peck, I slip back through the trees, jogging back to my place. I now have a date with my shower and my hand.

Chapter 34

Thea

Moira and Scott both showed up on campus today. They've come to campus at least once a week to follow up on the investigation into what happened to me; but I haven't seen the both of them here together since the day they dropped me off at the beginning of the semester, and I liked it that way.

They've been asking me to come to their home and talk, but I haven't been in the mood. I'm still angry and confused because my life has only gotten more complicated since the news broke that I'm their kid. God, can a girl just deal and process in peace? "I'm still not ready to talk about it." I say, moving to sit on my couch.

Scott's running point on this conversation. "Well, it seems we don't have the luxury of waiting until you *are* ready. We need to set some ground rules."

Bolting to my feet, I yell, "What am I, eleven, and staying home for the first time by myself? Fuck your rules. I've gone this long without them, and I'm sure as shit not entertaining them now."

"You will sit down and listen to what I have to say, young lady."

"Or what? You gonna stop paying my tuition. Send me back to Nags Creek? Great. Let's go."

His brows pinch together. "What? No. Why would you think that?"

"What do you mean, *why*? That's what people do when they pay your way and find out they can't control you."

"Thea..., you're not here for us to control. We didn't bring you here so that you..." He takes a breath before continuing. "First of all, you're here because we want you here. Your education is important to you and to us. We wouldn't stop paying your tuition or throw you out on the street because we're having difficulties. Families fight. They don't always agree and we realize you're used to taking care of yourself, but we're your parents. We have an obligation to your safety and well being and we care about you."

I snort at that. They cared so much; I spent nineteen years of my life not knowing they existed. Oh wait, *eighteen* years. They cared so much they had someone lie about my age.

He continues on. "Our dynamics notwithstanding, and yes, I know we owe you a huge apology, a lot of answers, and your anger is warranted. But the way you're going about rebelling... it's not safe."

"Safe? Are you serious right now? I didn't go out looking to get beat up!"

He rakes his hand through his hair and says, "I'm not talking about that, but your behavior since returning to school is drawing attention. A *lot* of attention. And... we sacrificed a lot to keep you off of certain people's radar. Now that you're on it, there are certain things that are expected of you. As our daughter."

Moira chimes in, "You don't understand the way things work around here."

"That's absolutely true, and that's probably because- *one*, I don't care and *two*- you haven't told me anything."

She looks at Scott before giving me the bullshit line, "It's for your own good."

"Yeah, well, that shit doesn't work for me, since I'm the only one who has given a damn about *my own good* for a very long time."

Moira steps in front of Scott. "Thea, we owe you answers. We're gonna give them to you, I promise. But it's a lot and right now things are still raw between us all."

"If you just tell me the truth about everything-"

"It may send you running away from us."

I can't even refute that. Haven't I been threatening to do just that since that first phone call? My jump bag has been ready since the moment I got back on campus. Well, my second jump bag. Hurricane Eloise destroyed the first. "What can be so bad that I'd run?"

Moira steps closer. She reaches out for me, then quickly tucks her hands behind her back. "I know you think we were selfish or irresponsible or didn't love you and sent you away while we lived this fabulous life. But it wasn't like that. I promise I'll explain everything. I just need some time before dragging it all up."

"Fine, it's your trauma. If you're not ready to spill; I get that. But what does your villain origin story have to do with what I'm doing for fun?"

Scott answers. "Because The League of the Daggered Ravens has appointed you the title of a legacy student."

"The League of the- You're talking about the secret society you said didn't really exist?"

"Oh, they exist, and they have an active recruitment program through Rho Beta Psi."

I manage a laugh. "Well, rest easy. I didn't make it into that fancy little sorority Moira was a part of, nor will I be getting an invite to hang with them anytime soon. I am definitely persona non grata, so you don't have to worry about me dating any of the guys that are a part of the stabbed birds."

Moira's lips twitch at me intentionally butchering the name. Scott's not so easily amused. "They also recruit based on skills." He gives me a pointed look. "You know, like if a person shows an affinity for lock picking, and hot-wiring motorcycles that don't belong to them."

My eyes cut to the set that I still can't get over look just like mine. Moira nods, "Yeah, we know about that."

"Having me followed, huh?"

"Actually, a few days ago, I overheard some girls whispering over lunch about a Trium's bike being stolen from campus. That's what sparked us coming here today."

Wow. Just blatant distrust. I mean, I did it. Of course I did it and will probably do it again. Okay, I'm *totally* gonna do it again, but that's my business. These two will never understand why I stole the bike. They'll never understand me. "And you assumed I was the thief?"

"There's not another person on this campus, let alone in this town, who would be bold enough to do it. And, since I have some idea of the things you were dealing with from The Trium before your accident... well, let's just say, stealing Paxton Cox's bike is something I would have done in retaliation."

Scott tucks Moira against his side and kisses the top of her head, while I stand here gaping at her. Did she just confess that she's stolen shit? "Now that's a conversation I'd sit down and have with you."

The tension around her mouth eases a little. "You'll have to be in town at Christmas for that to happen."

I nod. Knowing full well she just got me to agree to something I wasn't willing to agree to before. Because even though I had every intention of finishing out the semester here, I wasn't sure what I'd be doing or where I'd be at Christmas. My aunt-slash-mother is a crafty one. I'm gonna have to keep an eye on her. Where were these little gems of personality when I first came to town?

Side eyeing her, I say, "Fine, don't get caught borrowing vehicles. Any other rules I need to know?"

"No more fighting."

I arch a brow and Moira quickly says, "I swear we're not having you followed. But there are eyes and ears everywhere."

I tell her the same thing I told Wolfe. "I won't go looking for a fight, but if someone brings one to me, I will vigorously defend myself." Provided I don't freeze up like a block of ice before they do too much damage.

"Understood."

"What else?"

Scott joins in. "We're very proud of the grades you've earned even with missing three weeks of on-line learning while you recovered. Just focus on that. Don't give up on your goals, no matter what else is happening. Going to classes and getting your degree so you can travel the world like you plan. *That's* the most important thing."

I nod. I've been cutting classes, but part of the things I've been thinking about during my rides is whether my plans for the future are still the same. They are. No matter what bullshit is happening around here, I want that degree and the life I've envisioned for myself so many days in Nags Creek.

They've gotten to say what they want. I've agreed to consider it, and I still don't know anything. Moira steps forward and shoves a photo in my hand. "This is Joshua Laurent. My father." She looks nervous when she says, "He wants to meet you."

"Okay... do you not want me to?"

"The League has already announced to its members that they're investigating the circumstances surrounding your birth and disappearance. My father's bloodline is reactivated on a provisional basis. He'll be spending more time in town as he campaigns to be restored to his previous position, which means you'll be seeing a lot of him."

"That doesn't answer my question."

She gnaws her bottom lip before answering. "We want you to make your own decisions about your relationships with members of our families."

Members? Yeah, that sounds like a lot, and I'm not ready for that. I've already met Scott's mom, and we were getting close, until I found out she was lying to me too. I liked Van, and even though I avoid the diner and hotel when I go to the beach, I still think about how much fun we had talking over tea.

"Are any of these family members gonna tell me what happened?"

"If you ask, I'm sure they'll give you their version and understanding of events."

"How sure are you about that? Because Van didn't say shit when I asked her." Talk to your parents is such a cop out.

"Van was trying to be respectful of our position. But we've suggested she be more forthcoming." Moira's staring at me, trying to gauge my reaction. "And you're willing to let me hear all these other versions of events before you tell me yours?"

"We'd prefer to tell you, ourselves, but you're not one to sit on questions for long, and we don't want to influence your thoughts or opinions about any of our family members you may interact with in the future."

I fold the slip of paper she handed me and shove into my back pocket. "I'll think about it."

Chapter 35
Thea

I lower the lid on the washer and hop up on the table to wait for the load of darks to finish. I've taken to washing my clothes late at night to avoid people. That's basically what my life's become. A series of decisions that have me interacting with the least amount of people possible.

The door opens and Finn walks in, a laundry bag thrown over his shoulder. I watch him drop it in a corner and shake my head when he walks back towards the door. I guess he hasn't learned his lesson about trusting other people to wash his shit.

He comes back in with a second bag and drops it in front of an empty machine. He reaches inside and pulls out laundry soap, bleach, and the same brand of dryer sheets I use. Maybe he learned his lesson after all.

With his back to me, he asks, "How long are you gonna stay mad at me?"

"How long are you gonna be an asshole?"

"Probably for the rest of my life."

"Then, there's your answer."

"Pet-"

"Stop calling me that!"

He straightens and faces me. "*Pet,* I'm sorry for what I did. I'm sorry I jumped to conclusions. What else do I have to do to get you to talk to me again?"

"Talk? Gee, that's an idea. But where was the talking that night, or any time since? Because every time I see you, you're butting into my business. Speaking for me, telling everyone what I am and am not interested in. There is no talking with you. So I'm just gonna sit here and be the dummy while you do your ventriloquist act."

He steps closer. "Now we're getting somewhere. I'm happy to control your body and pose you any way I want."

"That's not what I said."

"It's what I heard, and it can be arranged." He pushes my legs apart and steps between them.

"Back up, Finn."

"That's not what I want you to say."

I scoot back and swing my legs around the table. "God, I wish I had my knife."

He whips his out and extends it towards me, reminding me that he's not afraid of a little blood.

One of the other washers I'm using chimes and I scurry past him to change the load and put it in the dryer. He crowds me against it from behind. "I am sorry, Pet, and I'm not going to stop apologizing until we're friends again."

"Were we ever friends? Because we don't know shit about each other."

"What would you call it?"

"An entertaining annoyance that ran its course." I say, ducking under his arm and moving to the other side of the table.

He comes around the table towards me, slowly backing me against the wall. "Then I'll just add that to the list of things I need to fix with us. You just decide who you're replacing."

"Huh?"

"LJ or Austin? I vote Austin. You'll have me filling the roll of the guy with a dick."

"Uh, what the hell are you babbling about?"

He yanks my hair, forcing my head back. "I'm saying you're gonna forgive me and we're gonna be best friends, Pet."

He kisses the tip of my nose, then releases me and goes back over to his own machine.

I've been trying to figure out how the conversation Finn and I had in the laundry room went off the rails. Three days later and I'm still just as baffled as I was when he made his pronouncement about me forgiving him. Does he actually think he can force me to be friends with him? That he can snap his fingers and make me get over him being an absolute dick to me when he found my birth certificate? As if *sorry Pet* just magically undoes it all?

The thing is, I don't care about him being mad about that piece of paper. I'm upset too. What bothers me is that he didn't at least try to talk it out like an adult, and he's the one walking around here sulking like I'm being irrational. If he's expecting me to be the bigger person, the joke's on him; I'm as petty as they come.

I think it's time to bring in some visual aides because he's just not getting it. I don't just *get over* shit. I'm not a roll with the punches kind of girl. I'm the kind of girl that hits back, *hard.*

What I'm about to do is gonna hurt, but it's the least he deserves. When I add up the value of all the shit The Trium did to me, and what they had their flunkies do, this won't even put a dent in it. It takes no time at all to climb over onto his balcony and let myself inside. My wrist is still tricky, but it's getting better each day, and there's nothing like practicing a bit of fine motor skills to help get it back in shape.

My body buzzes as I close the door behind me. What is it about doing something so wrong that excites me so much? I was always told I was acting out, but maybe it's infused in my DNA. Moira said stealing a bike was something she'd do in retaliation for being wronged. Would she do this too?

I loved my mom, Hailee, and no matter what, I will never change the time we had together. But other than Sasha, there's nobody who knows this side of me. Or rather, nobody who hasn't paid me for my services. Nobody I could talk to. Could Moira and I share about this? If she knew, would she accept me for this, or turn me in?

I don't need a mom, but maybe I could have an adult friend who gets me. I push those thoughts away and get to work looking for my prize. Finn's out at another one of his frat parties, so I have some time to work.

He's proud of his knife collection, so it's on display in his living room. The hardest thing for me to do is decide which one I want to make prettier.

I settle on the Cold Steel Espada. Without hesitation, I jab the press plate. The speed at which the blade unfolds is breathtaking. She's a beauty. All shiny and spot free. I hate to do it, but I can't let my affection for sharp, pointy objects win.

I slip my backpack off my shoulders and get to work. It takes an hour and the mold definitely needs to cure, but I admire my handy work. I carefully place the knife back on its stand and let myself out the way I came in. After a quick shower, I'm ready for some more fun.

Finn

Somebody's fucking with us. First it was Holden's computers, then Pax's bike, and now I'm standing here staring at my knives, and one thing is definitely *not* like the others.

"Nothing on the cameras, man." Holden says, closing the cover on his tablet.

"There has to be something. My knife didn't just bronze itself and I promise in all the years I've been alive, never once have I shown signs of having Midas' touch."

I walk around my display case, making sure nothing else was tampered with or missing.

Pax cracks his knuckles. "Okay, then it's time we confront Austin and his frat. I don't know how they're bypassing the cameras, but it's time we put them in their place."

Holden sighs and says, "It's probable that it's Austin, but we need to make sure before we just go after them."

"Who else would be stupid enough to come after us?"

I chime in, "I can think of a few people who fit the stupid category, but..."

"But what?"

"But this feels personal." I stop in front of my display stand again. Staring at all of my knifes. Slowly, my anger evaporates and I smile. "She forgives me."

"What?"

"I don't know why I didn't realize that as soon as I walked in."

"Where are you going?" Pax asks as I head to the door.

I turn to look at him. "Didn't you hear what I said? Thea has finally accepted my apology."

He and Holden share a look, then he says, "You're reaching, man. This isn't Thea's doing."

"Yes, it is. This is exactly something she'd do." I can see he doesn't believe me, so I explain, "Before things went to shit, she and I were pulling these types of pranks on each other, all the time. She's clearly thought about my offer to be best friends, and this is her way of saying yes."

"That makes no sense, and even if it did, how would she get in your room without coming through the front door?"

Holden speaks up, "The balcony. That's how she got to his favorite beanie the last time."

Pax yells, "What the fuck do you mean, the last time? How many times has she broken in?"

"This is the second time that I know of, but it could be more." I look around the living room, trying to spot other things she may have messed with.

Pax turns to Holden. "And you knew about this?"

"I did."

"And neither of you said anything?"

"What was there to say? She broke in, scented my beanie and went on about her business. It wasn't a big deal."

"Scented? Like put perfume on it?"

I grin, remembering what she did. "Only the best kind. *God*, I need her to do it again."

"You want to walk around smelling like her perfume?"

"Yes, but only you've got the wrong P word."

He looks to Holden for clarification. "He wants to smell like her pussy because apparently, she wiped his hat against it."

Pax shakes his head and rubs his hand through his hair. "Just like a female version of Finn."

"Exactly, which is why I know this is her doing, and it means she's forgiven me."

"That logic doesn't track for all of us. I haven't apologized for shit, and neither has Holden. So even if she did this to your knife, it's someone different who fucked with our stuff."

Holden interjects, "We could just ask her, instead of assuming we know the answer, since that didn't work out so well the last time."

I nod. He's right. We jumped to conclusions and now we have to undo the shit we did based on those wrong assumptions. Even though I know I'm right, we can't just go over there and accuse her. She'll think we're attacking her again and the plan is to soften her up.

I'll have to think of something. Thea retaliating is progress, and I refuse to lose the ground I've gained.

Chapter 36
Deacon

I hated having to put the breaks on what was happening the day I watched Thea steal Pax's bike, but there was no way I could let it go further. Not where we were and not when I know she's still got shit to work out. But, *goddamn*, it was hard to walk away, when all I wanted to do was rip our clothes off and slide home.

My sweetness has the fire of a dragon in and out of the ring, and the more time I spend around her, the less I care about getting burned. My hand and I have become damn near inseparable since our time in Palisade Shores.

Tonight will be another solo mission, as I envision her lips wrapped around me. Of course, the devil on my shoulder says, why think when you can do? The campus is full of dark corners and secret alcoves and passageways. I could drag us to one and put myself out of my misery.

And because karma is a such a bitch, I'm coming out of the faculty dining hall at the same time Thea's exiting hers. I feel the rage slide through me as Austin Kincaid puts his arm around her shoulder, tucking her against his side. I may have ruled him out as a suspect in her attack, but that doesn't mean I like how cozy he is with her.

Four days ago, she was clawing at me, inviting me to fuck her, and now she's moving on to him? She should, and I don't have a right to be pissed, but I am. No, pissed isn't the right word. What I *am* is losing my mind. I have to be, because that's the only way to explain why I pull my phone out and text her.

ME
I'm thinking of all the ways I can break his arm

I see her reach into her pocket and retrieve her phone. She's always so in control and tries not to give anything away. That's why she's the perfect fighter. But I see the way her body goes on alert, trying to figure out where I am. They stop to talk to some of Austin's friends and she sends me a reply.

THEA
Could've been your arms, but you made it clear you weren't interested. Now it's someone else's turn.

To hammer home her point, she steps closer to him, and this time he places a possessive hand against her lower back. She doesn't flinch at the touch. She's a lot more comfortable around him than she is around anyone else. Is it because they've been fucking or because she's so determined to antagonize me?

ME
I'm warning you

She tucks her phone away and the group breaks off. Austin's friend's head left and he and Thea go to her dorm. They linger outside for a while, talking, then he leaves. At least that's one thing he's got going for him. He's smart enough not to cross The Trium by stepping foot in their dorm. That just means I need to spend some time outside of his frat house to see when she's going in and out.

Fuck! I sound like a stalker. I tamp down a groan as the memories of our hook up in the alley come back to me. Stalker it is.

It's after ten at night and I've been waiting for Thea to come out of the library. When she does, I watch her stick to the middle of the path directly under the lights as she walks back to her dorm. *Alone.*

I follow a safe distance behind. She wasn't much of a people person before her attack, but now that little fact bothers me. We tell all students sticking in groups off campus is important. Now we need to tell them to follow the same rules on campus too. Until we find out the truth of what happened, Thea shouldn't be out here at night, alone.

I lose sight of her when she crosses The Circle, and hurry to catch up. I realize too late that she's made me and turn around seconds before the backpack she's wielding connects with the back of my head.

She goes to swing again and I grab the edge of the straps, pulling it from her hands. She throws a jab -which I deflect- and anticipating her hook; I sidestep it, but she's anticipated *that* and aims lower, giving me a nice punch to my side.

I can't believe we're out here fighting. She *shouldn't* be fighting. She can see it's me, but she doesn't stop charging at me. I'm both proud and turned on that she's coming at me so hard.

She throws her whole body into the next punch and when it connects; I double over as it knocks the wind out of me. She's ruthless and goes in for the kill, wrapping her arms around my neck, trying to choke me out. I straighten, which lifts her feet off the ground, taking away her leverage.

In a move that can only come from a trapeze artist, or stripper, she swings her body up and around, and ends upon my shoulders, her legs locked around my neck, her arms around my head.

Her voice is breathless from exertion. "Tap. Out."

What kind of trainer would I be if I let my students win? I stumble towards the treeline and when we're far enough away from the sidewalk, I lower us to the ground, leaning my weight into her so she can't roll out. She squeezes even tighter, and tugs my hair, which brings my nose in direct contact with her cunt. There's a damp patch in sweats. Is she turned on from the fight or something else?

I think of Austin and how she's been flirting with him all day, and snap. I break her leg hold and yank her pants down, before tossing her legs over my shoulder and burying my face between her thighs.

I eat her like she's my last meal, and my favorite dessert, using my tongue, teeth, lips and nose. There's no part of my face I want left dry. It's like drinking from a never ending well. She closes her legs again as she gets closer to detonating. I'm dying to feel it around my cock. I let out a strangled growl, because I don't have a condom.

After tasting her again, there's no way I'm finishing myself off tonight. I drag her upper body through the dirt until her head is between my legs and shove my pants down enough for my dick to spring free.

I don't give her time to think and position the tip at her mouth and push in, hissing through the scrape of her teeth. I push in until I'm lodged in her throat and feel her fighting it. Then I lower my head back down and latch my mouth around her clit, using my tongue to tease it into submission. I feel her relax around my cock, then slowly start to move in and out of her mouth.

I lick her slit, humming at the feel of her tongue on me. "That's it, sweetness. Breathe through your nose." I say, as I continue to strangle her with my cock.

She sputters a few times, trying to fight the feeling, but I continue my assault on her clit and she forgets she feels uncomfortable.

"Clench your lips around my cock like this cunt is clenching my fingers." My eyes roll back in my head when she does. "Yeah, just like that, sweetness."

She does it again, and I reward her with another finger in her cunt, while my dick pushes further down her throat. "I didn't know anything could feel as good as this sweet pussy, and then I met your mouth."

She moans at my compliment. The vibration shoots up my spine and across my dick. I'm not gonna be able to hold out much longer. "Are you close? God, tell me you're close."

Of course she can't say actual words, because her mouth is stuffed. She rocks her hips and I latch onto her clit again, tugging it into my mouth, sucking on it like the sweet candy coated gift it is. I can't hold off anymore. I bite down on her clit and she shatters with a scream. I press that last inch into her mouth, shooting my hot cum down her throat. I hear her sputtering and gagging like she's being waterboarded, which just prolongs my release. Her walls are still clenching around my fingers. "That's it. Choke on *all* of it."

When the tremors finally stop, I slowly withdraw my fingers and place a soft kiss against her inner thigh. I climb off her and help her to sit up, before scooting back, to brace myself against a tree, and gathering her in my arms. I slowly massage her jaws because I know they have to be sore by now.

"You okay?"

"I don't know. Nobody's ever tried to drown me with their dick before."

"You did so good, sweetness. Such a good girl." I say, peppering kisses along the top of her head.

She snuggles closer. "You did good, too."

Something lights up inside me. Is this what girls feel when they get praised? Warm and like they'd walk barefoot over hot coals to please us again? We sit in silence for a few more minutes, then I push her away to climb to my feet.

"Spooning over so soon?"

I'm amused at the tone in her voice, considering the first time we hooked up, she left me standing with my dick out in an alley. "The folks who prowl the campus at night will be making their rounds soon. I don't think you want them to see you like this."

"Why not?" She asks, climbing to her feet. "I'm freshly fingered and cute."

She's got crusted semen on her chin. *My* crusted semen on her chin, and she's right. She looks stunning wearing the evidence of my arousal on her face, but I don't want anyone else seeing her this way.

When she's done fixing her clothes, she takes a step away, putting distance back between us. It's good. We need it, because nothing good can come of this. Maybe now that I've shot my load, I'll be able to focus. "Come on, I'll make sure you get back to the dorm safely."

"I can protect myself."

"I know." I scrub a hand through my hair. "Me escorting you makes sure everyone else stays safe."

"From me?"

"From me. I meant what I said about Austin's arm."

"That's the most fucked up shit I've ever heard. I don't need a body-guard, and what I do with the guys on this campus doesn't have shit to do with you."

"You shouldn't be doing anything with anyone on this campus."

"Except for you?"

"Especially me." The reality of our situation fully sets in. "We shouldn't have done this."

She takes another step away and I see the last wall slamming into place between us. "Fine by me. As far as I'm concerned, it never happened at all."

She walks away without looking back.

Chapter 37
Holden

I canceled our eight am statistics class and sent an alert to everyone's phone except Thea's. It's time for us to have a little chat about her redecorating our rooms. I'm in my seat when she walks into class. A few minutes later, Finn enters, closing and locking the door behind him. She stiffens but makes no move to leave.

"Will the head Coxsucker be joining us?"

I love that she's putting on a brave face. It just reinforces my theory that she'd be the perfect prey. Finn hops onto the teacher's desk and bites into the Granny Smith apple he's holding before saying, "We didn't invite him to this little meeting."

"And why is that? Are you two staging a mutiny? I approve."

Her head whips around when I say, "We wanted you all to ourselves."

She struggles to hide the surprise on her face. It's there every time I talk to her. She studies my face, waiting to see if I'll say more. I usually let Finn or Pax do all the talking, but I enjoy watching the way her face changes and her eyes brighten when I do. I'm just out of practice holding conversations with girls.

I want to tell her we're doing this without Pax because he doesn't want her the way I do, the way *we* do, because I have to consider Finn's stake in this. He was always vocal about how much he wanted Thea. This will be the first time I express an interest in the same girl. We may have shared women, but I never wanted those women when it was over.

"Wanted me, so you could do what hurt me? Punish me?"

Finn cocks his head to the side. "Did you do something that has earned you a punishment, Pet?"

"In the nineteen years I've been on this planet? Plenty."

"Eighteen." I correct. "The eighteen years you've been on this planet."

She mulls that over and a small smile flits across her lips. It's quick, then gone. "What were you just thinking about?"

She scowls at me. "Nothing."

It's my turn to smile, and she asks, "What are you smiling at?"

"I'm gonna have so much fun with you."

Her brows shoot up. "We're not gonna have any kind of fun together."

"Yes, Thea. We are. But first we need to set some ground rules."

She laughs. The first laugh I've heard from her since her attack. "Ground rules? Seriously? I won't be listening to your ground rules, sky rules or any other kind of rules. So if you're done playing your royal asshole-ness, I'll be going."

"Rule number one, honesty is very important in our group. If we can't trust you, then we can't trust your family, and The League will intercede."

"You can trust me, pretty boy. Trust me to do the exact opposite of anything that makes you happy."

It's a slip of the tongue, but it's a significant slip, and I'm careful not to react. This makes Finn's theory more plausible that she's the person who's been messing with all of us. If I work off of that assumption, then I have to dig deeper into how. Although I guess the how isn't as important as the why.

Finn asks, "Is there something you've done recently that you need to be punished for?"

There's a calmness that comes over her face. No trace of emotion. She's preparing to be interrogated. I ask the next question. "Have you done something since you've been back on campus that you think *we'll* think you deserve to be punished for?"

"You three are such cry babies so, I'd say yes. I sneezed and didn't excuse myself yesterday. What's the punishment for that?"

Finn asks, "Anything more serious than that?"

"I tried to punch your daddy in the face last week. But in my defense, it's a pretty punchable face, and he was begging for it."

"Pax failed to mention that."

It's my turn to be surprised. The words tumble out, "You call Pax, daddy?"

"I call him *Finn's* daddy. Though I guess he'd be yours too, since he's the boss of you, too."

This conversation just keeps getting more interesting. I know she's directing it away from the topic, which means she's guilty of something she doesn't want us to know about, but this is the most we've ever said to each other and I'm fascinated. "Is that what you think? That we're mindless minions for Pax, just doing whatever he says?"

"Aren't you?"

"We're all on equal footing."

"Well, that's not what I hear."

I arch a brow. "No? Then enlighten me. What have you heard?"

"That the legacy system has stages. Some are higher than the others."

"That's true. But we're The Trium, meaning there isn't anybody higher than us, not even within the group."

"Sure." She drawls. "If you say so."

"Why is that so hard for you to believe, Thea?"

"Because everything has a hierarchy. Even when the presumption is that you're on equal footing, at some point and time, someone will always have more or less than the others."

I encourage her to continue. "Go on."

"Let's look at Finn and his apple. All things being equal, you don't have an apple. So he has more than you, thereby putting him ahead of you."

Finn pulls out his knife and says, "Very good argument, Pet, but there's one thing you haven't considered."

"What's that?"

He slices the apple in half and walks over and gives it to me. "We have no problem sharing the delicious things we eat; with each other."

Instead of heading back to the desk, he stops in front of her. "Shall we give you a demonstration?"

"Finley, you'll never get to taste my deliciousness again."

I climb out of my seat and walk over to her. "Shall we do a pop quiz and put that declaration to the test?"

She bolts for the door. That's the wrong thing for her to do. I shoot down the aisle and make it to the door before she does. She darts around the teachers's desk and I heft myself up on it, using it to transit to the other side of the room. She pushes a table towards Finn, which he easily jumps over. We box her in and crowd her against the wall. Her heart's racing and so is mine.

I toy with a lock of her hair. "You remember how this goes, don't you, Thea?"

She stares straight ahead and refuses to answer my question. "For every lie or refusal to answer, we'll deny you an orgasm."

"That's not torture. I don't want you, therefore I don't want to cum."

I lean in and whisper. "We both know that's not true. You love to cum."

"You're right. I do. What girl doesn't like a toe curling orgasm? What I meant was, the sight of you makes my pussy shrivel up and die."

"That's fair, but the sight of you makes me want to tear through your cunt. Natural lubricant not required."

She stiffens, and I put some space between us. "Don't worry, Thea. I already told you that you'll enjoy it in the end."

She gasps and I look down and see Finn's already worked his fingers inside her pants. He looks up and says, "I don't know, Pet. You feel a little wet to me."

"Silly boy, that's not because of you."

"No?"

"God, of course not. It's because I'm thinking of all the ways I'm going to make you pay for touching me."

"I love the way you make me pay, Pet."

I steer the conversation back to the reason we've locked her in with us. "Will this latest round of retribution involve you sneaking into our rooms again?"

She doesn't say anything; her face the picture of serenity and calm. Finn climbs to his feet, sucking his fingers in his mouth. I return to my seat and grab my backpack, and we leave the room without saying another word, ignoring the murderous look on her face. When we get to The Circle, I say, "Well?"

"Clenched up, just like you said."

An involuntary reaction to the question. She did it and the memory gives her pleasure. Did she touch herself afterwards? Now that we know she is the one who was in our room, I need to figure out how she got in. The secret passage would be an easy answer for my room, but I know that's not it. She doesn't know it's there. If she did, I'm sure she'd have already barricaded the door in her closest as a safety precaution.

Thea's been glaring at us all day. I'd be irritated if it were anyone else, but with her, I'm secretly eating up the attention. We're going to have to do something about her seating arrangements. It sends the wrong message to have a legacy sitting at a non-legacy table.

I'm pretending not to watch her, but Finn doesn't care about being discrete. When she finally looks in his direction, he sticks his fingers in his mouth and sucks on them. To which she sticks her middle finger up and pretends to gag. He nods and bites his bottom lip, the action she mimed not having its intended effect. I'm with Finn. Who wouldn't want her gagging on it?

When I notice Thea's almost done eating, I go outside to stand in front of the exit she uses. Once she and LJ are a good distance away, I step aside and let other people come out of the door.

Pax comes to stand next to me. "How long are you going to keep doing that?"

"For as long as it takes for her to stop looking over her shoulder as if she's expecting an attack."

"That may never happen."

"Then I guess that means I'll never stop watching her back."

"You know, even if she knew what you were up to, she'd be too much of a bitch to ever say thank you."

I don't need her thanks. I'm not doing it for recognition. My motives are purely selfish. I want her to feel safe enough to let down her guard, because when it comes time for her to be afraid again, those fears will be because of me. They will belong to me.

Chapter 38

Thea

I'm experiencing déjà vu as I approach the dorms. The last time these three were standing out here like this, was the day they wouldn't let me go after the guy who overreacted when that chick bumped into him.

As a precaution, I look around and make sure he's not out here. It would be just my luck if he were, and nothing makes me think Coxsucker one, two and three, would get between us again. If anything, they'd hold me down and let him do whatever he wanted.

My knees lock up. Dammit, when am I gonna stop having this reaction? I tell myself I'm fine. Remind myself I can handle it without my knife. It's like Wolfe said. I have years of experience fighting dirty. These pampered asses are *not* scarier than the crews in Nags Creek.

Straightening my spine, I force myself to look each of them in the eye and ignore the smile that flirts across Finn's face. I don't give a shit if he's laughing at me. I'm the one who's laughing hardest. I know exactly what kind of information they were looking for when they trapped me in our classroom. They're trying to figure out if I've been messing with their stuff. If they don't leave me alone, I'll find something else to tinker with.

I saunter past Finn and Pax and even bump into Pax's shoulder, since he refuses to move to the side to give me space. I hear Finn say, "Fuck, Pet. You're killing me here."

Holden is right in front of the doors, staring me down. My body lights up under his scrutiny. That part's not dead. The feeling I get when he looks at me. It's mixed in with the fear and confusion that I'm refusing to acknowledge, but it exists.

We rarely square off eye-to-eye like this, but today I stand still and let him look. I let him see me looking back. I ignore the crowd I sense gathering around us and just face off with him. He moves to the side and I walk by like that moment didn't just happen. It feels like a win. Not backing down. It feels like greeting an old friend. Fearless me.

I get a calendar reminder on my phone just as I'm stepping off the elevator. I'd forgotten all about the party I'm supposed to attend tonight. I want to skip it, but I agreed to attend it months ago. I called Moira for suggestions on what to wear, and she took over.

The hair and makeup team will be here in two hours to help me get ready. That gives me an hour in the gym to burn off some aggression. I change quickly and head down to the gym, which is currently occupied by the head Coxsucker.

I ignore Pax in the corner with his weighted speed rope. He's a big guy, but he's light on his feet. They barely make any noise when they touch the ground.

I run through a quick warm up then start on the heavy bag. Hitting it takes more coordination than the speed bag, because it swings around since no one's holding it steady.

"That's better, but you're still not completely centered on your feet."

I ignore Pax's comment.

"You don't have enough rotation in your hip."

"Why don't you come and put your face right here?" I tap my knee. "I'll show you how I roll my hips."

"You're not worth my time, Nem."

"That's what all the punks say when they're afraid of getting beat by a girl."

He walks to the door. "And that's what all amateurs say when they're deflecting away from the fact that the champs aren't going to waste their time on them."

"Come on, prove it, champ. Show me what you got."

"Keep practicing, Nem." He says as the doors swing closed. Once I'm alone, I readjust my stance, making sure my weight is centered over my feet and kick at the bag rotating my hip. I'm trying to perfect a move I saw in a fight, but it doesn't look as flawless as the person who did it on tv.

This is where training with Wolfe would come in handy, but since I still can't stand the idea of having people lock onto me or hit me, I'm practicing on my own.

It's like a 360 move. You start with a roundhouse, pivot all the way around to reposition your feet, and finish with a back kick on your opposite foot. I already knew there was something off about the movement. I hate Pax, but his input wasn't horrible, and this time, the kick comes easier. I almost make a full rotation around.

I practice a few more times before calling it quits, so I have time to shower and wash my hair before the glam team gets here.

Thea

Tonight, I'm getting a taste of just how many people fall under the legacy student umbrella, reinforcing my plan to stay away from them all. Holding court in the center of the room are the Coxsuckers and their queen. I caught the hate when I walked into the room.

When I asked LJ why they're here when I'm sure they haven't applied for any scholarships, she explained Rho Beta Psi and Zeta Nu help raise money that's donated to the scholarship fund.

I check the time on my phone, wondering just how long we need to stay here. LJ's off in the corner, taking pictures and talking to a reporter, and I'm trying to stay out of everyone's way.

The scent of metal hits my nose. I look over to see Finn standing next to me. "Hey, Pet."

"Fuck off, Finn."

"I would, but this is a mandatory function, and my disappearance would be noticed."

"Mine, won't."

I go to move away from him and someone else walks up to us. "Young Finn, good to see you."

"And you, Mr. Devereaux."

"I noticed you're not with your companion tonight."

"She's here, making her rounds, and I just came over to check on Thea. Since this is her first Merrill Anderson Scholarship event."

The man looks down at me. His eyes and tone less than friendly when he says, "Ah yes, the newest legacy. How are you adjusting? I'm sure you've found your peers to be quite helpful after your accident."

"What I've found is-"

Finn cuts in. "You'll have to excuse us. Right before you walked up, Thea agreed to a dance."

He grips my hand and drags me behind him. I hiss, "Let go."

"Nope, because you still haven't learned when to bite your tongue. Do you have any idea who that man is? What am I asking? Of course you don't, because you refuse to accept that things are different now and learn the players around here."

I let him pull me onto the floor to dance. It's easier than throat punching him and making a scene. It's all I can do to stand here and let him even touch me. I'm more touch averse than I was before, and it's not just about what happened to me. I'd let my guard down around Finn and he tried to use our familiarity to hurt me.

"Keep your hands to yourself."

Finn is Finn. He lives to break the rules, so he does the exact opposite of what I said, pulling me flush against his body. One hand grips me by the nape of my neck, the other holds me by my hip. He exhales loudly. I can see the muscle in his jaw jumping as he struggles.

"If it's this damn annoying to be close to me, just let me go back over there and finish telling that guy how helpful you all are."

"Annoying?" He grits out. "Pet, I'm not close enough." His words sound the opposite of gentle. They're hard, full of malice and ill intent. "I don't know how many times, how many different ways, I can apologize for what I said and did. I'm confused about where things stand with us, and how to fix it. I'm angry that you won't accept my help, or anyone else's help."

His grip tightens, biting into my skin. He's definitely leaving bruises. "I'm struggling, because all I can think about is you and you don't feel the same way about me. If I could, I'd flay you alive and wear your skin. Transplant your organs with mine."

Finn's intense. I always thought he was just the left side of too much, but he's crossed right over. He wants to wear me as a skin suit? That's next level horror movie shit and yet, in an unhinged kind of way, why is that the sweetest shit I've ever heard?

Before I can do something stupid like dissolve into a pool of goo over his psychotic confession, I remind myself what brought us to this moment. He's trying to play me. His buddy has admitted to chasing me in the woods. Who's to say he didn't have some "fun" with me on Mayhem Night too?

"It'll never be like it was Finn. I started to like you and you fucked it all up."

"I know. I know." His lips drop to my ear. "I'm going to unfuck it and make you want me again. I don't care what it takes."

He ends our dance, and I don't even have to look around to know why. Pax and Holden come into view. Pax scowls at me, while Holden steps closer than he usually does. I can feel the heat radiating off of him as he walks by and feel the faintest brush of his hand over my lower back.

He's texting something on his phone as he walks away. Seconds later, my phone chimes. I wait until they're out of my line of sight before pulling my phone out. There's a message from Holden. How the hell is his name and number programed into my phone?

I read the quick text and stare at the latitude and longitude numbers on the screen.

HOLDEN

This is where our chase ended. You were heading northeast towards campus.

I jab at the hyperlink and grip my phone with both hands, waiting for my maps app to load. It's just a location. A dot in the forest, but it's a clue. Holden just gave me a clue. I may have been heading northeast, but I *could* have changed direction and gone back to the cemetery where Wolfe found me.

Somehow, that logic doesn't feel right. That's not something I'd do. If I were evading capture, I wouldn't necessarily double back, unless I was sure I'd have an advantage. If I didn't stand and fight, if I really was running -if I was doing what he suggested and heading towards the dorms- it was because there was something else happening in those woods that I didn't want to deal with.

My hands shake, my stomach churns, and my ears ring as I try to remember what it was. This happens every time I think too hard about that night. It's like my mind and body are trying to protect me from whatever happened.

I look around the room again. The people here, and anyone at school, could be the perpetrator. I hate feeling like this. I hate being afraid and on edge. I hate being stuck, like I can't breathe or move on. Taking a deep breath, I decide it's time I stop avoiding and figure out what happened.

Chapter 39
Pax

I fiddle with my cufflinks, trying not to look as irritated as I feel. Of all the things I'd like to be doing on a Thursday night, spending time at this party isn't one of them. I know it serves a purpose and with the end of the semester fast approaching, this is the perfect time to get some last-minute face time with important people and donors before everyone scatters for winter break.

My parent's included. Every two years the families go on a member only retreat, no kids allowed. They'll be back in time for the town's New Year's celebration and then school will be back in session. I'm looking forward to a month where all league business comes grinding to a halt.

I'm standing near the front of the room where I'll get the most exposure and shake hands with another senator who tells me he appreciates my support.

"What are they doing here?"

I keep my face impassive as I finish up my handshake and order a drink from a passing server. I need a drink, but I also need something to keep my hands busy. Why did I ever agree to let Eloise ride with me?

"Do you know what she's doing here?"

I nod at another person walking by before responding, "This isn't the place for your petty little squabbles."

"I-"

"You, nothing. I don't care that the two of you can't stand each other, you save that shit for campus. If you make us look bad, you'll spend the rest of your life regretting it. And before you try to hide behind your arrangement with Finn -let me be clear- your status as a future wife doesn't mean shit to me or anyone else if you can't act the part with Thea in the room."

"I've been trained to smile and hug my adversaries. It's her you have to worry about."

Thea might be as eloquent as a rusty fence blowing in the breeze, but she cleans up well. She's wearing an off the shoulder midnight blue cocktail dress with an asymmetrical hem and strappy shoes. She's always in sneakers or boots on campus, but she's gliding around on those heels just as confidently as the other women who wear them all the time.

She scans the room, then smiles when she recognizes someone in the corner. It's one of the other pledges from Zeta Nu. I look over at Eloise and see her glaring at Thea, LJ, and the pledge. "Fix your face, Eloise."

"Why are they talking?"

Finn walks up with his father, and says, "Why wouldn't they be Ellie? Aren't the Zeta Nu's trying to convince our newest legacy student to re-pledge?"

The investigation into Thea's accident is over, and to appease the council, we've all agreed to redo the entire rush season. Eloise's vote is next week. I think the Zeta Nus are waiting until after the vote to make an official decision about inviting Thea to re-pledge. If it's up to Eloise, the answer will be no. Finn putting her on the spot in front of his father, pretty much guarantees she has to send the invite.

I don't care if Thea's a Zeta Nu or not. What I do care about is that she's not joining the Lady Lions or any other sorority. She can say no to Zeta Nu, but it better be a string of no's to everyone else, too.

Finn walks off to mingle, leaving me to deal with his *fiancé*. I should not have agreed to let her ride with me. I didn't know it meant she'd act like we're together.

"Pax?"

"What?"

Eloise huffs again.

"Clearly you're not having a good time with me, Eloise. Perhaps you should go hang with one of your lackeys."

"Where's Finn?"

It's on the tip of my tongue to say he's somewhere avoiding her -like I wish I was- until I see him dragging Thea into the throng of bodies dancing stiffly in the middle of the floor.

I look in the direction they came from and see Barrett Devereaux staring at them. I can read Thea's body language well enough to know she's uncomfortable dancing with Finn, just like I could tell whatever Deveraux said to her was about to get an answer he wouldn't like.

This is one time when Finn's obsession with this girl may have come in handy. The league members here will see us interacting with her, and it keeps her bitchy comments under control for a few more minutes. Holden walks over to where I'm standing and says, "Eloise, you'll need to find your own way home."

"Why?"

"Because I said so."

I don't question Holden. In fact, I'm glad he's said it. I follow him across the room to grab Finn, and we make our way to the valet stand to retrieve our cars. I wait until we're alone to ask, "You wanna tell me what we're doing?"

Holden looks over at the entrance. "I think it's time to give Thea a nudge. She was on edge in there, barely keeping it together, so I sent her the coordinates to where I last saw her."

"You think she'll bother checking it out, knowing it came from you?"

"I offered to help, but she's too stubborn to admit she's scared, or to come right out and ask me what I know. But she will go off on her own just to prove a point."

Finn laughs. "Ain't that the truth?"

As we're talking, Thea comes out of the building with LJ. They say their goodbyes and head off in opposite directions. I step towards my car. "Okay, let's see what the troublemaker gets up to for the rest of the night."

Thea

I made it through most of the party LJ dragged me to. It was some kind of mixer for a scholarship she applied to. She didn't get it, but since she was in the top ten applicants, they gave her an award. I'd rather have had the cash, but LJ was happy with the piece of paper and the envelope, with the contact information for somebody who will act as her mentor next semester.

After she smiled prettily and shook some hands, she agreed I'd been on display long enough. She drove to her parent's place, and I came back to the campus and changed into something breathable and comfortable. Now, I'm stuck at the tree-line that separates campus from the woods.

I exhale deeply, willing my body to move forward. It's just trees, and birds and squirrels out here. I know this, because I've walked these woods plenty of times at different parts of the day. Never once have I come across a bear or lion or anything that might eat me. I was safe from the forest life. The only threat to me in these trees walks on two legs. That's why I'm doing this. To figure out who that threat is.

The woods are more crowded than I thought it would be. Then again, around here, any night is a good night to party. I guess people are letting off steam leading up to finals. If I'm going to do this, now is the best time, when I won't be the only person out here.

Not that strength in numbers did me any good the last time, but this way I can go into the woods and don't have to admit to LJ or anyone else that I'm afraid of them.

I follow the crowd. I'm far enough away not to be spotted, but still close enough that they'll hear me call out for help. The group heads towards the left and I keep straight. My destination is deeper into the woods. Back to the last place somebody saw me. Thinking about that night head on doesn't help, so I'm hoping if I work backwards something will click.

I blink, trying to get my tired eyes to focus. It feels like forever since I've gotten any sleep. I miss the days when my only complaint was that I was a light sleeper. I'd gladly choose to wake up at the slightest sound over being too afraid to close my eyes. But that's why I'm here. To confront my fears and take back another piece of control.

I'm here to confront my fears. I'm here to confront my fears. I repeat that mantra over and over again as I make my way to the cemetery that I'm sure has a starring role in my nightmares.

It's just a place. The scenery isn't scary. These tombs and the woods didn't hurt me. The people I stumbled across after I ran through them are the reason I have a pin in my wrist and anchors holding the tendon in my shoulder in place.

I repeat that as well. But it does little to calm me when I know I'm getting ready to force myself to remember what happened that night. Taking a deep breath, I let my mind wander as I walk through the aisles. This is where Wolfe found me. I pull up the text Holden sent and hit the link, letting the GPS guide me to the last spot he saw me in. As I walk, nothing feels familiar. The uneasy feeling in my gut has more to do with my current state of nerves than anything I'm remembering about that night.

I'm at the coordinates now. I spin slowly, trying to feel which way I went. As if the breeze in the air, or the rustle of the leaves, will guide me. A branch snaps behind me.

My heart rate kicks up. Someone else is out here. I scan the trees, trying to pick out a form. I can't see anything, because I'm too far from the party and the extra planters they're using to light the way.

I stand still, listening for any other movement. Did I really hear it, or am I imagining things? Another twig snaps. This time, the sound comes from ahead of me. I'm definitely not hearing things. Someone's out here with me.

My phone buzzes with one word.

Run

My heart gallops in my chest as a masked figure comes into view. Is this them? Have they followed me again? Have I done the stupidest thing ever and given them the perfect opportunity to finish what they started?

Pax is right about me fighting shadows. I don't have a target because I can't remember any details about who was there that night. Zeus, the baseball guy, was and I only know that, because my teeth marks were etched into his dick. But if Holden, Finn and Pax are innocent, and I'm not sure they are, I can't even begin to guess who the other people were.

The figure steps closer, and I almost weep in relief when my flight response kicks in. I run now, much like I probably did that night. Trying to come up with a way to throw whoever it is off my trail. I hear whoever it is laughing behind me. It's a deep laugh. A man's laugh. I stumble over a tree, but keep running, sure of where I'm going. I'm just trying to get away. My chest burns. It's been too long since I've run. I should've gone back to Wolfe Pack and suffered through Wolfe's mandatory treadmill warm-ups.

My pursuer catches up to me way too soon. I hiss at the sharp sting from my hands and knees as he tackles me to the ground. My body tenses, but I work on my breathing, refusing to let my fear immobilize me. It's a struggle. My body strains, and tears burn my eyes, but I drag myself to my feet. A weight lands on my back, pushing me down again. I scramble forward on my hands and knees, trying to get away. He grabs my ankle, dragging me back towards him, and turns me over, so I'm on my back. My shoulder throbs. The jarring I've experienced reminds me I've been overworking my shoulder in the gym.

I came here to relive that night and the universe delivered. I have no idea why it hates me so damn much. I wanted to remember that night, not experience a 3D re-enactment.

"I don't know what kind of cultish sacrificial bullshit I stumbled on, but I do know if you don't let me go, right now, you're gonna regret it."

The masked freak just tips his head to the side. Yeah, I know there's probably no reasoning with him. I'm not even gonna try. I grip a handful of dirt and fling it at him. His hands fly to his face, forcing him to release my ankle, giving me enough time to get back to my feet and run. His long legs have him catching up to me in no time.

"You're gonna pay for that."

My adrenaline spikes at the threat in his voice. He's fast as fuck. He must've run parallel to me, because somehow he's now in front of me and is coming at me head on. I change course, and this time when he catches me, he slams me to the ground, his chilling laugh freezing me in place. "Caught you."

The cadence of his voice causes my brain to fritz. It's excited and menacing all at the same time. I turn over onto my back, dragging myself backwards, then pull to a sitting position, bracing myself against the tree. I'm gonna have to fight him off. I've been training on my own, telling myself I'm physically ready to fight. I guess I'm about to find out if that's true or just wishful thinking. He kneels down, unfeeling eyes blinking at me from behind the mask.

"Move." I hiss, slowly inching my fingers behind me.

"Can't do that. You see, you were at the cemetery tonight. There wasn't a ritual going on, but it's still a sacred space. Since you've sullied it with your presence, *twice*, I think it's only fair that you offer yourself to be cleansed."

He nudges a strand of hair behind my ear. "I can't wait to spread you open for everyone to see." His head tips to the side, then he looks to his right and I follow his gaze. The appearance of two more cloaked and hooded figures fills me with dread. I'm not gonna let them beat me down again. I won't stop fighting until one of us is dead.

"The rules regarding Mayhem Night were posted all over campus. You broke those rules, and look what happened to you. Why didn't you go back to the dorm like I told you to?"

He removes his mask, and my heart stutters to a stop before galloping again. Holden's in front of me. I suspected it was him, but a part of me hoped it wasn't. The calm, impassive face I'm used to seeing is contorted into a mask of rage.

"You're out here alone, again." His lips twist into a sneer. "Now it's my turn to break you."

The cold bite of his voice with psycho undertones is nothing like the guy from class. The other two masked figures step closer. "Ready to play, boys?" He asks, his voice mocking.

I push down my fear. How did I survive my chastity vow and get LJ out of a damn flop house only to have to deal with this shit twice?

The other two remove their masks, revealing Pax and Finn. If this is a do-over. If we're truly about to finish whatever the hell they started that night, I'm ready. A part of me hoped they were innocent. A part of me hoped I wasn't so out of touch with reality, so blinded by my personal problems, that I lost the ability to spot a threat living right next door.

"Are you giving up already, Thea? I thought for sure you had a little more fight in you."

I go over what I know about them again. Finn said some fucked up shit to me and I know he's partial to knives and violence. Pax has never hidden his feeling about me, and now here's Holden. His grey eyes swirl with hate.

The miscalculation, ignoring my gut, might have cost me dearly. I flick my gaze over to see what the other two Coxsuckers are doing. They hold their place. For now. Turning my attention back to Holden, I bite back a sigh. I hate to mess up his pretty face, but there's no way in hell I'm staying here for an encore version of whatever sick, twisted game they've been playing with me. I just need to stretch my fingertips a little more. I finally grab the branch behind me and swing.

My shoulder's on fire, as if I've re-torn the muscle with the force of the blow, but who cares? It does its job and I take advantage of his pain long enough to get back on my feet.

I finally make it back to the trail, but there's still quite a way to go to reach the edge of campus. Even if I evade Holden, one of the other two might find me. God knows I don't want to be wandering around with knife boy still lurking around. I already know he'll get off on seeing me bleed, too.

Holden laughs again. His voice carries to me. "You can't get away, Thea."

I'm freaking out, but underneath it, a buzz of energy thrums through me despite the danger I'm in. Is this the way it was the last time? How did I get away? What did I do to throw him off my trail?

I make the last minute decision to run deeper into the woods, parallel to campus, hoping to get away from them. They'll assume I headed toward campus and while they're looking for me on school grounds, I can circle back around behind them.

It's deathly quiet out here. My ears strain to pick up a sound. There's nothing. Not even a breeze to direct the smell of their cologne or aftershave my way. I must be safe. I brace my hand against a tree, taking a moment to catch my breath. I should be far enough away from them to be safe. I'll wait a few more minutes, then head back to campus. A twig snaps. I whip around, the smugness I felt at having gotten away, evaporates.

"Hello, again." Holden's arm snatches out, and I freeze the way I do so often now. He grips my throat and pushes me back against the tree. My teeth rattle from the force of my back slamming against the trunk. I smack at the hand he has to my throat, but it's useless. I look around frantically, waiting for his buddies to appear.

"They're off the other way. Looking in the wrong place. It's just you and me, but we should probably go somewhere more private, don't you think?"

He doesn't wait for an answer. Not that I could, since I'm struggling to get air into my lungs. He pulls me to his body, dragging me through the woods, heading back the way I came. I don't want private. Private is bad. I squirm, bucking, and fighting the entire way. We pass a tree and I try to wrap my arms around a branch to break out of his arms. Ignoring the pain in my bad shoulder. His hold on me tightens around my middle, pulling me more securely against his body. I reach back blindly, trying to find his eyes, but he moves his head around, avoiding my hands.

When we finally come to a stop, he drops me on the ground. He's on me quickly, maneuvering me onto my back before climbing on top of me. His knees press against my arms, pinning me in place. He's breathing just as hard as I am as he stares down at me.

"Warm-ups over, Thea. It's time to play."

I try not to flinch when he reaches out to touch my face.

"I'm going to have so much fun with you."

My brain short circuits at the change in his tone and the soft way he's touching me. He bites his lip, shyly smiling down at me. My stomach flips, warmth spreads through my belly from being gifted with such a sweet look on his face. What the hell is wrong with me? Feeling warm and tingly is not a normal reaction after everything that just happened.

Did I hit my head? I must have. I don't want to be here, don't want to play whatever game he has in mind, but for the life of me, I can't seem to make my body move. I've never seen Holden smile, and I'm caught. Trapped. Enthralled in the snare of his beautiful face. I don't come back to my senses until he pops the button on my jeans and shoves his hand inside my panties, dragging his finger between my slit. "I think you're gonna have fun with me, too."

The shock of his touch activates my fight response. I thrash around trying to buck him off of me. He shifts to the side. Half of his body leans on me, one hand's at my throat, and the other works my pants down my legs. I hear the strain on the waistband of my panties as he yanks them to the side, before slipping a finger inside me with ease.

"You're wet, already? I knew you would be."

I'm horrified that I'm finding him even the slightest bit attractive right now after he hunted me through a creepy ass cemetery and the woods, and threw me to the ground multiple times. I turn my head, not wanting him to see that I'm reacting to him.

"Oh no, don't hide it. I want to see every emotion. The disgust, the confusion, and the surrender."

He slides two fingers inside me and scissors them as he moves them in and out. He never removes his hand from my throat and never stops looking at my face. I'm trying to fight my body's reaction to him and what he's doing. I can't fight him.

He's immobilized me with his hand around my neck and my fear. Is it fear? I'm so confused about what I'm feeling. If I'm scared, then why do his fingers feel so good?

"You hear that sound, Thea? Hear how wet you are for me? Your pussy is slopping all over my fingers. I'm at two." He gives me a quizzical look. "Can you take more?"

I shake my head no. Why am I even answering him?

"I think you can." He smiles. The dark glint in his eyes is at odds with the analytical way he's talking to me. "How many can you take? Three, four? My whole hand?"

My pussy clenches around his fingers. "Fuck, your greedy cunt wants more. Do you think it'll hurt when I stretch you?"

"Don't you fucking dare."

"I dare. I totally dare."

He adds another finger to join the first two. Three of them, moving inside me. *Oh god.* It burns and I whimper at the stretch.

"You're a trooper. Thea. I can do more. Do you want more? I'll give you whatever you want. All you have to do is beg. "

I'll play this game just to get free. "Stop, please stop." I whimper. The broken sound is familiar to my ears. I made it before. I made it that night. I have a flash of a memory of being on my back and imagine the pressure of a body holding me down. I can almost remember how I felt. The full memory is just out of my grasp. The nausea in my stomach is mixed up with this desire for him to continue.

"Do you really want me to?" He leans closer, capturing my gaze, then shakes his head. "No, I don't think that's what you really want, and I don't want to stop. I'm gonna keep going and add another finger."

My throat hurts, my voice comes out in a strangled whisper. "It's. It's too much."

"I know." He does as he said and adds another digit. I'm full and aching. No longer able to hold back the groan of pleasure that's been building. "Mmm." He purrs. "Almost, there."

"Please, no more. I can't."

"You can. You're gonna look so pretty when you cum. I just know it."

He releases my throat and shoves my shirt up. His head dips down, and he latches onto the soft flesh of my side, biting me on the skin below my ribcage. The area where the ugliest bruise on my torso was. The area I was likely hit repeatedly as I tried to protect my injured arm. Pain slices through me and I give him what he wants. I scream. His teeth locked on my skin hurts like a sonofabitch.

He lifts his head. "Yes, Yes! That's it." He pulls his fingers out of me and shoves them in my mouth, cutting off my cries. "Suck them clean." He rasps.

He's crazy if he thinks I'm gonna suck his fingers like this is a normal hookup. I go to bite down on his fingers, but before I can, his mouth is against mine, in a weird ass kiss.

His fingers are between our lips, his tongue slips in and out and around his hand, and mine follows. What the hell am I doing? This isn't right. He removes his hand from my mouth and pins my arms down with his knees before freeing himself from his jeans.

"Don't do this. You don't want to do this."

The look on his face says there's nothing he wants more than this. His hand returns to my throat, his fingers flexing against it, until he finally settles on the amount of pressure he wants. I'm struggling to breathe. He settles between my legs and grinds his erection against me. His free hand pinching and twisting the spot where he bit me.

My mouth falls open, but I'm unable to make a sound as the pain ricochets through my body. But that's not enough for him. He pushes my bra up and latches onto my nipple. I can't keep back the tears as he suckles and bites at it and the surrounding area of my breast. He raises his head to look at my face and groans, taking pleasure in my misery.

His tongue darts out, licking my tears. Then finally, mercifully, he releases the skin he was pinching, placing that hand on my hip, holding me in place, as he rocks against me. His other hand flexes, allowing me enough air to take two ragged breaths before he constricts my airway again.

"There are lessons to be learned here, my lying little whore. I want to spell them out, so you'll understand the cause and effect of what's happened."

He moans, dragging his length through my folds. "Fuck, Rey. Your cunt is begging me to fill it, and your tears taste like the sweetest wine. I knew you'd be the perfect little prey."

My nerve endings are misfiring as he toys with my clit, my whole body vibrating, but instead of fear, it's with the buildup of my release threatening to break me open.

"Damn," He groans, rocking against me twice more, then buries his face in my neck and groans, a deep satisfying sound.

He releases a shuddering breath that fans across my skin. When he pulls away, there's a look on his face that can only be described as content. It's only there for a second before the cold, uncaring look from earlier is back in place. He climbs to his feet, tucks his dick back in his pants and turns to walk deeper into the woods.

"Wait. Where are you going?" I ask, slowly getting to my feet. My head is spinning and my body is sore. "You just attacked me and you're gonna leave me here... like this?"

My mouth stalls over the word horny because I won't give him the satisfaction of knowing I was reacting to what he was doing.

"I told you, there are lessons to be learned. First one. Be more careful about where you go when you're wandering around in old cemeteries and the woods. You never know what predators are looking to devour you."

I'm pissed he's leaving me, but I don't know why I'm upset. It's not like I want him to hang around. Not like I want him to be the one to make me cum. He's one of them. The stupid ass Trium and is a suspect on my list of who attacked me that night. Shit, after what just happened, he's the *only* suspect on my list. And I don't need a guide out of here. I can figure it out for myself.

The ache in my side mocks me as I pull my shirt down and pants up. I have plenty of marks and bruises on my body, but for the next few days, this one will be a shameful reminder of what happened to me in the woods. What I allowed to happen to me in the woods.

I fought Holden off, as much as I could considering my fear paralyzes me at the most inopportune moments. But I worked through it. I was fighting back as much as I could until my body betrayed me and a small part of me wanted him to overpower me. To take me. To fill me with his cock the way he was using his fingers. Why didn't he?

Sure, he chomped on me like I was a fucking hamburger, but Holden never demanded I do anything for him but scream and cry. Even the kiss was controlled. Designed to torment me. His hand was in the way so I could barely kiss him back or bite him, which is what I would have done if his fingers weren't in the way of my teeth connecting.

I walk back to campus. There's no way I can run right now. My shoulder hurts from hyper-extending it when I was reaching for that branch. I brace my arm against my body to keep from jostling it too much.

I'm sore between my legs, too. Four fingers stretching me was a lot. I feel it every time I take a step. But it's a familiar ache. A good ache. One I haven't felt in weeks. Like my pussy has been well used, but it's also sadly empty, my body unfulfilled.

I imagine I hear heavy breathing behind me, again, the pound of footsteps getting closer. I turn to see if Holden's tracking me again, but no one's behind me. When I turn back around, I bump into someone. Another set of hands grab me. I scream and fight.

"LaReaux. Look at me, Thea. It's me." I'm shoved backwards, my arms pinned overhead against a tree.

"Focus on me, sweetness."

Chapter 41
Holden

I told her I was leaving her alone, but I lied. I wanted to give her space after what we did, but there's no way I'd let her wander around out here alone. I keep my distance, trailing her deeper into the woods near the faculty buildings. I must not have been as quiet as I thought, because she stops to look and see who's behind her. I'm covered in the dark and the trees. She can't see me, but I can sense she's still on edge. From our chase and the denial of her orgasm.

She runs again, and I jog a nice pace behind her. She zigs and zags, probably with no destination in mind, her only thought to evade us. To evade me. Just as it should be.

Her flight comes to a halt when Coach Wolfe comes running towards her on the path. I'm too far away to hear what they're saying, but I know she's still trapped in whatever terror now has a hold of her. It's the only explanation for why she'd take a swing at a teacher. Her hands fly around in a flurry and then they're pressed against a tree. I watch in disbelief as Deacon Wolfe does the last thing I'd ever expect to see. He drops to his knees, yanks her pants down her legs, then shoves one leg over his shoulder, before diving onto her clit.

I hear her moan when reality penetrates her psyche, her hands grip his head, her hips buck against his face. Before she's even done, he pulls her to the ground and flips her onto her hands and knees. I watch as he sheathes his dick and slides into her. He pounds into her, one hand around her throat, the other fisting her hair.

The sounds she's making are louder than she made with us at her chastity vow. Louder than any sounds I ever heard her make at my oasis. She's been holding back.

My thoughts turn to Coach Wolfe. We all know students throw themselves at him. I've never seen him so much as look at anyone with more than passing disdain and wondered if maybe he was into men. But obviously, I got that shit wrong. He likes women. And from the sounds he's making, he likes this woman and the way her cunt feels. *A lot.* How long has this been going on?

I bite back the anger I feel that he's just taken my hard work and ruined it. I wanted her restless, needy, wanting. I wanted her in her room, touching herself while I watched.

I also feel a pang of jealousy. Watching them is a reminder of just how alone I am. I have the guys, but I've never had someone risk it all for me. To be so desperate to help me, or so needy for my cock, that they'd drop on all fours, right where they are.

I creep even closer, to watch her be her true, authentic self. No holding back. And until just this moment, I hadn't realized how badly I've wanted to see or hear that. The women we're with enjoy themselves, but it's not the same. It's not *this.* This reckless passion. Utter abandon. Between lovers.

"Have you been a naughty girl tonight, sweetness?"

Coach's voice holds a hint of affection I've never heard before. Everyone knows he's a gruff, sarcastic bastard, forceful and rough. Sweet isn't how any of us would ever characterize him. This entire night is obliterating, how I think of him.

"I told you no fighting outside of me training you."

Thea pants, "I haven't been fighting."

"Then why is your skin flushed and your eyes bright? They only get that way if you've been bashing someone's head in. Or after I've made you cum."

"Or when some assholes try to pick a fight in the middle of the woods and I have to fight through my horrors and desire to hurt them, to get away from them."

My lips twitch. I'd love to see her when she's no longer afraid, and as for her desires; she wasn't fighting in the end. She was embracing them.

"Whatever you were up to-" He grunts, "I'm glad you came this way. I really needed this."

She sasses. "I'm glad my trauma gets you off."

He pushes her between her shoulder blades so her chest hits the ground. Each snap of his hips punctuating the words, "You. Wouldn't. Be. Dealing. With. Trauma. Alone. If. You'd. Talk. To. Your. Shrink."

She moans, "Assssshole."

"Yeah, I am. I'm the asshole who owns this pussy."

That remark angers me more than seeing them together. I don't know why. I have no claim to her, but I want to be the one balls deep in her right now. And the thought of why I can't has me pissed and hard at the same time.

She's afraid of everyone. Well, everyone except Coach Wolfe. I pull my cock out and work it in angry strokes. I circle around the tree to get in a better position, where I can see the look on her face.

"Wolfe."

She grabs his hand and shoves three of his fingers into her mouth. Sucking on them the way I imagine she'd suck cock. She bobs her head up and down, forcing them to the back of her throat. I just about lose my shit. It takes a considerable amount of control to fight the urge to go over there and join in.

This is one time when it wouldn't feel like a chore or an obligation. I'd jump in, because having my cock down her throat while she's getting rutted from behind would make *me* happy.

"Please," she begs.

"What do you need, sweetness?"

"More. I need. More. Let me suck your dick."

"That would mean pulling out, and it doesn't feel like you want me to do that. Do you?"

"No. *Yes.*"

I can hear how conflicted she is. He pulls out and I can see he understands, too. He lays back and brings her hips down to straddle his face in reverse. I watch as she rips the condom off and tries to deep throat him.

"Easy babe." He says when she gags on his length.

She doesn't want easy. She tries again and again. Her moans echo in my ear. "Yes. My ass. Finger my ass."

Deacon Wolfe now has every one of her holes filled. "That's right, sweetness, give me what I want."

I'm not sure what else he could want. Her body shakes, her moans getting louder. Her body tenses. Somehow she's squatting over Deacon and from my vantage point, I see something I've only ever read about or seen in the movies.

Theona LaReaux's pussy expels a gush of fluid like a projectile, and Deacon lies there with his mouth open, catching every drop.

Seeing that triggers my own release. I bite down on my lip as I cum all over the base of the tree I'm hiding behind.

I'm tucking myself back in my pants when a grunt comes from behind me. I turn to see Finn doing the same. *Shit.* I was so caught up in Thea and Coach Wolfe that I didn't even hear him creeping up on me. I walk past him, knowing he'll follow. When we're a safe distance away, I tell him, "I don't wanna talk about it."

"Me either. Talking's overrated."

We walk a few more feet, then he says, "Are we gonna tell Pax about it?"

Tell Pax that Thea is fucking a teacher? That's just the leverage he needs to find out what other secrets Coach Wolfe is hiding. Even if they have nothing to do with us. He's been looking for dirt on him for years. A few of those students he turned down. We may have set him up. Only he never took the bait.

We thrive on secrets and leverage. That's The League of the Daggered Raven's way. I meet Finn's gaze and he nods. Somehow, we come to the same conclusion. We're not telling Pax, and our reason has nothing to do with the Coach Deacon Wolfe.

Chapter 42
Finn

I'm sitting on the couch in Holden's room, waiting for Pax to finish up with his post workout routine. I've been up all night, fuming. While we've been playing it safe, trying to be nice and take it easy with Thea, The Big Bad Wolfe has her huffing and puffing on his cock.

If this were anyone else, any other student or teacher, I'd shut that shit down. But, my pet has been through a lot and if sneaking around with him brings her joy, who am I to take it from her?

She's had enough bad in her life so far. She deserves to be with someone who makes her feel wanted. I mean, *I* want her -so damn bad- but until she's ready to forgive me; I don't want her to feel lonely.

I glance over at my best friend. He looks just as conflicted as I do. We haven't addressed how he feels about her, but now might be the best time to do it. Without Pax around. "You like her."

"Yes."

"Do you feel guilty about chasing her?"

"Why would I? I chased Thea, because I like her. I'm upset I let her get away. If I would have caught her, she wouldn't have been hurt by anyone else."

"But you don't feel guilty about that?"

"No, Finn. What I feel is a desire to dish out a similar punishment to whoever touched my girl."

Holden doesn't make comments lightly. His girl. She's my girl. "Our girl."

He dips his head in agreement. Good. Now we need to figure out how to make her our girl, because right now she's Coach Wolfe's girl. "We have to get her back. She can't be running around here, hooking up with Coach Wolfe. If anyone found out..."

"It would be leverage against him. Do we care about that?"

"I care what they'll say about her. That whatever grade she's earned in his class is because they're sleeping together."

I've seen her grades. She's passing Physical Enhancement. The girls who are not in MISTIC rarely score as high as she has, without augmenting their training.

"Let them talk. It'll be the last thing they say about her. *Ever.*"

I can get onboard with that sentiment. Holden grabs his and Pax's coffee and walks toward the door. I snatch one from his hand. "I've been up all night. I need this more than he does."

We let ourselves into Pax's room just as he's coming out of his bedroom. He's dressed, except for his shirt. He probably didn't put it on yet because he was afraid to wrinkle it. Just once, I'd like this guy to be a little messy and chaotic.

He looks at Holden holding one coffee cup. "No coffee?"

"Finn took yours."

I shrug and sip loudly before passing the cup over to Pax. Those few sips should hold me until we get to breakfast and I get some fuel in my system. We ride down to the lobby and I take my seat to watch the show. This will be one of the last ones until next semester. I'm looking forward to taking a break. I don't even care about this shit anymore. There's only one girl I actually want to see half naked. Or fully naked.

Thea comes down just as the show's coming to an end. The memory of her last night with Coach comes back, tenting my pants. Fuck, it was hot. Holden gets to his feet, and Pax and I do the same. We walk to the door, knowing everyone else will catch up to us in the dining hall.

Holden's gotten into the habit of blocking off the line to wait for Thea to get her food. He does the same thing today, and we take our seats, letting the routine of the day settle around us. When she's done eating, he takes up position outside of the dining hall at the exit she uses. Today Pax goes with him. I finish my pancakes then join them, stepping outside in time to hear Pax telling Thea, "From now on, you're eating with us."

She snorts a laugh, and moves around him. His face morphs into a derisive sneer. He's angry about being ignored. "Did you hear me? What am I asking? Of course you heard me."

"Since you're all knowing, then you also know how stupid it is to invite me to do that."

"I haven't invited you to do shit. You're a legacy, so you're expected to sit at our table."

"I'm *me*, so the only expectations I'm following are my own."

He steps towards her, and I watch her flinch. "You think so? Let me correct you on that. You don't have a choice. You don't get to decide what you're doing. As long as you're in this town, this is the way it is."

"That's an easy fix, isn't it?"

Her insinuation isn't lost on me. I stand rooted in place, watching her walk away, even though everything in me is screaming at me to run after her and smooth things over. It's always about our reputation. Our appearance. Our unshakable bond as The Trium. I keep my face neutral so none of the people standing around know I'm ready to slit my best friend's throat.

We head towards the class we have together. When we're alone, I turn to him, "What the fuck is your problem? We're supposed to be guiding her. Convincing her we want to be friends. Not giving her more reasons to run the other way."

"She can't run. League is in her blood. She's a legacy."

"We're talking about Thea. The girl we didn't know was a legacy until a few weeks ago. Thea, whose parents somehow made her entire existence disappear. Thea, the girl who's been joyriding on your bike, broke into Holden's room to rearrange his computer things, and happily bronzed my $650 knife. That Thea? The one who's part ninja? You think she can't vanish into thin air? She's only here because she wants to be, not because she has any ties to anyone in this place."

I can see he still doesn't believe she's the one who did those things and his answer is simply, "Her parents are here."

Shaking my head at him, I say, "Refer back to the part where they hid her existence even from her, and lied about being her aunt and uncle. Those parents? She grew up without parents. You really think she's attached to them?"

He scrubs a hand through his hair as my words sink in. "I know, man, I... she just knows how to piss me off. I said the first thing that came to mind. Her stubbornness is messing with the mission The League gave us."

"I get that. I know we're behind schedule, but we're supposed to be a team, Pax. You need to act like it."

"I am."

"You're not. It's not just your status on the line. Holden's and mine are too."

"I know, and I promise I'm not trying to mess this up for us. Look, you and Holden handle Thea, and I'll just pass along the updates."

"You really want to do that? Be completely hands off after we ambushed her the other night?"

"That wasn't my choice, either. But like you said, we're all in this together and we can't have her doing anything stupid. She and I antagonize each other, and we need her to stop fighting it. Work your magic, get her to accept her status, and she'll be off our hands."

I squint at him. "And you won't interfere in the way we go about getting her compliance?"

I already have a few ideas. Ideas I know Pax would definitely not be okay with. But his word is binding, so once he figures out what I'm doing, he won't do anything to interfere.

"Whatever plan you come up with, I'll go along with it."

I take a deep breath before pushing through the doors to the lobby of the hotel. It feels like a lifetime since I was last here for work, but it's only been a little longer than a month. I miss it.

My stomach clenches at the thought of what I had to give up when Moira and Scott's lies came out. I walk up to the front desk and wait for some girl I don't know to acknowledge me. When I worked here, I'd just go straight to Van's office. Now that would just be weird.

"Thea?"

I turn and wave at Sam, the maintenance guy. "You here to see Van? She's in the back. Come on by the shop when you're done. I'll show you the latest pictures of the puppies."

"I um. Was just gonna wait to see if she's free."

"For you, kiddo, I'm sure she is. We've missed your face around here."

So I don't look like an idiot just standing around; I walk down the hall toward Van's office. She's standing in the doorway. "Oh, you're leaving..."

"No, I saw you on the security feed. I was trying to decide if I should come out to the lobby. I didn't want to assume you were here to see me or interrupt if you had plans with someone."

"I'm here for you. I would've called, but I thought it would be better to talk in person. If you're busy, I can come back."

"Thea, Honey, I'm never too busy for you." Pushing the door open, she says, "Come on in."

I skirt around her and drop into the chair closest to the door while she takes a seat on the small sofa. She feels none of the awkwardness I do, or if she does, she's good at pretending, because she jumps right in and asks, "What's on your mind?"

Since she dived in, so will I. "What do you know about this legacy shit?"

She nods and gets up and walks to the desk to pick up the phone. "Wait. Who are you calling? Are you supposed to report me for asking?" I bolt to my feet, then feel silly when she orders food.

I plop back down, blowing out a puff of air. When she disconnects the call, she says. "Thea, you have every right to distrust me. But I'm on your side. We're all on your side."

Looking at the plaques on her wall, I say, "It doesn't feel like it."

She returns to the sofa. "Then why don't you tell me what you need, so it does."

It can't be that easy, but I wish it were. "Fine. What does being a legacy really mean and why is it such a big deal around here?"

"Ah. That's easy. Once upon a time, a bunch of rich men settled on some land and decided they owned it. They raised money to build a school and the biggest donors got the biggest perks. As for what it all means, it's just words that say your family descends from those original men. What's expected... is for you to carry on the traditions that are important to those men. And what you're *actually* gonna do is make up your own mind about what being a legacy means to you and how you want to carry yourself."

"Everyone's telling me I have to sit with the other legacies at meal times, and go to all their little parties, join their bullshit clubs. Deal with the bullshit. It's just a never ending chorus of have to, have to, have to."

She flicks her hand in a move that I'd make, if I were dismissing someone from my presence. "That's how the children are raised.

They're told to only interact within that circle and outsiders find it tough to join in. But like any clique, there are leaders and followers, and just like in every group dynamic, people respond and react accordingly."

She grabs my hands. "You, my dear, were born into a family of leaders, rule breakers and hell raisers. No matter what you think of Scott, Moira or Hailee, just know that what they did, hiding you away and deceiving the council, it went against everything they've ever learned growing up here."

Hearing that helps a little. It doesn't fix anything, but knowing I'm not the only one who presses back against the status quo makes me feel a little connected to them.

"Moira said her father will want to meet me."

"I expect he will."

"How do I do this, Van?"

"Do what?"

"Live here with these rules? Moira and Scott said I have to stay low key and stop doing things to draw attention. Which is crazy to hear, because I am usually the definition of low key - no attention-, but I'm so mad right now at everyone and everything, and all I want to do is make noise. I want to find out who attacked me and make them pay. I don't know how to just roll over and pretend it didn't happen, but..."

"But?"

"But I don't want to cause trouble for Moira and Scott, either. I'm mad at them, but they say they have a good reason for what they did. I want to believe that. A part of me *does* believe that, because I think my mom was hiding from something. My gut is telling me that all the moves and the unpredictable behavior were because she didn't want people from this place finding us."

"That would be a yes to both of your unasked questions."

"I don't want to ask because I'll probably never get answers to them."

"Sure you will. Moira and Scott will share when you're ready to hear them out. And as for the bastards that attacked you... the one sure-fire way to get answers about *that* is to embrace your position as a legacy heir."

"What? No!" I get dizzy from how hard I'm shaking my head. "You're wrong. Those shits don't play well with others. I'm operating under the assumption that they're all in on my attack. For all I know, I'm still being targeted."

"Those kids don't play well with outsiders. Which you're not." She arches a brow. "And The Trium are your neighbors. They can help you get answers and would actually be the best people to talk to about what being a legacy means now. Befriending them also offers an extra layer of protection."

"So you're saying to get answers I have to pretend I like them? Pass."

"Oh, no." She chuckles. "I would never suggest that. I'm saying use them for information in whatever form you require."

I chew that over. "I can do that."

Our food comes and we eat in silence until my next question comes tumbling out.

"Did you ever think about me? I know you said everyone assumed I was dead, but..."

She gets up and goes to a painting behind her desk, pushes it to the side and turns the dial to open the safe.

I blurt out, "Are you hoping to get robbed for an insurance pay out?"

"Huh?"

"Behind a picture, Van. Really?"

"Is there somewhere more appropriate I should have a safe?"

"Well, yeah. A bank vault, preferably. But if you need to have one close by, you don't have it on the wall behind a Monet. You get a custom-built desk or bookshelf with a hideaway that you can only access by DNA or biometrics. Of course, that's not full proof. Someone might take your blood or eyeball, but you'd know that's happening and have a chance to prevent it."

Her brow quirks again. "And where would I get one of those? eBay?"

I chew my bottom lip and shrug. "Uh. I might know a guy."

She finishes pulling out whatever's in the safe and says, "This is why I'm not worried about your ability to navigate your position as a legacy. It might seem intimidating because those kids have been friends all their lives, but you've got your own network. Your own resources. You're not alone, Thea. You just have to remember that."

She hands me an envelope. "What's this?"

"Take a look."

I pull out a stack of birthday and Christmas cards, and pictures of Van, Moira, and Scott over the years. "I don't-."

"You may not have been here. But you were always on my mind, and I took pictures of our lives and put them in cards and mailed them to the last address we had for you, even after I knew they'd come back undeliverable. Then I just started writing them and putting them in the safe. Every year. On your birthday or holiday or any family get togethers. Just because."

She stares down at me until I meet her eyes. "I know this doesn't fix things. You missed a lot. *We* missed a lot. But if you want to see some of the things we did over the years. It's all right there."

I pull out a card and look at the picture inside of Moira and Scott blowing out a candle. I spot the date on the bottom. "This is-"

"Your actual sixteenth birthday. We threw a party here at the hotel and made it Christmas themed so nobody would get suspicious."

I look closer and smile when I spot LJ in the back corner. "What was LJ doing here?"

She looks over and frowns. "I... don't know a... Oh wait, Layla-Jean Breland? A few of the students from the high schools helped with a landscape project that year as part of their community service endorsement for college. I sent them an invitation to come. I guess she was one of the only ones to show up."

I stroke the picture. They threw me a sweet sixteen party and my best friend, who feels like an outcast in this world, was there.

"Can I keep this?"

"Of course. They're all yours."

I fall silent for a few moments, flipping through a few more pictures. "You know it sucks that I'm only eighteen, right? I mean, it's a good thing I didn't find out earlier because some people might take issue with suddenly finding out they could be facing jail time, but it still sucks for me that I'll be using my fake ID for three more years."

"Noted."

My eyes snap to her face. "That's it? Just *noted?* You're not gonna fuss about me admitting to hooking up with older dudes or drinking?"

"Lemme ask you something... Will fussing about it make you stop doing it?"

I snort, "No."

"Then why should I waste my time or breath telling you not to do something you're gonna keep doing? I *will* say be safe and use your best judgment when it comes to men. That goes for men at any age, and don't get caught using your fake ID. If you do, call me. That doesn't mean you won't face the consequences for your actions, but I will be there supporting you as you do."

She returns to her seat and picks up her burger. "Now you wanna tell me about this motorcycle theft ring I keep hearing about?"

Chapter 44
Thea

LJ has dragged me out to another party. This one is on campus and I'm in my normal clothes. I couldn't tell her no. Not when she's about to be gone for most of the Christmas Break. Her parents sprung a trip to visit relatives on her and she seems really excited about it. So I'm stepping out, showing my face at a party hosted by the frat house of some guy on the football team.

We spot Oscar right away and she goes off to dance with him. I love that she's feeling more comfortable in social settings. I stay on the fringe with my back to the wall while I nurse my drink.

There are a lot of jocks here, which I expected, but *they're* here too. The Coxsuckers. It's questionable if they were actually on the guest list, because I've learned they show up, regardless. I chat with a few people I recognize and decide to relocate, because this side of the room is getting crowded. I spot another section of unoccupied wall over by the stairs and head there, my drink raised above my head to keep from spilling it on people as I push through the crowd.

As careful as I am, I still manage to bump into a few people, but I make it to my new safety zone without freaking out. Progress. I take a congratulatory sip of my drink to celebrate. After a while, I feel myself relaxing enough to sway to the music, letting the beat wash through me.

I even smile and make small talk with a few people who drift by. The happy vibe of the room is contagious. This is the crowd we should have been partying with all semester.

I take another sip of my drink, once again raise my hand in the air, then move from against the wall, deciding to find LJ so we can dance together. I find her off to the side talking to Oscar, and grab both of their hands, dragging them onto the floor.

"Someone's found their party spirit." Oscar says, smiling down at me.

I nod, smiling back as I spin to the music, completely unbothered by all the people swarming around us, or the limbs jostling against me. I'm happy here in the middle of the crowd. I feel light, like I could float up to the ceiling and fly away.

"Hey, Thea."

I crack an eye open. "Hey person, I don't know." I say to the guy beside me.

"You wanna dance?"

I open my other eye. "I am dancing." To prove my point, I shimmy my shoulders and swirl my hips.

He chuckles. "I meant with me."

"Sure, you'll do."

It's a little hard to tell exactly what he looks like under the dim lights, but it doesn't matter. I'm not trying to judge how our future babies will look. The only thing I care about is that he's not a teacher, or a Coxsucker and my body seems to like him.

I hook my arms around his neck, pulling him closer, and grind against him. It doesn't take long before I feel him stiffen against me, his erection growing the longer we move together. I ask, "You a member of this frat?"

"Yeah."

"So that means you have a room here that you want to show me?"

My meaning is clear enough. With a smile, he grabs my hand and pulls me through the crowd. Before we make it to the stairs, Eloise steps in our path.

"Hey Blane. What you up to?"

The guy, Blane, looks down at her and smiles. "Thea and I are gonna go some place quieter to hang out and talk."

"Tramp, run. Got it." She cackles.

I'm really feeling the urge to ride a dick. She is not about to ruin this for me. I'll shove her out of the way to get where we're going, if I have to.

"You sound jealous, Eloise. How much longer do you have to wait until you're allowed to play with a penis, anyway?" I pretend to be looking for something around the room. "Don't worry. I heard a Lady Lion offering to keep Finn's dick company while your VV is turning to dust."

"VV?" Blane asks.

"Vanilla Vagina." I pat him on the chest. "No worries. Mine is like a trip to Baskin Robbins. You can sample multiple flavors."

He stoops down to kiss me, and I let him, just to show him I'm not full of shit. We're gonna have a lot of fun. His hand grips my ass, pulling me closer to his body, rubbing his still hard cock against me. Suddenly, he's yanked away, a growl coming from behind where he was standing. Finn is standing over him.

"What. The. Fuck. Number Three?"

"What the fuck is right, Pet. As in, what the fuck do you think you're doing?"

He's looking at me, but I get the impression the question is for Blane. That doesn't stop me from saying, "Will you and your boo please go cock block someone else." Looking down at Blane, I say, "Don't worry about this idiot spoiling our fun. I wanna fuck you twice as bad now."

He stutters, "See Finn. It's all good, man. She asked me-"

I tune out the rest of what he's saying when someone walks by and brushes against me. I grab his arm and pull him closer, nuzzling his neck. Eloise's annoying voice mocks me. "God, she really is a slut."

"Pet..."

I ignore Finn. Looking over my shoulder, I ask, "Blane, are you coming or what?"

He climbs to his feet and comes to stand next to the guy.

"Thea!"

"Dammit, fuck off, Finn!"

He growls at the guys, "Let's make something clear. I don't give a shit what she asked you. I don't care if she flashed her tits and shoved your face against them while palming your dick. You don't touch her."

Is this some more legacy shit? I whip my shirt off and fling it behind me, moving to stand directly in front of the guys. I palm their dicks just like Finn mentioned.

"Ignore him. Play with my tits all you want."

Eloise gets out another jab. "And this is why thinking you'd ever be a legacy, that you'd ever be good enough for any legacy man, is a joke. You are the common whore I always knew you to be." I hear a camera flash. "And now everyone else knows it, too. Congratulations, Thea. You finally succeeded. No one will accept you as a legacy now."

Chapter 45
Finn

I've been watching Thea all night. She started off against a wall, clinging to the shadows, keeping a safe distance from everyone, but after a while, her mood changed. She joined her friends on the makeshift dance floor and she seemed to have a good time.

I lost sight of her when she left the dance floor with Blane. It was Eloise's hysterics that clued me into her location. When I walked up, nothing seemed out of the ordinary. She was arguing with Eloise, like always. I thought Thea was fucking with me. Pushing back because that's just what she does when I told Blane to get lost. Until she turned around and started petting someone else.

That's not Thea. She's not the overly touchy type. Now she's fidgety. Her body looking for stimuli, her pupils dilated. I recognize the signs. She's been dosed. One of the more friendly party favors in her system. The drugs take hold quickly. In a few more minutes, she'll be too out of it to fight its effects. I don't have time to wonder if Blane is responsible. It would be a ballsy move, but I don't put anything past anyone these days.

She's swaying to the music, hands in the air. "Thea, you need to listen to me."

"Oh, I think I've heard everything I needed to hear from your future *wife*."

I slip my arm around her waist and drag her out of the room, looking for some place private. Her shirt's already off, her pants might not be far behind.

"Thea, you've been dosed. You're about to feel a lot of things at once. I need you to focus." We make it to the frat meeting room, which is empty. I flick on the light to get a better look at her. Her eyes are glassy. I don't even know if she's here anymore.

"LaReaux."

Where the hell did he come from? At the sound of Coach Wolfe's voice, her head snaps up, and she stands taller. Sort of. She's staring at him, waiting for him to say something else. I've never seen her like this before. Even leaning against me, I can tell she's in obedient mode.

"I want you to do exactly what Finn says."

She swirls her fingers in the air. "Fuck, Finn."

I readjust my hold to keep her from walking out the door. "You're on a very potent blend of drugs, Pet. It just may come to that."

She shifts from one foot to the other, and gasps when I accidentally bump her shoulder. She's feeling it now. She turns to me, her lower lip snagged between her teeth, her eyes hooded. An invitation to kiss her if I've ever seen one.

Coach Wolfe says, "This is important, Thea. Do what he says."

She moves, so she's standing in front of me. "I don't like Finn."

He nods and the look on his face says he doesn't like me either. "I get that. But you need him. You do what he says or I'm canceling that fight I promised you."

She squirms against me. More like drags her ass against me. "You can't do that."

"Sure I can. You haven't shown up for training. You told me you wanted to quit, anyway. Besides, if I have to take you to a hospital, you won't pass the drug test, which will automatically bar you from official events."

"You know I don't do drugs."

"The drink or shots you had, maybe both, were laced. Don't you feel your skin tingling? Your body getting worked up? Your clit starting to throb?"

Her brows furrow as she realizes maybe it's more than a little buzz she's got going on.

"Let Finn walk you through this and help you release."

She's shaking her head. "I had help for my throbbing clit, and he scared them off."

I ignore her pout and say, "I'll keep scaring them off, too."

She twists out of my hold. "I don't need a man. I can handle this myself back at my dorm."

I step in front of her so she can't leave, and Coach says, "If you walk out of here, I can guarantee there is a gang of people waiting to pounce on you, Pet. This cocktail shouldn't be taking effect this soon. So that means they wanted you out of it so they could fuck you without you fighting back."

"Isn't that what you brought me in here to do? How do I know you didn't do this to me?"

Coach answers before I can say anything. "LaReaux, if I thought he did this, I wouldn't let him anywhere near you."

He steps closer, stroking her cheek. "You might be fighting me about training you, but I'm still your coach and I still have big plans for whenever you're ready to return to the ring. I want you on my ticket. I want to give you what I promised you, but I need you safe." His voice drops. "Be a good girl and let him lick that pussy."

"Wolfe..." She pants his name, pinches her nipples, and presses her thighs together.

"I'll be close by. Making sure nobody interrupts."

He ignores the rest of her refusal and says, "Take care of her, Finn."

"Oh, god." She pants. "I don't want you, Finn. Don't touch me. Wolfe can do it."

I pull her back against my chest, gently caressing her breast, and tweak her nipple through her bra. She tries to pull away. I should let her. But Coach is right. If she leaves, she'll probably be walking into an ambush. She'll be so high and horny she won't even care. Maybe I should let her, instead of giving her one more thing to hate about me.

"Don't overthink it, Rhodes. She needs help."

Someone comes crashing through the door. Pax is weaving from side to side. Shit, was he dosed too? What the hell is even happening tonight? I don't have time for this shit. If Holden is cocked too, I'll be on babysitting duty all night.

Pax wanders over to us and glares at the hand I have on Thea's tit. He shoves my hand out of the way, replacing it with his. He's got no hang ups about touching her. He's definitely on drugs because he never touches her. He *hates* her and I'm sure he'd rather his dick fall off than put it anywhere near here. Yet here he is. Squeezing her tit with this awed look on his face, like he's never touched one before.

I meet Coach's gaze. Surprised he's really not going to put a stop to this. It's twisted. He's pushing a student to fuck people she hates. I know they're hooking up. But Holden and I have an agreement, not to mention it.

A grunt brings my attention back to the two people in front of me. Thea's still trying to run, and Pax is holding his nose. Coach steps up, and growls, "Why are you being so damn difficult, LaReaux?"

"Because I hate them. I said I can tough this out myself."

"You're being stubborn and trying to put yourself in danger. You know I don't tolerate that." He squeezes her face, likely leaving marks. "Mr. Cox. For that little stunt she just pulled, you get to dish out my punishment."

He never looks away from Thea when he says. "Fuck the foreplay. Pull out your dick and shove it into her weeping cunt." He chuckles when her eyes widen. "Mr. Rhodes. You get her mouth."

He was gentle earlier. Probably because he was trying to get her compliance, but *this* is the Deacon Wolfe I'm used to. Hard. Unrelenting. Callous. His voice drops a bit, but I still hear him say, "The longer you fight this, the worse it gets. Your body's on fire, isn't it? Your pussy begging to be filled?"

She whimpers, and Coach Wolfe steps behind her, hooking his arm around her neck. Without hesitation, Pax pushes his pants down, freeing his dick.

"Not him. Please, not him."

"Yes, him. Every. Single. Inch."

I wait for Pax to do the opposite of what he was told and take her mouth. He hasn't put his dick in a pussy in almost two years. But he breaks his pussy ban, rolls on a condom, and hooks her legs around his waist before shoving into her.

She's not listening to Coach. She's fighting it. He says, "Don't think about how much you hate them. Think about how much you love fucking. You can do that and get through this, right?"

She clenches her teeth, and nods.

"Finn, I'm waiting for you to come shut her up."

Before I can ask how he expects me to reach her mouth, Pax pulls her down onto the floor, so she's straddling him. Wolfe's hands are on her shoulders holding her in place. Tears gather in the corner of her eyes as she fights the need coursing through her veins. Tough and fragile. Perfect. I don't have to talk myself into what I do next, because the truth is I've been dying to feel her mouth on my cock again. I push into her mouth. Sliding against her tongue.

"I want your throat, Pet." I slide out, then push back in without giving her a chance to agree, fully expecting her teeth. She doesn't disappoint. My eyes slam shut, as they scrape across my shaft. "That's it Pet. You know I like some pain with my pleasure."

She moans. When I open my eyes, I see Deacon behind her, nuzzling her ear. "That's a good girl. Stop fighting and let them help you." He presses a kiss to her temple. "Let me see how you ride Pax." She moves and he tsks. "Don't be shy, sweetness. I know you can do better than that. You say you want a hard fuck, then show me. I wanna hear that ass meet his thighs."

He grabs her hips, lifting her slightly, then shoves her back down. She readjusts her weight then takes over bouncing up and down on Pax's dick, so hard, her jaw shakes.

Coach Wolfe says, "Don't forget about Finn."

She strokes me before wrapping her lips around me again, sucking on the tip of my dick. "Suck me harder, Pet."

She complies, hollowing out her cheeks, while continuing to slide up and Pax's shaft. This feels so fucking good and she looks amazing. I could finish like this, but I want that pussy, so I hold off, waiting for Pax to finish.

"I think you've got on too many clothes, sweetness." Coach pulls off her bra. Her nipples pebble as soon as they're exposed to the air.

"Yes. Fuck. Ride that dick. You're doing so good, Thea." He praises. "Dick in your dripping cunt. Dick in your mouth. I've never seen a more beautiful sight."

"Mmm," I hum in agreement.

She sucks harder. Her eyes rolling to the back of her head. Mine do the same, the suction and heat of her mouth pushing me closer to the edge. She has a praise kink? How did I not know this?

Pax grunts, "Fuck that." He yanks her off of me and pushes her onto her back. Ending my blowy. He spreads her legs wider, pounding into her.

"Deke." She moans.

"Fuck him." Pax growls. "I'm the one about to make you cum."

Pax is usually so good at sharing. I guess he realizes the only reason she's getting off is because Coach Wolfe is coaching her. That doesn't bother me. I like that he's here. I wouldn't be touching her if he wasn't. It's not the reunion I hoped for. But I'm happy to roll with it. Thea and Pax are going at it hard. Her nails dig into his back, drawing blood.

Even spread the way she is, she's lifting her hips to meet his thrusts, giving just as good as he is. It's so hot. But this isn't supposed to be about him. Or not just him.

"Deke." She moans, making me harder.

Her words only make Pax madder. He bites out, "I'm the one in you. I'm. Fucking. You."

She laughs at him, unfazed by the threat in his voice. God, the balls on my girl. His control snaps. She's pushed him too far. He ruts into her. Her body slides across the floor with every snap of his hips.

"Not so funny now, is it? Splitting you with this cock. More fucking trouble than you're worth. Not worth a legacy dick."

"Then why are you. On top. Of. *Me?*"

Good question. It's a hate fuck, but it's not that simple. I'm watching Pax now. Really watching him. His words don't match the look on his face. He's caught up in her. I know just how good Thea's pussy feels. I remember the way I wanted to get closer and stay buried inside her.

"Don't fight it Thea." Coach says, encouraging her on.

"Shit." This time, the strangled gasp comes from my best friend. "No. Fuck No. What are you *doing*?"

Aaah. It's happening. He can't power his way through this.

"You're. Shit. *Fuck*, Nemesis. One more. Inch." He moans, then chants, "Shit. Shit. Shit."

I hear the pride in Coach Wolfe's voice when he says, "Good girl, sweetness. I knew you could take all of him."

"Finn." She pants.

Hearing my name like that from her mouth, god I could nut right now. "Yeah, Pet?"

"Fuck my mouth."

I chuckle and straddle her face. "Since you've asked so sweetly."

"Make me jealous, Thea." Coach commands. "Make me regret letting them touch you."

Somehow, Pax and I make it work. My knees are on either side of her face, which I'm holding steady, as I rock into her mouth. Pax is between her legs, holding her hips up off the ground, wrecking her pussy. I feel her tense against me, then her mouth goes slack as her release ricochets through her. Pax finishes a few moments later. Then pushes away like he's been burned. Before she can start bitching about it, I roll on a condom and take his place. My strokes are slower. Gentler than his. She has to be sore after the way he rode her. Fucking barbarian.

"Finn..."

"Shh. I've missed you, Pet. Your mouth is good, but this pussy is heaven. I need to feel it."

I slide my hand up to her face and drop my forehead to hers. "Pet. You feel so good. Fuck, this pussy is so wet. I'm not gonna last. You make it impossible for me to last."

I wanted to go longer for her. Be gentle with her. But I can't. Everything I've been holding back comes rushing to the surface and I take her body. Using my touch and every stroke of my cock to apologize and to show her she's mine.

She locks around my dick, and I blow my load. Twitching against her. When the fog clears, I hear crying. I stumble away from her. Shit. Did I hurt her? I didn't mean to. Or is this the aftermath of forcing her to do what she said she didn't want?

"Come here, sweetness." Coach Wolfe gathers her in his arms, rubbing circles on her lower back. "You're good. You did so good. How do you feel?"

"I'm on fire. I need... you." Her voice cracks on that admission.

Pax is over in the corner. He looks like he's coming down, but she's still in the middle of it. It's gonna take a minute before I'm ready to go again.

"I can't, Thea."

"I won't tell anyone. You know I won't."

A look crosses Coach's face before he presses her back to the floor and delves between her legs. Devouring her. She holds onto his hair, riding his face, her body convulsing as she cums. He's got the patience of a saint, because he's down there long enough for me to get hard again. I'm stroking my dick, counting the number of times she cums by his mouth alone. I'm at three.

"One more sweetness."

She's writhing around. Finally, trying to get away from him. Insisting she's too sensitive.

"One more sweet girl. Fuck, you taste amazing. You want me, happy right? One more will make me so happy."

"Your cock."

"No, sweetness. This. Your taste in my mouth. Your juices dripping down my face. This makes me so happy. Stop fighting me and let this sweet cunt take over. You know what I need, baby. You're my good girl, right?"

"Yes!"

"Damn right you are. Oh, look at that. More sweet juice for me. So good. I'm about ready to make a mess in my pants for you, Thea."

He's not the only one.

"You're so close. I can feel it."

"Deke... shit. Like that."

"I know, sweetness. I know just how to do it. Oh, look at that."

I wish I were closer so I could see what he's seeing. Whatever it is, has him in awe. He flips them over, so she's riding his face. He's now only capable of grunts and garbled noises. But he seems to love being suffocated by her. She rises up a little, throws her head back and screams so loud, I'm sure someone can hear us.

"What the fuck?"

I look to where Pax is staring, in time to see her... squirt. Coach Deacon Wolfe leans his head up, pressing his lips to her lower ones, like he's shotgunning it. With a ragged groan, she collapses against him. His hands hold her to his chest, as he resumes rubbing soothing circles on her back.

"So damn, good. You did so damn good. That will always be the sexiest thing I've seen. The way you gift me with that sweet, tasty cream. Fuck Thea. You're so perfect."

She sounds unsure when she asks, "You happy?"

"So fucking happy, Thea." His arms tighten around her. "You make me so damn happy."

Now, I feel like I'm intruding. Pax and I fucked the shit out of her, but she's curled against Deacon Wolfe and glowing because he's praising her.

He whispers something in her ear, to which she replies, "I don't want to."

"I know. But they helped you. Maybe saved your life. You can still hate them, but thank them for doing something I couldn't do tonight." He kisses her forehead, and she climbs to her feet, walking over to where I'm standing. Tits out, skirt still bunched up around her hips.

"Thank you for helping me. You too, Pax." She says, looking over at him. He's scoffing like an idiot, refusing to recognize the gift her apology is.

I'm not an idiot, so I say, "You're welcome, Pet. I'm glad I could help, so is Pax."

Shooting a glare at him, she says, "He doesn't look happy."

"You know he's a man of few words and he's coming down too, so..."

Pax butts in, "I was dosed too. That's the only reason I touched you."

Her back stiffens, her chin lifts. "Whatever you have to tell yourself. But we both know you'll be replaying this memory for the rest of your life."

He grumbles that he won't, but I know I will. Wolfe hands her, her bra and says, "Somebody give her a shirt."

Before I can move, Pax yanks his off and tosses it to him.

Chapter 46
Pax

I half listen as Thea mumbles a half-hearted thank you. Trying to work through what just happened. I don't know how I wound up with a poisoned shot. That's what we call the jello shots with the cocktail in it. Someone must've switched out the colors because only the blueberry ones are supposed to be tainted.

I only took half of a jello shot before I had to take a call from my dad. The effects came over me just as the call ended. I was looking for a room to ride it out in, because there was no way I wanted to hook up with any of the girls at the party. They're all opportunists, and I knew they would only use the situation to their advantage. By the time I found an unlocked room, I was well into the throes of it. It was pure bad luck that the room was occupied by Finn and Thea.

My gaze drifts over to her. She's still out of it. I have more body mass than her and had less of a dose. I was pretty much sober before I even nutted.

I could have stopped, but she was talking so much shit, I wanted to prove a point. I was gonna leave her high and horny and take Finn with me, but then she stopped fighting it. She opened up and took me to the hilt. It's been so long since I've slipped into some pussy. It felt better than I remembered and sliding home was like something clicked.

I'd gotten used to girls who pushed back. They refused to let me go deep, as if they thought it would preserve this illusion of purity they needed to project. Or they would tell me it hurt too much, and screech the whole time.

Finn laughed at their cries. Holden wanted their tears, and me. I ignored what they were saying. I always blocked out the sounds, focused on one goal. To nut. It's the same thing when I'm in their asses, but that crevice was designed for deep penetration, so their protests don't mean shit.

But Thea took me, and she let me have my way with her, while Finn used her mouth and Deacon Wolfe sat there encouraging her on.

I almost wish I was high and that I'd imagined it. But I didn't. The most fulfilling fuck I've had in months is with the someone I can't stand. The woman The League is expecting me to be friends with. To bring her in. Shit. I'm handling this wrong. This is the perfect peace offering.

I grumble, "You're welcome," as she walks away. I toss Coach Wolfe my shirt when he asks for it and, leave before she's finished dressing. I need to get back to the party and find out who fucked with the standard set up. All parties follow the same protocol for poisoned shots. It's easier to keep things straight. Poison shots are *always* blue raspberry. I had an apple shot. I should have been safe.

Finn, Coach Wolfe, and Thea return to the party shortly after I do. I watch as Coach Wolfe snags a couple of bottles of water and gives them to her, standing guard in front of her while she drinks them down.

I chug my own water, my mind feeling clearer than it did when I stumbled into that room. Finn catches up to me, a glint in his eye. "We about to bust some heads for what they did to Thea?"

"Thea? No. For what they did to me. If she wants to get high, why do I care?"

"After what happened? Seriously Pax."

I glance over at him, noting the look of disapproval on his face matches the tone in his voice. "What's your deal? We fucked. It doesn't mean anything."

"We'll come back to that later. I'm talking about how much of the cocktail she probably has in her system and how it got there. She's still out of it, man."

I scoff. "That's an easy answer. She had too many blue shots."

"She didn't take any blue shots."

Scanning the room for anything suspicious, I say, "Okay, neither did I. Obviously somebody screwed up by deciding to change the poisoned shot colors without telling people."

"I'm telling you, man, she didn't have *any* shots. She had one beer, a cocktail, and a glass of water."

My head whips around. "What?"

"Somebody dosed her straight up, man. Not by giving her a jello shooter either."

"You're right." Coach Wolfe says as he walks up to us. What the hell is he even doing at this party? It's not unheard of that faculty patrol the campus during certain events, but a little frat party shouldn't even be on their radar. Even then, they don't come to the parties. Finn scans the room. "Where's Thea?"

"Over by the door with LJ."

I temporarily ignore the question I have about why he's here, focusing on what Finn was suggesting. "You're saying someone put something in her drink?"

Coach Wolfe shakes his head. "I'm saying someone injected her with enough of the cocktail to keep her out of it for hours."

My blood simmers with that wild accusation. Is he here to start rumors and drama? "You don't know that. She could have popped a pill."

"Thea already has a prescription for enough pills that she could mix with booze to give her a high, and she knows better than to do that." He taps his right shoulder. "I saw the needle mark top deltoid."

Finn looks around, a murderous look on his face. I ask, "How the fuck would someone be able to prick her with a needle without her knowing?"

"In here, pressed together? A lots of ways. With a ring hiding the liquid concoction. A hand shake or friendly pat on the back, multiple times over and no one would know anything was happening."

I consider that answer. A hypodermic needle would be noticeable to a random bystander unless multiple people were in on it. But Thea hasn't been comfortable around crowds. That's one thing I know about her since her accident. "A ring?"

"Sure. A ring modified with a secret compartment under the jewel."

I work that answer over in my head. "Like some spy shit?"

Coach Wolfe looks at me like I'm an idiot. "Yes, like some spy shit. Why do you sound so surprised? You've gone to school here for three years. What the hell do you think they're learning over at MISTIC?"

When neither of us answers, he says, "It's not just military customs and courtesies or how to salute."

We've all interacted with students from MISTIC from time to time. They're on a separate side of campus, but some of the students are in our classes, and they show up to our parties. Thea could have been dosed before she came here, or it could have been somebody here. There's no way of knowing what happened.

I continue working over what I do know. If Finn says she didn't take a shot, I believe him. He watches that girl closely enough to know if there's lettuce stuck in her teeth. I took a green shot which is apple flavored. I have a memory of Finn mentioning Thea likes apple vodka. I thought it was a weird bit of trivia. But now... if I operate on the assumption that she didn't do this to herself, that means someone intentionally mixed up the shots to cover their tracks.

"We're all thinking the same thing, right?" Finn asks.

I scrub my hand through my hair. We probably are, but it's hard to wrap my mind around. She's a nobody. "You're thinking someone targeted her. But why?"

"Isn't it obvious?" Wolfe gives me his patented glare. "Someone's trying to take out the newest legacy."

The look on his face says what remains unsaid. "You think it's me? I took half an apple shot and got dosed too. But thanks for your concern, *Coach*."

"Half a shot?" He snarls. "That little interlude back there only took the edge off of what she's feeling, but you nutted, and you look all rejuvenated. So spare me the righteous indignation about how you're a victim, too. This is supposed to be your school. You're the almighty *Trium*. Find out who keeps coming after her and fix it."

I hear the threat in his voice. I pull myself up to my full height and step closer, growling, "Or what?"

"Or I will."

He stalks over to Thea and walks her and LJ out the door. I hate his attitude. I hate that he thinks he has any right to tell us what to do. But if his theory is correct, we have a big problem. I can't stand Thea. I don't understand what she's doing here, or why or who, even the fuck she really is. But The League says she's one of us, and we protect our own, which means this attack on her, if it was an attack, is an attack on us.

Great, just one more mess, I have to clean up and pray the council doesn't find out about it.

Chapter 47
Deacon

I watch Thea drink her third glass of water, then order her to get into bed. She's holding the phone with one hand and lifts the blankets back with the other. "Why?"

"Why what?"

She's been rambling on about how much she hates The Trium and hopes Pax gets drunk and vomits all over himself. I've tuned those rants out because I don't have anything helpful to offer. "Why would you just sit there and let them fuck me?"

I let my head fall back with a heavy sigh. I didn't want to let them do anything, but where we were, with all those people around. Anyone could have walked in, and it was easier for her to be caught with them. Even going down on her was a risk, but she looked so lost, so needy, and they were in no position to help at that point, so I did what I had to do. There was no way I was going to let another guy fuck her. Those two were hard enough to watch.

That's the thing about this cocktail a chemistry student created years ago. It drops your inhibitions and keeps you lucid while you're under its control. But as soon as you fall asleep, the after affects are the same as HGB. Thea and Pax probably won't remember anything. The shit that happens while under the influence has been the catalyst for plenty of blackmail schemes. Around here, in this town and this school, blackmail and secrets are currency.

Do I think Finn would have told anyone if I would have stuck my dick in Thea? No. I've been following her around in my free time. Watching her. Watching them, and every one else she's come in contact with, trying to find out who attacked her Mayhem Night. I see the way Finn looks at her. It irritates me how much he looks at her, but it's without malice.

I get the impression he really likes her. He's a Trium and a Wren, so I'd be stupid to trust him. Stupid to trust any of them. But, I trusted him to take care of her, while I was there. In answer to her question, I say, "Because you needed them to."

"I needed *you*. They could have been the ones watching."

"Thea."

"What?"

"You're my student, and I'm your trainer outside of school. It would be unethical of me to fuck you while you were under the influence."

"But it's not unethical for you to lick me like an ice cream cone?"

"It is. But I wanted to reward you for being such a good girl, and letting them help you." I drop my voice, and let my question rumble through my chest the way I know makes her shiver. "Didn't you like your reward?"

"Yes."

"And I liked giving it to you. How are you feeling, sweetness?"

"I'm still turned on."

"It'll pass. Just try to get some sleep."

"I don't think I can."

"Then rub one out first."

"That's not enough. I need dick, and I can't figure out where the hell my dildo is."

My brows arch. Am I shocked Thea plays with toys? No, not really, but I am surprised she just volunteered that info with me. She sounds so aggravated about it being missing too. Her bottom lip pokes out in a pout. Her reaction pisses me off. I'm glad it's misplaced. How pathetic is it that I'm jealous of a toy?

Maybe I'll offer to buy her a new one and let her use it under supervision, if she does something I want. Like sit down with her psychologist for thirty minutes. I'll circle back around to that.

I guess it's pretty twisted. I don't want her fucking her toys, but I let two of The Trium do it. Part of me wanted to rip their heads off. The other part loved watching her face and seeing how good they were making her feel.

Everyone got off tonight. Except me. My balls are aching from holding back. I drop the phone to my lap. "Someone wants to say hi." I chuckle at her sharp intake of breath.

"Fuck, Wolfe. Warn a girl before you pull that thing out and start playing with it."

She should be trying to sleep it off. The more worked up she gets, the hornier she'll get, the cycle continuing until all the drugs are out of her system. But, I can't seem to stop. I need this connection with her. "Did you like Finn and Pax fucking you like that tonight?"

"You already know I like sex. It was sort of like an out-of-body experience because I hate them but I was so horny. So they served their purpose."

She makes it sound so basic. Clinical. I admire that she can compartmentalize, but she doesn't need to do it with me. I heard what Pax said when she tried to thank him. He's lucky he still has both legs to stand on. "I meant, together. Did you like Pax in your pussy, while Finn was in your mouth?"

"No."

Arching a brow I parrot, "No?"

"No. Wolfe. I didn't like it. I wanted more."

"How much more?"

"I wanted you too, Wolfe. I wanted you to touch me, too. I wanted you fucking me."

God, I love when she's open and honest with me. It's like a rare gift because she doesn't bare her soul easily. "Away from them. Or with them? No lies, Thea."

"With them. I wanted you in my ass, calling me your good girl, *okay?*"

"You are my good girl. And for that truth, you've earned a reward."

I fuck my hand, *hard,* the way I want to pound her sweet hole. Her ass. Her mouth. "Thea, if our situation ever changes, you get all this dick. Any time and anywhere you want it. I'm gonna take you so hard and long and deep, you'll think we're fused together. There won't be a part of you I haven't touched, licked, or spit on."

"Yes. Please, Wolfe."

I glance down at the phone and see her face contorted. "Lower the phone. Spread those lips. Let me see you cum. Fuck your hand, Thea. Pretend I'm there. Pretend I'm inside of you."

She's chanting my name, the springs on her bed squeak as she thrusts her hips. Her hand stills, and I watch as her arousal coats her fingers and her body quivers.

"Fuck." The sight sets me off and I release my load on the screen. She raises the phone and now it's like I'm aiming for her tits. Then, finally, her face.

She giggles, a carefree sound, as my cock softness, and I struggle to catch my breath. "Good night, Wolfe."

"Sleep well, sweetness."

The loud thud of my pulse in my ears is like a soundtrack to my death as I drag myself out of bed to the bathroom. I know better than to drink too much, although I didn't think I did. The last drink I remember getting was the rum and coke I fixed. Then I went... I went to find a bathroom, came back to LJ, who was dancing. We danced ... a lot, and...

I rub my temples as if that will unclog the foggy spots in my memory. Hopefully, a hot shower and caffeine will help me work through what else I did last night. I step under the shower spray and tip my head back to wash my hair, which feels gross and drier than it should, considering I washed it yesterday.

I take my time letting my mind wander as the routine of cleaning myself grounds me. Sometimes, my best thinking is done when I'm not thinking at all.

Nothing comes to me, but I feel better once I'm done in the shower. I brush my teeth, giving extra attention to my cottony tongue. Once I'm dressed, I head out for food and caffeine, shooting LJ a text to let her know what I'm doing. She responds with a thumbs up emoji and says she'll meet me there.

The campus is still quiet. I'm guessing everyone's sleeping in this morning before final exams start tomorrow. Good, I'm not in the mood for people right now. My steps slow as I approach The Rock. Finn's standing in front of it. The person he's talking to has their back to me. He spots me and the guy turns around. My steps falter.

Coach Wolfe rarely hangs out on this side of campus. The way they're looking at me leaves me unsettled. I shake the feeling off and walk through the doors. I sit in my usual seat after grabbing coffee and two breakfast croissants to help soak up the remaining alcohol in my system.

They both walk into the dining hall. Finn takes the seat across from me and Coach Wolfe stands off to the side, his arms folded across his chest. "Whatever it is, I just woke up, so I couldn't have done it." I say before taking a sip of my coffee.

"We need to talk about last night, Pet."

"I was at a party. I have witnesses and a hangover as my alibi, so I didn't do whatever happened last night, either."

Wolfe's jaw clenches. I'm already tired of this game. "What? Spit it out?"

"It's not a hangover LaReaux. Someone drugged you last night."

My focus snaps to Finn. Is that why Wolfe's here? Because he has proof that Finn drugged me? Sitting back in my seat, I fold my hands across my chest. God, I need my knife. I scan the surrounding tables to see if someone left a knife out. I wonder if Wolfe would keep Finn from running off while I go grab one. I look over at him again. He promised to find my attackers and let me get revenge, so I think he would. I stand to my feet.

Wolfe asks, "Where are you going?"

"To get a knife." His brows furrow, and I explain. "You brought Finn here so I could hurt him like he hurt me, right?"

His lips twitch. "No, LaReaux. Finn isn't the person who drugged you last night. But my promise stands."

I lower back into my seat. "Okay. Then what's going on?"

"Last night when I noticed you weren't acting like yourself, I tried to keep you from walking off with a bunch of idiots, and I took you into a room where you'd be safe, but the drugs were already taking effect and the only way to get you through it was to..." Finn's voice trails off.

"To what? God, will somebody just grow some balls and tell me what I did!"

Finn looks at Wolfe. "She's gonna hate me for this."

"Probably. But she'll hate me more."

"I hate you both equally because you're stalling. Now spit it out."

"Fine. We were trying to ease you into this. Last night you were drugged with a very potent drug combination that lowers your inhibitions like molly and blacks you out afterwards like HGB. You were high, and horny and determined to act on those feelings. Finn stepped in to keep you from fucking a pair of asshats."

I work through what he just said. "I had sex. With Finn?"

"And Pax."

My stomach lurches. "No. No, I didn't. I'd remember having sex. I don't..." I check in on my how I'm really feeling. The aches in my thighs, the heaviness between my legs. I am a little sore, but I figured that was part of my hangover.

"Tell me this is a sick joke." Looking to Wolfe, I say, "Please tell me this is a prank The Trium is making you to play on me."

"I would never joke about something like this, and I certainly wouldn't do anything The Trium said. You had sex with Pax and Finn last night."

"Is this what they told you? Wolfe, you can't believe anything they say. They lie. They cheat. They steal and they live to make me miserable. They somehow figured this would make me miserable, but jokes on them. I would never-"

He leans down to get in my face. "Look at me, LaReaux. It's not a joke. This happened, and I know it's true because I was there. Watching them do it." Before I can say anything else, he adds. "I was there, coaching them through it."

My blood freezes in my veins. "You watched them violate me?"

"I watched them please you, and then when you told me you needed more, when you begged me to fuck you, I gorged myself on your cunt. I devoured you until you couldn't take one more ounce of pleasure." He leans forward and whispers. "Then you did that thing I love. You know what thing I'm talking about, don't you?"

I do. He means that thing I've only ever done for him. "Then what?"

"Then I made sure both you and LJ got to your rooms safely. I went back to my apartment and video called you to make sure you were drinking water. I talked to you while you got ready for bed, and when you told me, you couldn't sleep. That you were still wired, and pissed because you wanted my cock, I pulled it out and jerked off to the sight of you dipping your fingers into your cunt."

My mouth parts, a small gasp floating from my lips. "Why would you let them fuck me?"

"That's the same question you asked me last night. And my answer is the same. It was the safest option, considering where we were."

"Safer for you, Coach?" My question drips with sarcasm.

"Safer for you, LaReaux. You have enough to deal with already. The last thing you needed was someone walking in on you riding my cock, and the trouble that would cause for you here at school. Your education is important to you. I won't do anything to jeopardize that or your reputation."

"What about the rumor if someone would have seen me fucking two Trium? What about my reputation, then?"

Finn answers, "We already have that reputation on lock. We've shared plenty of women. Nobody would have batted an eye at us together."

Looking back at Wolfe, I say, "You should've just done it yourself, because if they were in the room, they're gonna use it against me, anyway."

Finn shake this head. "Thea, if I wanted to use your relationship with Coach Wolfe against you, Holden and I would have said something last week."

We both turn to look at Finn. "What do you mean last week?"

"I mean, the night we found you traipsing in the woods. After you punched Pax and ran off, we followed you, and saw how much of a teacher's pet you are."

"What do you want?" I stiffen my spine, waiting for him to tell me what hoops I have to jump through to keep him quiet. I'm not worried about my reputation. I own my shit, but I won't drag Wolfe down with me.

"Pet, I don't want anything." He quickly amends. "Okay, so that's not true. I want something, but I'm not going to use this as a way to get it. What I want, I want you giving freely and willingly."

"So you don't want me to do anything in return for keeping quiet about what you saw? Why? Why wouldn't you take this chance to get something out of it?"

Wolfe speaks up. "It's because you're a legacy and the perception is they don't do anything to cause a scandal. Telling anyone would go against that mandate."

"Is that true? Are you keeping quiet because you think it's going to force me to be a *legacy*?" Could I do it? Accept that stupid title and conform to keep this a secret? I'd have to talk to Wolfe and see just how bad the damage would be if it came out.

"This has nothing to do with being a legacy. I don't want to force you to accept that title. I want you to embrace it on your own, because it's who you are. I'm not going to say anything, because I want us to be friends, and I don't hurt my friends." Looking to Wolfe, he says, "I don't let other people hurt my friends either, so if you're just fucking with her because she's a hot young piece of ass..."

"What I'm doing is none of your fucking business."

I see this about to turn into a pissing match, so I say, "Wolfe and I are on the same page about it being none of your business, and all you need to know, is he's my trainer at his gym, and he's my friend." I pause, letting that sink in, before saying, "I think you're familiar with how far I'll go when someone hurts my friends."

With a curt nod, some of the tension oozes from Finn's body.

Wolfe says, "You're taking this calmer than I thought you would, LaReaux."

"I'm the opposite of calm, but this is just one more incident I don't remember, so I'm putting it in the box with the other one."

Finn's face morphs as he and Wolfe share a look. "What now?"

Finn's blade makes an appearance when he says, "I think it's suddenly occurred to us both that your inability to remember what happened that night might be more than a trauma response."

I catch on quick. "You think it's because I had these same drugs in my system? Wouldn't it have shown up on a toxicology report?"

"No. The way this cocktail synthesizes it would have burned through your system without a trace by the time you got to the hospital. That's why it's so popular around here."

"You're suggesting whoever was there wanted to make sure I wouldn't remember?" My eyes drift to Finn. This could be his buddy's doing. "I wonder who'd be smart enough to plan that detail out. Maybe someone who drugged me during a chastity vow ceremony?"

Finn's already shaking his head. "It wasn't Holden."

"You-"

"Yes, he gave you a beta blocker, but trust me, he did you a favor. And you remember everything about that night, right? When it comes to things like this cocktail, he has his own issues with being drugged and losing control of his body. He wouldn't do that to you."

I'm not alone. I reach under my pillow, grabbing for my steak knife. I'm in bed, but I'm wide awake. Hearing Finn and Wolfe recount what happened was painful, especially since I don't remember any of it.

I hate to think I was so out of it I would have fucked a stranger. I mean, sure, I've done it plenty of times, but I've always been cognizant of it. The choice has been mine. Being under the influence of whatever drugs I was given, takes my choice away, so in that regard, I'm glad Deacon was there to supervise Finn and the head Coxsucker while they helped get me over the worst of it. I hate them, but if anybody had to see me vulnerable like that, who better than the devil, you know, right?

The figure in my room walks over to my bed and stands there. Just staring at me. He doesn't say anything, but I feel the anger vibrating off of him. I turn over in bed, letting his herbal scent waft over me, but maintain my grip on my knife.

He was unaccounted for at the party, and he's already admitted to chasing me through the forest like I'm some helpless little bunny. I don't care what Finn says. Holden's at the top of another suspect list.

"What are you doing in my room, Holden?"

"I heard what happened, so I came to check on you."

"You heard? Or you're responsible?"

His gaze drops drown to my knife, his jaw ticking. "I heard."

"Why should I believe you, after you've chased me through the woods and already admitted to wanting me incapacitated, so you can do whatever you want to me?"

He ignores my question, pulls the covers off of me and pushes me onto my side. "What are you doing?" I try to push back over, but he flips me onto my stomach and holds me down with his elbow on my back.

I'm not scared, he's not hurting me, I'm just confused as to why he's here and how he got into my room. Then I remember the last time he came in here with Finn through my balcony. He pushes my t-shirt up, running his hand over my shoulder in the spot where Wolfe says there's an injection sight.

When he backs away, I scramble to sit up in bed, my back against the headboard, watching as he paces back and forth. Once again, I'm reminded that as unpredictable as Finn is, it's Holden that holds back the most. He's the deadliest. The real loose cannon. I study him, trying to figure out what's going on in his head.

"Why are you here?"

"Nobody's allowed to drug a legacy. They keep breaking the rules."

The legacy rules. Right. "I'm not a legacy, so your rules don't apply."

"Just because you say you're not doesn't change the fact that you are, and it doesn't give anyone the right to pretend otherwise."

Following his logic, I say "You're suggesting my refusal to accept this legacy title is the reason I got drugged?"

"Yes."

"Doesn't the almighty Trium's words trump everything else? So in that regard, you saying I'm a legacy should be enough to make sure these things don't happen."

"Usually, but not in this case. There are some other legacies that are providing contradictory information to what we're putting out."

I snort and roll my eyes. "You mean Finn's boo thang and her glitter posse?"

"Their parents too. It's unheard of for a legacy bloodline to become defunct without the family actually dying off, and with the mystery surrounding your birth still under investigation, they are well within their rights to voice concern and disbelief."

Smoothing my blanket across my legs, I say, "I'm with them. I disbelieve."

"That's why it's in the hands of the validation committee, but Finn, Pax and I are here to help you adjust. Why don't you want to be a legacy?"

"Seriously? Do you not think about the shit ya'll say and do around here? Have you seen Eloise and her crew? I'm nothing like that. I would never want to be anything like that."

"The title doesn't make you an annoying bitch."

"I have friends. I have a life. I'm not turning my back on that because of some title."

"You mean Layla-Jean?"

"And Austin, and the things I like to do, which don't include fancy brunches and manicures every Tuesday."

"You don't do those things anymore."

My brows furrow in confusion. "What?"

"Hiking. Why don't you do that anymore? You haven't been to the oasis in the woods."

I pinch the bridge of my nose. "How do you know about that?"

"I saw you."

"Don't you mean spied on me? When was this? Back when you were digging up shit to implode my life?"

He shrugs like it's no big deal. "You were with Pax and Finn. Are you okay?"

"Huh?" I'm not following the topic shift, because I'm stuck on him spying on me and wondering how long and how much he saw.

"Last night, when you were on the poisoned shot. You let them fuck you. I thought you hated us."

"I do."

"So you're upset? Is that why you're still awake? Because you think one of them will come in and touch you again?"

His jaw ticks, his hands clenched at his side. Wait, is he mad? At them? This is hilarious, and I'd love to see him go after his friends, but I'm not a manipulative bitch. "What? No. I... I don't remember all the details yet, but I believe Coach Wolfe when he said they didn't hurt me. Finn and Pax helped me."

"Coach made you comply."

"He did."

"You didn't want it?"

"No. I don't think so. Not at first."

"Eventually?"

I inspect my knife, and shrug.. "Maybe a little. Wolfe says I had a good time. I had to have wanted a part of it in order for that to happen."

"But not me. You asked Coach to finish you, and didn't ask them to call me."

My eyebrows pop to the top of my forehead. Am I getting this right? Am I actually hearing this correctly? I'm tripping. It's the drugs. It *has* to be the drugs, because there's no way he's saying what I think he's saying.

"Uh, Holden, are you here because you're jealous, and not because you're concerned that someone's drugging legacies or because your friends took advantage of me?"

He thinks about the answer. I know nothing about this guy, but I get the impression that dealing with women is new to him. So, I just let him work it out for himself. It doesn't take long. "Yes. I'm jealous and *mad*. I want to choke you out for putting yourself in danger."

Shit, wasn't expecting that much truth and self reflection. He sounds like Wolfe. "How the fuck are you mad at me? I didn't *know* I put myself in danger. I was drugged."

"That's why I take my own food to the cafeteria, and don't take drinks from people at parties."

"Didn't you just see the scab from the pin prick? Didn't you just finish telling me I'm a target because of that shit ya'll pulled before Mayhem Night and that it's gonna keep happening until I say the magic words?"

He looks towards the window and grumbles, "I don't let people touch me."

"Usually, I don't either."

"I'm going to touch your throat now, Thea." He says, changing topics again.

The way his brain shifts around is fascinating. To the average person, it may seem like he's just going off on a tangent, but I'm beginning to understand that this is actually a linear conversation. "Why?"

"Because you didn't see a doctor and I want to be helpful, too."

My heart stutters as he comes back over to the bed. His hand darts out, closing around my neck, then squeezes. Just a little pressure as he hovers over me. Looking up at him, I say, "I'm okay, Holden."

He looks down at his watch, and I wait for him to finish taking my pulse. Counting my heartbeats. My breath. When he's satisfied that I'm not actually freaking out about anything that happened last night, or on the verge of a medical emergency, he says, "Go to sleep. I'll keep a lookout for you for the rest of the night."

He sits with his back against my bedroom door, like a sentry. Rather than argue, and fight to get him out of my room, I slip back down in bed, and close my eyes even though I know there's no way I'll be able to sleep.

Holden is gone when I wake up in the morning. The bottle of water on my nightstand is the only evidence that I didn't hallucinate his visit.

Chapter 50
Holden

Finn huffs again as he paces around the bunker. He's been doing that since he got here. I'm trying to ignore him, but the constant movement and sound is distracting. "Why are you so restless?"

"Why are we here? Everyone's gone. There are no challenges to do. So what gives?"

"What gives is I need to run a software update, and you need to do inventory on the stuff we have."

He huffs again. "You already know everything we have. Nobody broke in and stole it. The security system would have alerted us if they did."

"The way it alerted us to what Thea was doing in our rooms?"

He stops pacing and smiles. "Good point." Walking to the other side of the room to get the clipboard, he says, "Why are we doing this now?"

"To get it out of the way so we can enjoy our break with no distractions. The longer we put it off, the less we'll want to stop whatever fun we're having and come here and do it."

"Another good point. I just have one more question. Why isn't Pax here too?"

"Did you want to be the one to stay on campus and deal with Eloise?"

"Holden, my man, you are a genius."

We work in silence for about an hour. Then I ask the question that's been swirling around in my brain for days now. "Were you serious about Thea?"

"I'm always serious about Thea, but be more specific."

"When you said she belongs to both of us."

I'm glad he takes his time answering. That means he's really thinking about how to respond instead of just going on emotions. "I was serious. I like Thea. I want her, but I can tell you like her too, and I think she'd fit right in with us. Pax too, if he stops being all confrontational and broody long enough to realize what a gift she is."

"The night they were drugged, how was he with her?"

"Totally wrapped up in it. He's acting like it was a chore, but I know he had a good time, man. None of that just stick it in their ass stuff, either."

My head jerks around. "What?"

"He was in her sweet, sweet pussy and was In. To. It. She took every inch, man."

My pulse stutters. A feeling of hope blossoms in my chest. Pax is a big guy, so if she took all of him, maybe she can... I shut that thought down. She might have, but I don't know what her experience was. It may have hurt her too badly. "How was she after?"

"I don't know. She was still out of it with the poisoned shot, but she didn't cry and do all that other shit girls did when Pax was inside them. Of course, that could be because I was working her mouth."

"And she didn't freak out about you both being with her at the same time?"

"Not a peep, other than how much she didn't want us because she hates us. She didn't even care that Coach Wolfe was there, or that we watched him go down on her when it was over."

That makes sense with what I know about her. She wouldn't be shy about having her body exposed. You can't be shy and fuck your hand in the middle of the forest where someone may walk up and see you.

I miss watching her do that. I miss watching her period. I might need to escalate my plans. She's slowly coming back around, but I'm getting impatient. I'm not sure how much longer I can keep my urges at bay.

We go back to working in silence and by the time Finn finishes with the inventory list, I'm on my last software upgrade. I can follow its progress remotely, so we exit the bunker and go to our cars to head back to campus.

This time away from campus was relaxing, and our conversation was enlightening. I feel good. I'll need to hang on to my zen feelings to get me through tonight.

Chapter 51
Pax

I'm at lunch, alone for one of the first times ever. Alone, meaning my brothers aren't here. Eloise and everyone else are. The semester is almost over and I'm looking forward to having some peace and quiet.

Eloise whips her head back and forth, scanning the nearly empty dining hall like she's looking for something. I know who it is. But I keep my mouth shut. I know better than to start a conversation with her. She'll never shut up.

My hopes that I'll get through this meal in silence are dashed the moment she asks, "Where's Finn?"

"When did I become his secretary?"

Someone down the table says, "I saw him driving off campus on my way here."

Everyone watches our moves too damn closely. It's a wonder we can even shit without the entire school gossiping about it. Somebody mutters, "Now there's someone who needs to take a long drive. Right, Eloise?"

She glances over at me, but doesn't respond. It's a very delicate situation to navigate. Openly trash talking a legacy. The wrong person hears it and reports back to The League, then your affiliation comes into question.

We don't pretend to like everyone, but we don't broadcast it. Thea walks over to her usual table. I finish my meal and then go over to her. "Finn told you why you need to eat with us. No more hanging out on your own like you're unaligned."

"And I told Finn to get fucked. Are you Finn's spokesperson today? Because you can get fucked too."

"I already did."

Her mouth pops open. I know Finn and Coach Wolfe told her what happened. I guess she didn't think I'd mention it. Since I had a smaller dose, I remember it all. "And since I have, I can say with certainty it'll never happen again."

"That life altering, huh? Afraid you'll become addicted to me?"

"It was that boring and forgettable. I wouldn't waste the erection on you when my hand shows me a better time. You might convince inexperienced boys that you're a good lay, but I've fucked lots of women and you're the worst I ever had. If I hadn't of been dosed, I wouldn't even have nutted."

"Finn had a good time, and he was sober. Both times."

"Did he? Then why was it so easy to dismiss you when he found out the truth about you? Finn doesn't let anything get in the way of a good fuck." I twist my lips, mocking her further. "I guess that's why he's not here now. He's avoiding the girl he pity fucked."

I dig one more nail under her skin. "You'd think fucking someone as old as Deacon Wolfe would have taught you how to please a man. But I guess it's just young pussy and the thrill of it that he's chasing after."

Eloise walks up in time to hear her say, "That speech is the opposite of convincing me to sit over there with your cult."

"Oh, make no mistake, whore. Pax doesn't want you over there. None of us do, but it's expected. Now feel free to skip every meal here and we won't need to have this conversation again. Or better yet, leave school like we told you months ago and sit wherever you want in a new location."

Thea purses her lips in thought. "You would like that, right? Me away from this school and Finn?" She shakes her head. "I think I'll stay a little longer. Things are just getting fun.."

Her bravado waivers when someone yells and a tray drops behind her. Eloise laughs. "Awe, is the little baby afraid of the big bad sound? You're so weak and pathetic. Did you learn anything at all in Coach Wolfe's Physical Enhancement Class?" She laughs. "What am I saying? Of course you didn't. Not even how to keep your balance or dig a hole. That's why you had to visit the infirmary after you fell into a coffin and couldn't dig your way out on Mayhem Night, isn't it?"

I stiffen. I give Thea shit. I can't stand her. But the idea of someone else taking shots like this pisses me off. I know why I'm antagonizing her. It's to get her to act in her own best interest because being reasonable isn't part of her personality. She won't do shit we want her to do, so I have to reverse psychology her ass into it.

Eloise is saying this shit just to tear her down. Turning to Eloise, I say, "Did I ask you to come over here and give your input? You're sitting with us is a privilege, based on your relationship to Finn, not because you've earned the right."

"I have more rights than she does."

Glaring at her I say, "When it's time for the Zeta Nu's to send out the invites for Thea to pledge, next semester, then you get to haze her. Until then, go back to the table. Stay in your seat and stay out of Trium business, or we'll send you back to where you were sitting before."

As I'm watching Eloise walk away, Thea gets up from her seat. "Where are you going?"

"Gonna finish my food someplace where there's less bullshit and bravado in the air."

I hate that she's walking away, but I'm not about to run after or call out to her and cause a scene. I keep my mask in place so nobody knows how livid I am. How did I get stuck on campus with the problem children?

When I exit The Rock after my meal, I walk through The Circle to get to my car. I pass Thea on a picnic bench stretched out on top of it, staring up at the sky. Her fingers tap against her right leg, but other than that, she looks completely relaxed and calm. I resist the urge to walk over and continue our conversation.

I have a Wren meeting, and I don't need to be in a worse mood than I'm already in, when I get there.

Chapter 52
Pax

I'm on the way back to Vale Tower after my last exam. Finn sent a text saying he intercepted another package from The Prides and Lady Lions. They're really going overboard trying to woo Thea. She seems receptive to them too, which only creates more chaos and drama every time we intervene. There's no way we can let a legacy princess, no matter how low and annoying, join a rival sorority.

Nothing says ineffectual rule as much as that happening on our watch. I come from a long line of Triums. There's no way in hell I'm letting the history and reputation my family has built around here go to shit behind this trouble maker. I rub the pin clipped to the underside of my shirt at the collar. It's the symbol of my family's legacy, a show of our power.

My grandfather has been a member of the high council for over thirty years, having taken over the position from his father. He's ruthless, has a dry sense of humor and doesn't suffer fools.

His relationship with my father is strained. There's always been tension there, but it's been getting worse over the years. They keep up appearances at events, and around other people, but in private, my dad is barely civil.

I thought it was the usual tension that comes from the new, thinking it's time to get rid of the old. It's the same dynamic I expect to have with my father when it's time for me to take over. Sometimes it's uncomfortable to be around them, but even as hard as Malcolm Senior is on his son, he was always kind to me.

That is, until I started the process of joining The League. He's never been overly affection, but at least I don't feel like I'm walking on eggshells around him either.

It might be because I haven't given him a reason to direct his hostility towards me, but I'm not in the mood to test that theory. Which is why I know I fucked up this afternoon. I shouldn't have been antagonizing the troublemaker. She just makes it so damn hard to be cordial to her. Why can't she just accept this change and be grateful like anyone else would?

I know Finn thinks she's the one who broke in and bronzed his knife, and I guess he could be right. But there's no way she's the one who was stealing my bike or breaking into Holden's room and messing with his computers.

One of his security cameras would have definitely alerted him to the intrusion, and the cameras never even flickered. So unless she can teleport, she's not the person who messed with our stuff.

And if she is, that just proves that winning her over is an impossible task. Hell, shouldn't she be more compliant since Finn and I helped her at the party? I was trying to get a rise out of her. I had no business saying Finn didn't enjoy it, because I know he did. I just didn't want her to get a big head about it.

Thea's in the gym, swinging on the punching bag again, ignoring the limitation of her wrist and shoulder. I'm a little impressed as I watch her. I know grown men who would wimp out from the pain, but she just grits her teeth and keeps punching.

I stand in the doorway and watch her form. She's good. Despite what Eloise said, I know for a fact that Thea's better than most of the girls I've seen take Coach Wolfe's class, but she's nowhere near ready to take me on. She freezes up whenever anyone moves too fast, or like today with unexpected loud noises. Plus, she's skipped out on the last few weeks of Wolfe's class. If she were healed, I'd be happy to knock her down a few pegs, literally.

"Are you just gonna stand there staring at my ass or do you plan to do something about that beer belly you spend every weekend working on?"

I wasn't even looking at her ass, but now that she's brought it up, I do and say, "It needs some squat work."

I pull my shirt over my head with one hand, watching her in the mirror as I go through my warm up. She doesn't say anything else, and barely acknowledges me as she settles into her routine. I like that she's focused and not chatty when we work out. It lets me concentrate on what I'm doing.

An hour later, I'm moving to my cool down and she's in the ring still working on combos. Her feet trip up on the third one. I recognize the pattern and offer a suggestion. "You're shuffling too soon. Plant your back foot, pivot, then shuffle."

"Who the hell asked you?"

"You look like a newborn giraffe stumbling on your feet. If you don't set your balance correctly, you're gonna fall flat on your face."

I climb into the ring and move to reset her feet. Her fist darts out, but I duck out of the way. "I'm trying to help your crazy ass."

"I didn't ask for your help."

"And I'm not in the mood to call in a clean-up crew when you split your face open. You just recovered from a bunch of bruises. Do you want to go back to having to wear all that cover up shit again?"

"Didn't you hear? I'm a *legacy*. Extra caked on face paint is part of the uniform."

"They need that shit, you don't."

She goes back to what she was doing and when she gets to that third combo; I strike out, sending her off balance and catch her by the back of her sports bra before she collides with the floor. When she regains her footing, she swings. "What the hell is wrong with you?"

"Nothing. I told you if you didn't plant your feet correctly, you'd hit the floor."

"You pushed me, you ass."

"Do you think if you were in a real fight, they'd play fair? That they'd say 'oh, she doesn't have her feet planted correctly. Let me wait', or do you think they're going to take advantage of you being off balance? And before you answer, did the people who attacked you wait and be fair?"

"The more you talk, the more you convince me that you're one of those attackers."

"If I were, I'd own up to it. If I wanted to kick your ass, I'd do it in broad daylight with everyone watching."

"Is that a confession that you beat women?"

"What it is, is me telling you again that I'll give you a chance to go toe-to-toe with me just as soon as you're healed."

She stands taller and puts on a brave face. "I'm ready now."

I climb out of the ring, shaking my head, and grab my stuff off the floor. "No, Nemesis, you're not. As long as you're out here reacting to Eloise's snipes at you, and swinging at windmills, you'll never be ready for me."

I can't believe I'm here. Shit, I can't believe I let the lead Coxsucker get in my head enough that I even considered coming here. He accused me of attacking imaginary enemies. I want to disagree on principle, but he's basically said the same thing Wolfe has been telling me. I need to get my head on straight and figure out who I need to be fighting.

I can't do that if I'm mad at everyone. So I came to the house of horrors to hear their side of the story. I probably should have come sooner, but I haven't been ready to see them, or hear anything they've had to say. I even convinced myself that I was okay, not knowing. That I didn't care why they gave me away.

I've spent years perfecting this aura of I don't care, and for most things I don't. But on this. I care. I care just as much as I care about why my mother disappeared on me.

I might not tell people, but there has always been the tiniest voice inside my head saying I wasn't good enough. I wasn't good enough for my mom to stay sober, or for the foster homes to keep me, or the group homes to protect me, or even for the friends I used to try to make, to accept me. Yesterday, Eloise and Pax both poked at that scab.

I know they're all lies, because I *know* I'm good enough, but sometimes the lies and self doubt scream louder than the truth. So when I found that birth certificate, all the years of building myself up, all the work I did to be okay about being on my own, came undone, just for a little while.

Then I was attacked, and it's like I can't climb out. Like I'm buried in the doubts. But I have to crawl out. I have to be done.

I find Moira in the living room, reading a book. "I'm ready to listen now." I hold up my hand to warn her, "If you say one crappy thing about my mom, I'm out. Got it?"

"Thea, I loved my sister. I looked up to her and I'm grateful to her for keeping you safe for as long as she could. I know I haven't expressed that or given you any reason to think I care about her, but it wasn't Hailee that I was mad at. All that anger was actually at myself, for not finding you sooner, and keeping you from going into the system. I was mad at myself for being weak. Too weak to fight my father. To step out of line and bring attention to myself with The League."

That's the part I don't understand. How this billionaire boy's club wields so much power and why everyone seems so afraid of them. That's the part of the story I need to hear before I can even consider calling myself a legacy anything. "Start at the beginning."

"I've already mentioned that Hailee was my half sister."

I nod. That's the part I know.

"But I'm five years younger than she is."

"Did your father have an affair with your mother?"

"Surprisingly, no. Hailee's mom and my dad divorced when she was around three, and they split custody. He met my mother on a business trip. She worked for a subsidiary of one of his companies and fell for him. A little more than a year into their relationship, I came along. I didn't know anything about Canyon Falls or the way he and Hailee lived. He was always just my dad, who lived away and traveled for work. He called me all the time, and when he came to visit, he called me Princess and treated me like I was a princess. When I turned eight, his visits to us slowed down because I was old enough to come to him."

"Is that when you met my mom?"

"Oh, no." She shakes her head, a small smile on her lips. "Hailee was in my life from the beginning. I had pictures of her, she came to my parties, and we had sleep overs. Of course I annoyed her because I wanted to be just like her. I thought she was so cool."

She sips her coffee. "When my mom got sick, she told me that I would be coming to live here permanently. I didn't want to. Not one bit. I refused to leave her, so I got to stay in Savannah until she passed away. I was miserable after she died, but Hailee was there for me. She took care of me. God knows my dad didn't know what to do for a grieving pre-teen girl."

"What happened when you moved here?"

"I was thrust into this life with rules and expectations I wasn't used to. I started going to these fancy parties, and meeting dad's friends. I thought it was so glamorous. But Hailee didn't like it. She went from being this happy person to being quiet and reserved. She was nothing like the sister that came to see me or went on vacations with me. She used to pick fights with dad to let me stay home with the nanny. I thought I was embarrassing her since I didn't grow up in this fancy world, but then I turned twelve."

"What happened?"

"There was this boy at one of the parties. He smiled at me and I smiled back. It was the first time anyone had seemed to take an interest in me. The person they all still called the new girl. He asked me if I wanted to hang out with him. Of course I said yes, and I started following him to the pool house where I knew the other kids were hanging out. The next thing I know, Hailee's there dragging me away and saying this was not happening to me. I had no idea what she was rambling on about. Later, she explained that the guy was fifteen and from a legacy family. Then explained that his dad told him to talk to me, so they could get my dad's attention. That's the night she told me how the people in this town would try to use me as a pawn and explained about The League of the Daggered Ravens. Of course I thought she was nuts. A secret society, like on television? It was just too farfetched to believe. But I started paying attention and noticing things, like all the girls in my classes that had boyfriends shared a common theme. Their parents did business together. It was cute when they first hooked up in junior high. I went to an all girl's school so everyone thought having a boyfriend was so cool."

She gives me a rueful smile. "But I didn't have one back then. Hailee scared them all off."

"Did that change in high school?"

"No, and when I confronted her, she had tears in her eyes and admitted she had been meddling. When I told her to stay out of my life, she told me that would never happen, and that she'd always do whatever she needed to, to protect me, even if I didn't like it. I was *so* angry. I was so mean. She was already at CaFa U and living on campus, so I didn't see her as much and froze her out for months. Then one day I heard her and my father talking about the deal she made with him to hold off on arranging any relationships for me so that I could stay a kid for a little while longer, and in return she'd do whatever he wanted."

"Lemme guess, in return, he had a specific marriage planned for her, didn't he?"

"Yes." Her lips pull taut. "To a horrible person. Even I knew what a sociopath he was, and he'd never be faithful to her. But he was already a Wren and his family was hirer up in The League."

"Did she go through with it?"

Shaking her head, she says, "The guy, her *intended,* wanted to wait until after graduation. We thought that was perfect. It brought Hailee some time. And then..."

Whatever she's thinking isn't good. I definitely didn't get my poker face from her. "Then what?"

"Then I heard someone talking in the bathroom during one of the Ladies' Guild garden parties. They said he wasn't really waiting for Hailee to graduate. It was the lie he'd told his parents to get them to agree to stall the marriage, because he liked them a little younger. Then they said my name."

My stomach clenches when she looks at me.

"Thea, it took everything in me not to barge out there and ask them what the hell they were talking about. I had to force myself to be still and listen to it all. I waited until they left and then went to find my dad."

Her voice turns sad. A bitter hint to it. "Turns out he already knew about the rumors. The husbands were joking about it too."

"But he wasn't gonna go along with it, right? I mean, aren't these things usually contract based like in the movies?"

"Yes, but I don't know how The League decides things. I've seen enough situations over the years where people start off intended for one person and end up with another. Mentioning what I heard got me grounded for eavesdropping. My father craved power, just like everyone else. He was still a lower ranked member, and I had no way of knowing what he'd allow. I just knew that I wasn't gonna be someone's pawn. Not after watching what Hailee was going through."

"What did you do?"

"I acted out. Went out. *Stayed out* too late. I drank too much, drove too fast. Sometimes the cars weren't mine, and I got caught kissing boys."

I feel myself smile. That sounds like something I would have done.

"I was raising hell and successfully pissing my dad off, but Hailee was getting worried. So, being a good big sister, she convinced our father to let me go away for the summer. She said it would give me a chance to clear my head. He agreed, and the week after I graduated high school, I hopped a plane to Greece."

Going to Greece sounds amazing. Maybe I should go instead of sticking around here for my own version of league drama. "Did that calm you down?"

Her smile covers her entire face. "It was life changing. It's where I met your father."

"What?"

"He was making his way through the European and Mediterranean country sides. He had his own family issues to work through. We met on a tour and figured out we were from the same town. We've been inseparable ever since."

"Love at first sight, huh?"

"There was a connection, yes. But I was still feeling foolish and reckless. He sensed that and made me wait. I had a lot of growing up to do. It was the longest year of my life."

"A year? He resisted you for a year?"

"I was still only seventeen. He was nineteen, so he only offered me friendship. But I took it and clung to it. Scott was my safety net."

"What happened when you got home?"

"Hailee had somehow gotten my father to get a firm signature on her marriage contract. She was gonna marry the guy, but dad was still searching for someone else for me. He was determined to get two powerful alliances out of the deal. I had a lot of eyes on me, but Hailee helped me sneak off to see Scott whenever I could, as long as I promised to be careful."

I already see where this is heading. "You weren't careful."

"Dad found me a match and there was no way out of it. I ran to Scott, determined to do one last thing *for me.* We made love. You were conceived, and there was never any question in my mind that I was having my baby. There was also no way I'd be able to hide my pregnancy for long, so I told Hailee, and she donned her big sister cape again and assured me she'd handle it; just like she handled everything else. The next thing I know, she's telling people she's pregnant. Dad was furious. Her announcement made him look like a fool, especially when she refused to name the father. "

"Was she?" A small part of me wants there to be hope that this is all a crazy nightmare and I'm gonna wake up and find out nothing since the moment I found that birth certificate really happened. But hope's a sadistic bitch.

"Hailee lied to help me hide my pregnancy. Then somehow she once again convinced dad to do something to save face. He sent her away in shame and I went with her so she'd have a support system."

She smiles. "Scott joined us and he and I had four months where we didn't have to hide our relationship. But we still weren't free. Dad was looking to salvage his marriage deal with that family and decided I would be the substitute. Hailee knew it. I knew it. It was a no-win situation. We'd already said you were hers. I couldn't say she lied. It would've made things worse for the both of us. So we planned to run.

Her first with you. Then Scott and I were going to follow. Van was a godsend. She helped us make all the arrangements." Her lips turn down. "I hated letting you go, but there was no way I could subject you to this life. There was no way I'd make my sister stay here and live a life with someone she didn't want, when she'd been protecting me the whole time. You were the way we were all going to escape and have the lives we chose for ourselves."

"If all of you were leaving, how did I wind up growing up thinking my mom was my mom?"

"All of us leaving at once would have been suspicious. I was supposed to come back to Canyon Falls and say you didn't make it, and that Hailee took off in the middle of the night. We had a death certificate saying the baby, a boy, was stillborn. Our plan was foolproof. We had pre-planned meet up locations, dates and times and backups. Hailee was supposed to keep moving until we could eventually join her. Dad all but ignored me because he was too busy trying to save his reputation. Hailee had disgraced the Laurent name, and that made me tainted goods, by league standards, so my marriage deal was called off too."

"Are you still in this secret society that everybody and their doctor knows about?"

With a shake of her hair, she says, "We're not active members, we were never asked to join, but we live in town and smile and play the game. We live by their rules, with none of the perks. It's my penance for Hailee."

"Does your father know the truth about me?" I can't call him my grandfather. I don't know that man, and nothing I've heard makes me want to get to know him.

"He does, now. It was stupid of me to think I could continue to lie about you being related to Scott's cousin. The minute we brought you here, it was only a matter of time before The League uncovered the truth."

"And now they want me to be one of their legacy brats?"

"Yes."

"What happens if I say no? If I keep saying no?"

"Thea, I know you like your autonomy and making decisions for yourself, but on this, there is no telling them no. You were born into this bloodline, and I don't have any leverage, or anyway to hide you again, since the truth is out there. I can only hope that whatever role they want you to play isn't too bad."

I snap my fingers and say, "Now we're getting to the conflict in the story. I'm not playing any *roles*. I'm here for school -and I'll be honest- every day I wake up I'm ready to say *fuck this school*. So there won't be any roles or assignments that I'll be accepting around here. This is all just the free trial period, and I'm ready to cancel my subscription."

"I wish it were that simple, Thea. God, how I wish you could just say no, and tell them all to go fuck themselves. But this town, The League of the Daggered Ravens, once they get their hands on you..."

"They'd have to catch me first, and if they did, it would *only* be because I let them."

With a sad smile, she says, "That's entirely your choice, and if you decide to leave, we'll help you get settled somewhere new, but I hope you'll stick around."

Narrowing my eyes, trying to see through the bullshit, I say, "You don't want to fight me about this?"

"Of course I do, but I have the feeling pushing back will only make you more determined to go. It would make *me* more determined to go. When you make your choice, I want it to be rational, not based on your desire to tell me to kiss your ass."

My lips twitch. "Fair enough." I take in the room and the paintings on the wall. "So what do you do for the not so secret society?"

"Pretty much the same thing I do at my day job. I use my design and marketing skills to create content, like flyers and mementos for their parties."

"You said your father was all about status. Do you think he'll want to marry me off to someone?"

"I love my father. It took a long time for us to rebuild our relation-ship after I married Scott, and we're on shaky ground now, because I lied to him for all these years, so we haven't really talked about what it means for The League to acknowledge you as a part of his bloodline. I just hope he's learned his lesson about how far people will go, how far *I* will go to keep you from the same fate Hailee and I faced. But a part of me worries that if he decides it's an avenue worth pursuing -to regain the footing he lost- then, *yes*, he would definitely try to match you with someone."

"Even though I'm not his daughter?"

"You're still a Laurent. So you fall under his authority with the council. As the oldest male of our bloodline, he'd have that responsibility over you."

I grimace at the words, *authority*. "Not Scott?" He and I have a prickly relationship, but I'm pretty sure he wouldn't be trying to pimp me out. He keeps telling me to *stay away* from boys.

"Males married into a bloodline have no power outside of what The League gives them, because women don't hold leadership positions. I know you don't want to hear this, Thea, and I'm gonna sound like a hypocrite saying it, but the best way to keep The League of the Daggered Ravens from looking too closely at you is to blend in. Keep your head down. Go to class. Don't do anything that gets you noticed."

Too late for these warnings. I bat my eyes and give a demure smile. "I'm all about existing in obscurity. I'm already declining invites to their parties."

She laughs and says, "I'll make a list of the ones you should attend."

My smile drops. "Maybe you didn't hear me. I said I've been *ignoring* the invites."

"Oh, I heard you, and I said *don't* do anything to get noticed. Turning down every invite will get you noticed." She picks up her phone and types. "I'll let you know the events Scott and I are attending. That should make it easier."

She invites me to stay for dinner, but I decline, needing some time to sit with what I just learned. I feel a little better after having talked to her. I still don't like being lied to, and I'm even less enthused about this legacy crap, but I have a little better understanding of what a young Moira would have been thinking. I would've made plans to run away from some perverted asshole, too. Of course, my departure would have involved bloodshed.

I go over the conversations I've had with Van, Moira and even the Coxsuckers. Everyone's saying the same thing. There is no way to avoid having to tangle with this league while I'm in their town. I already feel the weight pressing down on me, taking away my ability to breathe.

I pull out my phone and send a text. I need oxygen. I need a life raft.

I'm walking the perimeter of the woods, debating whether to venture into them again. I know I'm not alone. This time, they're not even trying to be subtle about following. "Come on out and face me, instead of stalking through the shadows like a pussy." I don't have Clint, but I'm not out here empty-handed. I pull the butcher knife out of my makeshift hilt.

The Coxsuckers step from behind the building.

Finn eyes the knife. "I can see what you're thinking, and after what happened the last time, I understand your assumption, but it wasn't us on Mayhem Night."

"Right, so you're following me now because..."

Pax snarls, "Because your stupid ass is out here once again, prowling through the woods alone like you're just asking to get attacked again."

"Attacked? I thought you said I went through a little *hazing.*"

"Or maybe you were out in the woods beating up on yourself. I really don't give a shit, but we're responsible for you now, so whatever happened, we're here to make sure it doesn't happen again."

"I don't need you babysitting me."

"Then stop acting like a fucking toddler who's refusing to eat their peas."

"If I'm a toddler, what does that make you?"

Finn steps forward. "Thea, what Pax means, is you have to stop operating like you're unaligned. Until we figure out what happened to you, on Mayhem Night and who drugged you at the last frat party, you shouldn't be walking around alone. There is safety in numbers. You're a legacy, and just because you ignore it, won't make it go away."

"Do you think if you say that word enough times, it'll seep in and I'll automatically start acting like it?"

"Pet, trust me, if I wanted those words to make you do anything, I could. I'd rather give you the choice." He raises my chin. "But don't tempt me."

"Finn..." Holden's voice holds a note of censure.

"It's fine, Holden. I said I *could*, not that I will. I happen to like her the way she is, and plan to use other ways to persuade her to give in. Ways that we've both found enjoyable in the past." Finn leans in. "You remember some of those things, don't you, Pet? Like the way you clawed at my back and dug your heels into my ass, as I rode you on the pool table? Or how many times I made you cum that night. What count did we make it up to?"

"What I remember, Finley, is you turning into a full-blown asshole afterwards."

"You're right. Shall I drop to my knees right now and start my penance? Lick you until you forgive me?" He lowers to the ground. "Come on, Pet. Punish me."

He grabs my hips, pulls me to his face, and bites my inner thigh. I feel the sting through my jeans. "I'm gonna stab you in the back of your neck if you don't let me go. How's that for punishment?"

He moans, then bites the other thigh. "I know you don't mean it, so don't tease me like that."

I'd forgotten who I was talking to. Stabbing turns him on. Holden steps around us, holding a tablet in his hand, and asks, "What do you remember about what happened that night?"

"Why don't you man up and tell me what you and your merry band of attackers did to me that night and save me the headache I'll get trying to remember?"

Instead of deflecting or refusing to answer, he says, "You were in the cemetery, watching the Tao's crossover ceremony. You turned to leave, but weren't as stealthy as you thought you were. They started chasing you, but I caught you first and dragged you deeper into the woods."

None of this sounds familiar. But, it's exactly what he did the last time. "What happened next? These two were waiting for you to bring someone back and I just happened to be the person you grabbed?"

"I gave you the option to run. I told you I'd be chasing you and if you made it to the dorms, I wouldn't punish you for being out on Mayhem Night, or tell anyone I saw you. Where we talked last week is the spot you were in when I let you get away."

"Talked?" I scoff.

The corner of his lip moves, but he doesn't say anything about using that bullshit word. "So you sent me the coordinates to relive it like a psychopath. Did you get your kicks?"

Pax growls, "Will you just shut up and listen!"

I sneer at him. "No, I won't. I'm not one of your mindless blow up dolls, just accepting whatever you say. I'm *not* a legacy." Without looking down at Finn, I say, "If your hand moves one more inch, you're gonna lose some fingers."

Climbing to his feet, he huffs, "Damn, Pax. You had to go and ruin my fun." I think he's going to go stand next to one of his friends, but he doesn't. He yanks me against him and kisses me. I bite down on his lip, drawing blood, which spurs him on. He moans and pushes his tongue into my mouth. My body locks up as the coppery taste hits my tongue. I can't breathe. I'm choking on blood.

"Pet? Thea? Thea!"

Hands grab me, and I swing, catching Pax in the jaw. He grabs me and spins me, pinning me to his chest from behind. "Easy Nemesis."

I twist, trying to break his hold, his arm across me holding me so I can't escape. "You're still not ready to fight me, Nem. Your form still needs some work, but that was a halfway decent hit you got off."

His words break through my panic. "Let me go and I'll show you just how good my form is."

He shoves me away, crossing his arms across his chest, and Finn asks, "What just happened?"

"Nothing."

Pax says, "What happened is you proved my point. You've got no business being out in these woods by yourself. Now go back to the dorms and stop being a nuisance."

"And if I don't?"

"There is no don't. You're going, even if I have to carry you there myself." He steps toward me. "So what's it gonna be?"

I don't want him touching me. Don't want any of them touching me, but I know this isn't an empty threat. They'll do it. "Fuck you."

"Never again. One time on the crazy train was more than enough."

I ignore his attempt to insult me and head back to Vale Tower. I need to come up with another plan. They show up every time I go into the woods. Help my ass. Maybe they're trying to stop me from finding clues and piecing together the details of that night.

Chapter 55
Thea

Campus is abuzz with everyone packing their cars to leave for the holidays. In forty-eight hours, it'll be like a ghost town around here, as the last students finish their final exams and leave for winter break. LJ and I shared a tearful goodbye this afternoon. She had tears. I kept mine on the inside. But it was still hard to watch her drive away.

I stare at the package wrapped with a huge silver bow outside my door. It's not my birthday. It's not either of my birthdays. My newest one and Christmas are still two weeks away, so why is my aunt sending me gifts?

I take it inside, grab a water bottle from the fridge, then sit on the couch to open it. I damn near fall out the chair when I see what's inside. It's *not* from my aunt. There's no card or note, but it can only be from one person and the message is pretty clear.

Shit, shit, shit. I'm not ready to forgive him. Even after he interceded when I was roofied, but this is a *huge* apology. I go from shocked to pissed off. How dare he. I grab the gift and stomp across the hall, banging on the door with the heel of my hand. He opens it and smiles.

"Don't smile at me, you manipulative piece of shit." I hold up the box. "I don't accept your apology gift."

"Oh-kaay."

"That doesn't mean you're getting it back."

"Of course not."

"I'm only keeping it to teach you a lesson."

"As you should. I'm open to any and all lessons, Pet."

"I should use it to cut your heart out, but you don't have one."

"I've heard that. A lot. And I started to believe it. But I have one. It's just walking around on the outside of my body, exposed to the world and I fucked up bad so I can't be there to protect it." His gaze drops to the knives. "I'm hoping they'll do in my absence."

A quick flick of my wrist has one of the blades at his throat, the other at his crotch. The crazy psycho just smiles. "What are you smiling about?"

"I'm glad you like the gifts, Pet."

He backs away, humming to himself like I didn't just tell him this changes nothing about how much I hate him.

I go back to my room and step onto the balcony to get some air. The gift is over the top, but it's the most thoughtful thing he's ever done and it's exactly what I needed, even though I didn't say anything. A small fracture heals in my heart. I miss Clint, but Finn's just made sure I can protect myself. Even after fucking with his knife. He thought enough about me to arm me.

I'm staring off, watching the sunset, when I hear what sounds like grunts coming from his balcony. The grunts and moans intensify. Did he have someone in there waiting for him while we were talking? Once a man whore, always a man whore.

I walk closer to our shared railing to call him out on his shit. My steps stall as the full scene comes into view. It's not Finn making noise, although he and Holden are on the balcony, too. It's Pax with his dick out this time, with some chick. She and Moira have similar taste in underwear, because she's wearing a bra and panty set like the one I had that went missing from my laundry when the guys were messing with my car and shit. Hers fits a little tighter than mine did. When Pax pulls her by the hair, forcing her to arch her back, I get a better look at the side of the bra and snort a laugh. The bra and panties don't fit because they *are* mine. In group homes and juvie, you learn to label your shit so it doesn't get stolen. I still do it out of habit. Moira was appalled at the idea and sent all my stuff off to get little monograms on them. For some of the lingerie, she had tiny charms sewn on the front of them so I could thread a belly chain through it. This set has the charm.

There are so many thoughts I'm having about what I'm seeing. First. Eeew. I hope they burn that when they're done. Second, and this is the weirdest thing that needs to be unpacked. Did Finn make her dress in my underwear, or did she steal my underwear to catch Finn? And uh, if she was after Finn, why is Pax the one pounding her into the concrete?

"I'm a low-class slut, Paxton. That's right. I'm trailer trash, desperate for your cock to elevate my status."

Is that supposed to be me? On what planet does anybody talk like that?

"I'm a grimy whore. I don't belong. Put me in my place with your masterful dick."

Oh god. This is the worst dirty talk I've ever heard. I'm bent over, leaning on my knees. My silent laugh constricts my chest so hard I can barely breathe. When I finally regain control, I straighten, swiping tears from my cheeks.

These three never let me have any rest. They keep stooping to new lows. Pax said I was the worst lay of his life. That the drug coursing through his system was the only reason he could finish. Well, fuck him, he doesn't get to enjoy this moment either. I'm about to fuck his shit up.

I dart inside to grab my free standing mirror, dragging it back onto the balcony and angle it so he can see me, but from her position on the concrete, she can't. She doesn't need to see me. She'll be able to hear just fine. I stab the number 4 on my speed dial.

"What can I do for you, LaReaux?"

"I need your help."

"With what?"

"My neighbors are having a party."

"You want me to send campus security to shut it down?"

I hold the phone out so it'll pick up on her moans. "I want you to help me drown out those sounds."

"Are you jealous they're having a good time?"

"I'm insulted. You missed the part where she's pretending to be me. So my *fake* me needs a lesson from the *real* me on how I sound when I'm getting a good dicking down. Think you can help me with that?"

"Help you fake it? No."

"That's why I'm calling, Wolfe. I want you to help me do the real thing."

"Sweetness, are you saying you wanna have phone sex with me while your neighbors are listening?"

"Yes. Is that a problem?"

"Not at all. You know how much I love to make you cum."

I shift in my seat. I don't know how he does it, but the minute he turns the sexy voice on, my panties get wet.

"Are you sitting?"

"Yes."

"What are you wearing?"

"Don't be cliché."

"Since I can't see you, I need to know what you're wearing so I can visualize what I'd do to you. It won't work if I tell you to lift your skirt when you're wearing pants."

"Good point. I'm wearing sweatpants and a t-shirt."

"Bra?"

"Nope."

"Mmm. So you have free access to those pointy nipples. Play with them for me."

I tug at them the way I like. Panting out a breath at how good that feels.

"Are they hard?"

"Yes."

"Wet your thumb and roll it on your nipple. Imagine it's my tongue."

I close my eyes, imagining he's here with me. I pretend he's latched onto my nipple, sucking it.

"These pants are in my way. Take them off."

I do, lifting my hips to push them down my legs and kick them onto the ground.

"God, I need a taste of this pussy."

"Taste it."

"I will sweetness. I'll taste you while you're swallowing me down."

I groan, as I think about how he tastes. I finger myself, slowly rubbing my clit, and shove my thumb in my mouth, pretending to suck him off. I need to buy new toys, but this will do for now.

I whimper as he praises, "Fuck, Thea, you suck me so good. Spread that pretty pussy for me."

I do, draping my left leg over the arm of the chair I'm sitting in. "You're so tight around my two fingers."

I dip two fingers inside myself, work them in and out as I work my clit. "I need to be inside you. Are you ready for this dick?"

"Yes."

"Mmmm." He chuckles. "You're already clenching around my dick."

I rock against my hand.

"One more inch, sweetness. Let me all the way in."

I tilt my hips, pushing my fingers in a little further. "That's it." He grunts. "Take it all. Shit, will you look at that? I love watching my cock disappear inside this tight cunt."

"Shit, Wolfe. I'm so wet." I rasp into the phone. "I wanna come around your thick juicy cock so bad."

"Shit, is right." He grunts, "Damn, you feel like heaven. You feel how deep I am?"

"Mmm-hmm. So deep."

"Fuck." I hear Finn say from the other side of the balcony.

"Are you close, sweetness?"

I'm tingling all over. I curl my fingers hitting delicious nerve endings inside me, his voice like velvety goodness in my ear. "So close. Don't stop." I pant.

"This pussy is gripping me like a vise. Fuck, I'm gonna cum." He groans in my ear and sets off fireworks in my body. My mouth falls open as the first tremor rushes over me. I inch another finger inside and pinch my clit, pushing myself completely over the edge.

I ease my hand out as my heart rate slows. My eyes fly open as my hand is snatched away, a thick warm tongue working over my fingers. Holden's looming over me, sucking them clean. He drops my hand, then jumps back over the railing. I blink, still a little dazed, when I hear a shriek. Then I remember the reason behind this show of exhibitionism. Whatever just happened to fake me did not sound pleasurable.

Wolfe's voice brings me the rest of the way back to reality. "Are you done causing trouble for tonight, sweetness?"

I smile into the phone. "Your mouth is amazing."

He chuckles. "Good night, LaReaux."

I disconnect the call and stand, stretching out my muscles. I love the way I feel after a good orgasm. Boneless and free. Fake me is also on her feet, and I can see what the hysterics was all about. I clamp my hand over my mouth, smothering my laugh.

She looks like a melting vanilla ice cream cone. I open the door to go back in as she screams, "Do you know how much these lashes and hair extensions cost?"

Chapter 56
Pax

She's a fucking menace. I can't even bust a nut without her intruding on the moment. Until I fucked Thea, I hadn't let myself dwell on the fact that I might actually miss the feel of pussy. I thought I was cured of my disinterest, so when the girl who crashed the lingerie show at the beginning of the semester approached me, I thought, why not?

She's the one who brought up role playing and asked for an audience while I gave it to her rough and dirty. There was no way I was taking her to my room, and I knew better than to ask Holden. That's how we wound up on Finn's balcony. He said he didn't want her pussy smell in his room.

I let her suck me off to warm me up, but the more she talked, the softer my dick got. I was about to send her home when Thea started up. At first I thought she was mocking me, but the image in the mirror told a different tale. Her leg hitched up over the arm of the chair, her shirt pushed up, exposing her tits. I had the perfect view.

My dick got hard again, watching Thea, and I completely zoned out while the girl did all the work. The guys refused to touch her, but Finn had no problem pulling his dick out and jacking off. We were clearly in sync with her. Thea. Probably both remembering the night of the party. It might not've been my choice to hook up with Thea at that party, and despite what I told her, I remember enough about what happened to know that I thoroughly enjoyed how tight her pussy was.

It's Holden whose behavior shocked me. As soon as Thea started cumming, Finn walked over to the railing and blew his load all over her potted plants. I shot mine in the girl's face, but Holden jumped onto her balcony and sucked the juices right off of her fingers before coming back on our side and picking his book up like nothing happened.

I look up as Holden enters my room. "You all packed, man?"

He plops down on the couch. "I'm not going."

My brows lift. The campus will be operating on a skeleton crew. It's closed, but there are always some students who don't go home, because they take an accelerated class or live on the east coast and choose to stay in California for easier access to the slopes at Big Bear. But Holden isn't one of those students. He always goes home for winter break. He says it's the only place he's completely at ease. "Why not?"

"Dad's away on an assignment and mom's taking my sister to New York to catch the nutcracker, so it'll just be me."

"That's never bothered you before."

"Thea's not going either."

"Why does that matter?"

"There's still a lot of people on campus. We shouldn't leave her here alone."

Finn walks in and says, "She won't be. I'm staying on campus for the break."

What is this shit? "She'll be okay. She's not talking to either of you. I doubt she'll notice if you're gone."

"It's not about that. I just don't want to leave, okay? She might not be talking to us, but she doesn't hate us. She just needs time to get used to me again, and rebuilding our relationship when campus is relatively empty is the perfect time to do it. No distractions. No, Eloise."

Finn shifts in his seat to face me. "Think about how the new semester can be a totally different vibe if we can put in the work now with no one else around trying to sabotage us."

I don't like the look in his eyes, or where I think this is going. "What we?"

"You're staying on campus, too. None of our parents are in town this year, so what's the sense of going home when we can hang out here?"

I can't even argue with that, but my reasons for not going home have nothing to do with Thea. I'd rather be here on campus in my comfort zone than wandering the halls of my father's domain. In fact, I was looking forward to her being gone too, so I didn't have the constant reminder of the assignment from The League hanging over my head. I tell them both, "I just want to chill for the next five weeks. No drama, no putting out fires, or mediating fights. I'm on vacation."

Finn nods, quickly agreeing. "All the troublemakers will be gone."

I point out, "Not all of them. The main one lives right across the hall."

"Thea won't give us any trouble. Holden and I will make sure of it."

This is it. This is the day I ignore everything in me that's screaming at me not to do this, and march over to their side of the room. Today is the day I dip my toe into their world. Squaring my shoulders and lifting my chin, I walk up to them, feigning an air of nonchalantness I don't really feel.

Finn gets to his feet when I get closer. "Pet, I just want you to know that I-"

I hold my hand up to silence him. Whatever he's about to say isn't important. I don't want to hear any more apologies. Van said if I want answers about the people who attacked me, this is the way to get them. That's the only reason I'm here.

Pax is sitting there, his ever present scowl on his face when he's not running things. "I'm not ready to just forgive any of you for the shit I went through, but I also know I can't navigate this legacy thing without you. If I have to sit at your table and pretend to have a stick up my ass, then you're gonna damn well run interference with the future ex mistress club. So whatever you gotta do to make them happy, you do it. I don't have time to deal with jealous bitches right now."

Holden speaks next. "Define... whatever..."

I look him square in the eye and say, "It means if she likes for you to suck her toes and tickle her kneecaps under a full moon while yodeling, you do it."

"That goes against any way we've ever treated them before."

"That's not my problem." I scan the table for a place to sit and choose the end farthest from them. "I don't want there to be any confusion about where things stand with us. So you stick to your corner of the table with your people. I'll stay at the other end with mine."

Pax smirks at me. "You have people now?"

I swear I wanna punch him in his face. But we're supposed to be communicating. Tryna find some common ground. "Yes. LJ and Austin will be joining the table when they get back to school." I fix my gaze on him and dare him to say something. He tries to hold it back, but fails.

"Austin can't sit with us."

"That's why he's sitting *with me.* Or under me. Or on top of the table. The point is, your rules govern you and your friends. My rules are for me and mine."

"You can't have two different sets of rules. It creates chaos."

"So you keep telling me, and yet the only chaos I've seen is the shit stirring you've been doing since the moment you ran into me. Which is why it's best if we stay separated. You and your minions get this side of the table." I wave towards the other end. "Me and my friends will get that side. It's a win-win."

Holden and Finn are looking at me. Holden's face is just as unreadable as usual, but Finn's wearing his thoughts and feelings on his sleeve. "Look, Finn. I know you're sorry. I know you're apologizing, and I'm really grateful for the knives. But that doesn't just magically fix everything. We have to coexist, and I'm willing to try when you get back from Winter Break."

He smiles now. "Oh, we don't need to wait that long. We can start now."

"It really wouldn't make a difference. Nothing's going to change in one or two days."

His smile widens. "Then it's a good thing I won't be leaving campus, isn't it?"

"You're staying here?" He nods and I look at all of them, my stomach tightening. "You're all staying here?"

Holden tilts his head and Finn says, "Pet, you didn't think I'd leave you here alone, did you?"

"Yes. Finn, that's exactly what I thought. In fact, I was looking forward to it."

Holden's still staring at me, like he's trying to penetrate my mind, my soul. I have to remind myself not to get lost in his stormy gaze. The longer he stares, the hotter I get. Why am I reacting this way to him? Sure, he sat at my door like a sentry the other night, but that doesn't absolve him from all the other shit he's done. I didn't ask him to play guard dog.

"Why aren't you leaving?"

His cryptic answer leaves me confused. "Because I'm ready to play."

Chapter 58
Finn

Thea wakes with a stretch, then stiffens. I see her hand moving under her pillow. I know what she's going for.

"Morning, Pet." I let her hear the smile in my voice and brush my lips across the nape of her neck, so she'll know there's no need to stab me this early in the morning. I've been here patiently waiting for her to wake up. I know she took some sleeping pills. The bottle is still out on her night table. I was getting worried she took too many.

I snuggle closer. This whole time she's been mad at me; I've been missing out on the chance to rub my dick against her in the morning.

"What are you doing in my bed, Finn?"

"Isn't it obvious? I'm waking up to the face of the most beautiful woman I've ever seen."

"Don't try to be cute."

"I'm not trying. I *am* cute. Sexy. A god among men."

"I told you at lunch yesterday that things aren't fixed, that I needed space, and it would take time to work on forgiving you. And your move was to just disregard all that and let yourself into my room and crawl into bed with me?"

"After that little display on the balcony the other night, did you really expect me to stay away? You all but screamed, Finn, come play with me."

"What I did had nothing to do with you and it wasn't some mating call."

I press closer, letting her feel my morning wood. "Yes, Pet. It was." She presses her ass against me, despite her attempts to pretend she's unaffected by our proximity.

"Finn, if you don't stop humping me like a dog in heat, you won't be able to use that thing in your pants on anyone."

You'd think she'd know by now that her threats have the opposite effect of what she's intended. I grind harder, gripping her hip to hold her against me. "You can cut me, make me bleed, and it will only make me want you more."

I suck on the skin on the back of her neck, but not hard enough to leave a mark. "Now the only reason I'm not going to bypass this waiting game and speed up the timeline of our reunion is because I want you to want me just as badly as I want you."

"You can't speed it up. It'll take as long as it takes."

I chuckle. If only she knew. "I can. I've done it plenty of times to others. It's a testament to how special I think you are that I want you to choose it. That I'm giving you the option to choose it in your own time, instead of hacking your brain."

I'm keyed up and close to spilling. With a shuddering breath, I stop moving against her. I hate that I'm going back to my room sexually frustrated, but I think my point is clear. With one final nuzzle of her ear, I say, "I'll wait for you, Thea. God, it's gonna be so damn hard to do it, but I will."

I climb out of bed and stroke my dick. She turns around to face me, eyes snagging on the movement of my hand before drifting up to my face. "Get really friendly with that hand, Number Three. You'll be waiting a long time."

I release my shaft and wink before turning towards the door. "Maybe, but I know it's worth it."

. . .

I'm in a great mood. Waking up with the girl you're crazy about will do that to you. Who knew? I've got excess energy, so I briefly consider taking Pax up on his offer to join him for a workout.

"Nah. I'm good. I think I should burn this energy off at the parkour course."

I haven't been out there in weeks. Not since Thea got hurt. I haven't felt interested in having fun, knowing she wasn't having fun. But things are turning around for us.

"Why are you so damn peppy this morning? You know you shouldn't be drinking those energy drinks if you're gonna go push yourself on the course."

"I haven't had an energy drink. I actually just got out of bed." I smile even harder. Thea's bed. Maybe I should have finished rubbing one out, but I want to wait until later, when I have time to think about it and really draw it out.

"I get it. Eloise isn't here, so you're sampling again." He chuckles. "I'm surprised you've held out this long."

"I haven't fucked anybody since Thea."

"Okay, so you let them suck your dick. Same difference."

"Nope. The only mouth I've had is Thea's, and I'm not interested in hooking up with anyone else." He laughs at my confession. "What's so funny?"

"You. You almost had me, man. We both know how much you like variety. It's why Eloise walks around with her face cracked. Because no matter how much she tells you to keep it in your pants, you won't. Sometimes I think you do it just to be spiteful."

"Sometimes I do. But this isn't a joke, Pax. I want Thea. I only want Thea."

"Yeah, now while you can't have her. The minute she gives in, you'll be on to the next one."

He's not getting it. So I spell it out for him, as clearly as I can. "There is no next one. Thea's it for me. And before you say it, yes, I know I'm promised to marry Eloise, but that won't change anything about how I feel. That girl's perfect. Perfect for me."

I bite back what else I want to say, knowing he's not ready to hear it yet. It's always been something we talked about in passing. About how we'd find the perfect woman and have to share her, because that's the only way we'd be able to fully focus on our goals.

One woman to rotate between us. It's always been an option for The Triums, but none of them could ever agree on a woman. Our dads couldn't. Pax's father has widely different views on how women should be treated. It's a wonder he even created an heir. Ultimately, the women they marry enter this place where they're pitted against each other. And that pulls The Triums apart. We plan to be different, to do things differently than any other Trium. It's all we think about. All we talk about.

I guess it's why we even started sharing women to begin with. First, to see if it would even work between us, and then it became the only way we could get someone to give Holden a chance. The dream; it could be a reality. We could make it happen.

Thea's strong, brave, protective of the people she cares about. She gets me. She doesn't back down or turn her nose up at Holden and engages with him on a level nobody ever has, and she gives Pax as much shit as he gives her. I know in my soul that she's perfect for all of us.

We have to all agree to it, and petition the council for permission. I know Holden is interested in Thea right now. If it works out between them, if she can truly accept him, then we'd just have to get Pax on board.

Hell, he doesn't even have to be with her. He can just sign off on the arrangement and continue to do his own thing. But none of us would have to worry about marrying women we don't want.

Chapter 59
Thea

School's empty and so are the streets of Canyon Falls Annex. I walk through town happy to have space, a reprieve from all the bustling bodies and long lines and wait times. I'm treating myself to lunch today at a restaurant that's always crowded.

I have my playlist ready to go, so I can listen to music while I eat. I can't seem to bring myself to open a map yet and finish marking out the layout of town or finding that hiking path I was so excited about when I first moved here. The woods and I still aren't on speaking terms. I don't know how I'm going to get over that hurdle.

I'm mulling over options when a body stops at the end of my table. I take in the man wearing a black on black suit and a dark blue tie. He holds himself with an air of importance and looks down at me expectantly. I don't know what he's expecting, but I do know he's at the wrong table looking for whatever it is.

My phone chimes and I glance down, seeing a message from Moira.

MOIRA

My father's in town. I've been putting him off,
but he's getting impatient about meeting you.
He'll probably seek you out.

I take an educated guess and reply

ME

I think he already has

I sip my water, ignoring him. Since he's looking for me, he can break the awkward silence, or stand there until I'm done eating. I really don't care. He tires of being ignored and says, "The first thing we'll need to work on are your manners, or maybe your wardrobe. I can't believe Moira lets you walk around town like this."

I continue to ignore him, breaking off a piece of my garlic butter roll and popping it into my mouth.

"The way you dress is a direct reflection of yourself and this family."

I finally raise my gaze to meet his and answer, enunciating every word, "I don't have a family."

Shaking his head, he scoffs, "Just as hardheaded and stubborn as your mother, I see."

"That's right, I'm a chip right off of Hailee LaReaux's block."

I watch his jaw clench. If he expected this to go a different way, he should have done some research on me first. A phone call, a text message. Something to warm me up, instead of coming up to me with nothing but put downs falling from his lips.

The server comes over with my appetizers. "Sir, shall I set another place?"

I answer for him, "No. He's leaving."

When she walks away, he says, "The correct thing for you to do would be to invite me to sit."

He wants to play this game? Okay, I'll play. "The correct thing for you to do would be to not approach a young woman sitting alone and expect her to engage in a conversation with you when you haven't even introduced yourself. The correct thing to do is to not expect her to share her space, or be comfortable in your presence just because you think she should. The absolute correct thing to do is to *not* engage in behaviors that predators would."

I say the last part loud enough for the couple at the next table to hear me. His eyes widen, and he turns a little red in the face. "I." He clears his voice. "I apologize, you are correct. I should have introduced myself first. I assumed you knew who I was."

"You know what they say about assumptions."

"I'm Joshua Laurent. I'm your grandfather." He smiles and tries to lighten the mood. "I apologize for alarming you and you're right. I should have contacted you to arrange our first meeting." He chuckles. "I was just so excited to meet you, and when I saw you sitting here, I couldn't let the opportunity pass."

I blink up at him. I have nothing to say to any of that. He was excited. He couldn't wait. He never once took into consideration how I would be feeling.

"I have your number, Mr. Laurent. I haven't used it because I'm still trying to get my head around all of this. You forcing the issue doesn't make me any more interested in using it. If anything, your approach has made me even more leery about it."

Cocking my head to the side, I say, "Perhaps you should speak with Moira and Scott and let them catch you up to speed on what's been happening around here, and that would give you better insight into why ambushing me was the wrong move."

"I know everything I need to know."

"Is that so? So you know about my attack on campus and still thought jumpstarting our acquaintance was the way to go?"

"I'm aware that you were involved in an unfortunate hazing incident the night you were supposed to cross over."

"So you follow the school's version of events. Great. Now I know I won't be using your number." The waitress approaches with the rest of my food. "I wish I could say it was nice meeting you, but it'd be a lie. Now if you'll excuse me, I'm famished."

He looks like he's about to say something else, but something over by the door grabs his attention. I turn around to see what he's looking at, but don't see anything. He gives me one more smile and says, "Enjoy your meal, Theona. I will reach out to you again in the next few days. Perhaps you'll be more receptive to a conversation then."

I don't bother telling him not to hold his breath.

Thea

I haven't left my room all day. I had big plans for this week, but Joshua Laurent ruined all that with one ill timed introduction. What an ass. He might have changed his tune when I pushed back on his bullshit, but he's definitely still the guy who thinks he can make the women in this family do what he wants.

I know he's gonna try again, instead of waiting for me to extend the invite. He thinks mom and Moira were a handful. He hasn't seen nothing yet. Nothing in my life has made me docile or compliant. I'm not a people pleaser. I cannot, I *will not*, be controlled.

I stomp into the gym, ready to pound my frustrations out on the heavy bag. What I really need is someone to swing back. I miss it. The more I come to the gym, the more settled I feel in my abilities. It might be time for me to get back to training at Wolfe Pack.

I warm up and then get to swinging. Every hit soothes me. The steady exhalation of my breath relaxes me. Grounds me. I weave and bob around the bag, staying light on my feet. I'm in the zone. For the first time since my attack I'm aware and in the moment, so when Pax walks up to me and reaches for me, instead of freezing, I dodge his hand.

I readjust my feet and go back to the heavy bag, but he reaches for me again and I side step, slipping by him. He does it again and when he gets within reach, I swing, connecting with his jaw. I didn't put a lot of power behind it. Just enough so he'll know that I'm serious about this fight. A warning to back off.

He doesn't listen and I snap, going after him, rotating my hips, putting my weight into the swing. Now he's on the defensive, trying to avoid my blows. He can't dodge all of them and I connect more times than I miss.

I'm sweating, my chest burns. It's been too long since I've fought like this and I've lost stamina. But the burn feels good. The movement is like coming home.

"Enough!"

I ignore him. It'll be enough when he's on the ground. I go for his ribs, determined that he'll feel the lingering traces of this tomorrow. He rocks with the blow and when I go to follow up, he sidesteps me, getting behind me and puts me in a bar hold. Pulling me off my feet as he stands to his full height. With my boxing gloves on, I can't get traction on his arm to assist me with getting out of the hold he has me in.

"You're a stubborn little thing."

"I told you I'd kick your ass."

"I wasn't fighting back."

"Then why are you sticking behind me, afraid to face me head on?"

"Because I have better things to do with my time."

"Then go do them. You attacked me. I just defended myself."

"Attacked?" He snorts. "So now you're playing the victim? It won't work. I see right through you, and whatever you're planning this time won't work either, so you can stop pretending to be on board with being a legacy."

"Make up your mind, Pax. Do you want me in your club or not?"

"*Not,* but we don't have a choice. You sitting with us doesn't change who you really are. It doesn't make you special, and it won't elevate your family's status. Neither will trying to get your claws into Finn again."

"What's he got to do with it?"

"I'm just reminding you that his thoughts about you haven't changed. He's bored because of that shit you pulled with his fiancé and has decided that the person who should satisfy his needs is the one who tied his hands to begin with. Once he's done taking his frustrations out on you, he'll discard you all over again."

"If that's true, then why are you so worried?"

"I'm not worried about Finn. I know what he's going to do to you."

"Then this hug you're giving me is out of what? Jealousy?"

"That he's fucking you? Don't flatter yourself."

I grind my ass against him. "I don't have to. You're doing it for me."

He pushes me away, and I turn to face him. Laughing at the look of disgust on his face. "Your brain might not like me, and you might've blamed your reaction to me on the drugs in our system the last time, but you look stone cold sober right now. You know exactly what Finn sees in me."

I slip off my gloves and stomp towards the doors. "But don't worry, Coxsucker. There's plenty of dick on campus, so I'll never be forced to endure either of your touches again."

I shove past Finn on my way out, flipping him off as the doors hiss closed.

Chapter 60
Thea

Winter break started eight days ago. I thought I was getting a full month of vacation from all the legacy minions. I was wrong. Six of them showed up on campus today. Whether they've moved back into the dorms or not is unclear. But they're here at The Rock, so I won't be sitting at that table today. Shrimp scampi was on the menu, and I'm not about to let them ruin my meal.

Finn wanders over to my table and slides into the seat across from me. Before he can utter a word, I ask, "Are you lost?"

"Lost? No. But I am on a journey much like Odysseus trying to get home to his one true love."

"Okay.... So I'm gonna go out on a limb and say this table is one of the challenges you face on your way to Ithaca. Which one?"

"Pet. You know your Greek poems?"

"Doesn't everyone know that one and The Iliad?"

"Finn!"

Right on cue. The minute he breathes in my direction, somebody has something to say. With a twist of my lips and a grand sweep of my hands, I say, "And there goes Penelope. The deceiver of men awaiting your return. Off you go, Odysseus. The contests await."

Finn looks at me, that boyish smile I haven't seen since my return, firmly in place. "If you're casting the roles, what does that make you, Pet?"

"Take your pick of whichever calamity you want."

"Go on."

"I represent the distractions, the pitfalls, the obstacles you encounter along the way. Call me Siren, Poseidon, Cyclops. Chronos."

"Time."

"That's right. And you're wasting it sitting here."

"Or perhaps you're Helene."

"Treacherous cheating bitch? Yeah. Pax definitely casts me in that role." I purse my lips as if thinking, then say, "But then so did you." I flutter my fingers and say, "So off you go. Save yourself."

He stands and comes to my side of the table. "Helene was a woman worth going to war over. Of course, I think Marlowe says it best." He leans forward, brushing his lips against my ear.

"Sweet Helene, make me immortal with a kiss. Her lips
suck forth my soul: see, where it flies!"

Eloise has had enough of being ignored. She's finally made it to this side of the metaphorical sea. "Finn. What are you doing over here?"

"Discussing poetry."

I blink several times, digesting what he said before she interrupted, then smile. "You're welcome."

Finn's brows furrow. "Did I thank you for something?"

"Sounds like you were." I cover the top of my straw with my finger and pull it from my milkshake. "You know, with the whole soul sucking with my lips, speech." I put the end of the straw in my mouth and suck. Then smack my lips as I drop it back in my cup.

Finn drags his beanie off his head and shoves it in his mouth, muffling whatever he says as he walks back over to his table. I catch Holden staring at me. I fan my fingers open, swiping them across my throat and up over my face, flipping him off before they collapse on the other side of my neck. He drops his head back down to his book, but not before I see a small smile play across his lips.

Holden's not a smiler and a small part of me preens over being the one who made him do it. Weirder still is me even entertaining the idea of finding ways to make him smile again. My musings are interrupted because Eloise didn't walk off with Finn.

"Let's get something straight. Finn is mine and will always be mine. Throwing yourself at him and the other Trium won't change that."

"Perhaps you should think about what you're saying. I'm over here minding my business and everyone keeps coming over here demanding my attention."

"Nobody has come to you."

"Finn, has. Pax has, and you have, too. So maybe you three are the ones throwing yourselves at me."

I drop my gaze to her feet and slowly drag them back up her body. "Don't get me wrong, you're cute and all, but you're also not my type. I don't know how many more times I can let all of you hit the metaphorical pavement before you get it in your heads that I'm not interested. You wanna write that down or something? Or should I say it louder for the people in the back?"

Finn calls her back to the table. "Eloise, get your ass over here before I give your seat away."

That threat gets her moving. I snort because it's just a seat, but she's scurrying off like she's trying to win musical chairs and the prize is an emerald studded throne.

Chapter 61
Thea

I wince from the bite of my nails digging into my palms. The pain serves as a reminder to keep it together, instead of going off on the two adults riding in the car with me. I can get through a night of food and stifled conversation, just to say I've done it and therefore there won't be a reason to do it again.

They have Van to thank for why I showed up tonight. I wish she could have come too, but she insists her presence might cloud my opinion of Joshua Laurent. I don't see how. My opinion of him is already in the dirt.

Moira glances over at me. She's had this docile expression on her face since they picked me up from the dorms. It's creepy as fuck, and Scott is acting weird, too. We should've had at least one heated exchange by now, seeing how I kept them both on read, and haven't called to check in this week. But he barely squeaked out a hello when I got in the car.

We pull in front of the restaurant and I let out a breath before letting myself out of the car. I peek through the doors to see if Joshua is standing inside, but the hostess area is empty. Of course he's not here yet. "How long do we have to wait until we cancel this whole farce?"

Moira says, "We wait until he gets here, no matter how long it takes. If we need to reschedule, he'll let us know."

"Seriously? You just stand around waiting for him?" I shake my head. "You know what? He's your dad, you do you. But I'm not about to stand here and let him disrespect my time like that. He's got five minutes, then I'm out."

Scott mutters something that could pass for a string of cuss words. "What? Did he already reschedule?"

"No." He holds out his phone to Moira, who grimaces.

"Wanna share with everyone standing here?"

"It seems the restaurant is hosting a going away dinner for some of the families."

"Where are they going?"

"On vacation. Most of the diners tonight will probably have some affiliation to legacy families or The League."

That's the most information Scott has volunteered to share with me ever. I can't help but think it's a warning of some sort. I go with my gut and say, "It's not a coincidence that he picked tonight, and this restaurant is it?"

Is that approval I see on his face, that I've figured that out on my own? God, he really needs to spend more time talking to me, instead of at me. "I'm not gonna play some game, or pretend to be some docile little lamb."

"No one's asking you to. But you do need to be mindful of where you are and who's in attendance tonight. They'll be looking at us. At Joshua, and at you."

Moira's staring at the town car pulling up to the curb when she says, "Remember our goals, Thea."

"Our goals?"

She squeezes my hand. "Stay under the radar. Graduate. Get the hell away from this town."

I repeat those words over to myself. That is the goal. That is the plan. That is why I'm doing this, and forcing myself to be in the presence of all those idiots at school. I'm playing the game, so I can get what I want. I square my shoulders, and face the curb, watching as her father unfolds himself from the car.

I watch as he addresses Scott first, with a firm handshake. One I imagine hurts, but Scott doesn't show it. Then he steps in front of Moira, forcing her to reach up to kiss his cheek. "Hello, daddy."

Then he's wheeling around to look at me. He stares at me, and I stare back. I don't know what protocol he expects me to follow, but I'm damn sure not kissing him.

Scott breaks through the tension. "Thea, this is Joshua Laurent. Moira's father."

I appreciate that he didn't say "Your grandfather." I'm not accepting that title. I haven't even accepted Scott and Moira as my mother and father yet.

"Theona. A pleasure to see you again."

"We'll see."

His left eye twitches, but he doesn't say anything else. Scott pulls the door open. "Shall we go in?"

Joshua struts up to the door, walking in ahead of Moira. She goes second, followed by me, then Scott. When the hostess says our table is ready, I hang back, letting them all walk through the space ahead of me. I'm looking straight ahead, avoiding the stares. I am so over being looked at like I'm a spectacle.

Our table is in the back corner of the restaurant. Joshua takes the seat facing the room, Moira and Scott on either side of the table, which forces me to sit with my exposed back to the door.

I study the menu, tuning out the conversation. Not that Moira's father seems to be all that interested in talking to me to begin with. He's too busy grilling Scott on business and throwing cheap shots at Moira for not making more of an effort to nurture her former friendships now that the Laurent family status is changing.

"I have friends, daddy. We enjoy each other's company. I have no need to force myself onto anyone else."

"It's not forcing, it's an honor and an expectation."

"It would be forcing them to include me, if I just show up without being invited."

"That's to be expected. You need to rebuild their trust. Make yourself available in whatever capacity they need. You can't walk around here too prideful. There are amends to be made, Moira."

"Why?" They all look at me, and I continue, "Why does Moira need to regain these women's trust? In fact, how did she break their trust?"

Moira calls my name, softly, "Thea."

I give it a beat. Take a breath, then push on. "Are you not answering because you don't have one? Or because you don't think I'm entitled to having my questions answered?"

"Young lady..."

"If you're about to chastise me for questioning you, then maybe you shouldn't have said you wanted to get to know me. Because me... I ask questions when I don't know or understand something."

Joshua says, "It is quite appropriate to ask questions in class when you don't understand the material being presented, but this situation is different. We won't rehash all the details, but Moira knows why she can't be trusted, and she knows that she must face the consequences of her actions. That's what happens when you make choices. There are consequences."

He sips his drink. "Now I understand you may not be used to structure or parental authority because you bounced around all your life. That's another consequence to her and Hailee's actions. But..."

"Daddy..."

"I'm talking, Moira, and since she's so inquisitive, this part she needs to hear."

My fingers inch across the table towards my fork. "Go on, finish what you were saying about my mother."

Chapter 62
Holden

I'm stunned, watching Thea and her parents walk into the restaurant. I knew they'd have to interact with the families, but it's jarring to see her here. The man who walks in first is a legacy through and through. I can see it in the way his head tilts up, his chin jutting forward, his shoulders square as he walks in, taking up space. He projects an aura that makes people want to obey and get the hell out of the way.

This must be her grandfather. I study Thea's face and demeanor. She doesn't want to be here. She scans the room, her eyes widening when she sees me. Pax and Finn are here too. Our families are sharing a table. It's sort of an unofficial farewell dinner for the parents going out of town for the holidays.

It's a smart move, Laurent making tonight his reintroduction to The League. The families will spend the next few weeks thinking about it, but he won't have to answer any questions about Thea's disappearance right away. What is he going to say? The League's stance is that he's provisionally reinstated, but that doesn't mean they don't suspect he had a hand in her identity being hidden away.

They settle in a corner in the back of the restaurant, but I can still see Thea's profile from where I'm sitting. Her hands are clenched in her lap. I assume it's because she's sitting with her back exposed.

I take in Moira and Scott Hughes' posture, too. They're good actors, pretending to be perfectly calm but their micro expressions belay the strain they're feeling. My father's laughter draws my attention back to my table, and I catch Finn and Pax staring in the same direction I was. Malcom takes a sip from his glass, sits it on the table, then steeples his fingers together. This is his signature move before he says something boastful.

I catch Pax's eye. He gives a small shake to his head. He doesn't know what his father is about to say. That means it's probably got nothing to do with us, so I tune out and dig into my food, keeping an eye on Thea through my peripheral vision.

"We're nearly done with our investigation. I finally tracked down the last witness and will interview them when we get back from our trip. I expect to announce good news at the New Year's ceremony. We can finally move forward with the official advancement of last year's prospects and start planning this year's induction ceremony."

That gets my attention. I notice he said a lot of he did this and he did that, even though it was supposed to be a team effort. It's like this with all the former Trium members. It's like they graduated and no longer remember what it's like to work together. Everything's a competition.

I glance over at my father. He doesn't seem bothered by Malcolm's announcement. Finn's dad rolls his eyes and shakes his head. I've heard him say on more than one occasion that Malcolm has never played well with others.

Pax, Holden and I give the expected platitudes and then the wives dominate the next thirty minutes of conversation, talking about the stores they'll visit and massages they'll be getting on vacation, while the men are off golfing, smoking cigars and sipping brandy.

Whatever they'll be doing, I hope they have fun. I don't mind hanging out with my family, but this year I have plans of my own. Plans that include the woman across the restaurant. I don't know what's happening over there, but I can read her body language well enough to know things are about to turn violent. She's gripping her fork like she's considering using it as a weapon.

That wouldn't go over so well in this room, with anyone other than Finn. If we don't intercede, everyone in attendance tonight will see just how Thea reacts when she's feeling threatened. I, for one, don't care. If whatever the older Laurent is saying is hurting her, he deserves to get stabbed, but it's not the first impression Thea wants to be making to the rest of this room.

Holden

I snag Pax's attention and subtly tilt my head in Thea's direction. He rolls his eyes and I arch a brow. Finn picks up on what we're doing and tilts his head towards me. Pax jerks his chin, and Finn excuses himself from the table. Eight minutes later, he's back, and settles in his seat as if he doesn't know what's about to happen.

At family dinners, all phones should be on silent or vibrate, but of course there are always people who forget to turn them off. The first two go off in quick succession. The combined buzzing of the rest adds to the noise, amplifying the sound.

Chairs push away from the tables, the younger diners offering hasty goodbyes. Nobody wants to miss out on the pop-up party they've just got notifications for. The guys and I remain seated, finishing our meals, pretending like we have nothing to do with the hasty retreat of our school mates.

Ten minutes later, we rise from our seats, wish our parents a safe trip and stroll over to Thea's table. Finn smiles at the adults and offers a greeting. My attention is on Thea. I stand at her back, hoping it will settle her nerves a bit.

I study Moira, and Scott Hughes and the older gentlemen. The

Hughes' brows pinch and they share a look when Finn says, "Thea, we need to head out now or we'll be late."

He doesn't say anything else, offering no further explanation about what we'll be late to. I wait to see if she'll push back the way she usually does. Does her discomfort here outweigh the animosity she has for us? I doubt she sees this as the rescue attempt it's meant to be.

Pax's voice shows he has no patience for the delay. "Let's go, Thea."

She must really need an escape because she pushes her chair back without hesitation. The older man says, "Theona, we're in the middle of dinner."

"Right, but you know how much I hate to be late. Oh wait, you don't, but I'm sure Scott and Moira can fill you in on everything they know about me and ya'll can make up the rest. Enjoy your steak salad."

She marches towards the door ahead of us, and I can't help but admire the confidence she displays as she walks by the tables filled with influential people from our world. Thea didn't grow up here with our privilege, but she'd fit right in if she ever truly embraced the life before her.

When we're in front of the restaurant, she says, "I don't know why you guys showed up and crashed my awkward family dinner, but whatever shit you're getting into tonight, just scratch me off the list."

Finn holds out his phone. "There's a pop up party and you're my plus one."

"No, thanks."

Pax says, "That restaurant is full of some of the most influential people in town. Since you never looked at your phone and left with the other legacies, we had to come get you. Now you can go with us, or go back in there and publicly declare that you're not one of us. I promise the decision they'll make regarding your family will be swift and loud and long lasting."

"First of all, they're not my family, second it's just a party. Those happen all the time."

"Tonight is a statement to the parents in there that we're united on campus, and you've already seen what happens when you broadcast that you're not one of us. Trust me, if the parents think that's your stance, things will get much, much worse."

She huffs out, "Fine. I'll meet you back on campus."

Finn snorts. "Oh no, Pet. You'll be riding with me so I can make sure you show up to the party."

I expected to have to bang on Thea's door to get her to come out of her room after we broke off to change our clothes. She met the thirty-minute deadline Pax gave, but I'm not stupid enough to think she's suddenly decided to be compliant. She's got that look in her eye that says we're probably gonna regret making her come along.

There are enough non-legacy students at the party that she can ignore us, but I'm still cognizant of where she's standing, and what she's doing. I don't think I'll ever be able to ignore her. I wonder how Pax manages to do it.

The compulsion to watch her is the reason I notice she's walking away, dragging someone by the hand towards the cover of the trees behind us. I follow and watch as he kisses her, rubbing his hands up the sides of her body.

It makes sense now. Why she didn't put up a fight. She came to a legacy party with the intention of doing the worst thing she can. Hooking up with someone who's not a legacy. It's a huge slap in our face.

I watch him slip his hand under her shirt, kneading at her breast. She's not enjoying it. I see the tension in her body. The way he's touching her. It's too soft. Too delicate. My Rey likes to feel. I don't know why she's suffering through this. There are other ways to rebel.

I'm tired of watching. I step from behind the trees, making more noise than necessary. The guy takes one look at me, then runs off, knowing he crossed a line, touching a legacy. When Thea tries to do the same, I grab her arm and drag her even deeper into the woods, ignoring her protests, sucking in that first hint of fear.

I've been tolerant. I've been patient. Now, I'm pissed that she's being so cavalier about her safety and letting a complete stranger put their hands on her. Her first mistake was walking off into the woods with someone she doesn't know and letting him touch her out in the open, where anybody could see.

When I find a spot away from prying eyes, I trade out my hold on her arm for her throat. Before she can complain, I crash my lips against hers. Of course, she resists my kiss and tries to evade my mouth. That doesn't stop me. I bite her cheek, her nose, whichever part of her face she turns my way.

"What are you doing, Holden? You can't just interrupt my hookup."

"I can, and I *will* every damn time. You wanna fuck in the woods? I'm your guy."

"I don't want you."

"Too bad, because I'm who you're getting." I wedge my leg between hers. "If you want someone else, you'll have to get away from me."

I ignore the rest of what she's saying about not wanting to fuck me. She's not trying to escape. I know her. I know what she needs and what she likes. She slaps at my hand, trying to push it away, but I work my hands into her pants, past the waistband of her panties, and jam my long middle finger into her dry cunt. "He wasn't even doing enough to get you wet. Don't worry, I'll have you dripping in no time."

I pull my hand out, spit on my fingers, then shove two of them inside her. The confines of her jeans making it a tight fit. The heel of my hand presses against her clit. It feels so good to be touching her the way I want to.

"Holden. My god." She gasps around my hold on her throat.

"Oh baby, save the exaltation for when you're on your knees worshipping me."

I yank her to the ground, pinning her arms to her sides with my knees as I straddle her. I push her shirt up, exposing her tits. "No bra? It's like you wanted me to have easy access or something."

I pull out my dick and wedge it between her tits, smashing them together, and slide it back and forth, tapping her lips with the head every time I push forward.

"Open." I don't give her time to think about it. I help her along by tugging her nipple. When her lips part on a pant of air, I push my cock head past her lips. I groan when I brush along the roof of her mouth and feel the barest scrape of her teeth. Then pull out.

"Get up, get up." She moves her head side to side, trying to prevent me from sliding into her mouth again.

"No." I see the panic in her eyes, the fear because I'm pinning her down. But I'm not getting up. She doesn't need to be scared of me. "Suck me, Rey. It'll make you feel better."

"A blow job makes *you* feel better."

"Me rewarding you in the end will make you feel better." I hold her head still and push in again, sliding against her velvety tongue. "Come on, let's play. Suck me hard and deep into the back of your throat while I squeeze the life out of you."

I pull out and squeeze her cheeks, forcing her jaws to hollow. "You need a little more lube on your tongue, so I don't get stuck."

I spit into her mouth, then stuff her with my cock again. "Our combined spit feels so good on my shaft."

I drop more spit between the valley of her breasts, making the slide easier. I keep one hand on her throat, and rake the other through my hair, my eyes falling to half mast. God, her mouth feels so damn good. My balls are tightening up already.

I really need to stop denying myself like I've been doing. Now is as good a time as any to tell her we're locked in from here on out. If I want to cum, she's gonna give me whatever opening I want, and if she wants to cum, I'll make her see stars. Any time, any place.

"It's done, Thea. No more using other guys to stuff down your feelings and doing shit to help you numb the pain. I want you to embrace it. Feel it all. I'm your pain management from now on."

I grab her arm, dragging it to my mouth and bite down on the skin at the bend of her elbow. "I'll give it." I kiss the same spot, sucking the flesh, soothing the sting of the bite with my tongue. "And I'll take it away." I go back to moving in and out of her mouth. "All you have to do is hang on for the ride."

I pinch her nostrils and damn near spill down her throat when I push further into her mouth, preventing her from taking a decent breath of air.

"I love the look on your face you get when you can't breathe. It's like acceptance. Peace. Like you're ready to let go permanently." I pull out, then shove back in. "But you won't be dying on me anytime soon, Rey. There's so much for us to discover about each other. So many more ways to play."

She hums around my cock. Her eyes widen as she realizes what she's done. I pull out again, already missing the feel of her mouth, but I have rules and number one will always be that I don't cum until she does. "Time to taste that pussy now. See what all the fuss is about." I stare her down. "Keep your hands on the ground. Don't even think about moving them."

She squirms as I tug her pants and panties down to her knees, exposing her glistening, wet pussy. "So pretty."

I kiss it reverently. Happy that it's here waiting for me to give it pleasure and pain. Because I will. Her clit is pulsing. Just asking me to take a bite out of it. I start with slow, soft licks, savoring the taste of her on my tongue, the smell of her in the air. Testing her ability to listen. She moans and lifts her head off the ground but her hands stay in place.

Coach Wolfe was right about how amazing she tastes. I scrape my nails across the inside of her thigh and plunge my tongue into her hole, adding a finger to grab some moisture, before smoothing it down to her ass. I repeat the process, moving more of her slickness, then push a finger deep into her ass.

"Oh shit, oh shit, oh shit." She chants.

I work my finger in and out while sucking on her clit. She groans, and raises her hips off the ground, thrusting against my hand. Her hand moves and I stop what I'm doing. "What did I tell you about your hands?"

She lowers them, and I chuckle, as she clenches around my fingers. "Such a dirty, girl, aren't you? You like being bossed around while my finger's in your ass? You know what'll feel better? My cock in one hole, my fingers in another and a ball gag in your mouth. All your holes filled at once, while you fight to breathe."

I slide my hand up to cup her breast. "Your skin on fire as I turn it pink with my hand, belt, or zap you with my taser."

My dick jumps at that thought. "Yeah, I think I want to cum deep in your ass while you're strapped down to my bed, still convulsing from a zap on your clit."

She stiffens, the fear of being subdued rearing its head again. My cock swells. I need more of her fear. "I'm gonna blindfold you so you can't see me. Bind your hands so you can't touch me. You'll be stretched out, forced to endure whatever I do to you. Helpless. Unable to fight back."

She cries out as she struggles in my hold. Writhing, trying to get away. "Are you reliving that night again, Thea?" I take her whimper as a yes. "The people who hurt you, do you think they held you down? Do you think they tried to take this cunt? Your mouth or ass? I bet they did. Just like somebody wanted to the night they drugged you at the party."

My hand trails up to her neck. I squeeze her throat, taking away her air. "I'm gonna do what they couldn't. I'm gonna make you do the one thing your stubborn ass probably refused to do. I'm gonna make you beg for it."

I dive back between her legs, feasting on her. Working my thumb in and out of her slick heat. It's not enough. Not nearly enough. I need to feel her. I replace my thumb with the tip of my cock. He hands leave the ground. She pushes against my chest trying to put space between us.

I tighten my grip. "That's right. Fight me baby. Make me work for it." I pull her closer, slowly work my dick around. Pushing just a little of the way in. "You feel amazing, Rey." I stare down at where the head breaches her opening. "Just the tip and I'm leaking."

"Don't. Don't. Don't, fuck me raw. Don't cum in me." She repeats over and over. Her broken sobs fuel my lust.

I hadn't considered it. Now she's put the thought in my head, and I can't get it out. But she's right about one thing. I can't cum inside her tonight. We have a few things to work out first. This is already reckless enough. Once again, I'm losing my ability to stay detached and think rationally. She does that to me. Makes me irrational.

I won't lose control like that. I won't even push all the way in. I just needed to feel her a little bit. After four more shallow thrusts, I pull out and resume gorging on her taste. "We were up to three fingers last time. Right? Let's add another."

"Oh, god, Don't!" Her plea blends into a threat.

"I have to. I have to see how much you can take." I glance up from my favorite view, taking in the confusion on her face. She's flushed, her hair fanning out, with wisps sticking to her forehead. She's beautiful. "Don't be scared, Thea. Not of this. I want you to crave pain. *My* pain. Only mine."

Smiling up at her, I say, "Let me hurt you." I don't wait for her to answer. Shoving four fingers at once into her swollen cunt. Her body jolts as I ram them in and out. Not at all gentle. Her wails of protest turn to moans of pleasure as I work her over. And just because I'm all about pushing her boundaries, I work two fingers into her ass.

"How does it feel?"

"It's too full, too much." She pants.

"I know," I moan, when her walls clench around my fingers. "Isn't it perfect?"

I lean over and bite down on her clit. She screams as her body convulses around my hands. I abandon my plans to come down her throat. Using the hand covered in her juices, I stroke myself and erupt, aiming my load at her stomach and tits. I smear my seed over her skin. Like I'm an artist painting my canvas. When I look up, she's staring at me. Her eyes clear, the tension gone, if only for a few minutes. It'll all be back. I know that better than anyone.

As the fog clears, she asks, "Are you gonna just take off and leave me out here, like you did the last time?"

It's a valid question and I'm glad she's smart enough to ask it. "Yes."

"Why? Why go through all the trouble to hurt me and make me cum, then run off?"

"Because you're gonna be pissed when you come down from your sex high, and I don't have a death wish."

I kiss her, because I'm not a total dick. I know she doesn't need me coddling her, but I also know that she's still in a vulnerable state of mind. "Next time, I promise to let you choke on my dick, and I'll cum down your throat."

"Next time? Are you fucking crazy? There is no next time."

Her blatant attempt to lie puts a smile on my face. It's normal for her to struggle with this. Her body wants to be owned. She likes being used, but she thinks there's something wrong with it. That's why we'll do this again and again until she finally feels safe in admitting it. I kiss her again. "Thank you, Thea. You can go back to hating me now."

I go to pull away, but she surprises me, pulling me down for another kiss. I have to break it off or we're gonna go into round two and I'm not sure I'm strong enough to resist fucking her for a second time tonight. "If there's no next time, then why did you kiss me?"

"It was a kiss off. A kiss of death. My promise that if you try this again, I'll kill you."

That's so adorable. Her threatening while she's underneath me. Getting to my feet, I say, "Head straight back to the dorms."

She stands and brushes her hands across her ass before pulling her pants up. "I'm going back to the party."

Always fighting back. It's time she learns that I fight back, too. "If you do, then we'll be on *next time* before you've fully recovered from this time, and everyone will find out how much of a pain slut you are."

Her knife makes an appearance. She jabs it in my direction. "I'm not a pain anything, unless it's a pain bringer."

"I'm looking forward to testing the validity of that statement. But I need to get back to the party. Go to the dorm, Thea."

I'm caught off guard, again, when she grabs my hand, keeping me from walking off. She drops it just as quickly. I pretend not to notice the small tremor. She doesn't want to seem weak, and I won't make her feel that way.

"No wandering around, no searching out any new hookups. Keep to the path straight ahead for maybe a quarter mile, and it'll bring you by the guard shack near the front gates. If I see you lingering around out here, I will chase you and catch you, and I won't show as much restraint as I have so far." I grab her shirt, pulling her closer. "Don't fucking try me."

I ignore the insults she's hurling at me, and walk through the clearing towards the party, without looking back.

I'm not some damsel in distress and I haven't been afraid of the dark since I was six, but I'm glad Holden gave me directions for how to get to a well lit portion of campus. The canopy of trees isn't as dense as the way we entered the woods, so I have plenty of moonlight to help me navigate.

As I walk, I go over what happened to distract me from the pounding in my chest. This is the second time Holden's rammed his fingers into me. It's like he's fixated on how many I can take. Determined to stretch my pussy out of shape. But why?

I'd also like to know why he keeps dragging up my attack, and why I don't stab him the minute he holds me down and threatens to hurt me. Just because he hasn't yet, doesn't mean he won't. And as LJ said, I haven't completely ruled out that The Trium was behind what happened to me.

I reach the pathway that leads to the dorms. There are a few people out tonight who aren't at the party and a security guard goes by on his bike. The school made this big show about upping security's presence on campus between sunset and one am. I think they're still flaky, because the only places I've seen an increase in security are around Vale Tower, The Rock and The Library.

I swipe myself into the building. Everyone in Vale Tower goes to any party the Trium attends, and I'm assuming the people here for Winter break are still operating under that stupid rule. But just in case somebody else cut out early or stayed home, I set the elevator to secure mode to take me to the top floor without stopping. I'm not in the mood to deal with the snide comments about the way I look with leaves and dirt in my hair, or the offhanded questions about what happened to me. Everyone's so damn nosy, and after Pax's comment, I'm wondering if these students report back every detail about what happens on campus to their parents.

Moira, Scott and Wolfe have all been clear on one thing since I woke up in Palisade Shores. Don't take anything anyone says or does at face value. They all have agendas. Until I can completely rule them out as suspects or accomplices, trust no one.

I slip into the shower, washing the dirt and grime off my body and out of my hair, taking special care between my legs. I'm sore, and the soap stings where I have scratches from Holden's fingernails.

I close my eyes, replaying what happened. The weight of his body against mine. His hands on my skin and in my hair. The way he smiled up at me and said, "Let me hurt you." As if he was simply asking me out on a date.

Why did I let him? Why did my body react? Why did I enjoy it all? Even in those moments when I couldn't breathe, my throat stuffed with his cock, his fingers pinching off my nostrils. He could have killed me, and yet I didn't feel like I was in any danger. I wanted to see how far he would go. Wanted him to continue. Wanted him. Until the panic set in, and he came dangerously close to slipping inside me with no protection.

How screwed up is it that my issue was with him going raw and not with him trying to make it a trifecta of me having fucked each of the Coxsuckers. Although Pax doesn't count. I wasn't in my right mind when I slept with him.

I finish with my shower and take time to squeeze the excess water out of my hair, before twisting it up into a bun on the top of my head, throw on some shorts and a t-shirt, then pop a sleeping pill before climbing into bed. I read until the pills take effect, pulling me into a deep, dreamless sleep.

Chapter 64

Thea

I push through the doors of Wolfe Pack, doing my best to ignore the nervous flutter in my stomach. I changed my mind a million times this weekend, but I finally admitted to myself that it's time to get back to training. Watching videos online will only get me so far.

It's not my regularly scheduled day, if I even have a day anymore, but I figure Wolfe won't refuse to train me if I'm in his face. I give a courtesy knock before stepping into his office. He takes one look at me and says, "LaReaux, have you been breaking my no fighting rule?"

"No, coach."

"Really? Because you just walked in here, like you got your ass kicked last night."

I mumble, "That's because I did. Literally."

He must've heard me because he stands and walks over, lifting my shirt. I swipe at his hand. "Don't."

I'm sore and don't move fast enough to keep him from seeing the bruising on my ribs from Holden pinning his knees against me. I avert my eyes as he takes in my torso, rubbing his hand along the mottled skin.

"Did you want this?"

I chew my lip, thinking over the best way to respond. If he'd have asked when Holden was giving his evil villain monologue, my answer would've been hell no. But by the end, I was wet and needy just like he said I'd be.

"No judgement, sweetness. I just need to know if I'm adding to my body count."

"You don't have a body count."

He tilts my head up, eyeing the faint hand print I know is on my throat.

"Not yet, but I have a list I'm building of future victims." He forces me to look at him. "Now answer the question. Did you feel safe, and did you want it, or did someone come back to finish what they started?"

I could lie. I could tell him no and send him after Holden, but that would be a bitch move and manipulative as hell. I'm still processing everything, but dealing with Holden falls to me. And I'm safe now. Strange as it may seem, I know I was safe then, too. "Yes, I wanted it."

He curses and growls, "Lucky bastard."

"It's not. It's not like that."

"You don't owe me any explanations about who you hook up with."

I grab his arm to keep him from walking away. "Wolfe, I- It just happened."

His smile is forced. "Thea. It's your life. Your body. As long as you were safe and are happy with your choices, you won't hear anything else from me about it. I told you we couldn't happen again and I'm glad we're on the same page."

"I didn't do it to spite you. We didn't even have sex. He..."

"I don't wanna hear about it. Any of it. Ever."

Maybe coming here today was a mistake. I was so focused on needing to get back into fighting. Pushing myself to prove that I'm ready to train, that I didn't think of what Wolfe would say if he saw the bruises. I guess I thought he wouldn't say anything.

There are so many things I haven't said. That I should have said, especially since he's been there for me all this time. He saved me from the coffin, but it's not some hero worship thing. I've been drawn to Wolfe since the moment I saw him in the bar.

"I think about the night we met, and how things might have been different for us if I would have dropped your Physical Enhancement class."

"I'm not that difficult to work with."

"You are. You know you are. And you like it that way."

He studies me and asks, "Why didn't you drop the class? You know, when you quit after your accident, I thought... well, it doesn't matter what I thought, because you're ready to train again. That is why you're here, right?"

"I like training. You've worked with the best." Do I dare say the rest of it, knowing nothing will change? I need to tell him. I need him to know it's not just the fighting. "And because some sick, twisted part of me can't stand the idea of not seeing you." I step closer. "I think about that night, Wolfe. I think about all the nights in Palisade Shores, the phone calls we've had. The nights we stole on campus. What I did last night doesn't change that. It doesn't change how much I wish I could have another night with you, which is ridiculous because you've made it perfectly clear that you don't want me. But if you did, I'd want you too. I know I've never said it. But I do."

"What are you saying, exactly, Thea? That you want me to lay you out in the middle of the octagon and fuck you into the mats?"

I nod my head, and smirk, "Yes."

He steps closer, crowding me until my back is against the wall. "Think about what you're risking for a few moments of pleasure. What if The Trium decides to tell people I went down on you at a frat party? What if someone finds out that I just spent an entire semester in class struggling not to touch you? What if your grades get called into question, or they toss you out of school?"

Our lips are inches apart. I brush my mouth against his as I whisper, "I. Don't. Care."

He growls and jerks me closer, pressing his lips to mine in a feverish kiss. I groan into his mouth as he slips his hand under the waistband of my yoga pants. His rough fingers gather up the moisture already pooling between my legs and, swipes it across my clit. It's so similar to what Holden did to me, and yet so different. How does my body react to two different people? I push that thought away, and lower the front of his shorts enough to free him, stroking him to match the pace of his fingers on my clit.

"Fuck sweetness." He groans. "We shouldn't be doing this. Here, of all places, but damned if I'm gonna stop before I get to see you fall apart for me again."

I nod. I'm all for us to keep going until that happens.

"I think about it too." He says. "About how fucking good you felt bouncing up and down on my cock and how incredible you taste." He grunts against my ear as my thumb circles the crown of his shaft. "I should have kicked you out of my class and never agreed to train you. I fight every goddamn day not to do this to you."

"Because of your job."

"Because I know every time I do, I'm one step closer to…"

He cuts off what he's saying and I don't press for an answer, too caught up in the feeling of his hands on me. His mouth on my neck. I'm close. I wrap my arms around his neck and hitch a leg up on his waist, trusting him to keep me upright as I ride his fingers.

"Wolfe!" I pant.

"I know, I know." He presses his forehead to mine. "Cum for me, sweetness. Let me feel you lock down on my fingers."

I do, my head falling back, mouth open as I find my release. As I catch my breath, I reach for him, but he shifts away, sucking his fingers into his mouth with a contented hum. He places a chaste kiss against my temple, then whispers in my ear. "You're gonna do that on my cock real soon."

He lowers me to the ground and slides my pants back up before taking a step back. With a smirk on his face, he taunts, "Now stop stalling and go get on the treadmill."

Chapter 65
Holden

I cast a furtive look over at the table where Thea usually sits. I know she said she'd be sitting with us from now on, but there are plenty of reasons for her to change her mind. I think back to our second chase through the woods. She was perfect that first night. The way she ran, and hid and eluded me for as long as she could. But those are my woods. I'm comfortable in the dark. Alive. There's no place among those trees that anyone can hide from me.

Next, my mind drifts to her failed hook up attempt at the party. She was carrying the knives Finn gifted her, and could have pulled them out at any time to protect herself from me. But she didn't. She fought, called me names, and begged, and then she gave me those sweet tears and that *scream*. I was still hearing, like the sweetest lullaby, as I drifted off to sleep.

She's not here for breakfast, but I know I'll see her, eventually. I'm happy about the temporary reprieve. I've never been in this position before. Uncertain of how someone will react. She didn't confront me right away, but I've learned Thea likes to act strategically. So her retaliation could come at any moment. If she's trying to lull me into a false sense of security, enough time has passed where that has happened. Except I never let my guard down.

Will she have security with her or will she dish out her revenge herself? Approach me in public and out me to the students on campus about what I did? Either way, I'm prepared for the looks. The hate. The disgust. I controlled myself as much as I could. I didn't take it too far, although everything in my body was telling me to fuck her into the dirt.

I can be cruel in bed. I have a savagery in me that wants to toy with women and break them over and over again. But they're so soft and fragile around here, I can never allow myself to go too far. Holding back leaves me unsatisfied and hollow. I've learned to deny myself. To ignore my needs. I'm okay with being celibate until Pax and Finn drag me into a hookup, thinking it's what I need. I do it for them, because I know they think they're doing it for me.

I eat my food and sip my tea while reading my book. Thea enters the dining hall and goes to get her food. The Rock is empty so I stay in my seat instead of blocking off the line, but my senses are on high alert. Her head is down, and she's wearing a ball cap pulled over her eyes. Did I succeed with her already? Did I break her? I feel a twinge of trepidation. I thought she'd be stronger than this. That thought is followed by a sense of guilt. My father would be so disappointed.

This is not how a Sullivan man acts. League members have their vices, but Sullivan's are supposed to be above it all. It's why my dad works for the government. Our bloodline has always been without blemish. Without reproach. It's bad enough I hack into things I shouldn't. But my dark desire... this would be the thing that someone could use against him.

I've played with girls before, but they always know ahead of time what's about to happen. It's one thing to do it with someone who's trying to get closer to a Wren or The League. They know how things work around here and we pay to keep their silence. I didn't take any such precautions with Thea. Both times, I just went on instinct.

She sits at her usual table. I'm glad I didn't have them remove the partition yet. I suspected it would take a while before she fully committed to sitting with us. Should I apologize? Get her to promise not to tell? Or is it too late? She drops a napkin and winces when she bends over to pick it up.

Why is she in pain? Any soreness from that night should have passed by now. Did someone else touch her? She straightens and catches me staring. I don't bother trying to pretend I'm not. I can't get a read on how she's feeling. I can't tell if the anger on her face is directed at me or someone else.

Somehow I make it through my meal, without going to her. When she's done, she comes to stand next to my seat. She leans close enough that I smell her unique apple scent. It's not as good as how it smells when her essence mixes with the apples on my hand, but I like it all the same.

She waits until the last person leaves the table, then pulls my hair, baring my throat and pressing a knife against my Adam's apple. I see the darkness swirling in her gaze and hear the promise of retribution in her voice. "I hope you had fun, pretty boy. Because the next time we meet in the dark, you'll be the one running and limping out of those woods." She pulls the knife away from my throat and taps me on the cheek with it.

I lean into her hold and kiss of the blade. "I'll text you my schedule for the rest of Winter break, to make me easier to track. But if I get the drop on you, the two nights we've had will seem like pillow fights compared to what happens next."

Her pupils blow wide, her tongue darts out to wet her bottom lip, a little gasp escaping through her parted lips. She releases her hold and hurries out the door. I follow soon after, meeting up with Finn on the sidewalk.

He stares at Thea's back as she walks aways, and asks, "What the hell was that all about? I could feel the tension all the way out here."

A smile slowly makes its way across my lips. Thea sought me out, and despite what she may think, she didn't tell me to stay away. I can't wait to exploit that loophole every chance I get.

So apparently those consequences Joshua Laurent is so fond of have found me. As a punishment for leaving dinner, I'm stuck attending another function with him. He calls it family bonding time. I roll my eyes, knowing this has nothing to do with him wanting to get closer to me, and everything to do with trying to be seen.

Moira came tonight, but Scott's stuck at work. "Please try to keep your cool, Thea."

"I'm cool. I'm calm. I don't know how much chit chat we're gonna have watching the ballet, but I'm here as requested." And I'm only here because I'd be stupid to give up a chance to see The Los Angeles Ballet.

I've watched plenty of clips online, even caught a few ballets on television, but this will be my first time seeing one live. I keep my face blank, though. Never let your opponent know what you're feeling because they'll take that good thing away from you.

We push our way through the crowd hovering in the lobby, and go find our seats. We've barely settled when Joshua excuses himself, saying he sees someone he needs to speak with. Moira smiles and I roll my eyes. He's so damn obvious.

"Is this as bad as it gets?"

Moira looks up from her phone with a sigh. "I wish I could answer that. He's making the rounds, putting his face back out there. I'm happy he has this chance to get involved again. The League meant a lot to him, and my actions took that away from him."

"Do you feel guilty because they kicked him out of the clubhouse?"

"A part of me does, but I'd do it again."

"Even though I'm like this?"

Her brows furrow. "Like what?"

"Tough, abrasive, say whatever I want. Rule breaker. You name it, I'm it. I'm not sweet and light and airy. I'm heavy and dark."

"Thea, you're smart, brave and strong. Resilient. You stand up for yourself. You make sure everyone knows where they stand with you. You are everything Scott and I dreamed you would be. Don't let what you see and hear from the other legacy students or their parents make you feel otherwise."

I settle back in my seat. Did we just have a moment? I feel like we did. Maybe I should say something. Joshua returns before I can. I watch Moira's face transform back into its plastic mask. When the lights dim, I reach over and squeeze her hand. I've been around enough kids and they're disapproving parents to know this must be uncomfortable for her.

I'm not ready to make any decisions about our relationship. I haven't heard Joshua's side of things, and I probably should, before passing judgement. I will, when I'm ready. But no matter what happened, nobody should have to act like they've been body snatched just to keep the peace.

He's droning on and on. The ballet ended fifteen minutes ago and now we're standing around waiting for Joshua to finish babbling about what he's been doing all these years away from Canyon Falls.

He spins a lively tale. It's hard to tell if they're all impressed by his story or standing around hoping to press him for details about his suspension. Moira's off to the side with some of the wives. That just leaves me standing with my back against the wall, waiting so we can all walk out of here together.

Moira breaks off from her group and walks over to me. "Why don't you head out?"

"You sure?"

"There's nothing else for you to do around here. Daddy's gonna talk until everyone walks off or we get thrown out of here. You showed up wearing a dress. You've done more than enough today."

It's a pretty dress. Another of Moira's picks. "Thanks, Moira."

She smiles, then goes back over to her group, and I slip out the door. I pass my ticket to the valet and pull my phone out, waiting for him to bring my car around. My hand hovers over my contact list, trying to think of who I should call to talk to on the ninety-minute drive back to campus.

I climb into the driver's seat, snap my belt into place, and set my phone in the holder before pushing the call button. It rings four times, then connects just as I'm reaching to disconnect the line.

"LaReaux."

Just hearing his voice calms me. "Why do you sound like you're asleep?"

"Because it's after ten at night. I was asleep."

"Well, wake up."

"Why? Is my gym on fire?"

"Not that I know of."

I switch lanes and pull onto the freeway. "What are you doing LaReaux?"

"I just left the ballet and I'm heading back to campus."

"That's right. Plans with the grandfather. Tell me about it."

"He pretty much ignored us, but at least I had good seats and saw a fantastic ballet."

"In that world, women are accessories. They're rarely seen as people with something to contribute."

"Then I guess it's a good thing I'm not part of that world."

"The more time you spend around them, the more influence they'll have over you."

My whole body shivers, rejecting that thought. "Awe, Wolfe. Are you scared they're gonna woo me away from you? I promise that will never happen. I'll always be a stubborn pain in your ass."

He chuckles. "I hope so, sweetness. I hope so."

My eyes drift open when the timer goes off, letting me know my time in the sauna is up. I climb to my feet, stretching the tendons in my neck, groaning when I hear that satisfying pop.

When I grab the door handle and tug, it doesn't move. I pull again, confirming it's locked. I smear my hand across the steamy window, peering into the gym. I can't see anything with how quickly it keeps fogging up.

I bang the heel of my palm against the door, trying to get someone's attention. There has to be someone else here, because I didn't lock myself in.

After a few minutes, I add my voice to the banging. Nobody comes, and I watch with a sense of dread as the lights in the gym flick off. I swipe at the beads of sweat running down my forehead.

I glance at the thermostat. It's getting hotter in here. I resume pounding on the door and yelling until my voice goes hoarse. The last light clicks off. My next breath is heavy and thick. I'm back there. Back in that moment. I feel the heat on my feet and struggle to breathe as the smoke fills my chest. My vocal cords shredded from yelling for someone to help me. Just like I'm doing now.

"Let me out, let me out!!" I plead, straining to be heard. Nobody's coming. There is no saving me this time.

"What the hell?"

"Thea! Thea! Wake up. Wake the fuck up." Arms grab me, shaking me. My head lolls to the side. I try to open my eyes, but I'm too tired. "You are not doing this shit to me, Nem. Not today. Look at me! Dammit, look at me! We need to get your body temperature cooled down, but I need you to wake the fuck up!"

My eyes flutter open. I move my mouth, wanting to tell him I don't take orders. My words slur. "Gid you shtrug me again?"

I miss his response because I finally pass out.

I know that beep. I'm intimately familiar with that beep. I hate the beep. "Easy, Thea."

A cool hand presses against my shoulder, keeping me prone. "What?" I try again. "Did they catch him?"

"Catch who?"

I fall back asleep.

Hospital. I'm in a fucking hospital.

"You're awake."

I push myself up in bed to get a better look at my surroundings.

"Thirsty?"

I nod. My mouth is dry and my throat hurts. She holds the glass while I sip through a straw. She takes the cup away and says, "I'll let the doctor know you're up."

She returns with him a few minutes later. "How are you feeling?" He asks as he takes my vitals.

"Fine."

"You gave Mr. Cox quite a scare. Do you remember what happened?"

"Someone locked me in the sauna.."

He gives me a pitying smile. "No one did anything to you, Miss LaReaux. You stayed in the sauna too long and passed out. There's a reason we don't recommend exceeding twenty minutes. You run the risk of dehydration, heat exhaustion and, in your case, heat stroke. It's a good thing Mr. Cox found you."

"I- I couldn't get out. The door was locked."

"I'm sure the fatigue you felt made it seem that way. We've given you some fluids and cold compresses. We recommend you continue to hydrate throughout the night with water and electrolytes. Probably just broth for food to make sure you can keep it down."

My head still feels foggy, and the details of what happened are fuzzy. Was I so overcome by the heat that I lacked the strength to open the door? "Mr. Cox has volunteered to see you safely back to the dorm. Now, if you'll excuse me."

I swing my legs over the side of the bed and get my first look at what I'm wearing. "Um, Pax." I look around the room. "Where are my clothes?"

He snarls, "How the hell should I know?"

"You didn't grab my gym bag before your brought me here?"

"I found you delirious on the floor. Sure, I thought, let me go looking through the girl's locker room so I can find your shit."

My legs are bare and I'm swimming in a zip up hoodie. "Whose nasty ass clothes am I wearing?"

"Mine. I carry a sweatshirt with me, so I yanked it on you. Good thing too, because the towel came off on our way here."

My head snaps up. "You carried me all the way here from the gym?"

"No, I teleported. Now if you're done asking stupid ass questions. Let's go."

"The doctor's gone. You can stop acting like you're some kind of hero, when you're probably the person who locked me in to begin with."

I struggle to hang on to my attitude. The truth is, my nerves are shot. I feel like I did when I first came back to school, and I don't want to be anywhere near Paxton Cox, or anyone else on campus right now.

"Go on. You're dismissed."

He stalks over and gets into my face, leaning close enough that I get an extra whiff of his body wash. "Look here, you little brat. I'm about sick and tired of you getting yourself into trouble and having to come put out the fires. I don't want to spend a second more with you than necessary, but the only way the doctor would release you was if someone escorted you back to the dorms. And since your friends are off campus, I got stuck doing it. Or would you like Mr. Laurent to come sign you out?"

"What?"

"That's right. As a legacy heir, school policy says the infirmary has to release you to the head of your bloodline."

"Then why did the doctor agree to leave me with you?"

"Four months and you still don't know the answer? The Trium is at the top of the food chain here. We're the exception to the rules. Now either get off your ass, or stay here for the rest of the night."

Chapter 68
Finn

I pace back and forth. I can't calm myself enough to sit still. Not after the phone call we got from Pax. Somebody did it again. Some dead man locked Thea in a sauna and left her there. But once again, we're saying it was an *accident* to keep everyone else from overreacting and causing a panic. Not that they should be panicking. So far, these near-death experiences have only happened to Thea.

"She's okay, right?"

Holden nods, still staring at his tablet screen. "Her medical records are clear from any lasting issues. She's on fluids and bedrest for the next twenty-four hours, and could probably benefit from a massage to offset the muscle cramps, but other than that, she's fine."

"You didn't see anything on the cameras?"

"A bunch of people entering and exiting the gym, but there aren't any cameras over by the sauna."

"Another blind spot. How many more of them are there on campus?"

"Enough to be concerning."

"We need to fix that."

"I can't mount cameras in bathrooms and shower areas, and we shouldn't need cameras in any of the other areas. Thea's status should be enough to keep her safe."

"Well, it's not."

"And we need to figure out why that is."

"That's an easy answer. Somebody's gone rogue."

"Or somebody's about to make a move and officially challenge our position here. They might be orchestrating these attacks on Thea as evidence of why The League should pick a new Trium. Or finally pick another family to rule alongside us."

I hear Pax's voice in the hall and jump over the couch, rushing to fling open my door. She's got that look on her face again. The one she had after her attack. The look in her eyes that lets me know she's not really here. She's detaching, shrinking back on herself. Pushing me away is sure to follow. I can't stand the idea of her going back into zombie mode. I grab her, crushing her to my chest. "Thank god you're okay."

She's stiff in my arms, but I ignore it, lifting her up. "Let's get you settled, Pet."

"Finn, I don't need help walking."

I tilt my head, capturing her gaze. "I know exactly what you need and I'm going to make sure you get it."

"I don't need..."

"Hush, Pet. There's no fighting me on this." I tuck her head in the crook of my neck and carry her into my room, past Holden sitting on the couch and into my bedroom. I don't put her down until we reach the bathroom, lowering her onto the counter.

I start the shower, making sure the water isn't too hot. I'm sure she's had enough of heat, but she smells salty from the workout and steam. I know she wants to wash the grime off.

"Finn, I can't shower here. I don't have any of my stuff."

"You can just use mine and I'll get you a t-shirt to relax in."

I squeeze my dick. Thinking of her smelling like me and wearing my shit is the ultimate turn on.

"We've already talked about it, sending the wrong message when girls wear your stuff."

I look down at what she's wearing now. Pax's zip up. Maybe she should have this conversation with him, since she wore it across campus. That definitely sent a message. I pretend not to notice that the jacket is all she's wearing.

"Just shower, and then come out and we'll come up with a plan."

"A plan for what?"

"For figuring out who keeps fucking with you!"

"According to Pax and the doctor, I was overheated and couldn't work the doorknob."

"Is that what you think happened?"

She worries her lip and shakes her head. "I just can't figure out why people keep coming for me."

"Neither can we, but we're gonna get answers. Now shower, and when you feel more like yourself, come out to the living room."

Her hand snaps out, snagging my shirt and pulling me to her. Her lips crashing against mine. She works her hands under my shirt, her nails raking across my skin. "Pet, what are you…"

"Trying to feel more like myself."

"This isn't the way. You need to rest."

"Are you really about to talk yourself out of this, Number Three?"

There are so many reasons I should. A good guy would. But I'm not that guy. I'm the guy who is happy to take advantage of a situation to get what I want. For the moment, it seems we both want the same thing. I back away, stripping out of my shirt and unbutton my jeans, shoving them to the floor, then unzip Pax's hoodie, pushing the fabric off her shoulders as I lean forward, claiming her nipple.

Her legs part and I step between them, groaning at the feel of her stiff nipple in my mouth and the heat from her pussy. I toy with her clit until she's grinding against my hand, wet for me.

She strokes me until I'm painfully hard. I reach into the drawer on the left and pull out a condom, happy that I have a handful stashed in here. I love the flush of her cheeks, the look in her eyes as she watches me roll the condom on. When I'm done, she grabs my dick and lines me up with her opening. Slowly, I push inside.

She groans, and grabs my ass, rushing me. Denying me of the experience of taking my time. "You want hard and fast, Pet? Say less."

I have a knife in the same drawer where I keep my condoms. I pull it out to play, dragging it across her nipple. "You gonna bleed for me, Pet?"

I cut a slash across the top of her breast and lean forward, fusing my mouth to it. Lapping at her life force as if it has the power to replenish me. Her walls clench around me, sucking me in deeper. I pull out and plunge in again and again, riding a high, mindlessly fucking her into the mirror.

"Finn." She gasps.

"This dick feels good, yeah Pet? Because your pussy feels like nirvana." I lift her and lower the toilet seat lid, sitting down on it so she straddles me. "Bounce up and down on my cock, Pet. Ride me hard."

She braces her legs on either side of the bowl and rises and lowers herself up and down. Her tits bouncing with the movement. I reach between us and rub her clit. "Fuck. You close? Tell me you're close." I pant, grinding my teeth, trying to stave off my eruption.

"So close." She groans. "Stay right there, Finn. Right there."

At the first flutter of her pussy around me, I shove the knife into her hand. "Finish me, Pet. Finish me."

She presses the tip of the knife against my jugular, just as she locks me in place. The force of my release steals my breath. She grinds against me then stills, her head thrown back, eyes closed as her body detonates. The mirrors, fogged, our hair sticks to our foreheads from the steam from the shower. I wasn't thinking. What if the steamed room triggers her?

But she doesn't look upset. She looks content as I press kisses to her jawline.

The banging on the door interrupts my post orgasmic bliss. "Fuck off." I growl, pulling her closer.

"Let's go, Finn."

Thea was chill. Melting into my touch, as I gently kneaded her lower back. Now she stiffens at the sound of Pax's voice. I try to keep the mood light. "At least he waited until we were done."

She shrugs as she climbs off my lap and steps into the shower. I yank my pants up and open the door, stepping into the hall. "Dude, whatever it is, can't it wait?"

"No, it can't. Holden wants to inspect the gym."

"Fine, let me grab my shirt and shoes." While I'm in my room, I snag a second shirt for Thea, and pop back into the bathroom, peeking my head into the shower. She squints at me with one eye, trying to keep the soap from getting in it, from the bubbles coating her hair. "We're going on a run. I'll bring back snacks. Make yourself comfortable."

She closes her eyes and tips her head back, going back to her shower.

I join Pax and Holden at the front door. "Let's get this over with." I stomp out of my room, ahead of them. If we tackle this from three sides, we should be done quickly and I can come back and chill with my girl.

Chapter 69
Deacon

I stare at Thea's gym bag trying to work out what the hell it's doing here in the lost and found area. The gym is open to students from six in the morning until eleven at night, but I haven't seen Thea today.

The front doors slide open and the lead assholes on campus stroll into the gym like they're up to no good. I can't help but be distrustful of them, since nothing goes on around here without their knowledge. Which is why I know them all being here together has something to do with this bag.

"Where's Thea?"

Pax answers, "Why are you asking us?"

"None of you are here to work out, and Finn's fixated on her gym bag."

"It's an interesting bag. Maybe he was working up the nerve to ask where you bought it so he could get one, too."

"And maybe you're full of shit. What am I saying? There is no *maybe* about it. So I'mma ask you again, try answering truthfully this time."

"Or what?"

The thing with these guys is they think they're untouchable. That everyone is afraid of them or afraid of losing their jobs. I'm off the clock, we're in the gym and, as I have to keep reminding people, I'm not technically a teacher. I'm here on contract. I don't care if the school terminates it.

Instead of answering with my mouth, I drop Thea's bag. It falls with a heavy thunk. The split second Pax allows his eyes to track the movement is the same second my fist snaps out, connecting with his jaw.

His head snaps to the side, the other two step towards me. "Are we all having this conversation? Or is just one of you the spokesperson for the group?"

"Oh, we're all having this conversation." Pax cracks his neck and throws his guard up.

"Good. I've been wanting to hash this out since the night I found Thea in a burning coffin."

Pax goes to lunge for me, but Holden juts his arm out, holding him back. "Wait. We didn't come here looking for a fight. We are here about Thea, and going to blows won't get any of us the answers we're looking for."

"You sure? Because I think smashing your faces in until one of you spills the truth is the perfect way to get to the bottom of things."

Pax bites out, "None of us had anything to do with your little girlfriend getting buried in a coffin. We didn't even see her that night."

"Then explain the rumor I heard about Holden chasing her through the woods."

Pax's face gives nothing away when he says, "It's a rumor. Nothing else to say." His head tilts to the right. "Oops, I lied. I do have something else to say. If you ever put your hands on me again, I'll end you."

I scoff at his threat, and the lie he just told, since I got my information directly from Thea. They're so used to being the scariest people in the room that they're unwilling to consider that there is always a bigger predator out there.

"None of those words explain why you're here and since none of you are dressed for a workout, get out."

Finn reaches for Thea's bag, but I snatch it off the floor, tossing it over my shoulder. "Nah ah, ah. This doesn't belong to you."

He says, "We're taking it back to Thea."

There's no way she sent them to retrieve her stuff. Just like there's no way she left it here on purpose. "If LaReaux wants this bag, she can come get it herself."

I can feel Holden's gaze, drilling holes into the side of my face. "Something to add, Mr. Sullivan?"

"I need the log for who swiped in and out of the gym between six this morning and two this afternoon."

"Why?"

"Because one of those people locked Thea in the Sauna."

He's the only one of the three that has any fucking sense. They should let him do the talking more often. "That explains why her bag was in the lost and found, but none of you answered my original question. Where is she now?"

"At the dorms. Resting."

I chuckle. Just as I think to myself that I gave him too much credit, he says, "No, I don't believe she's resting either. She's probably plotting a very painful retaliation for whoever did it."

"So lemme guess. The Trium is gonna help her get those answers by covering up and helping the guilty party get away with it?"

Finn says, "We're not trying to cover for whoever did it. We honestly want to know who keeps messing with our girl."

My body shakes with the effort it's taking to not smash my fist into his mouth when he calls her his girl. Thea doesn't belong to him. She doesn't belong to anyone. But if she did, if she's anyone's anything. She's mine. These fuckers don't deserve her. They don't deserve the taste of her they were given.

Pointing to Pax and Finn, I say, "I warned the two of you about what would happen if she got hurt again."

Pax is still talking like they're in control of this conversation. "We don't take threats or orders from you, or any other teacher on this campus." He rubs his jaw. "And since you've clearly crossed several lines with your behavior concerning students, maybe it's time to end your employment here."

I pull out my phone and hold it out to him. "Go on, make your call. You can even use my phone to do it. I stand by everything I've ever done at this school with any student and will do it all over again."

"You admit you broke the rules? The termination letter is just writing itself."

"I admit I found a student broken and beaten in a burning coffin and I admit the school covered it up. I admit there have been no list of suspects and the investigation closed without a satisfying resolution. And I admit that when Thea and the Hughes' decide to sue the school, I will be more than happy to testify as a witness to what I saw and experienced that night and the weeks following, during her recovery."

"What?" Finn frowns and looks at the other two. "What do you know about her recovery?"

"More than you. More than the doctors here. More than the teachers on campus. More than the administration."

My gaze sweeps across their faces as I let the implications sink in. "That's right. I'm not operating on rumors or hearsay. I know what she went through. What she's still going through." Addressing Finn, I say, "Firing me hurts *your girl*." I put those words in finger quotes. "Not me."

Holden's posture changes. He's still on edge, but he loses a fraction of the aggression. "How close are the two of you?"

"I train her at school and at my gym. I'm always available for my clients, coaching them through whatever fights and battles they're facing."

His jaw clenches, then he says, "I chased Thea through the woods on Mayhem Night, but she was unharmed the last time I saw her."

"And today?"

"We don't know what happened. Pax is the one who found her in the Sauna, and he took her to the infirmary. We're here for her bag because her keys are in there and right now she's locked out of her room." He gestures towards the door. "And I need the access log because we're trying to figure out who tried to bake her like a potato.

There are no cameras pointing to the sauna, so the access log is our best chance at finding out who was here."

I toss the bag to Finn and tell Holden. "Let's go. I'll pull up the list in my office."

He falls into step beside me and says, "You believed all that? What if I'm lying?"

When we step into my office, I say, "The benefit to not playing the games the other teachers play, and not turning a blind eye to what's happening, is that I see everything going on around me."

Walking over to my desk, I ask, "Hard copy or digital?"

"Both."

I pull up the admin account and the access list, waiting until the printer spits out the pages, before saying, "Play your little legacy games, make her a part of your group. Find the assailants. But if I find out, any of you are involved in what's been happening to Thea. They'll never find your bodies."

"You're threatening us over a student?"

Handing him the printout, I make my point as clear as can, "I wouldn't waste my time or my breath over a student. I'm telling you how far I'll go to avenge *my* girl."

I rummage through Finn's dresser for some shorts. He's crazy if he thinks I'm hanging around here in nothing but his t-shirt. In fact, I don't wanna hang out here at all.

After a few more minutes of hunting around, I find what I need to get myself into my room. I climb over the balcony and pick the lock on the glass door. I don't know why I didn't think about doing it before. Before I slipped up and had sex with him.

It felt good in the moment and now I feel guilty because of my situation with Wolfe. He says he doesn't mind when I hook up with other people, but I'm not sure how that can be true or how long he'll feel that way.

It's one thing to only be casually fooling around, but I see him all the time. It's gonna get weird. Right?

The message notifications are pinging on my laptop when I walk into my bedroom. I flip it open and pull up the messages on the school app.

WOLFE

I heard what happened

ME

Great news travels fast

WOLFE

I expect conjugal visits while I'm serving consecutive life sentences

ME

I slept with Finn

WOLFE

Okay. Strictly training it is.

ME

No. That's not what I'm saying. I'm not with him. I'm not choosing him. It happened because I'm a mess. And it was a mistake. I just don't want to lie to you about it.

WOLFE

Why do you think you owe me an explanation?

ME

Because we're

WOLFE

We're what?

ME

I don't know. Sort of together. I think.

WOLFE

You think? Do you want us to be together, sweetness? For me to lay claim to you?

Do I?

ME

Yes, and no. I want you and I don't like the idea of you hooking up with anyone else, but I'm a hypocrite because I have issues with monogamy. So…

WOLFE

Do you want to see a bunch of other people or is your interest more specific to your neighbors?

ME

Just Finn

WOLFE

Not Holden?

ME

I don't know. He's… it's complicated, but I've always thought he was cute

WOLFE

Pax?

ME

Fuck that Coxsucker

WOLFE

You did. Which is why I'm asking.

ME

I was under the influence of some lab made drug. I wouldn't have if I were in control

Wolfe

I don't like the idea of you with other men, but I won't ask you to choose when I can't promise you any kind of future

ME

I understand. That's the male conundrum. Women have to be faithful while men seek out variety.

WOLFE

Is that your roundabout way of asking if I'm seeing other women?

ME

I don't have to ask. I see you with other women, and I expect it because we're not a couple.

WOLFE

This conversation's getting heavy

ME

Lol, no. It doesn't have to. It's good we're having it and clearing the air so things won't be awkward while we're training

WOLFE

Why does it sound like you're trying to end things?

ME

Because I won't agree to keep my legs closed, and you're ending things. Right?

WOLFE

Fuck no. I'm saying I guess I'll figure out how to deal with it while you work through it. Like I said, I can't promise you anything more than a good training session and a great fucking session.

I stare at the screen. This seems too easy. Too good to be true. Maybe his account was hacked.

My front door flies open. I bolt to my feet, reaching for the lamp to use as a weapon.

"How the- Why the fuck are you here?"

"This is my room Finn."

"Do you know how worried I was when I came back and you weren't in my room where I left you?"

He's holding my gym bag. Thank god he found it. I point to it. "Can I have that?"

"Yes. It'll be in my room."

"No Finn, I want to be in my room. I need to be around my things."

"Fine, I'll hang out here with you."

I push against his chest, pushing him out. "Alone. I need to be alone."

"Pet."

"Look Finn. I appreciate you getting my bag and helping me earlier, but I need space."

"Why does it sound like you're wanting space from me? After what happened, I thought we were done with the space thing."

"We had fun. Hooking up. It was a great distraction. But I don't want to give you the wrong impression."

"Are you trying to tell me it was a mistake?"

"I was needy, and I used you. I'm sorry. I-"

"I was worried, and I needed you. We needed each other. Don't try to run now, Thea, and don't think your little space speech is going to keep me away from you forever."

"I'm seeing someone, Finn. We can't hook up again."

"Who? Coach Wolfe?" He chuckles. "Yeah, Pet. I already know all about it and that doesn't change anything for me. What about you, Holden?"

I look over his shoulder to where Holden's leaning against the wall.

"Nope. Although, I actually like when Thea runs."

Shit. My walls clench because I'm fucked up in the head after everything that's happened. I like when I run from him too.

He pushes from the wall, takes my bag from Finn and hands it to me.

They both retreat to Finn's room. I drag my phone from my bag and dial Wolfe's number.

. . .

"I see the boys delivered your bag."

"Yeah. I need to make sure nothing is missing."

"It's not. Unless they let it out of their sight. And if they did, I'll kill them."

"So they're the ones who told you what happened?"

"I knew something was off because your bag was in the lost and found. You're not careless with your shit. They gave me the brief rundown, and I gave them your bag and a copy of the gym's access logs."

"Wolfe, you can't trust them."

"I agree. They're a bunch of entitled pricks, but anybody trying to help you helps me, too. I made you a promise, didn't I?"

"Yes."

"And I always keep my promises. This temporary alliance is just one tool for me to do that."

"I don't want you to get into trouble for me. It's not worth it."

"But you are, sweetness. You're worth it, and so much more."

He switches gears. "Now. Treating dehydration for the rest of the evening. You've got plenty of fluids?"

"Yes."

"No strenuous activity. Just relax in the AC for the rest of the day and tomorrow."

"That's the plan."

"And call me if you need anything."

I don't answer. I don't need to be babied.

"Thea.."

"I'm fine."

"I'm giving you an order. You will not compromise your body by overexerting yourself. Dehydration is serious for an athlete. You will call me if you need anything. No matter how small. I don't want you leaving your room. Understood?"

"Yes, sir."

"Good girl."

I whimper at his words.

"Oh sweetness. I can't wait to say those words in your ear when you take my cock."

"Fuck, Wolfe. You said no overexertion. Talking like that makes me want to be a bad girl."

He chuckles. "Alright. I'll behave."

I settle on my bed as he tells me about a fighter he's tracking and the upcoming competition season, then reaffirms his promise to get me on a ticket as long as I stick to his no unsanctioned fights rule.

I don't know why he's stuck on that. I know other fighters at his gym fight at Dredd. He's even recruited some people from there. But for me, he's not even willing to entertain the idea of me getting into the ring, even though he knows I can win. I could win before my attack. But this rule was in place before then.

I miss making all that cash, but it's not worth the argument or losing my spot. Plus, the chance for a pro fight comes with more money and will be the validation I need that I can stand toe to toe with the best in the business.

We end the call because his next client walks in, and I crack open the book I'm reading. It really is one of the best ways to check out of reality for a few hours.

Chapter 71
Finn

I launch myself onto Thea's balcony. I don't know why I didn't think about doing this before. Waiting for her to come to me is out of character for me. I'm not the wait guy. I'm the tell them what I want and enjoy letting them give it to me guy. I just spent the evening listening to Eloise drone on about this life she's dreamt up in her head for us. Now, I just want to spend time with my pet.

She's laying on her side, one hand tucked under her face, the other under her pillow. One leg and foot sticking out from under the blanket, which has slipped down to her waist. Thea's eyes pop open when I reach my hand out.

What the hell just happened? One minute I'm pulling the blanket up to her shoulder and the next I'm on the floor with a knife against my carotid. I'd usually say something funny, but right now the demons in her eyes are dishing up a nice dose of keep my fucking mouth shut. I doubt she's even seeing me.

"I told you never to touch me." She growls, pressing the blade closer. The cut of the edge letting me know just how close I am to losing my life.

"Pet." I soothe. I don't wanna spook her from whatever dream she's having. "It's me, Pet."

Her chest heaves, the knife digs deeper. She's still trapped in her head. "Thea." I move to touch her, and that sets her off. "Don't fucking touch me!"

I feel the slick warmth of blood trickling down my neck.

"I'm gonna cut your dick off and then you'll never flash it at anyone ever again, big man. Or how about I watch you bleed out until there's nothing left?"

"Neither of those sound appealing right now, Pet."

"Nemesis!"

I can't turn my head to see him or even wonder how the hell he got in here, but the way Pax just barked at her has her focusing on him. He steps closer and leans down, reaching for her, and earns a punch in the face for his trouble. She springs to her feet, swinging again.

He dodges the second blow and just misses getting gutted with her blade, taking her wrist and pulling her in close before gripping her tight, pinning her arms at her sides like she's in a straight jacket.

"What are you gonna do now?"

She head butts him, making him back away and launches at him. They go falling to the floor, with a crash I'm sure the people below us can hear. Then she's got him pinned under her.

Pax grabs her hair, forcing her head back and grunts, "Are you awake yet, or do I need to knock you around some more?"

She's breathing hard. The air thick with tension. "Pax? What the fuck are you doing in my room?"

"Keeping you from catching a murder rap." Her face pales as she looks down at the blade in her hand. He sits up, bringing his chest closer to hers, and pulls the knife from her hand as he whispers something in her ear. I'm glad he showed up to help, but I'm also jealous that he's holding her so closely. When he's done, she scrambles to her feet, gives a curt nod, then walks to her bathroom, mumbling an apology to me.

"What's a little spilled blood between friends?"

"What the hell was that?" I ask, still not sure what happened in such a short amount of time.

"Night terrors." Pax says, staring at the closed bathroom door. "Aren't you two hooking up? How do you not know she has them?"

Rolling my eyes at him, I explain, "It was three hookups. You were there for two of them. None of them ended in sleep overs." I strain my ears trying to hear what's happening behind the door. "And how do *you* know she does?"

He walks over to inspect the cut on my neck. But avoids answering my question. Stepping back and crossing his arms over his chest, he tells me, "She didn't go too deep. Just make sure you clean the wound so it doesn't get infected."

"I'm sorry, Finn. I didn't realize it was you."

My head whips around. She's standing in the doorway of her bathroom, looking small and uncertain. I hate that. I like when she's Belinda Badass. My scratch your eyes out, little pet. "It's fine. I've tasted the edge of a knife before."

"Maybe, but not one that was really intent on killing you."

Shows how much she knows. I've definitely been almost murdered once or twice. "Were you going to kill me, Pet?"

"Yes."

All this time, I played off her threats as a joke, but after watching her and Pax fight, I'm realizing how naïve that might have been of me.

Thea returns to the bathroom. The shower comes on, and Pax drags me back to my room. I have a hard time falling asleep, fighting the urge to go back over to her room.

She avoids me at breakfast, and I'm on edge for the rest of the day. Not because I'm worried that I need to watch my back, but because I don't know how to let her know that everything's okay with us.

If anything, seeing her like that just made me fall a little harder.

Chapter 72
Holden

When I let myself into Thea's room, I find her huddled under the covers, her hand under the pillow where she keeps her knife. I see another on her nightstand next to a bottle of sleeping pills. A quick check around her dorm room shows several more knives placed in discreet locations.

She doesn't feel safe in her own room. She is. Nobody's getting on this floor without us knowing, and no one other than me and Finn are coming in here while she sleeps. I can't believe he let his guard down like that and nearly got himself killed.

I go back to the bedroom and climb under the covers, rolling Thea onto her back the way I like, and settle on my side, putting my hand against the pulse of her throat. It's steady, albeit a little too fast, her anxiety spiking because she knows she's not alone. She's slow to wake with those chemicals in her system. It's why I prefer to make my own natural blend, and I only dose myself when absolutely necessary.

"It's me, Rey." Her face scrunches up, but her breathing slows. Instinctively, she knows she's safe. Even if she's not sure why. It's all the nights I've come in here. Talked to her. Touched her. It's seeped into her soul. Her body's conditioned to recognize my voice. My touch.

"How was your day?" I ask, resuming my usual greeting. "Mine was crappy. This research I'm doing for a friend keeps leading to a dead end. But I'm not quitting. I just need to get my mind off of it for a while."

I look over at her nightstand. "Finn told me what happened with your night terrors. That's unacceptable. I'm supposed to be the scariest thing in your dreams. I understand why you're taking sleeping pills. Believe me, I do. Because it gives you a deep dreamless sleep, but you need to stop taking them. You need your nightmares to help you remember what happened on Mayhem Night."

She flinches as if just the words have triggered a dream. "Don't worry. I'll give you something better to dream about."

I sit up in bed, hovering over her. My right hand holding her by the throat, my left tweaks her nipple. "You wanna play?" I lean forward, tracing the shell of her ear with my tongue. "Wake up and let me make you feel good."

I pinch her nipple a little harder, hoping the pain drags her from the hold of the sleeping pills. Her little gasp lets me know it registers, but she's not awake enough for me to start. I want her in a lucid dream state. I pinch her again, simultaneously biting down on the side of her neck. Her hand darts up, the knife swings towards me. I'm prepared for it and grab her wrist, pushing it back against the mattress. Her eyes widen and I feel her pulse hammering where I'm holding her wrist. Good. Now she's ready to play.

"What the hell are you doing in my room?" Thea's voice is thick with sleep, but I catch the angry undertones.

"Watching you."

"Get out."

"No."

"What do you mean, no?"

"I mean, I'm not leaving until we've had some fun." I tug her nipple. "You like games. Right? You and Finn were playing them all semester."

"Finn doesn't sneak into my room."

"Doesn't he?" She looks over my shoulder towards her door. "He's not here tonight. This game is just for us."

"I don't want to help you with any more experiments. I'm a liar and you hate me, remember?"

"This isn't an experiment, because I already know the results." I tighten my hold on her neck. "You're gonna enjoy everything I do to you. You'll fight and curse in the beginning, but we both know you'll be begging me when I'm done." I transfer my grip to her other hand, holding them both above her head as I settle my weight on her chest.

"Get off of me, Holden! Get off!"

She thrashes around, but she's not getting free. I let her work herself up. She hates being subdued. It has to be more than the coffin. I make a note to find out what other trauma she's endured.

Tonight, I focus on the now. My erection grows as I watch her fear eclipse her anger. Waiting for that first tear to slip free. I groan when it does, leaning forward, I lap at with my tongue. "They've still got a hold of you. The people who hurt you. They don't deserve your fears, Thea." I brush my lips across her tear stained cheek. "But I'm gonna savor every tear you shed. Break you down and break you apart."

She gives me a look that implies she's already broken before hiding it away again. I kiss her. Kissing the lie away. She's not some fragile thing. She's a fighter. It's why I chose her for this game. It's how I knew she'd be strong enough to break over and over again. Tonight, she gets her first lesson in that. Tonight, she'll realize she doesn't have to hide her darkness from me. I'm rock hard just thinking about how much fun this is gonna be.

"You remember our first kiss?"

"I remember you punking out when I touched you."

"Our second kiss was better. The way I held you down. Controlling your every breath. Were you wet for me?"

"Nope. I was feeling sorry for you. I could tell you'd never been kissed before."

She's not wrong. I hadn't had too many kisses and I'm glad about that. None of them compared to hers. I feel her breathing evening out. Can't have that. I want her hovering in a state of panic.

I stroke a finger across her nipple. "Tell me about Mayhem Night."

"You were there. You tell me."

"I wish I was there after our chase to see what happened. Did they touch you, Thea? Play with your cunt? Is that why you're drugging yourself to sleep? So you don't remember? Or is it to block out their warnings that they're coming back to finish the job?"

I lean closer, dropping my voice. "Perhaps they promised to drop you off at the same place they took your friend, and planned to keep you there until your pussy's been good and used. I hear condoms are optional in those types of places."

She shakes underneath me.

"Were you ever fucked without a condom in your old life?" I chuckle darkly. "How does it feel? Knowing you moved here to escape your old life, thinking you were being offered better opportunities, only to find out it was all a lie? You're still gonna wind up somebody's whore."

Forcing her to look at me, I say, "Or is the lie this new reality you've been told? The pills in the nightstand. The empty bottles under the sink. Seems to me like you really *are* your mother's daughter."

I press more of my weight against her, letting her feel how hard I am. "The only thing missing is the baby stroller, but I think I can help with that." Against her ear, I whisper, "I'll be an amazing absentee dad. You'll be stuck with a kid I'll never claim, and I'll be happy here with a more acceptable wife. I think I wanna start tonight."

"Don't you dare. Don't fucking touch me, Holden."

I squeeze her throat, cutting off her screams and kiss her the way I've dreamt of kissing her for weeks. With her trying to get away. Denying me. She bites my tongue and I pull back, tasting blood. I gather saliva on my tongue and grip her jaw, forcing her mouth open. Dropping the blood tinged mixture into her mouth.

Her eyes widen. Her body shaking underneath me. The fear is winning. This time when the tears fall, I let them run down her face but take away her ability to make a sound. I force my fingers inside her sleep shorts. This is the last night she'll sleep covered up like this.

"You think you can keep this pussy safe? It'll never be safe from me." I slide my fingers through her folds. She's dry, but she won't be for long. I know how she likes to be touched. Just how much pressure to apply. What rhythm to use.

She tries clamping her legs closed when she realizes she's getting turned on.

"That's right. I know this cunt and it wants me. You can tell yourself you don't, but you do. Your thirsty cunt is begging for my fingers. My mouth. My cock."

I pull my fingers out and shove them in her mouth. "Suck them clean. Don't leave a drop."

I push her shirt up, my mouth mirroring what she's doing to my fingers on her nipples, before moving lower.

"Boot mark. Hand print. Scratch. Broken rib." I quietly recite every injury she sustained, biting the area, re-marking it. Mentally, this has to be fucking with her. I'm making her relive the scars, but she has no idea how she got them.

I concede I'm a bastard for playing on her fears. Of abandonment, of unplanned pregnancy, and of that night. When I'm done with her, she'll still be crying, but I'll have replaced the reason for those tears, if only for a little while. I'll come back and do it night after night until her fears no longer have a hold on her, and she's my fearless supernova again.

I lied about putting a baby in her. I would never father a child and leave her to raise it on her own, and there is no wife that would make me happy, unless I chose her for myself. The League's matchmaking will ensure a life of loneliness.

She swallows thickly and rasps out, "I'll do whatever you want. Just promise not to hurt me."

"I can't promise that. I'm gonna hurt you. A lot." I stuff her cunt with my fingers, moving them in and out, and watch as the shock gives way to pleasure. I continue my assault, pushing her towards release. It doesn't take long, the fear heightening her passion.

She cums with a little moan, still holding back. This time I withdraw my fingers, licking them myself, before dragging off her shorts and panties. I free my erection and settle myself between her legs, grinding my arousal against her drenched core.

The weight of my body holds her in place. My fingers pinch, and bruise. My teeth, bite, all the while playing with her breath. The tip of my cock toys with her entrance. When she rubs against me, I pull away and flip her over, giving a punishing smack to her ass. Then another. And another.

"You think you can turn this around on me? Like I don't know you're trying to distract me to get to your knife?" I arch a brow. "Your fake acquiescence and greedy cunt won't make me take it easier on you." I spank her ass cheeks until they bloom a deep pink. "Beg me to stop."

She refuses, earning another smack. "Stubborn brat. I'll do this until you beg. Beg and grovel the way you should've groveled before The Trium in the beginning. The way you should've begged your *attackers* to stop on Mayhem Night. The way you should have begged your mom to love you enough to stay sober. To stay. Beg me the way you should be begging your real parents to explain why they gave you away. Beg me the way you have never begged a single day in your life."

"I hate you. I hate you!"

The words pierce my dark heart because I know they're not directed at me. Not just at me. They're for every one of those people or situations I've named. I turn her back over, diving between her legs, working her towards another orgasm. I use my tongue, mouth, fingers and scrape my teeth across her clit. "Just spanked your worthless ass, and this cunt is weeping for me. That's all you're good for, Thea. To feed me this pussy."

I bury my face between her thighs, inhaling her scent. Getting her juices all over it. Her walls clamp around my fingers. "God, Rey. You're so full of cream and I haven't even fucked you yet."

As she comes off another orgasm, I climb to my knees and finish myself off. My seed landing on her chin and tits. Before sliding the tip between her lips. Her wide-eyed gaze meets mine. She's confused about what just happened. I'm not. She was perfect. Just like I knew she'd be. I lean down, kissing her, until she's panting. "You're a dirty little pain slut. But you're mine." I growl. "I'm never letting you go."

I climb off the bed and lift her in my arms, carrying her into the bathroom. Her eyes droop, but she's fighting to stay awake. I sit her on the vanity while running a bath with some bubbles, then strip her out of her soiled t-shirt before putting her in the water and climbing in behind her.

Chapter 73
Pax

My jaw clenches as I watch Holden emerge from the hidden door. Now I know why he's been behind schedule lately and it's got nothing to do with computers. "How long have you been doing that?"

"Since after her chastity vow ceremony."

"Holden."

"I don't need a lecture. I know what I'm doing."

"Sneaking around like this, isn't you, man. This isn't us. This is the same shit all the other Trium went through. You've gotta come clean with Finn. Don't let her play you like this."

"She's not playing me, and Finn already knows I'm playing *with* her."

"He does?"

"Of course he does. We've already talked about it."

"He's backing down?"

"No. We're sharing her."

"You're what?"

He gives me a look that says I'm crazy. It feels crazy to be having this conversation with the most level-headed person in our group.

"You heard me. We both want her. So we're sharing her. Thea can't come between us, because we're not forcing her to choose one of us over the other."

I try to wrap my head around what he's saying. No woman in the history of The League of the Daggered Ravens has ever been okay with that type of setup. They always prefer one league member, one Trium member, over the other. Even when my friends and I share women, they have a preference and it's not usually Holden with his degradation kink.

"Is Finn still over there?"

"I haven't seen Finn. I'm guessing he's in his room."

"I just came from Finn's room. He wasn't in there, which is why I came over here, thinking he was with you. So, he wasn't with you?"

Holden looks confused when he asks, "Why would he be?"

"To um, moderate?"

Now the look he's giving me says I'm an idiot. "Thea doesn't need to be coerced into letting me touch her."

"Not yet, but we've seen how they react once you—"

"Thea knows what she's getting into. She's had adequate time to tell me to stop. She hasn't yet."

"She will, when things get too intense."

"*If* she does, then our playtime is over."

"Did you at least get an NDA? You didn't, did you? Fuck, Holden. At least take care of that before you decide to trust her."

"You're right. I have the paperwork printed, and I meant to talk to her about it last night, but she wasn't in the right headspace."

"What do you mean?"

"I mean, she's taking sleeping pills, probably more than the recommended dose, because she doesn't want to deal with her life or her dreams."

"That's not true. She wasn't medicated the night she almost cut Finn."

"If you remember, we were all at a party and she was drinking. She's smart enough not to mix the two." He pinches the bridge of his nose. "At any rate, that's the reason I was over there last night. I went to check on her and I fell asleep."

"You fell asleep?"

"Mmm." He moves to the coffee maker.

I don't know how to process that statement. It's small, but it's huge. Holden doesn't sleep and refuses to take sleeping aids because of how they make him feel, which explains why he's invested in Thea's use. "Did you take a pill too?"

"No. I just laid down on the bed and dozed off after we got in the tub."

"The tub?"

He throws up his hands. "Geez Pax. What are you struggling with here?"

"Everything! How are you so calm right now, talking about this? You bathed together? You slept in her bed? Those things require touching..."

He's got issues with touch. We all know this. The girls on campus gossip about it and they still freak out when he ties their hands.

"I'm fine, Pax and so far Thea respects my boundaries. She didn't ask me to stay the night and didn't try to push me into letting her touch me. She keeps her hands where I tell her, bitches and screams at me, and threatens to stab me."

"And what do you do?"

"I explain in graphic detail everything I want to do to her and sometimes I do it, then I get off on pointing out just how wet she gets for me."

I can tell he's getting annoyed at my questions. I'm not trying to get into his business but, it's been six years since the last time Holden has tried to hook up with a girl on his own.

He hands me a coffee and sits on the couch to put his shoes on. "You ready?"

I jerk my head, yes. We're having brunch with the legacies that stayed on campus. This'll be interesting.

. . .

Finn's waiting for us at the elevator, which we ride in uncomfortable silence. When we step into the lobby, Finn asks, "Do we need to fight it out before we go to breakfast?"

Holden's fingers fly over his phone. Without looking up, he says, "Pax is worried because he caught me coming out of Thea's room this morning."

He looks Holden up and down. "His pretty boy face is intact. Were there stab wounds?"

I let out a frustrated sigh. "No."

"Then whatever happened, Thea was okay with it."

"The two of you can't be this naïve. We can't trust her."

"It's not naïveté. I trust Thea to defend herself if she feels threatened or attacked. Holden's not hurt. He's not plotting her demise with his online friends on his tablet, and he's wearing his glasses."

"Didn't have time for my contacts."

Finn grins over at him. "Oh... you overslept? Good for you, man."

This is monumental news. I want to show him the same support Finn is. I want to be happy for him, but it's hard to do, because one of us has to be prepared for the worst. Women in our world have proven they're only loyal to the man with the most power. That means their goal will always be to divide us. Pitting Finn and Holden against each other, and me assuming the role as the voice of reason, is the easiest way to do that.

We enter the dining hall, and I scan the room for Thea. She's in line waiting for her food, instead of making someone bring it to her. Standing in line is a luxury of time we don't have.

She carries her tray, and I watch. Waiting to pounce on her. This is the moment she crushes Holden's tentative trust when she goes to sit at another table or at the end of the table, ignoring him. Or worse, sits next to Finn.

She does none of those things. She drops into the empty seat next to Holden and scowls at Finn, who steals a piece of toast off her plate. Then plugs her ears to drown out the conversation. Holden's reading his book. Finn's chattering away, but I keep my eye on her. She doesn't do anything out of the ordinary until she picks up Holdens coffee cup and drinks from it when she's finished with hers.

He doesn't react. He doesn't complain. He casually turns the page in his book, like sharing his coffee is the most natural thing in the world. Thea finishes eating and leaves without so much as a goodbye. Wait, I lied. She flips me off as she walks by on her way to the trash bin.

I take in the room, trying to see if I recognize anyone in the restaurant of the Bianci Hotel. This is a legacy family hot spot, and Moira suggested eating here is the easiest and least obtrusive way to fake like I care about my newly appointed legacy status.

I don't care, and I'm only here because Van says it sends a message that I'm one of them, which might make them more willing to help me get answers about my attack. I'm here for as long as it takes to eat a meal and then I'm out.

I'm sitting at the bar having a coffee, trying to ignore the old man sitting two seats over who keeps staring at me. Total creep vibes. I roll my eyes at him and wait for the hostess to come back and tell me a table is ready.

"You're Joshua Laurent's granddaughter, aren't you?"

I give the old man my best fuck off face.

"Aren't you?"

"No."

"You're not Theona Laurent?"

"Nope."

The hostess waves me over and I slide off my seat to meet her across the room. The man grabs my arm, sneering down at me. "Lying to a high council member is a punishable offense."

Ah. The sour look on his face as if I'm covered in shit all makes sense now. He's one of them. But I'm not and I don't care who he is, he's not gonna get me to answer to a name that isn't mine.

"Look here, mister. I'm not Laurent's anything. And my name isn't Theona Laurent. Your intel is shoddy as shit. If you want an answer, how about finding out who I really am instead of who you want me to be? Then you'll see I'm the life of the party, able to hold an intelligent conversation." I glance down at his hand. "Now would be a good idea to let go."

"I heard you were a disrespectful little bitch."

"Oh?" I smile at him. "Yeah, that sounds a lot more like me. But you still need to let go."

A throat clears behind me. "I think the young lady has expressed her displeasure at being touched by you."

I turn my head left and see future Pax sitting two tables over. He also has that 'I'm better than you' vibe going on, but grandpa Pax has a little more oomph with his. I wouldn't want to get stuck with him on a life raft. He definitely gives off -he'll kill me to survive- vibes. But he's at least pretending that he's not looking at me like I'm a science experiment gone wrong.

The other man slides back up to the bar several seats away from where he was before and I head towards the table that's waiting for me. As I pass old man Pax, he says, "You'll have to forgive my colleague's behavior."

With a vehement shake of my head, I say, "No, I don't. He was wrong to put his hands on me and wrong to call me a bitch when I was simply establishing boundaries. I'm not going to make excuses or allowances for it."

"Indeed. You are correct. Those actions were uncalled for and I assure you they'll be addressed in our next meeting."

"No offense, Papa Pax, but your assurances don't leave me feeling anything but skeptical."

His brows raise at me calling him Papa Pax, but instead of calling me on it, he says, "And why is that?"

"I don't know you, so I don't trust you."

"But I take it you know my grandson. Do you trust him?"

"I trust him to be an asshole. He's consistent with that."

"And what of the other two members of The Trium?"

"They show their asses right along with him, and I trust them to be in lockstep with whatever bullshit they're getting into."

He nods, looking pleased about that. "May I ask why you told Randall Collins your name isn't Theona Laurent? And that you're not Joshua Laurent's granddaughter?"

I'm looking down at him, but there's no power struggle. He's confident he's in charge. "You may."

"Will you answer?"

"Yes."

He folds his napkin and sets it on the table. "Why did you tell him your name isn't Theona Laurent?"

"Because it's not. My name is Theona *LaReaux*. It's the name I've had my entire life. And I don't even use Theona, so I don't answer to it."

"And the second question. Why did you say you're not Joshua Laurent's granddaughter?"

"Because that would presume a relationship we don't have. I just met the man a few weeks ago. We've spent a grand total of six hours in each other's company, and never once has he tried to get to know *me*, and that includes my name. He's operating with this image he has in his head, and the hell with the reality of it all."

"Yes, knowing one's name is important. What name do you prefer?"

"Thea."

"I see. Well, Thea. May I call you that?"

"Sure. If you're gonna interview me, might as well."

"Then perhaps we should sit together?"

I plop down in the chair across from him. "Next question."

I understand nothing at all about this organization, but I recognize a big shot when I see one. That other dude backed off without hesitation and ran to the other side of the bar. And from the way people are avoiding this table, giving it a wide berth. Stuttering hellos to Papa Pax. I'd say he's pretty high up, too. Was he one of the men making deals with Moira's father? Did he have a hand in me getting thrown away like trash?

If so, he'll be higher up on my list of people to hate and avoid.

"How are you adjusting?" He asks, finally breaking the silence.

"To what?" It's a question inside a question. I can see that, but it'll be more fun to play stupid, just to see how much information he wants to reveal.

"To the news of your heritage."

I shrug. I'm adjusting. He doesn't need to know what I'm doing to cope. Moira and Scott, whether they be my aunt and uncle or my parents, are still relative strangers. Now I know they're strangers who lie. They're sorry, they're trying to make amends. That's between us.

In answer to his question, I say, "It's a little hard to wrap my head around, but in the end, it's just historical data that has nothing to do with me. I'm still the same person I was before someone went poking their nose in my business and decided I'm suddenly *worthy*." The words drip with sarcasm. The thoughts and opinions of this old fart and his cronies don't mean shit to me.

"I imagine the change in your status is jarring. And I can respect that you're getting demands from so many people. Are the other students at school helping you acclimate?"

Ordinarily, I wouldn't engage with someone trying to get all up in my business, but I appreciate Papa Pax taking time to ask me questions. God knows nobody else has.

"You strike me as a man who knows the answers to most of your questions before you ask them, so I have a question for you."

"By all means."

"Do you want my honest answer and for me to tell you, my favorite people on campus are normal kids and the guy in the kitchen who makes the cheese fries, or do you want me to tell you they've all been lovely?"

"Do you always say every thought that passes through your mind?"

"Ninety-seven percent of the time, I do."

"And the other three?"

We sit in silence. Him trying to get a read on me. Me making sure he can't. With a decisive nod, he simply says, "I see." He finishes his water, then says, "Enjoy your meal."

My gaze darts across the table. There's no money or credit card envelope on it, and the server hasn't brought one over since I've been sitting here. "You'd better not be leaving me with your check."

His eyes crinkle at the corner. I can't tell if it's humor or anger. His tone measured and even when he says, "I wouldn't dream of it."

He leaves and I stay at his table and order my food. I scroll through my phone while I eat and text Sasha, LJ, and Austin. When I ask for my check, I'm told the old man already covered it.

I pigged out at the restaurant yesterday, now I need to work off the extra calories. I groan as I stretch my arm across my chest, to loosen up my shoulder. Wolfe has upped the resistance on the bands, and my shoulder and arms are stiff. Pax enters the gym. I'm used to my appearance pissing him off, and I've come to the conclusion that he can't help himself. Whenever he sees me, he feels compelled to talk to me. It's always bullshit that he's spewing but he's incapable of walking by and keeping his mouth shut.

"What are you up to?" He snarls as he stalks over to me. "Why the hell are you stalking my grandfather?"

He always shows his hand. He makes it too easy to harass him. "Heard about our little lunch date, did you? I gotta say. He pulled out all the stops." I fan myself. "He really knows how to make a girl feel special. I'm too young to be called grammy, so when we get married, you can just stick to calling me by my first name."

"Cut your shit, Thea, and just tell me what you said to him."

"Why don't you ask him?"

"I already have. Now I wanna see if you lie about it."

Pax has a great poker face. His grandfather's is better. Pax wants answers and hopes I'm stupid enough to give him some. You'd think he'd have learned by now that I'm a fucking vault when I want to be.

"You're so full of shit. You didn't ask him a damn thing." I pat his chest. "But I'll throw you a bone. *He* asked me stuff, and *I* gave him my honest answers."

"That's probably a lie. You're never honest."

I don't let him see how much that stings. One thing I pride myself on is my honesty. I didn't have shit growing up, but I always had the integrity of my words. People may not have liked me, but they could trust that when I spoke, it was the truth. "I'm always honest. You guys are just too busy trying to shut me up or too pigheaded to listen, so you can't hear the truth when it's offered to you."

I step into the ring, done with talking to his bullheaded ass. He climbs through the ropes and stands across from me, critiquing my form. He's trying to get a rise out of me, and when I grow tired of hearing his mouth, I taunt him back. I've learned two things about him from all the time he spends harassing me in the ring. His ego can't handle being ignored, and he gets pissy when I call his manhood into question.

Last week, I decided that if he was gonna stand there and criticize me, then he needed to make himself useful. I threw a punch which he barely dodged- and every time since then- we've spent twenty minutes in the ring, with me pounding on his ass. I like that he fights back. I haven't won any of our sparring matches yet. Pax is good, but I would let someone pull my nails off with rusty pliers before admitting it.

He's also an obnoxious winner. I don't get upset about him teasing me after he wins, because I take each loss as a learning opportunity. With every fight I know I'm one step closer to taking him down to the mats. With that goal in mind, I swing, slamming my fist into his cheek.

Chapter 75
Holden

I'm leaning against the wall of the library on a call when I hear someone say, "Little Thea LaReaux. It's so nice to finally see you."

Moving to the edge of the wall, I see Thea walk past the guy, ignoring the garbage he's spitting.

"Where's all that sass I keep hearing about? Is it in your ass?"

He grabs a handful of her right ass cheek, then grabs her tit when she turns to confront him. Before she can react, I'm on him, tossing his ass against the building.

I don't think about the consequences of what I'm doing, operating on pure rage and instinct. Every punch echoes. Every hit produces a crunch. "Don't you ever fucking touch her." I hit him again. "Got some fucking nerve touching my girl. Your daddy should have told you to keep your hands to your. Self."

The satisfying sound of his nose breaking is not enough. The heavy wet squishing sound as I pulverize his face is not enough. The rage consumes me. Overpowering and suffocating. Once I let it out, there's never any way to tame it without knocking me out. And that's exactly what's going to need to happen. I'm cognizant of movement on my left. People should know better than to approach me.

I glance over to see whose ass I'm kicking next. It's her. Thea's standing next to me, looking down at him. I want to hit him again, just so he can never look at her again. I raise my fist and she jumps in front of me.

She's protecting him? After all this? Now I'll kill him. She steps with me, keeping between us, so I can't exact another blow.

I look at her face and see her lips moving. Whatever she's saying is lost on me. My chest heaves as I hold the guy by his bloody shirt. I can't hear shit through the ringing in my ears. The rage has me firmly in its grasp. But I feel something on my hand. I look down to see Thea's holding onto it, rubbing her thumb across my damaged knuckles. She's trying to calm me down. I blink and shake my head, trying to clear the fog and focus on what she's saying.

"Hey pretty boy. His dentist has enough work that he can retire off of. How about you stop making the rich richer?"

What is she talking about?

"You need to feed your monster? Wanna play with your food? Come play with me. You don't need to beat the shit out of him. He might deserve it, but that's not satisfying you. That's why you can't turn it off." She steps closer. "I know what you need. I know exactly what will put the monster back in its cage."

She tugs my hand. "Come play with me."

I can see clearly enough now to know Finn's here. He says, "Pet, you don't want-."

Thea holds her hand up to stop him from coming any closer and continues pulling me towards the path that leads to our dorm. I can feel him following, but he doesn't try to interrupt again. Not until she ducks off the pavement and pulls me behind a tree.

"Thea..."

She ignores his warning and drops to her knees, rubbing my cock through my pants. My dick hardens. The haze is still in front of my eyes, but I can see her through it, staring up at me. She strokes me up and down, curiosity on her face. What could she possibly want to know? Why I'm like this? Why I beat that piece of shit the way I did?

"I wanna know what your rage tastes like." She says, answering the questions swirling in my head.

My voice rasps out, "You don't."

"Yes. I do. Do your worst, pretty boy."

Instead of calming me down, she's riling me up. And because the anger is still at the surface, I dive into it, wanting to make her hurt. "You're such a fucking tease. Did you wear this shirt, tits hanging out and these tight ass jeans to get noticed? You were trying to get your ass grabbed. Begging for attention."

I fist her hair. "I split my hands open because of you. His blood is on my hands." I tip her chin up. "But his blood is on *your* hands, too. This is your fault." Her eyes are hooded. "Did you like it? Did you like seeing me turn into a monster because of you, you little slut?" I tug her hair so hard that I'm sure I dislodged a few hairs. She winces through the pain. "Oh, did that hurt? You haven't felt anything yet."

I release my grip long enough to yank her shirt over her head and lower my zipper. I fist my dick, stepping closer, then shove it into her mouth in one forceful stroke.

"You're gonna have an aversion to cock by the time I'm done with you."

Ever the fighter, her teeth scrapes against me and she bites down. I grab her head, squeezing it between my hands. "You're gonna pay for that, you brat."

I force her to swallow me down. My strokes aren't tame or tentative. They're aggressive. Hard. I shove in deeper, chuckling as she gags around my length, trying to suck in a breath. "Oh, no you don't. If you can moan or breathe, that means I'm not in far enough."

I plunge forward, closing off the rest of her airway. "Oh fuck. There it is. You don't need to breathe. Just embrace the darkness."

I pound her face, working out the rest of my anger on her. Not because I'm angry with her, but because I'm angry at myself. She's under my skin. In my head. In my dreams and nightmares.

She's mine and someone keeps trying to touch what's mine. The anger slips into that feeling of obsession. I need to possess her. I hold her head steady, fucking her mouth. She holds it open, taking the punishing slide of my cock without complaint.

I grunt. "God, your throat feels amazing, the perfect place to store my dick." I hiss when her tongue flexes around me.

This is why she's perfect. Made for me. She sees the monster in me. Knows it thirsts for pain and she's encouraging me to let it out to play. I graze her cheek with the back of my hand, leaving a smear of blood behind. His. Mine. Doesn't matter. It's proof of how far I'd go to protect her from anyone and anything. Except me.

Thea's nose flares as she tries to take in enough air. Her eyes water, her chest heaving. I can imagine there are spots dancing around the edge of her vision. That she's struggling with the lightheadedness that precedes blacking out. I stay lodged in her throat. Watching. Waiting for the perfect moment. Her eyes widen and I know she's there. The sweet hint of panic dances in her violet eyes.

"I'm gonna pump my seed straight into your stomach. And you're gonna hold down every single drop. If you spill any, you'll be licking it from the ground. Blink once if you understand."

She does and with one final push; I let go. Flooding her mouth, her throat. Snarling as she sputters around my cock. Rope after rope of hot cum shoots down her throat, cutting off the last of her air. But she doesn't let it come out of her mouth, sucking and swallowing as fast as she can.

I groan as I spill the last of my relief. "So fucking perfect."

Her mouth goes slack, and she slumps over. I release her head and pull out of her mouth, tucking my dick away. Then scoop down to pick her up, cradling her in my arms until she gets her bearings back.

I can sense Finn freaking out behind me. He knows I go dark, but he's never seen this side of it, because no girl, no woman has ever had the guts to see how far I'd go. Thea blinks up at me, the sweetest smile on her swollen lips, like I'm the one who just gave her a killer orgasm instead of it being the other way around.

"All better?" She asks, her voice scratchy from the number I did to her throat.

I nod my head once in response. She looks over to where Finn's standing. "You okay, Number Three?"

"Am I ok? I don't know if I should be appalled that he fucked your mouth until you were unconscious or turned on and jealous because I wanna do the same thing." He steps closer. "Are you okay, Pet?"

"Why wouldn't I be?"

Finn looks at her, then at me, then back to her. "Uh, cause he fucked your mouth until you were unconscious."

I set her on her feet and step away, giving her some space in case she needs it. Her hand massages her throat and jaws, trying to work the stiffness and soreness out. My chest puffs up. I did that.

She waves her hand dismissively. "I'm fine. I've been unconscious before. Besides, I barely passed out. I just have to work up to holding my breath for five minutes." She smiles. "But I'd say four minutes nineteen seconds means I'm no slouch."

Finn looks over at me before asking, "How do you know how long it was?"

"I was keeping time on Holden's watch."

She's still rubbing her jaws, so I step up and take over. My chest leaning into her back as I work the mandible joint. She melts into me with a sigh and I say, "I'll steep you some tea and honey when we get back to the dorms."

Finn steps in front of her, reaching out his hand. "Come here, Pet."

I stiffen. Is he scared I'm gonna hurt her? The rage is over. I didn't black out. I was totally in control with Thea.

She doesn't move toward him. Instead, she grabs the hem of my t-shirt with her right hand. "I can't move right now, Finn."

"Why not?"

"Because Holden's hands feel amazing." She groans that last part as I move my hands to work the kink in her neck.

I appreciate her trust, but I need to explain why Finn's being clingy. "He's worried I hurt you."

"You did. But I told you too, and I liked it."

"He doesn't believe that."

"What's he want? Proof? I can pull off my drenched panties and give them to him." She tips her head back to look at me. A devious smile on her lips. "Or pull my pussy lips apart and let him see it up close."

"Don't you dare," Finn growls.

Thea teases, "Dare what?"

"Pull that pretty pussy out, right here."

"Why not?"

He rolls his eyes at her. "We're not deep enough in the woods. It's one thing for someone to walk up on you giving Holden head. But he's just calmed down. He'll probably kill someone if they accidentally see or smell that sweet pussy."

"You've seen it and he hasn't killed you."

I grumble, "Sometimes I think about it."

She tilts her head back to look at me. "Really? He's your best friend. One of the Coxsuckers. I thought it was all for one and all that jazz."

"He is, but since your attack, I feel a tad homicidal when it comes to you."

She turns in my arms. "I'm gonna tell you like I've told Finn. I can take care of myself." She rises on tiptoe and kisses me. It's quick and sweet, and over before I realize it's happened. It's also not at all appropriate for the conversation we're having.

"But I appreciate you using your fist to apologize." She takes my hand and drags me back onto campus. "Let's go have some tea."

I let her lead me, staring at where our hands are connected the entire time.

Chapter 76
Pax

My phone chimes with a message from Finn that he and Holden are heading back to the dorms. He's finally answering my texts, but I'm still pissed off. I had to do damage control for the beat down Holden gave Leo.

I walked up on the end, but enough people told me it was over the troublemaker. Then he took off with her, still raging, with only Finn to handle the situation.

When he didn't answer, I didn't know what to think. But now he's saying they're heading back. He didn't have to knock Holden out and they'll be in Holden's room making tea. Tea!

I step through the door, ready to intervene, but things look normal. Holden's at his stove, the tea kettle is on, and he's flipping through the tea bags. Thea's on the couch next to Finn like she belongs here.

"He's fine." Finn says from his spot on the couch.

"How? Because that beat down looked like Holden went nuclear. He's gonna need something stronger than chamomile tea to take the edge off."

Thea snorts. "Relax. He's already had his stress reliever. The tea's for me."

"What's that supposed to mean?"

Finn chuckles, because he's in on the joke.

She sasses, "It means Holden's fine. He doesn't need you to come in here and treat him like he's not."

It's time we have this out once and for all. Now that we're all here, maybe they'll see her for what she is. Dangerous to everything we've built over the years.

"You've been here five minutes and have been stirring shit up since the beginning. Do you have any idea what happens when Holden loses control? No. You sit there and spin him up and then run off when you see the damage you've caused." I slam his pills on the table. "Here Holden."

"What are those?" Thea sniffs, suspiciously.

"His pills to calm him down and even him out."

"He doesn't need them."

"Yes. He. Does."

She gets to her feet and shoves them onto the floor, crushing them under her foot.

"No. He. Doesn't. Have you even looked at him?" She points to the kitchen. "Does he look pissed off? On edge? No! He's fine. Mellow. Or he was until you came in here messing up our vibe. Now I'm gonna have to practice holding my breath sooner than I would have liked."

She rubs her throat, Finn chuckles, and Holden makes a sound that sounds a lot like appreciation. What the hell is going on? I look over at Holden, who is now standing next to me, holding a cup of tea. He passes it to Thea and takes over, rubbing her throat.

He really does look fine. Not a trace of the wild rage I'm used to seeing when he loses his temper. And he walked to the dorm with Finn. Maybe they took a trip to the infirmary first. "Did you already take something to take the edge off?"

Thea makes a derisive sound while she sips her tea. Stalking closer, I growl, "What was that?"

She pulls the cup away from her mouth. "I *said* the only illicit substance he came into contact with was my throat around his piercings."

"You..." My steps halt.

She flutters her lashes as what she's saying finally registers. "Sucked his rage out through his penis."

Finn snorts, "Wasn't much sucking going on."

"My jaws disagree."

I work my own jaw loose and blurt out, "You gave him a blow job?"

"I did. I deep throated the monster. Literally and figuratively until the pearly gates came calling."

I snap my gaze to Holden. "While he was pissed off? Damn near feral?"

"Yup." She pops her p, staring at me like it's no big deal. And she's here. Drinking tea. She goes back over to the couch. Puts her feet up in Finn's lap and pats the seat cushion next to her. Holden joins them, sitting in the empty spot. She drapes his arm around her neck and settles against his chest as she sips from her mug.

This has to be a joke. Except Finn says he was with Holden the whole time. I believe him. He would never leave Holden alone in a blind rage like that.

"Heads up."

I snatch his phone out of the air. Hitting play on the video. It's barely two minutes long, and it's clear the footage is from today. Thea's on her knees, Holden standing over her, holding her face in a punishing grip as he fucks her mouth. I'm getting ready to launch into damage control when I reach the end. Thea's slumped over. I watch as Holden picks her up, and she blinks, smiling up at him.

I take in the trio on the couch again. Thea's looking at me. There's none of the usual bitch on her face or snark in her voice when she says, "I always take responsibility for the hurt I cause."

I jolt awake, straining my eyes in the dark to make out what woke me. I pick out the shadow against my door, recognizing the silhouette. "Holden, what are you doing in here?"

He comes over to the bed and yanks the cover off of me, sliding his hand between my legs, cupping me through my panties.

"I didn't get to thank you for today."

"I'm the reason you got into a fight in the first place, so I thanked you for defending me." Giving him a pointed look, I say, "I didn't need it. I can fight my own battles, but I guess your heart was in the right place, so that matters."

"Maybe, but your gratitude went above and beyond. I feel like I owe you, and I don't like owing people anything."

I can relate to that. "Okay, then I guess you can buy me a donut and a cup of that fancy coffee you were drinking at breakfast or something."

"I make my coffee in my room, and I'm happy to make a cup for you when I fix mine."

"There. Good. We're even. Now get out."

While we've been talking, his hands have been creeping up my body. He's now playing with my tits. My nipples pebble against his palms. "I can't leave until I've thanked you."

"We've already discussed this."

"The coffee is because you asked. My thanks will make you feel as good as you made me feel. I'm not leaving until you've cum for me. How does that sound?"

I mull that over. I'm feeling a little horny from earlier. "Sounds good. Since you woke me up, it'll be hard to get back to sleep. An orgasm might help."

I lay on my back, linking my arms behind my head, mindful that he has to work himself up into being okay with my touch. I'm actually kind of surprised he let me lean against him on the couch earlier.

He climbs onto the bed next to me and stares at my face. "I liked watching tv earlier."

"You barely paid attention. You were reading a book."

"I know, but I liked the company. And since Finn had you to talk to about the movie, he didn't try to get me involved."

"Yeah. Finn and I like action flicks. We had a fun movie thing hanging in the beginning, and he surprised me with tickets to Graffiti Warehouse once, but that was before things went to shit."

"You and Finn were dating?"

"Not dating. We were just at some of the same places at the same time and hung out."

"For Finn, that's considered dating."

Curiosity that I shouldn't be feeling has me asking, "And what would you call dating?"

He lays his head next to mine on the pillow. "I don't know. I never actually thought about it. My parents will pick my future wife, so when they find someone for me to court, we'll go to dinners and things like that. Probably a few parties here on campus. I don't know, the usual stuff other people do."

He lists each one like an item he has to check off. "I'm not asking about the stuff other people do. I'm asking what you would do on a date you took the time to plan."

"I'd take her to work in a community garden for the day. Pick some veggies and then come back and cook. Or go on a hike and have a picnic and read a book. Go to a tech convention, or a yoga retreat."

"That sounds like fun."

He dismisses my comment. "Sure it does."

I roll onto my side. "No, I'm being serious, Holden. I would have so much fun at a tech convention, looking at all the gadgets from the security vendors. Or even hiking and putting my hands in the dirt. Or going to visit an excavation site or museum exhibit with one of those fake digs that kids get to play in."

"I understand your interest in the museum and hiking, because you want to be an archaeologist, but why a tech convention?"

"My best friend Sasha is into technology and gizmos. We went to a few conventions in Vegas and we had fun."

We had even more fun using the stuff we brought to do some other things we got paid to do. When I moved here. I left my gadgets with Sasha, and that part of my life behind.

"We'll go to a convention in LA."

"You assume I'd want to go with you."

"We both agreed it would be a fun, so my assumption is correct."

Rolling my eyes, I say, "You can try asking me, you know."

"Asking you to go with me makes it a date and comes with pressure and expectations. If I have an extra ticket and give it to you, it's us hanging out, and we'll have more fun."

I don't hate the idea. It's the type of suggestion I would have offered if he'd have asked me out.

"Why don't you talk to people?"

I feel his shoulder move. "Why don't you?"

"Because I'm comfortable alone and sitting in silence. I don't need a bunch of people around making unnecessary noise. Now your turn."

"I'm blunt and people don't know how to take that. I'm also usually the smartest person in the room, which makes them even more uncomfortable, and I don't have time for stupidity or games."

"But you like games."

"I like the games I choose to play, and the ones where I make the rules. I like games I know I'll win."

He parts my legs and rolls on top of me. "There are so many games I can play with you. So many I *will* play with you."

When his hand brushes against my throat, I know he's done talking. I stay still as he tightens his hold and leans down to kiss me, the way he did that first time. And just like that time, I get wet from the way his weight feels on top of me and the control he holds over my next breath. Holden's kiss consumes my mouth. Demands control. For this game, I willingly give in.

He yanks my shirt up, latching around my nipple. My hips roll against him as my body comes alive under the assault of his mouth. I fist my pillow to keep from touching him.

He moves his attention to my other breast and slips his hands inside my panties, toying with my folds, running his finger through the wetness gathering there.

"You're wet already? Did I wake you in the middle of a sexy dream, or is it the anticipation of our game that has you making such a mess around my fingers?"

He shoves his tongue in my mouth at the same time he shoves three fingers into me. I moan at the intrusion and clamp around his fingers, trying to keep them inside. He yanks his fingers out and shoves them in my mouth before kissing me again. I swirl my tongue around his fingers in tandem with his.

He pulls away, and stares down at me, darkness swirling in his gaze, before slowly climbing off the bed. I watch as he discards his clothes. A slow removal of each garment as he watches me, watching him.

I bite my lip, watching the strip tease. He gets to his pants, slowly unzipping them, and shoves them and his boxer briefs down to his feet. I get stuck on the sight of his cock bobbing free.

When Holden and I first met, I thought he was sweet and innocent. His quiet way of watching and speaking certainly lends to that fantasy. But, there's nothing sweet or innocent about the way he's looking at me, while he rolls a condom onto the length of his pierced cock. And somebody smack me, because even though I've had it in my mouth twice, I can't stop staring at it.

I didn't get a good look at it either of those times, but look my fill now. I swipe my hand across my mouth, in case I'm drooling, as I size his dick up trying to figure out the best way to play this. I'm being perfectly honest when I say I'm not sure it'll fit.

My gaze sweeps across the rest of his body. Muscled perfection. Holden's fucking jacked. Why he hides this magnificent body under baggy clothes is beyond my comprehension. Though I suppose skinny jeans won't quite work if he's trying to hide those thick thighs and his huge dick.

He calls my name softly, but I still don't... *can't* look away. "Huh?"

"Would you rather watch another action movie until you fall back asleep?"

Now my gaze snaps to his. "A movie?"

"If you've changed your mind, I get it-"

I scramble out of bed, damn near vaulting into the air, and wrap my arms and legs around him like a spider monkey. The way I lock my arms around his neck, making it impossible for him to look away. I know he has issues with being touched, but he's gonna deal with it for a few minutes before he splits me in two.

He grabs my ass, hoisting me a little higher. "I know people think I'm too big. I just-"

I nod. "It's not a think. It's a fact. Even right now, I'm worried it's gonna get stuck between my pelvic bones. I haven't changed my mind. This beast you're swinging between your legs might literally tear me a new asshole, but I'm willing to take one for the team. I just need. Shit. Lube. All the lube. And you'll have to give me a good stretch out, since it's like the size of a fist." Now his obsession with how many fingers I can take makes sense. "But. Nope. Not changing my mind."

He gifts me with his rare heart-stopping smile, his gray eyes taking on the color of a storm cloud, and I can't help but lean forward and kiss him. The beast between his legs twitches, letting me know he's enjoying the kiss. And since I'm a shameless hussy, I grind against him, knowing I'm not even close to wet enough to take the tip of this thing.

He grips my hips, moving me up and down, dragging the seam of my panties along his length. Up and down. Up and down. A tingle ignites between my legs and I groan into his mouth.

His tongue tastes divine. Man can he kiss. I'm so caught up in the kiss that I don't realize he's moved my panties aside until he's knuckles deep inside me. Two fingers stroking in and out. Then he adds a third, and it feels like he's spread them in the Vulcan sign. I'm stretched, and it's burning and good.

He walks us back over to the bed without breaking our connection until I'm lying flat against it. Slowly, he drags my panties down my legs. We're not separated for long. He settles between my parted legs and applies just the right amount of pressure against my clit as he grinds against me. I'm gonna combust any second now.

I squeeze my eyes shut, and with one last thrust against him, I'm coming. My eyes fly open in the middle of my orgasm. I'm being stretched beyond anything I've ever felt before. Looking down, I see it's literally just the tip. Instinct tells me to back away from the pain.

"Fuck, you're tight." He groans.

Fuck is right. I feel like I'm losing my virginity all over again. My voice is strained. "I told you, you wouldn't fit."

He kisses me again, waiting for me to relax. Stroking the side of my hip like he's not one-eighth of the way inside me. "God, just this little bit is already the best thing I've ever felt." He kisses me again. "Thank you."

My heart constricts, knowing he's probably always had issues with women, starting with his lack of interaction, and ending with his kink. At first glance, it looks like Holden's awkward and misses major social cues, but I can see that's a very narrow view. He has huge fucking trust issues and a low tolerance for bullshit. I don't blame him. It's their loss, anyway. Holden has a pierced monster peen.

"I'm sorry we don't fit. I really wanted to."

He leans forward, brushing his nose against mine in an Eskimo kiss that melts a smidgeon of ice around my heart. His hips flex and I arch against him as he pushes his way in another inch. "I'll fit. I'll take my time until I'm balls deep, and you feel like you're breaking apart, but I promise you'll love every minute of it."

After several slow thrusts of his hips, he slides all the way home. He's definitely touching my cervix. I'm breathing heavily and so is he.

But he holds himself still, like we're cuddling. His nose, buried in the crook of my neck, adds to the illusion.

"I never thought I'd find someone who'd be willing to try. At least not sober."

"What?" I gasp. Damn, it's hard to breathe. Is this thing in my chest? "Fuck those girls. You're incredible. Funny. Smart. So sweet when you want to be, and built like one of those Olympic gods."

"But I don't always talk or act the way people expect. If I were different... I try to be different."

"No!" I grab his face. "Never change. Never conform or dumb yourself down for approval. Not for me. Not for anyone."

This time, our kiss is fierce. Nipping, biting, dueling tongues. He slides back, then snaps his hips forward, driving me into the mattress, and all I can do is hang on. He shifts, putting one leg over his shoulder, and I see stars.

"That's it. Let me in."

In? He's already impossibly deep. Any further, he'll be inside my uterus.

"Look at that. All pink and stuffed by me."

I chance a look and *wow*. It's the sexiest thing I've ever seen, watching him disappear inside me. I look up to watch his face. It's a blend of concentration, ecstasy and pride. Scratch that. His face is the sexiest thing I've ever seen.

It comes out of nowhere. The need for him to move harder. Faster. I plant my foot on the bed and rock up to meet him. He growls, and it's then that I realize just how much control he's been holding on to. The bed slams furiously against the wall, our moans mixing. He suddenly stops moving and pulls away. It takes a minute to come out of my haze.

"What's wrong?" I look between his legs. He's still hard, so he didn't blow too fast. And if he did, I wouldn't care.

"This was a mistake. I can't..."

I push myself up on my elbows, trying to figure out what's got him so twisted up. "Holden. What's happening? Did you change your mind?"

That'll be a first for me. I'd hate it, but I wouldn't like, force him to finish. He clenches his teeth and shakes his head. "Then why'd you stop?"

A shadow crosses his face. "I wanna hurt you, Thea."

I remember him holding me down in the woods and how he promised to hurt me, make me bleed. I was appalled at the idea, but now I'm curious about what that really means. He's already stuffed my throat like a turkey on Thanksgiving and bitten my side hard enough to leave marks. He's had his hand on my throat, and fingered me so hard I've leaked tears. None of the things he's done were painful. Unless you count clamping my nipples when he had me strapped to the table during that stupid ass chastity vow prank. I thought that was Pax's call, but now I know that's more Holden's thing.

"I'm not some fragile thing. I can take a hard fuck." Lying back down, I say, "Do you want to hold me down while you fuck me, Holden?"

"Yes."

"What else?" I drag my hand across my throat, down between the valley of my breast and lower still until I reach the juncture of my thighs. He tracks the movement. The way he's looking at me sets my body on fire.

"I want to wrap my hands around your neck and squeeze."

"So what's stopping you from doing that? I've let you before." I spread my legs in invitation. "My pussy's feeling really empty. Why don't you come over here and fix that for me?"

His eyes darken in disapproval. Oh, he doesn't like being told what to do. Let's see what it takes for him to shed whatever remaining chains he's got on him, keeping him from showing me the real him. I got a glimpse after his fight, but that guy is buried deep again. I dip a finger into my pussy. "I said get over here and service me."

He stalks over to me and grabs me by the throat, lifting my upper body from the bed. "You don't tell me what to do with this cunt."

He flips me over onto my stomach, pushing my face into the mattress. "Your bratty ass mouth and greedy cunt are gonna be the death of you."

His other hand yanks my hips back, forcing me to get to my knees, presenting my ass to him. The patience he afforded me to adjust to his length before is long gone. He slams into me, holding onto the back of my neck, holding me in place.

"We've let you sass us too long. I'm finally going to shut you up. Show you who's really in charge around here. Whores don't demand. They're here for my pleasure."

"Who are you calling a whore?" My face is smashed into the mattress, muffling my question.

He reaches under me, grabs my nipple, and pulls. I yelp and jerk against him. "You, my little pain slut."

I'm pushed forward with every forceful slide of his cock, his grip on my neck pulling me back to him. My pussy burns, stretched wider than it's ever been before, but behind the pain is pleasure. The longer he's inside me, the better it feels.

"I want this cunt sore. Your throat covered in my handprints." He smacks my ass. "Your ass on fire when you sit." He's gripping my hip so hard it hurts. "You're here to service me. Now take this dick like a good little slut."

I clench around him. I should be disgusted that he's degrading me with his words and hands, but I'm not. His actions call to the part of me that craves danger and trouble. He adds a finger into my pussy even though his dick is already taking up all the room.

"Damn, I never knew a pussy could be as greedy as yours. It's just begging me to tear through it."

I mewl into the mattress because I'm a sick hussy and I want that too. I thought Deacon had a mouth on him. But where his words praise and encourage me to obey; I hear the violence in Holden's voice, the promise to inflict pain and take what he wants without remorse, and it makes me want to push him, to see how far he'd go. It makes me want to let him do naughty, naughty things to me.

He pushes my hips into the mattress, curling his upper body over me, as he lifts my face away from the bed. His hands circle my neck from behind. He squeezes, and my body convulses as I come apart for him, the force of my orgasm so strong I forget to breathe. His hands tighten, prolonging the depletion of oxygen. I'm light headed. Helpless.

As he continues to savagely thrust inside me. I struggle for air, my fight spurring him on.

"You're not going anywhere, little minx."

I feel the world slip away. My body is heavy. It's only his hold on my neck that keeps me from slumping forward. The edges of my vision slowly darken, then everything goes black.

I sputter, gasping for air, as the room slowly comes back into view.

"So good, so fucking good." Holden groans in my ear. I'm flat on the bed, his body shaking on top of me, coming to a stop as his climax ends.

Was he fucking me while I was unconscious? How long was I out? It couldn't have been more than a few seconds, right? I take a minute to check in with my body. I'm sore, but sated. My heartbeat steady. Shouldn't I be freaking out that he choked me out and kept going?

With one last kiss to the back of my neck, Holden rolls off of me and climbs off the bed. I slowly turn over, mindful of the stiffness and soreness I'm already feeling from being held down and contorted.

Once I'm on my back, I wiggle until I'm in a sitting position. Holden's now in the furthest corner of the room, watching me. His look guarded. I can't even begin to imagine what he's thinking. I sit quietly, giving him a second before asking what's on his mind, but before I can ask, he tugs his pants on, and leaves.

Chapter 78

Thea

I can feel Holden's eyes on me when I walk into The Rock for breakfast. I ignore him and sit at my table, the non-legacy table, and dig into my scrambled eggs. He walked out without a word, after our hook up, and he and all the other trust fund babies have been missing from campus for three days. I don't know why and didn't bother asking. I'm just glad wherever they were, they didn't expect me to be there too.

I chomp down on a sausage link and cut into my Belgian waffle, smearing it through the whipped cream. I'm in heaven with this food. The Belgian waffles are my second favorite menu item. The cheese fries are my first.

When I'm done eating, I feel energized to get through my day. I'm taking myself thrifting and then I'm stopping by to see Van, before stretching out on the beach to watch the waves. After throwing my trash away, I make a pit stop at the coffee station to refresh my cup. Holden's impersonating a sentry when I walk outside.

I had gotten used to seeing him hanging around on the pavement for no reason, and it felt weird that he wasn't here the last few days. He closes the book he's holding, his finger inside the pages as a placeholder.

Any hope I had to walk by and continue ignoring him is dashed when he asks, "Why did you sit at your old table?"

"I like the view."

"There was nothing in front of you but other empty tables."

I'm not doing this, shit. "Why are you suddenly talking to me?"

He looks at me like it's a stupid question and I guess it is. "Fine, why are you talking to me today when the last time I saw you, you walked away from me without so much as a goodbye?"

"I needed to go. I-"

I wave off the rest of his explanation. "It was a rhetorical question. I'm not even upset that you ghosted me. It's cool, but you wasted my time and yours pretending to want to be friends, just like Finn did. If you and your buddies had a competition or something, then you all won. I fucked all three of you. Good job. I didn't need you talking to me and defending me and all that shit to weaken my defenses. I like sex as much as the next person. We could've just skipped to the fucking part."

"Thea, I talk to you because I like to, not because I'm trying to win any points with you."

"Sure. Whatever. Like I said, I'm cool. But for the record, you didn't have to run off like you did. It's not like I was going to ask you to cuddle or anything."

"So, the reason you sat at your old table has nothing to do with me running off after sex?"

"Nope."

I shove my sunglasses on, pushing them up the bridge of my nose with my middle finger. "Later."

He grabs my arm, preventing me from walking away, and pulls my shades off, sticking them in his pocket. "What are you doing?"

"I should explain what happened." He scrubs his hand through his hair.

"Don't stress yourself out trying to come up with an excuse. I'm fine with it. Really."

"I freaked out after we had sex."

Freaked out could mean so many things. But I've only had one guy freak out on me before. "Did the condom break?" That would explain his MIA status for three days, but shit, a heads up via text the next morning, would have been nice. You know, in case a girl needs to get a morning-after pill.

"The condom was still intact."

"Were you embarrassed? Did you think you came too quickly?"

"I'm fine with how long I lasted, and even if I did, you got off first."

I shrug. "Then I don't understand what you were freaking out about."

"We fucked, Thea. And I didn't have all the protections in place I was supposed to, even though I promised Pax I would."

"I don't know why it's any of Pax's business, but you tell the head Coxsucker, that we used a condom, just like I'm told he did when he fucked me under the influence. I'm also on birth control. So what other precautions can he mean? Was I supposed to wear a female condom, too? Add some extra spermicide?"

"I was supposed to have you sign an NDA. I would have, and I meant to get that out of the way before I ever touched you, but... you were so lost when you came back to school. So shattered. I just wanted to help you mend yourself back together. Every time I saw you, I couldn't help myself. I had to touch you. And then you showed no fear of me when I beat that guy to a pulp or afterwards when you were on your knees for me."

"There was nothing to be scared of."

"I was out of control, Thea. With anger and with lust, and even though I said I was fine, I wasn't. I wasn't fully in control when I came into your room that night, but I couldn't stop. I needed that outlet. And when I finished and realized how far I went, I panicked, because I didn't have the paperwork in place. I didn't have a binding agreement that you wouldn't tell anyone."

His voice gets huskier the longer he talks, and by the time he finishes, the last words are barely a whisper.

"You freaked out because you're worried I'm gonna tell someone you have a pierced monster peen and fuck like a god?"

He's nodding. I chew that over and blurt out, "You know, most guys would love for me to brag about that, but whatever. You didn't need to stress out about it. I don't go around volunteering details about my sex life to absolute strangers."

"It's not about my dick. Enough people on campus know it's pierced. It's the other aspects of sex that I need kept quiet."

"What's so wrong about a little choking and degradation between consenting adults?"

He sighs, as if exasperated with the conversation, or with me, and averts his gaze. "It's something that can be used as blackmail, so like I said, I screwed up and I freaked out."

With a shrug I say, "Well, you can't put the toothpaste back in the tube. It happened. But if you need me to sign your little paper and back date it, I will."

That regains his attention. "You will?"

"Why do you look so surprised? Was Pax talking shit about me? Fuck, I wish he'd mind his business. If you were avoiding me for three days because you were afraid I'd say no..."

"I wasn't avoiding you for three days. I had some things to take care of at home, and it was easier to stay at my parents' house instead of commuting everyday just to sleep in the dorm."

"I notice you didn't say Pax wasn't talking shit about me."

His lips twitch. He's holding back a smile, so I know I'm right. "I'll sign your paper. Just bring it over to my room whenever you get it. And you have my word that I won't tell anyone that we hooked up between now and the time I sign the form."

"Thank you."

It's my turn to look away. "I hate to say this, and I will deny it if it ever gets back to him, but Pax is right. If this paperwork is such a big deal, you need to take the time to have this conversation with your future partners before you have them naked and squirming on the bed."

"Future partners?"

"Ye-es." I drawl.

"What future partners, Thea?"

"The next girls that'll be blessed with the gift of that pierced weapon in your pants."

"There won't be any other women seeing my piercings."

"Nothing wrong with celibacy. Sure, wait until your parents tell you that they've found the perfect girl, and you're ready to do it again."

"I have no intentions of denying my sexual urges. My cock will be getting a workout on a frequent basis."

"Lucky guy." He arches a brow. "Lucky hands?" He narrows his eyes. "Look, I don't know, lucky toys, whatever. My point is-"

He grabs my shirt, yanking me closer. "Go on. Make your point."

"My point is, I wish you good orgasms, however, they come along."

"I'll be having great orgasms in your mouth, that tight pussy, and soon your ass."

My mouth opens and closes like a fish. I pry his fingers off my shirt to give my brain something to concentrate on other than his words. When I'm able to make words again, I say, "Sure. Sometimes if I'm feeling it, and I don't have anyone else in the rotation, I'd be down for a little neighborly hook up."

He steps closer, eliminating the space I'd just reclaimed. "There is no rotation. You need dick. I'm your guy."

"See, that won't work for me. I like sex and I get mine when I want it too. I'm not built for sitting at home lonely and horny while some guy I'm supposed to be faithful to fucks his way through campus."

"Your pussy will be too sore to be useful to anyone else."

"I'll soak in that big ass tub I have."

"Thea, you're not hooking up with anybody else."

I drop my face in my hand and growl in frustration. I'm trying to be mindful that this may be a new situation for him. Lifting my head, I try to stay calm as I say, "Look, Holden. I'm not a monogamous type of girl. The fact that I fucked two of your friends should have clued you in on that. I'm not being flippant when I say I like sex. I do. And I like it with different partners. I can't be tied down to one person. I'd be miserable, bored, and find ways to make their life hell just to get rid of me. So, trust me, it's better this way."

"You wouldn't be bored with me, and Finn and I already talked. He's okay with you seeing me, too."

They talked to each other and made this decision instead of talking to me. Typical. "I don't need Finn's permission. He and I hooked up a few times, but that doesn't mean we're together any more than it means you and I are after you chased me in the woods."

"And where does Coach Wolfe fit in? Is he just a hook up too?"

"He's my trainer and whatever that entails is none of your business, just like whatever happened with you and I is none of his, Finn's or anyone else's."

I pluck my shades out of his pocket and say, "I've got somewhere to be. Let me know when those documents are ready."

Chapter 79
Thea

I'm humming to myself as I step off the elevator in Vale Tower. LJ comes back tomorrow, and I can't wait to see her. We have a group chat set up with Sasha, so we've been texting or talking every day, but it's not the same as seeing her face when she's here.

I've had plenty to keep me busy and occupy my time this last week of winter break. I've been doing extra training sessions with Deacon and taking short hikes through the heavily used run trails in town. The one and two-mile treks in the middle of the day with the tourists and locals have helped me rediscover my love of hiking. I'm not ready to go on a long walk in the dark, but the thought of being in the woods no longer makes me break out in a cold sweat.

The lobby and sidewalk are full of suitcases and boxes from the students who are already returning to the dorms. The sounds of laughter, squeals and chatter taints the quiet peace I've gotten used to. Of course, the loudest voice of all is Eloise's. My plan is to walk by and ignore her, hoping she'll choose to do the same. We can restart our feud next week when classes resume, and she has a full audience present.

I head towards The Rock, wanting to grab a quick bite before I leave campus. The students are back and so are their parents, which means Canyon Falls Annex is bustling with activity.

I'm taking a drive down the coast today. Getting away from the campus and the town is the easiest way to avoid running into Joshua, and anyone else dick riding the stabbed birds. I've had two more random people come up to me and ask me about the man who calls himself my grandfather. They were marginally nicer about it than the first guy, but the questions were still intrusive and annoying.

Moira and Scott have been keeping me in the loop. The League will hold a vote soon to determine Joshua's status. It sounds like they expect the vote to break in his favor.

I just hope whatever they decide, he leaves me alone. I want nothing to do with that shit. Sitting at the legacy table and going to their parties is about all I can handle. Especially when it's clear to me that women have no say about what they do and who they spend time with. Their sole purpose is to make the man look good. I'd be the worse arm candy in the history of the world. But he doesn't seem to understand that -so rather than repeating myself- I'm avoiding him.

Speaking of arm candy. Eloise stomps over to me. "Are you still here?"

"Depends. Are you still an annoying shrew? Oops, I guess you are."

Breathe. Deflect. Evade. That's the defensive sequence Wolfe and I are working on. It's supposed to translate to all parts of life. I breathed when she walked up to me. I deflected the question back onto her, and now it's time to walk away and evade.

I'm inches away when she yells out, "We'll see how funny you are when The League makes the announcement that your reject family is getting shoved back into the dungeon of obscurity. No matter how many hands your grandfather shakes, it'll never be enough to wash away the stench of shame and betrayal your family is covered in, or that you're tainted goods."

Family back in obscurity sounds amazing. It means I can go back to living my life in the shadows. It's the tainted goods comment that sticks in my craw. "What did you say?"

"Oh, come on. We all know that little *attack* you keep alluding to was bullshit. We've seen you throwing yourself at everyone around here. Why don't you just admit that you snuck out on Mayhem Night to hook up with Zeus and things got too rough? Then you lied and said he attacked you. It's clear to me you attacked him first. You have a history of fighting when things don't go your way. Zeus lured you out there as a prank and then you freaked out on him. Poor Zeus was just defending himself."

"Yeah, victim blame. There's clearly not enough of it already happening in the world."

"Am I making it up, though? The thing about you fighting? You assaulted me, after all." She steps forward and shoves her phone in my face. "And then there's this."

There aren't supposed to be any cameras at Club Dredd, but someone managed to get a few minutes of video footage of me ringside before one of my fights before security caught them. I remember that night. I had a good time.

"This little revelation is supposed to upset me? It's a fight. I was there watching and so were a lot of other people. It's not the first fight I've gone to, and it won't be the last one."

"You'll fit right in with the lower legacy families. You know, the ones who are servants and coffee runners to the upper bloodlines, because none of you would ever meet the standards for any other level."

I leave her standing there, smug superiority etched on her face. I text Moira when I get to the car.

ME

"You didn't tell me these bird people have respectable jobs like assistant and culinary chef."

MOIRA

"???"

Twisted Legacy

Eloise just told me the bird people are going to vote to make your dad a servant or coffee runner. I don't see anything wrong with those jobs. If you would have pitched that, I might've started sitting at their stupid table sooner.

Legacy families hire someone else to clean up their mess and fetch their food. It's not other legacy families, no matter how lowly they are

Yeah, I worked that out for myself. She's always trying to get a rise out of me

Don't let her. Don't let any of them.
Remember our goals

Stay under the radar, graduate, get the hell out of this town

How do you celebrate your best friend's return? By letting her drag you to a party. She's gotten more comfortable hanging out, thanks to her friendship with Austin and Connor. I call them her practice dudes, because she's able to laugh and talk to them without breaking into a sweat, which often leads to her talking to other members of the football team.

She'd probably pass out if left on her own, but this is a huge improvement over where she started. I love to see her coming out of her shell.

I sip my bottled water and smile as Austin and Connor argue back and forth about a football game they watched last weekend. I've learned my lesson about drinking at these events, and won't be straying away from my core group.

Holden, and Pax are on opposite sides of the room, Finn is leaning against the wall in front of me, watching the crowd. A song comes on, and Austin drags me onto the dance floor. He doesn't have to try too hard. I love to dance and we always have a good time in our little group. He spins and twirls LJ until she's transferred to Connor's outstretched arms, then it's my turn.

We dance until my shirt clings to my skin. I let them know I need a break and head to the bathroom to pee and splash water on my face. When I come out, Finn's leaning against the wall, with some girl I've seen hanging with the baseball team in his face.

I scowl at her, as she drags her hand through his hair. Finn's eyes widen, and I shake my head to clear the irrational urge to pull her away from him. This is Finn. He loves attention. It's none of my business what he does. I don't care what he does.

"Come on Finn, let me show you a good time, since Eloise can't."

I make it two steps and freeze, waiting to hear his response. Why is the thought of him hooking up with her bothering me? It shouldn't. *It doesn't.* I have Wolfe. Finn can have whoever he wants. He's allowed to change his mind about wanting me.

"I'll suck you so good, you won't be thinking about anyone else ever again."

I'm back over to them before I can think about what I'm doing. I politely tap her on the shoulder. She shrugs me off, and I tap again. I'm gonna be diplomatic about this. No fighting. Use my words. All the stuff that would make Wolfe call me his good girl.

In my nicest, firmest, non-confrontational voice I say, "Please remove your hands from Finn's dick."

She ignores me and sinks to her knees. Finn's mouth twitches. Is he laughing at me or her? He thinks this is funny, and probably laughing at me since he gets off on drama. Fine, he wants her sucking him off, now I wanna put a stop to it, because now I'm just annoyed that she's ignoring me.

She looks at me over her shoulder. "What do you want, Zeta Nu Dropout?"

"I want you to get up off your knees and find another dick to play with."

"I want this one. I hear it's amazing."

When she goes to turn back to Finn. He barks out a laugh when I yank her ponytail, jerking her away from him. "You don't need first hand knowledge about that. I can tell you it is, and it's off limits. Now get the fuck up and go play in someone else's pants."

"I suggest you do what she says. Thea's already claimed my cock, and it doesn't look like she's in the mood to share it."

He gives her an encouraging smile. "Don't look so glum, there are plenty of other people who would love to take your mouth. I hear it's quite an experience."

She straightens, and flips her hair, bolstered by his words. "Yes, it is. And when you're done with her, maybe I'll still be interested in letting you take it for a ride."

He shrugs, and I poke him in the side. "Ow. What was that for, Pet?"

"I didn't run her off, so you could leave the door open for her return."

"And why did you run her off? Did you think I couldn't handle her on my own, or worried I was gonna give in?"

"Neither. It looked like you were about to have fun and I live to stomp all over it."

He fists my shirt dragging me closer. "Do I get to do the same with you?"

My heart rate ticks up. Finn and I used to have fun, picking on each other. I'm sure he suspects I messed with his knives but he hasn't retaliated yet. Why hasn't he? Come to think of it, none of them have done anything to me at all. Is that why I interrupted him? Because I need the attention? I certainly feel more alive than I did before I walked up on him. I'm getting better every day, but something is missing. This push and pull with Finn might be it.

"You're welcome to try, but we both know I play these games better than you."

I bite his bottom lip, then ditch his hold, and head back to my friends.

Chapter 80
Holden

My conversation with Thea has been playing in my head since we talked. I wanted to chase her down and demand she take back what she said about not wanting to be tied to one person. I understood what she was saying, but for the first time in history, I had trouble expressing myself.

If she needs variety, I can give her that. We can give her that. Me and Finn, and Coach Wolfe. Because I know he's part of the deal. My dad finished his assignment two weeks ago and joined my mother and sister in New York. They got back last week, and I spent the last few days with my family, soaking up good vibes, before having to deal with everyone being back on campus.

Classes start in four days, but the first party of the new year, hosted by The Lady Lions, is in full swing. I read the last message on my phone from my father. He's checking on me because all the news that came out of our reunion wasn't good news. It turns out my mother was making connections and deals while in New York and some names are now being tossed around as potential matches for me.

I've always thought my parents would give me until my thirties before entertaining matches for me. My dad has been adamant that whoever they choose has to be compatible on and off paper. He didn't go into any details, but he alluded to my mother running into some of the council wives in New York, and using the time away from Canyon Falls to put some feelers out there.

Whatever happened, I'm definitely seeing the results. I've been waved to three times already, and someone across the room has been staring at me for seven and a half minutes. I guess she's finally done looking because she breaks off from her friends and walks over to where I'm standing.

"How's it going, Holden? Nice party, right?" She points to the bottle of vodka I'm holding. "Can I get some of that?"

I finish pouring some in my cup, then hand her the bottle. She tops off her drink, sets the bottle on the table and takes a sip, letting the juice dribble down her chin. With a tinkly laugh, she swipes at her chin with her fingers and pushes them in her mouth. "Don't want to waste any."

She's following me as I walk to the other side of the room. "Oh god. It's cooler over here. Can you believe how many people showed up tonight?"

I tamp down my annoyance. I came over here because there are less people on this side of the room and it's the perfect place for Pax, Finn and I to watch the room.

I sip my drink, and stare over her head, waiting for her to get the memo that I don't want to be bothered, and walk away. Instead, she presses closer. "So, how was your break?"

"Fine."

"Did Santa bring you what you wanted for Christmas?"

I shift my body, leaning against the wall, putting some space between us. She presses right up against my side. "I got almost everything I wanted."

"Good for you."

"Don't you want to know what gift I asked for that I didn't get?"

"Not particularly."

She touches my arm. "I wanted someone to ring in the new year with. You know, since they say whoever you kiss at midnight is who you'll spend the year with."

I press myself further against the wall. It's the only acceptable thing I can do when the alternative is snapping her wrists.

"I pouted for a little while, but then I thought about it. It was a good thing I didn't get it, because I've been hooking up with the same guys year after year and it always turns out the same. So I made a resolution to broaden my interests. Give someone else a chance."

"How nice for you."

"And do you know what I came up with when I started making my new list? Nice guys. That's who I need. A nice guy who's smart and athletic and doesn't do all that stupid shit I've had to put up with over the years. I deserve better, right?"

"Sure."

There's a couple making out on my left and a game of cups happening on my right. She's right in front of me, her scent invading my nose. Her touch makes my skin crawl. I'm gonna have to shove her out of my way to get free.

"I was wondering who would be perfect, and then I remembered you were eyeing me at the beginning of the semester, so tonight's your lucky night."

"How is that?"

"I'm gonna let you take me upstairs and show me a good time."

I snort. That's highly doubtful, and this entire conversation is ridiculous. I looked her way twice last year, and both times she turned her nose up at me. "You weren't interested then. What's changed?"

"I was foolish. Listening to rumors. Letting peer pressure guide me."

"Well, maybe you should let it guide you back to wherever the fuck you came from."

Her brows crease. "Didn't you come here to party?"

"I did, and I think we'd all like to leave here with all the limbs and body parts we came with."

She laughs and presses her hand against my chest. "Heard I was a man eater, did you? Well relax, Holden. Nobody complains when I swallow the bones."

I grimace at the imagery that conjures. That didn't sound nearly as sexy as she thinks it did. "I wasn't actually talking about my body being cut into little pieces. I was talking about yours."

I try to push her away, without having to put my hands on her. I don't want any of her perfume or makeup to get on me.

"Well, Finn's not here, and I doubt he's ever cut someone for wanting to give you a good lay. From what I hear, he's usually begging people to do it with all of you. Now you get me to yourself."

I laugh. I don't know what she has in her cup other than vodka, but it has to be the good stuff if she thinks this little seduction is working. "The danger isn't from Finn. Now, I suggest you back up. I won't be so nice if I tell you again."

She does the opposite. She yanks her shirt up and shows me her tits. One second they're on display, swinging at me, the next they're flying away from me. She falls to her ass, tits still out. The music comes to a halt, and I hear Thea saying, "Nice tits. I always wanted nipples like these. Maybe I should take yours."

Finn strolls over holding a beer and asks, "What happened?"

"Suddenly I'm worth a party fuck instead of a pity one." I heft a shoulder. "I told her not to touch me."

"You pushed her?"

"Never touched her."

Finn sputters his beer when Thea says, "Tell me why I shouldn't cut your tits off."

The girl on the floor shrieks, "What the hell is your problem, you crazy bitch?"

"My problem is, I could have sworn I told you to stay away from my toys."

"Finn was on the other side of the room."

I look at Finn. He nods, confirming she tried to hook up with him before she came to me. Thea taps on her forehead with the hilt of her knife. "Toys with an s." She grabs the girl's face, yanks it around to look at us, then turns it back to face forward. "Coxsucker one and two are not interested in you and your balloons. They don't want to play with your party favors."

The girl huffs, "There's only one of you. You can't have the two of them like they're a matching set."

My stomach flips when Thea says, "They are definitely not a matching pair, and I would never ask them to be. But you're right. My math is all fucked up. Did I say the both of them? I meant whichever one of your precious Trium members who've bled for me."

Pax finally makes his way over to us, with a girl tucked under his arm, and asks, "Who fucked with the music?"

Thea glances over at him with this strange look on her face. It's like a mashup of the one Finn has when he's about to do something crazy as fuck, and the determined gleam Pax gets in his eyes when he decides to fuck someone's life up. I think Finn and I work out what's gonna happen at the exact same time. Thea gets to her feet, walks right up to Pax, completely ignoring the girl he's with, and pulls him into a kiss.

His brain has to be short circuiting, because instead of pushing her away, he grips her hips, pulling her closer, deepening the kiss. Seconds later, he flinches and shoves her away.

Thea steps back and smiles, licking the blood from her bottom lip. She tells the girl he's with, "He tastes like butterscotch and caramel in case you were wondering," Then, turns her attention back to the girl on the floor who still hasn't put her tits away. With a condescending pat to the girl's cheek, she says, "I've bled them all. So don't fucking try me."

That's when Pax looks down on the floor. "What the fuck is going on here?"

Thea straightens and shrugs, "Desperate hoe down in aisle three?"

She walks off singing some made up song about if I bleed them, then I own them please, hoes try me.

The warmth in my belly expands. Thea came over here to protect me. In this room with all these people around, she *claimed* me. Pax looks over at us, his lip still bleeding.

Finn laughs, enjoying the destruction Thea left behind, while Pax scowls and barks orders for someone to turn the music back on. He's in clean up mode. Trying to show that things are still under control. I wonder how long it's gonna take for him to realize Thea claimed him, too.

The girl on the floor breaks out the tears, bemoaning how unfair it was that she was attacked unprovoked, and pretending to understand now why Pax hates Thea so much.

I'm not about to let her manipulate this situation. I look down at her and growl, "Stop with the fucking fake tears. I warned you Finn wasn't the person you had to worry about."

"But I."

"Touched me repeatedly against my wishes and flashed me your tits. I'd say you're lucky Thea let you keep your nipples."

When she looks at Finn, he flicks his knife open. "I suggest you put them away, doll, before I decide to gift them to my girl as a pair of earrings."

The only person left to get sympathy from is Pax. He shrugs. "A Trium gave you a warning you disregarded. The consequence is always someone putting you on your ass."

She climbs to her feet and swipes at her face. Switching tactics. "I'm gonna tell my daddy about this. She's a nobody. She has no authority here, so there will be consequences for *her* actions."

Thea's on the other side of the room with LJ. She looks likes she's having a good time, and I'm not gonna let anyone ruin it. Pax beats me to it when he says, "Maybe you and your daddy should brush up on the rules. Someone protecting a Trium will *always* get a pass."

Chapter 81
Finn

Thea went all vigilante justice on that girl, and I loved it. I guess she worked up an appetite, because I overheard her saying she and LJ were going out for pancakes before coming back to the dorm. Pax, Holden, and I left the party soon after that. She wound up spending the night at LJ's and has stayed gone for these last two days. It's almost like she's avoiding us.

Holden pinged her location on Prospectus. As of ten minutes ago, she was heading back to the dorm, so he's waiting at the elevator for her. She shrieks as they walk through the door and is threatening to murder him in his sleep if he doesn't put her down. He does once he reaches my bedroom and blocks the door so she can't leave.

"Unfucking believable." She's glares at me with her arms folded over her luscious tits.

"Don't be mad, Pet."

"Are you fucking serious right now? Holden just tossed me over his shoulder and fireman carried me over here. Mad is not even a drop of the amount of the rage I'm feeling right now."

"We wanted to talk to you."

"Try, um, I don't know... talking. There's this thing called a phone, or paper and pen."

"You're right. We should have just asked you to come over, but we didn't want you to say no."

"Of course I would have said no. I have things to do."

"You'll have plenty of time to do them, Pet. But we need to talk about what happened at the party."

"I know what it looked like, okay? And I heard the story she's been telling around campus, but that shit wasn't my fault. She had Holden pinned against the wall, and anyone could see he was uncomfortable. I was trying to help."

"Oh, we know." I step closer. "Which is why we want to thank you for coming to his rescue, and to say -once again- how truly, truly sorry we are, for all that shit we did to you in the beginning. Especially Pax."

Not even he can find fault in what she did, since it was to help Holden. She looks over at Pax and rolls her eyes. "He doesn't look like he's sorry."

"Trust me, he is."

"Are you sorry, Pax?," she asks.

He swallows and averts his gaze, too damn stubborn to admit he was wrong. Sucking her teeth, she says, "See? He stands by everything he's ever said and done."

"It appears so." I press a kiss to her temple. "His loss is my gain. I get you all to myself."

A throat clearing behind her disagrees. "Fine, I'll share you with Holden, but only because I know he has no problem admitting how badly he fucked up. Although he's been apologizing ever since you came back to campus." I turn her towards the door so she can see the sincerity on Holden's face.

"Never once has Holden said those words to me."

He walks over to us, a hard glint in his eyes, and says, "I'm a man of action, Rey. I've been showing you how sorry I am. You just haven't been paying attention. But tonight, I'll be more clear. I'm gonna leave your skin bruised and battered. A tapestry of my apology."

She sighs and melts against me, like that psychotic pronouncement was the swooniest shit she's ever heard. This is why Holden's obsessed with her. After that blow job in the woods, he confessed he's been playing his little primal games with her. Some kind of weird immersion therapy to help her heal from her attack.

Girls usually freak out and avoid Holden, if they get even a small glimpse of what he's into. It's why having them sign an NDA is so important. But Thea never once let on that it was happening. And the ways she took him down her throat and let him use her, it's clear she understands his needs and embraces it.

This girl is everything either of us could ever want. She lets him go dark, she goes stabby like me, and has some sort of daddy praise kink happening with Coach Wolfe that we're not supposed to know about. I guess that tracks since our girl has hella daddy issues.

I don't know what her thing with Pax would be. I don't even know if he has a thing, but if he does, I'm sure she'd embrace it and make it better. He's missing out.

I palm Thea's breasts, scraping my thumb across her nipples. She arches into my hands, but I pull her back flush against me. Tilting my head towards Holden, I say. "Let's see how long it takes to get our girl off, with all of our clothes on."

She snorts. Of course she does. Because she's never gonna take anything we say at face value. "What are we, fifteen? Trust me, Number Three, it's gonna be hard to get me off fully clothed."

I nibble on her ear and say, "You'll be naked, Pet. The rest of us won't."

Her breath hitches as my meaning sets in. "Whatever you have planned, it won't work. I need skin to skin contact."

"We'll see about that."

She shakes her head when Holden points to the bed. He warns, "I'm not opposed to giving you rug burns, but for what we have in mind, I think you might be more comfortable on the bed."

He snatches her up and tosses her through the air. I chuckle as she emits a little yelp when she bounces on the bed. I walk around the other side, climbing onto the bed beside her. Grabbing her shoulders, I pull her against me. If this is going to work, there's one more thing to take care of.

I grab my phone out of my back pocket and dial Coach Wolfe's number. "What?"

I ignore the terse answer and put it on speakerphone. "I'm about to have your star pupil panting my name. What's the record for the number of orgasms you've given her?"

Thea laughs and says, "In total or in one night?"

Wolfe's dark chuckles hint that these two have secrets. I place the phone on the bed. Holden has a quizzical expression on his face. He's probably trying to work out the orgasm number, based on what he knows about Thea's reaction time to sexual stimuli.

"Not only are we gonna beat whatever your number is, but we're gonna do it without removing a stitch of our clothing."

"You hear that, sweetness? Think they can do it?"

"They look very motivated to try," Thea says, in the most incredulous tone she can muster.

Wolfe hmmms then his voice drops when he asks, "Have you eaten today, sweetness?"

She squirms against me, biting down on her bottom lip. Just the sound of his voice has her flushed. Her hand slips between her legs.

"Because I'm starving."

She moans, grinding against her hand. I'm in awe. It's like some type of pavlovian response. "Are you touching yourself, sweetness?"

"Yes."

"I wanna hear. Bring the phone closer." Her hand flails out, looking for it. I grab it and hand it to her. She lowers it, putting it between her thighs so he can hear. God, now I'm gonna have her juices on my screen. It's gonna be like my own personal scratch and sniff. I'm never dropping it in water.

"Those noises sound so good. I wish I were there, to see you making a mess on your hands."

"Me, too," she pants.

"Finn says they plan to beat the number of times I've made you cum. What did you do this time to land in The Trium's clutches?"

Her free hand toys with her nipples. "Finn and Holden are making amends, trying to prove to me how sorry they are for the shit they've done to me."

"Mmm. If *I* were apologizing, you wouldn't be sounding so calm or compliant. I'd push you to the edge over and over, refusing to let you cum until you give me what I want."

I scoff. He clearly doesn't understand how to apologize. And they call us the assholes.

He asks, "Would you give it to me right away?"

"No."

"Of course not, because you never take the easy route, and that makes me so fucking hard for you. You know how much I love that fighting spirit, don't you? How much I love to hear you sing for me?"

"Yes."

"Yes, what?"

"Yes, sir."

"Damn right I do. I get so turned on by that fire. I wish I were there right now, to see the look on your face, to watch you try to reach that spot inside you that only I can. Are you trying to reach it right now, sweetness?"

"Yes. I need you, Wolfe. I need to cum."

"I need that, too. But I have a training session, sweetness, so Finn is going to have to take care of you. You get everything you deserve from them and not a thing less, you hear me?"

"Wolfe, please."

"It's okay sweetness. You be a *good girl* and enjoy your apology."

She cums. He said, *good girl* and she fucking came on the spot. My mind is blown. I mean yeah; I know the brain is the biggest sexual organ and all that, but never in my life have I seen a woman so receptive to words. He didn't even say anything all that riveting. But Thea is a shaking, moaning specimen of yummy goodness.

"That's one, boys, and you're welcome." Coach Wolfe laughs and disconnects the call.

Holden pulls the phone from Thea's hand and tosses it on the bed, climbing onto it until he's leaning over us, determination in his eyes. I've only seen him look like this once before and that was when someone bet him he couldn't hack into... well, I'm not allowed to say what he was hacking into. The point is, he stayed up three days straight until he did it, and this is the look he had on his face when he sat down at the computer.

"Oh shit, Pet. I think you're in trouble."

Holden pushes her shirt up, exposing her stomach and kisses a trail down her body, easing her yoga pants down her legs as he goes. She's propped against me so she can watch. Pax is sitting in the chair in the corner. He has a perfect view of everything that's going on. He doesn't want to join in. I respect that. But him being here shows we're in this together.

"Are you ready for what comes next?" I murmur against her ear.

"Depends. Is it more talking? Because I was promised orga-."

Her snarky response cuts off when Holden's tongue dives between her folds.

"Oh, shit." She moans, clamping her legs together and arching off the bed.

Holden presses his hand above her pubic bone to hold her in place while I grab her leg, spreading her wider. With my free hand, I pull her face towards me, leaning down for a kiss. I groan into her mouth as she opens to me, swiping her tongue against mine.

Thea said what happened between us the day Pax found her in the sauna was a mistake, but there's nothing wrong with the way she makes me feel. How can it be? We fit so well together. It feels *so good* to touch her.

How can it be wrong when my best friend is happily feasting between her legs and she's fisting the back of his shirt to hold him in place? Hell, him between her legs is damn near a miracle, because Holden has never bothered with foreplay. He and Pax both usually leave it to me, since I'm the most tactile one out of our group. But Holden's down there, his face buried in her pussy.

Thea breaks off our kiss to look at Holden. "Fuck," she pants. "That tongue ring should be patented as a must have toy."

Her head falls back against my chest as she grinds against my best friend's face. Her ass grazes against my dick with each undulation of her hips. I pull her shirt off and unhook her bra, pushing the straps from her body as I lean down and capture her nipple between my teeth. She grabs my head, digging her fingers into the hair curling at the nape of my neck as I suckle at her breasts. First one, then the other, going back and forth between them. Her body stiffens as she comes a second time. Holden lifts his head and looks at me. I swirl my finger to show I want her rolled over. He clambers up to the head of the bed and pulls her to straddle his face.

"Shit." She gasps, gripping the headboard as he impales her with his fingers. I bracket my elbows on either side of his knees and push her forward, presenting her ass. I swipe some moisture from the slickness between her legs, sucking my fingers into my mouth and humming as her taste explodes on my tongue. Holden gives me a nod as I push two of my fingers inside her pussy next to his. We're inside her from different angles. Our fingers brush against each other as they move in and out in alternate motions.

"What the fu-uck-"

"You like that, Pet?" I chuckle. "The beautiful thing is you have two more holes that we can find creative ways to fill."

I glance over to where Pax is sitting. This is a turn of events. It's usually Holden watching or doing the bare minimum. This would be the first time he's all in and Pax is on the sidelines. We could have so much more fun with Thea's body, if he'd get over his shit and come play.

She whimpers as we spear her with our fingers over and over again. Her cunt clamping down tight. I drag my hand from between her legs and tease the opening of her back door, slowly inching those same two fingers inside.

She mewls as I press inside. Holden's dark, husky voice asks, "Is her ass as greedy as this cunt?"

"Yes. She's trying to trap my fingers inside."

I press further and can feel Holden's fingers through the small membrane that separates her ass and cunt. "God," I hiss, pulling my fingers out and plunging back in. "It's gonna be epic when we fuck you."

"Do you want that, Rey?" Holden asks. "Do you want to feel what it's like for us to split you in two, while you gag on a twelve inch dildo with your nose plugged?"

He yanks on her nipple, and her body locks down around my fingers as she convulses.

Damn, I wish I was in her ass when it happened, with my knife carving lines downs the curve of her back. What am I saying? I can have that. I walk over to my dresser to get what I need. On the way back, I shove my sweat pants down to my hips, roll the condom on, and squirt a generous amount of lube on it.

Holden pulls a condom out of his back pocket. Good thing he has his own. I don't have a size to fit him. He surprises me once again when he removes his shirt. I watch as Thea gets to her knees and licks up his abs to his chest and captures his nipple ring in her mouth, giving it a slight tug.

Holden gathers her hair in his hand, but doesn't pull her off. His eyes are closed, his teeth digging into his bottom lip as she drags her nails down his pecs.

Miracle number two. She's touching him. She's touching him and he's letting her. I pull her onto her side and settle behind her. Holden is in front, claiming her mouth, as I press kisses against the nape of her neck and shoulder blades. He pulls back and I lean up to watch as he notches his cock at her entrance.

She tenses against me. I hook my hand under her knee, lifting it to give Holden room, and go back to dotting kisses across her skin as he pushes inside. Her hand grips my forearm. I check Holden's progress. "You're doing so good, Pet. Just breathe."

Her breath hitches, her body rocks as Holden pushes in further. Her body arches towards me. Holden grabs her face, yanking her back against his body, he says, "Where do you think you're going? You're gonna stay right here and take this cock. Both of these cocks."

His hips snap forward and from the quick exhalation of her breath, I know he's all the way in. I give her a second to adapt, smoothing my palms across her skin. He takes a few slow thrusts, letting her acclimate to him. I huff a breath when she rocks her hips, sliding against me. I grab the lube and squirt some between her ass cheeks, and add some more to my palm, smoothing it along my length, then set my tip against her opening.

"Hold her still, man."

Holden grips her hip and hooks her leg higher while I slowly push inside. "Relax, Thea." She pants and whimpers as I push in further. I can feel Holden and the ridges of his piercings. I don't know how he was able to get those damn things, but having them pressed against my cock from the other side feels amazing.

"Ready?" I hiss when Thea squirms between us.

"Yes." She pants.

I nod at Holden, and he pulls out, then slams back in, taking a few test strokes. Then I match his stroke, finding the rhythm we had with our fingers, his piercings adding to the friction against my cock. Thea's ass muscles quiver, and I groan at the same time Holden does.

Holden stretches Thea's hands over her head, and I shove my right hand under her head, gathering my hands at her wrist, holding them up, and hook her leg back around my hip, thrusting deep. Thea's body rocks forcefully between us.

Holden says, "Look at you. Taking two cocks at once. Such a needy little whore, aren't you?"

She's a whimpering, gasping mess, her pleas desperate and unintelligible. With my blade, I make two tiny cuts on her left shoulder blade. "You bleed so pretty for me." She clenches around me, breaking my rhythm.

"Fuck, man." I grit out. "I'm not gonna last much longer."

Holden clamps his palm against her face, blocking her nose and mouth, as he rasps, "Time to hold your breath."

I lap at the two dots of blood pebbling on her skin as her body convulses, clenching around my cock. I push deep and hold steady as her ass milks me dry. Her body goes slack as Holden slams home a few more times, before he finally releases with a heavy groan.

I feel like I just ran a marathon. I rub my hands across Thea's shoulder, trying to work the circulation back into it. Holden pulls out first, the slide of his piercings a little jarring across my soft and sensitive dick.

Thea's slowly coming to as I pull out of her ass. I push her onto her stomach, waiting until her eyes blink open before climbing off the bed to deal with the condom. When I come back, Holden gets up to do the same. I look over at the empty chair Pax was sitting in.

I'll talk to him tomorrow. Tonight I'm curling up next to my girl, who's sporting droopy eyes, and a blissed out expression on her face. I put my knife on the dresser out of her reach and crawl back onto the bed. Holden stares down at her. He's probably heading out, too. He has to be in bed alone, if he even sleeps.

I watch him get into bed. He pulls Thea against him, grabbing her breast like it's his teddy bear or some shit. I'm too tired to comment, so I slide my knee between hers, and link our hands together.

"Don't get comfy." She mumbles. "I'm going back to my room in a few minutes."

Given the possessive way Holden's holding on to her, there's no way that's happening. I peck her on the cheek. "Whatever you say, Pet."

My hand hits a warm body as I roll over in bed. I flinch and reach under my pillow for my knife. Where the hell is my knife? My body tenses, my panic mounting, until someone mumbles, "You okay, Pet?"

Finn. Why is Finn in my bed? Did he take my knife so I can't accidentally kill him? As my initial panic eases, I remember where I am and... what happened last night. Finn and Holden tag teaming me after my conversation with Wolfe. Although tag team might not be the right word. Sometimes, it felt more like a competition. They gave a good effort, but they both tapped out after my fourth "O" at their hands. The first one didn't count. I did that myself. With Wolfe's help. I wish he would've been here. The three of them together is what fantasies are made of.

Maybe next time. Next time? What, Thea? *No. There* is no *next time*. Not with them. Last night was a one off. They wanted to thank me for helping Holden out of that spider monkey's clutches. This isn't the start of any type of multi-partner arrangement.

Even if it were, Wolfe wouldn't be interested. He's made his position clear. He'll accept me hooking up with other people, because he can't offer me any kind of commitment, but he doesn't want to hear about it.

And yet, he didn't seem to mind that I was here and what they were planning to do. He even wished them good luck after talking me through my first orgasm. So would he go for it? Just one time?

My body heats just thinking about it. I shake my head, clearing my thoughts. It's not happening. Or I try to clear my thoughts, but now my brain is stuck on the idea of the three of them with their hands, mouths and dicks all over me.

I glance over to the chair where Pax was sitting. He saw everything. I don't care what Finn says, Pax isn't the least bit remorseful about how he's treated me. Is still treating me. I'm sure he'll have some snide ass comment when I see him again. I might not want a repeat, but I'm not ashamed of what happened.

I slip out of bed and hunt around for my panties, which I'm sure Holden took off and tossed onto the floor with my yoga pants. Maybe not. They could be on the bed which means Finn might be sleeping on them. I pull my clothes on, minus the bra, retrieve my shoes from where they landed by the chair, and walk barefoot to the front door to let myself out.

I have several missed calls and messages. I text LJ letting her know I'll meet her for breakfast in thirty minutes. I let out an exasperated sigh as I read the rest. I've still got a lot of shit to sort out with my life, like dealing with what I'm sure is gonna be an argument with Joshua about his failed attempt to turn me into some kind of bodyguard, my relationship with Moira and Scott, and the still unanswered questions regarding my attack.

I put out some clean clothes and brush my teeth while the water heats up in my shower. My muscles ache but in that way I welcome after a good round of sex. I'm smiling when I step under the shower spray, because despite all the bullshit I've got going on, last night gave me something I've been in short supply of lately. Fun.

"Oh, shit!" I yelp when I step into the hallway to head to breakfast. Finn's standing there smirking down at me. I move to sidestep him, but he pushes me against the wall.

"You snuck out on me, this morning." He nips my ear, and the hollow of my throat. "Now what was more pressing than waking up with me? Hmm?"

"A shower, for starters."

"I have one of those in my room."

"And breakfast."

"Are you saying we helped you work up an appetite, Pet?"

"I'm saying, I'm hungry."

"Me, too. Only what I want isn't being served at The Rock." He bends his knees, and presses closer. He rocks against me, letting me feel how hard he is. "Come back to bed."

Morning sex isn't a half bad idea, but I've already showered and confirmed meeting up with LJ. I can't bail on her for dick. No matter how good that dick is.

"I can't. I'm meeting LJ for breakfast."

"Then what am I going to do with all this pent up energy?"

He kisses me, his tongue sliding against mine, as he grabs my ass, pulling me closer. His erection hitting me with just the right amount of pressure against my clit. I'm panting when we break apart, but he's not done trying to convince me. He bites my neck, then sucks on the flesh, while his hand reaches between us to rub my throbbing clit.

"Finn!"

"God, I love the sound of you panting my name like that."

If I don't stop this now, I'm gonna be late. I can't be late. I need my time with LJ. I push him away, ignoring the heated gaze he's giving me. "I have plans. Now you can either take a cold shower, finish yourself off, or go work out. Hell, do all three. But you're not going to convince me to let you fuck me right now."

He grins down at me. "Fine. We'll put this on pause, and I'll convince you to let me fuck you later."

My mouth gapes open as I realize what just happened. He's in his room before I can clarify that that's *not* what I meant. Sneaky fucker.

Epilogue

Pax

'm really questioning my friendships right now. We thrive on antagonizing people. On finding that thing that makes them uncomfortable and pressing down on it. We hunt out secrets and use them to make the other students fall in line, to conform, or to punish them. But, we've never done it to each other.

Holden and Finn didn't come right out and say it, but I know that's what last night was supposed to be about. Getting me to admit to feeling regret about what we've done to Thea.

They should've known I don't. I stand by my decision. She wasn't who she claimed to be, and I was trying to prove it. Everything I did was to protect us.

Fuck, they really went all out last night. I didn't want to watch, but there was no way I was leaving and giving her the satisfaction of thinking that seeing her naked, her cunt dripping with her arousal, and that scent, was making me uncomfortable.

So, I sat there. Thinking of a million other things so my dick wouldn't react to the sight of my friends pounding into her. I sang songs in my head, to block out the sound of their pants and moans, and the noises she made when she was cumming.

I pretended to be bored and let my eyes glaze over instead of focusing my attention on the way she clawed at the sheets. I mastered control of my emotions and facial expressions at an early age, so it was easy to keep my ass in that chair. But when it was over -as soon as I got to my room- I let that control slip, over and over again, in the panties I swiped off the floor, when they were basking in the afterglow.

So *no*, I'm not sorry for what I did, and I wasn't going to pretend to be, just so I could join in. But, after watching them, I can admit I'd definitely fuck Thea again if I was drunk or high, or she just happened to be the closest warm body around. I'd have to gag her though, because I wouldn't want to hear her mouth, unless it's screaming my name as I drilled through her cervix.

I scrub a hand through my hair and focus back on my workout. It's done. It's over. I've already let last night take up too much space in my head. I bend over and pick up the weight restarting my arm curls.

Just as I'm getting in the zone, Eloise comes into the gym. I ignore her as she comes to a stop next to the weight bench. It's not unusual to see her in the gym. She's been up here plenty of times to drool over Finn, but that hasn't been since the start of the school year. Sorority shit keeps her busy and the Zeta Nus take yoga and spin classes at the main gym.

"Looking good, Pax."

I freeze, with the weight halfway between my thigh and my chest. "What do you want?" I ask, before completing my rep.

"This is why I like you. There's no lead up. You get right to the point."

She stands there like she's posing. I take in her outfit. Some kind of fancy short set with heels. I think they call it a romper. "Flattery isn't what gets me off. You know that. And if you're up here looking for someone to tell you how hot you look, go find someone else."

"That's precisely why I'm here. I do want someone paying me

compliments, and after that little display at the Lady Lions' party, the other night, I think it's time I remind you of our deal."

She's bringing this shit up again? I'd be more than happy to honor our agreement if I thought she could discreetly take care of my Thea problem. But there's no way for that to happen now. Not with the council watching.

"We're gonna have to hold off on that for a little longer."

She snorts, then laughs. The sound a bit condescending and unhinged. Something like dread starts as a funny feeling in my nose quickly morphing into a knot of discomfort in my stomach. "What's so funny?"

"You, and the fact that you have the nerve to try to back out of our deal."

"Nobody's backing out of anything. I said pause it. Not cancel it."

"Here's the thing, Paxton. We can't *pause* it, because I've already executed my part."

"How? By being catty and name calling? I could throw a nickel in any direction and have three dozen students do that with the promise of letting them suck my dick."

"Men are so stupid." She huffs. "Haven't you noticed your little project has an aversion to the athletic stadium and cemetery?"

"No, I haven't, and so what if she does? Her phobias don't have shit to do with me or you. And let me squash this shit now, before you start whining to me about Finn's behavior. He didn't do anything worth getting bent out of shape over at The Lady Lion's party. As far as I'm concerned, he was on his best behavior."

I press on making my point. "Now, I'm gonna tell you for the last time. I'll hold up my end of the deal, but in case you haven't noticed, there haven't been too many opportunities to push him your way. So until we can circle back around to getting rid of Thea, just sit back and chill the fuck out. I'm working on it."

She saunters forward and shoves her phone at me. "You're wrong about that, Pax. Her trauma has *everything* to do with me. And because I knew you wouldn't just take my word for it, I've brought you a little proof. Maybe this will motivate you to work faster." "

I snatch the phone from her grip and push play. My blood freezes, and that pit in my stomach settles into a lump of cement. My chest tightens. I can barely get out the words. "What the fuck is this?"

"That is a video of some very helpful people responding to your request to take out the trash on Mayhem Night. Just because you decided to bring it back in doesn't clear you of your part in our deal."

It's clear the video is spliced together, but that doesn't make it less disturbing. Finn's been looking for answers about Thea's attack, and something tells me Eloise knew this video existed all this time. She probably knows who recorded it. *Goddamnit.* If Finn finds out, he'll never forgive her. Or me.

I can't let him find out. Eloise won't hesitate to use this to her advantage. She's not just up here negotiating because she wants Finn. This is personal. She wants to get rid of Thea because she sees her as competition. Finn's not easy to forgive, and he's been looking for an escape clause. His marriage contract to Eloise is set, and if he tries to back out, it'll have lasting repercussions on his entire family line.

What is Eloise planning to do with this footage? You know what, it doesn't matter, because I know whatever she plans won't be good and will make us look inept. It's been two months and we had no clue it existed.

I need to find some way to stall her. Buy some time and keep this from getting out. Once again, I'm wishing Thea had stayed gone. Everything would be so much easier if she had. I don't like Thea. I don't trust her, but I never would have ordered this. The way she's screaming, in that coffin...

"What the fuck?"

My head pops up and I meet Finn's gaze. "What the hell are you watching, and why is Thea screaming like that?"

How does he know it's her? What am I asking? Of course he recognizes her voice. He's obsessed with the girl. Before I can come up with an answer, he walks over and snatches the phone from me. "What the fuck is this?"

Eloise meets my gaze. I shake my head, letting her know if she tells, then our deal is definitely off.

"What does it look like? It's the information you've been searching for regarding that slut's attack." She plucks the phone from his hand and tucks it away. "A very helpful individual forwarded it to me. I know how invested you've been in finding answers. I'm sure you recognize the robes, so I'll leave you to track down the identity of the offenders and to notify the school so we can finally bring this year's pledge season to a close. Aside from that, I think you'll both find the initiates who completed the season are very eager to take part in our first co-hosted event."

This is bad. So fucking bad. I can't even meet my friend's eyes as I say, "Of course. I'll have our committee contact you in the next few days to discuss."

She walks toward the door and I heave a sigh of relief, bending to pick up my weight.

"Aagh!!"

I shift on the bench and see Eloise pinned to the wall, Finn's hand at her throat.

"You're the least helpful person I know, Eloise, a terrible fucking liar, and you seem to have forgotten who the fuck I am." He pulls his phone out, and puts it on speakerphone.

Holden's gravelly voice says, "Yeah, man."

"There's a video on Eloise's phone. I want it. *All* of it."

He turns to look at me. My back stiffens as his chilly gaze takes me in. There's no trace of my best friend. Staring at me is the madman who wouldn't hesitate to leave me bleeding out at his feet. "If you've got something you want to say before he sends me that video, now would be the time."

Yikes!!!

What do you think? Will Pax come clean or continue to keep quiet about the deal he made with Eloise?

. . .

Join my Newsletter to be among the first to learn about release information for Ruthless Legacy, book three in the Heartless Heirs of Canyon Falls saga, or follow one of my social media accounts for updates on my writing status.

You can also catch me hanging out in my reader's group Dakota's Darlings. We'd love for you to join us.

Acknowledgments

I can't say this enough... To my group of *amazing* BETA Readers who took the time to read and provide feedback for this story, *Thank You!!!* Once again you got me over the hump. I wouldn't be able to tell these stories without you. I love you guys more than Finn loves his knives.

And to the readers, thank you for picking up this book, and for giving me a chance.

I hope you've enjoyed your time with me so far, and stick around for more adventures.

About the Author

Dakota Lee is an overworked mom of three human garbage disposals and a dog who thinks she's a wolf.

In the daylight, she loves paranormal/ supernatural books and tv shows, comic book movies, action movies, and the comfort of a good Hallmark movie.

When the sun goes down, she's been known to tune into some after dark deliciousness that she would never tell her co-workers about.

She's here to push boundaries through her words and hopefully take you on a twisty, thorny journey on the way to a happily ever after.

And if you happen to fall for the asshole before he's redeemed, that's okay.

Dakota's got a weakness for the bad boys too.